On The Wild Side

Martin Gardner

- The Big Bang
- ESP
- The Beast 666
- Levitation
- Rainmaking
- Trance-Channeling
- Séances and Ghosts
- And More . . .

Prometheus Books
Buffalo, New York

Published 1992 by Prometheus Books.

96 95 94 93 92   5 4 3 2 1

Library of Congress Cataloging-in-Publication Data

Gardner, Martin, 1914–
    On the wild side / by Martin Gardner.
        p.   cm.
    Includes bibliographical references.
    ISBN 0-87975-713-2
    1. Science—Miscellanea. I. Title.
Q173.G353   1992
500—dc20   91-43151
                                                                          CIP

Printed in the United States of America on acid-free paper.

Contents

Essays

Preface

I cannot recall when or why I first became interested in pseudoscience. It's a topic most scientists find too boring to investigate, and they certainly have no desire to waste valuable time trying to combat it. Not being a scientist, but only a science journalist, I have always been intrigued by fringe science, perhaps for the same reason that I enjoy freak shows at carnivals and circuses. Pseudoscientists, especially the extreme cranks, are fascinating creatures for psychological study. Moreover, I have found that one of the best ways to learn something about any branch of science is to find out where its crackpots go wrong.

For a brief period in my youth, when I was an evangelical Protestant, I took seriously the nonsense in George McCready Price's *The New Geology*, a masterpiece of crazy science. I can say truthfully that I first learned elementary geology by determining where Price's arguments were flawed. Although this is a roundabout way to learn a science, for some curious persons it is a technique I recommend.

My first book about pseudoscience was *In the Name of Science*, published by Putnam's in 1952. It sold so miserably that Putnam's remaindered it a year later. Dover picked it up and reprinted it as a paperback with the new title *Fads and Fallacies in the Name of Science*. It was a huge success, and since 1957 it has never been out of print. One reason it sold so well was that Long John Nebel was then hosting a late-night radio talk show to which he liked to invite cranks. Almost every night, for a year or two, listeners would hear my book blasted by one of Long John's guests.

I recall turning on the radio late one night, when I was bottle-feeding our first child in a Greenwich Village apartment, and hearing John Campbell say, "Mr. Gardner is a liar." Campbell was then editor of *Astounding Science Fiction,* and he had recently been the first to introduce and promote L. Ron Hubbard's philosophy of "dianetics." My chapter on dianetics got me on Hubbard's list of persons to whom his followers could do whatever mischief they liked. Fortunately, I escaped the serious harm done to others, like Paulette Cooper, who had dared to attack Scientology in a book.

My only other full-length work on fringe science is *How Not To Test a Psychic,* a detailed study of how poorly designed were the ESP tests by leading parapsychologists, over a period of more than a decade, of the Czech psychic Pavel Stepanek. The book was published by Prometheus, which earlier had issued two collections of my essays and reviews about bizarre science: *Science: Good, Bad and Bogus* and *The New Age: Notes of a Fringe-Watcher.* Prometheus also published *Order and Surprise,* an anthology in which most chapters are about literature, philosophy, and "straight" science, with some chapters on fringe science tossed in.

I hope no reader will suppose that my intellectual life is so sterile as to be dominated by reading crank literature. My scribblings about pseudo-science are a small fraction of what I have written or intend to write. I confess there are moods in which I agree with my wife that writing about weird science is indeed a thankless task. It may enlighten a few readers so untrained in science that they cannot tell good from bad; it surely has no effect whatever on cranks themselves or on their earnest acolytes.

Some cranks buy almost anything outside mainline science, but the more interesting ones are those who are crazy with respect to only one thing. Sir Arthur Conan Doyle is a classic example. I will not mention contemporary names for fear of libel actions, but every scientist should be able to think of several in his field to whom the following memorable passage from *Don Quixote* will apply:

The curate has just told Cardenio how strange it is that someone as intelligent as the don manages to believe all the absurd tales about knights of bygone ages.

"It is indeed," Cardenio replies, "so rare and unheard of a thing that if anyone desired to invent and fabricate it, in the form of fiction, I do not know if there would be any mind that would be equal to the task."

"But there is another aspect of the matter," the curate goes on. "Outside of the nonsense that he talks where his madness is concerned, if some other subject comes up he will discuss it most intelligently and will reason everything out very calmly and clearly; and, accordingly, unless the topic of chivalry is mentioned, no one would ever take him to be anything other than a man of very sound sense."

Martin Gardner

Skeptical Inquirer Columns

1 | The Obligation to Disclose Fraud

It is customary among editors of scientific journals to let their readers know when a published paper is found to have been based on fraud. It is the only way to prevent the paper from continuing to mislead later researchers. Such was not the practice of Joseph Banks Rhine.

Rhine outlined his policy of secrecy, in a note titled "The Hypothesis of Deception" (*Journal of Parapsychology,* 2, 151-152, 1938) as follows: "Certain friends of the research in extra-sensory perception," he began, "have recently informed us of rumors . . . that the subjects at Duke University and at other places were practicing deception . . . and that even when caught, these deceptions were deliberately withheld from the public. . . ." Rhine goes on to say that his researchers have become so skillful in safeguarding their experiments against both willful and unwitting deception that "no magician . . . is willing to attempt to work (as a magician) under such conditions." Indeed, he continues, so stringent are the controls that "the mere possibility alone" of cheating is "sufficient to bar data from acceptance. . . ."

That subjects and experimenters occasionally cheat is to be expected, Rhine says. It is not surprising, therefore, that his laboratory has "encountered a number of phenomena which on closer investigation proved to be fraudulently produced." Should such evidence be made public? "We do not feel," Rhine answers, "that any good purpose could be served by the exposure, à la Houdini, of these instances. . . . In a word, a research project in ESP does not become of conclusive scientific importance until it reaches the point at which even the greatest will-to-deceive can have no effect under the conditions. This criterion is the very threshold of the research field. It leaves us under no obligation to concern ourselves either with the ethics of the subjects or with the morbid curiosity of a few individuals."

My morbid curiosity was strongly aroused when I recently read in Louisa Rhine's *Something Hidden* (1983) a dramatic account of her husband's discovery that a paper he had published in his journal was based on deliberate cheating by the author. Mrs. Rhine refers to the dishonest parapsychologist only as "Jim." He had contributed many earlier articles

Joseph Rhine (right) testing Hubert Pearce, one of his most successful subjects, in 1933.

to Rhine's journal, and this new work was "considered one of the best of those recently reported."

Banks, as Louisa called her husband, intended to make Jim's paper the "centerpiece" of a talk he was scheduled to give at a meeting of parapsychologists in Columbus, Ohio. A few weeks before the symposium, Gardner Murphy asked Rhine for Jim's original records to consider for his own speech on record-keeping and -checking. Jim brought his records to Rhine a few days before the Columbus meeting. To Rhine's horror, when he and two of his assistants began examining the records, they found unmistakable evidence of fraud. "Jim had actually consistently falsified his records," Louisa Rhine tells us. "To produce extra hits Jim had to resort to erasures and transpositions in the records of his call series." Rhine journeyed to Columbus in great anguish. He had to scrap the paper he intended to read, and deliver instead, with visible nervousness, an entirely different talk. Jim's college professor, after seeing evidence of the cheating, was profoundly shocked and even blamed himself for not being more vigilant.

"Jim's name," Louisa Rhine writes, was never "again seen in the annals of parapsychology."

This simply isn't true. Jim (I learned from a disenchanted parapsychologist) was James D. MacFarland, then a young instructor in psychology at Tarkio College, in Tarkio, Missouri. His flawed paper, "Discrimination Shown Between Experimenters by Subjects," appeared in Rhine's journal

(*JP,* 2, 160-170, Sept. 1938), the issue following Rhine's piece on deception. No retraction of the paper was ever published. Did references to Mac-Farland's research vanish from the literature on psi? It did not. J. G. Pratt in *Extrasensory Perception after 60 Years* (1940), refers to MacFarland's work. And Pratt was one of Rhine's two assistants who originally discovered MacFarland's fudging!

In 1974 Rhine again suffered from unfortunate timing. His paper "Security Versus Deception in Parapsychology," published in his journal (vol. 38, 1974), runs to twenty-three pages. In it he dismisses deception by subjects as no longer significant. Self-deceptions by experimenters is more widespread, but this too is limited, Rhine says, to novices who form a "subspecies of unprepared experimenters" who "may soon be approaching extinction."

Turning to deliberate deception by parapsychologists, Rhine selects twelve sample cases of dishonest experimenters that came to his attention from 1940 to 1950, four of whom were caught "red-handed." Not a single name is mentioned. What papers did they publish, one wonders. Are their papers still being cited as evidence for psi? Rhine is convinced that such fraud diminished markedly after 1960. "We have at least got past the older phase of having to use detectives and magicians to discover or prevent trickery by the subjects." He applauds the growing use of computers, but although "machines will not lie," he warns against overoptimism about their usefulness in parapsychology. Complex apparatus, he cautions, "can sometimes also be used as a screen to conceal the trickery it was intended to prevent."

The warning proved prophetic. A few months after Rhine's paper appeared, Dr. Walter Levy, the acting director of his laboratory and the young man he had chosen to be his successor, was caught red-handed tinkering with an electronic recording machine. The tinkering had beefed up the scores of a test he was making on the PK ability of rats. Levy resigned in disgrace, though, again, references to his earlier papers (one on the PK powers of live chicken eggs) have not yet entirely vanished from psi literature. Rhine tried his best to hush up the scandal; but when it was obvious he could not do so, he wrote an apologetic article about it in his journal. As usual he did not mention Levy's name, apparently under the naive delusion that readers would not learn the flimflammer's identity.

Four years later, England's most distinguished parapsychologist, S. G. Soal, was caught having deliberately fudged the data for one of his most famous tests. I see no sign that Soal's other experiments are disappearing from the literature. Pratt, almost pathologically incapable of believing anyone would cheat, came to Soal's defense. He argued that Soal may have "used precognition when inserting digits into the columns of numbers he was copying down, unconsciously choosing numbers that would score hits on the calls the subject would make later. For me, this 'experimenter psi' explanation makes more sense, psychologically, than saying that Soal consciously falsified for his own records."

I have been told on reliable authority that the files in Rhine's laboratory contain material suggesting fraud on the part of Hubert Pearce, the most talented of all of Rhine's early psychics. Who knows how much data of this sort is buried in the Rhine archives? Let us hope that someday someone with a balanced sense of history, under no compulsion to regard Rhine as one of psi's saints, will be allowed full access to those archives and give us a biography of Banks that is not a hagiography.

Let me change the subject. Early in 1987 Random House published *Intruders,* by Budd Hopkins. It is one of the funniest and shabbiest books ever written about abductions of humans by extraterrestrials who visit Earth in flying saucers. Hopkins is easy to understand. He is a hack journalist of the occult. Harder to comprehend was a full-page advertisement that appeared in the *New York Times Book Review.* It is a long "Dear reader" letter signed by no less a personage than the then-publisher of Random House, Howard Kaminsky.

Kaminsky's letter bursts with praise for Hopkins's worthless volume. The book's events are "objectively set down." You might think the author is a "kook," Kaminsky continues, but it is "Hopkins' calmness, objectivity, and cogency—as well as the mass of medical, physical, and psychiatric evidence he presents—that makes *Intruders* so *un*kooky. He is as intelligent and thoughtful as anyone I know, and questions his own evidence as severely as any skeptic would. . . . There were moments, as I read the manuscript, when I actually got chills down the back of my neck."

Well, chills slithered down *my* neck when I read those incredible remarks by the publisher of one of our nation's most distinguished publishing houses. *Newsweek* magazine (October 26, 1987) devoted page 62 to the story of how Kaminsky had been suddenly fired from Random House by his superior, Robert Bernstein, chairman of the firm, to be replaced by Joni Evans, from Simon and Schuster. (Three months later Kaminsky became president of the Hearst Corporation's Trade Book Group, which includes William Morrow, Arbor House, and Avon Books.) I have no inside information about the personality clashes behind what *Newsweek* called the "rumble at Random House," but I suspect and hope that Kaminsky's idiotic letter played a role in the rumble.

Addendum

I have been told that all records of J. G. Pratt's famous experiment with Hubert Pearce have disappeared from the archives of Rhine's laboratory at Durham, North Carolina. Seymour Mauskopf and Michael McVaugh in their book about Rhine, *The Elusive Science* (Johns Hopkins University Press, 1980), refer to the "serious blow" of 1934 when all of Rhine's best subjects lost their psi powers. The following excerpt, in which Pearce is the unnamed student, underscores Rhine's extreme reluctance to reveal cheating in his experiments:

> In one case, indeed, when experimenters relaxed the test conditions some-what, the subject seemed to be taking advantage of the relaxation to obtain sensory information about the order of the target cards. Rhine reasoned that since the conditions for this experiment had been far looser than they had been for much of the work published in *Extra-Sensory Perception*, these suspicions could have no bearing upon the validity of the earlier work, and he quietly dropped the matter so as not to humiliate the student (although disconcerting rumors occasionally surfaced thereafter about the presence of cheating at Duke).

On Howard Kaminsky's personality, career, and power struggle at Random House, see "The New Protagonist at Hearst Books," in *Business Week* (April 4, 1988).

2 | Occam's Razor and the Nutshell Earth

I could be bounded in a nutshell and count myself a king of infinite space.

Shakespeare, *Hamlet* II:2

There is an old joke about a drunk who, late one night, found himself leaning against a circular pillar. He walked around it several times, patting it, then sank to the ground. "S'no use," he groaned. "I'm all walled in."

Incredible as it may seem, there was once a flourishing religious cult in Florida called Koreshanity, whose guru taught that the earth is hollow and we live on the inside. Almost as hard to believe is that this crazy theory still has defenders. But before explaining how the theory raises deep questions concerning the role of simplicity in science, and drawing a parallel with parapsychology, a few words about the Florida colony.

The founder, Cyrus Reed Teed, began his career as a Baptist fundamentalist and an eclectic doctor. (Eclecticism was a fringe medical school of the late nineteenth century that stressed herbal remedies.) In 1869 Teed experienced what he called his Great Illumination. An angel revealed to him that the earth is a hollow shell and that we live on its inner surface. The sun, moon, and stars are all tiny objects moving about inside the sphere, obeying complicated laws that Teed struggled to explain in his 1870 book *The Cellular Cosmogony, or the Earth a Concave Sphere.*

Calling himself "Koresh" (the Hebrew word for Cyrus), Teed was convinced that God had called him to be the founder of a new faith, that the scientific establishment was persecuting him just as they had persecuted Galileo, and that anyone who doubted the earth's concavity was in the grip of the Antichrist. In the late 1890s he began moving his colony of believers from Chicago to a spot south of Fort Meyers, on Florida's Estero River, where he established the town of Estero. The cult's magazine the *Flaming Sword* did not expire until 1949, after an astonishing life of some 60 years. According to an article in *Southern Living* (May 1984), eight of the cult's thirty buildings still stand and others are being restored. You can take a guided tour through them at the Koreshan State Historic Site, off U.S. 41, in Estero.

Old pseudosciences seldom die completely. In Hitler's Germany an aviator named Peter Bender became the leader of the *Hohlwelttheorie* (hollow-earth doctrine), which championed an inside-out cosmos. After his death the cult continued under the leadership of Karl Neupert, whose *Geokosmos* (Zurich and Leipzig, 1942) was the most widely read of his books. Other German books defending *Hohlwelttheorie* were published, and similar monographs popped up in Argentina.

Cyrus Reed Teed, "Koresh"

About ten years ago, a firm in Nevada City, California, was selling a 1972 English translation of a 1949 German book by Fritz Braun titled *Space and the Universe According to the Holy Scriptures*. The book went through several revisions in Germany, where the English translation was also published. I was unable to obtain any information about the Nevada City group. Braun's most unusual additions to the inside-out model are his putting God's throne in the center of the shrunken universe, within a metal sphere, and locating hell in the boundless region outside the earth. This conforms (Braun argues) to the Bible's picture of heaven as up, hell as down.

The inside-out model recently found its most sophisticated defender in Mostafa A. Abdelkader, of Alexandria, Egypt. Two of his papers were abstracted in the *Notices of the American Mathematical Society* (October 1981 and February 1982), and his article "A Geocosmos: Mapping Outer Space Into a Hollow Earth" was published in *Speculations in Science and Technology* (vol. 6, 1983, pp. 81-89), an Australian journal devoted to unorthodox science. The noted philosopher Paul Feyerabend is on its editorial board.

Although Abdelkader acknowledges his indebtedness to Braun, he gives to the concave-earth model a mathematical precision lacking in all earlier accounts. Imagine the earth's surface to be a perfect sphere. Using simple equations, Abdelkader performs on space what geometers call an "inversion" with respect to the sphere. All points outside the sphere are exchanged with all points inside. The sphere's center maps to infinity, and infinity maps to the center. Inversion theory is often used by geometers for proving

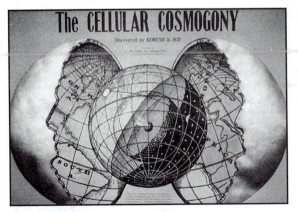 

Left: Drawing of Teed's concave-earth cosmogony. (Courtesy Donald E. Simanek.)
Right: Karl Neupert, another promoter of the hollow-earth doctrine.

difficult theorems, and it has been extremely useful in physics.

After inverting the cosmos, Abdelkader then applies the same inversion to all the laws of physics. The result is a consistent physics that cannot be falsified by any conceivable observation or experiment! Of course the equations for the laws become horribly complex. Light rays follow circular arcs, the velocity of light goes to zero as it approaches the center of inversion, and all sorts of other bizarre modifications of laws are required. To an observer in this inverted universe everything looks and measures exactly the same as in the Copernican model, even though the heavenly bodies become minuscule. Day and night, eclipses, and the orbits of the sun, moon, and planets—everything—can be explained by suitably inverted laws. Instead of the earth rotating, the shrunken celestial bodies revolve the opposite way around the earth's "axis." Because light follows curved paths, the sun seems to set as usual below the "horizon" as it travels a conical helix, six months in one direction and six months in the other. The Foucault pendulum, Coriolis effects, and other inertial "proofs" of the earth's rotation are all accounted for by the drastically modified laws.

Could you confirm the theory by taking off in a spaceship to see if you would quickly reach the other side by following a diameter of the sphere? No, because the closer you got to the center of inversion the smaller your ship would become and the slower it would move. You would soon find yourself traveling through what would appear to be vast galaxies. If the universe before inversion was open and infinite, you would never reach the center. It would be a singularity at which your size and speed would be zero, and time would stop completely. Of course you could avoid the singularity and get to the other side, but the trip would take as long as traveling to the outer edge of an expanding Copernican universe, and back again. The fastest way to get to the other side would be to fly around the inner surface of the hollow earth.

Abdelkader says his main reason for believing in his inverted model is the relief it brings from the anxiety of thinking the universe is so immense that the earth fades into insignificance. Braun earlier expressed the same emotion by writing that once you accept his model "the fearful distances of billions of light years, the infinite emptiness and senselessness" of the Copernican model disappears. A Freudian would say that the inside-out universe expresses an unconscious urge to return to the warmth and security of the womb.

Nowhere does Abdelkader invoke the Koran or his religious faith, though I suspect that Muslim fundamentalism lurks in the background in the same way that Christian fundamentalism underlies flat-earth theories and the cosmological models of Teed and the German concave-earthers. Teed liked to quote Isaiah 40:12, "[God] hath measured the waters in the hollow of his hand." Abdelkader also thinks that cosmic rays are best explained by his cosmology and that a definitive test of his model could be made by drilling a hole straight down through the earth. If his model is correct, would it not penetrate the earth's shell and open a hole to outer space?

It would not. A true inversion of infinite space would produce an infinitely thick shell of solid rock all the way to eternity. As the drill went "down," it would get larger and longer, and move more rapidly, until it passed through the "point at infinity," which corresponds to the earth's center before inversion. After that, the drill would start boring into the earth on the opposite side. The drill would emerge from the earth at a point antipodal to where it began drilling.

The matter is controversial, but most mathematicians believe that an inside-out universe, with properly adjusted physical laws, is empirically irrefutable. Why, then, does science reject it? The answer is that the price one has to pay in complicating physical laws is too high. A similar situation arises in relativity theory. There is nothing "wrong" in supposing the earth fixed, as Ptolemy believed it was, with the cosmos whirling around it. The question of which frame of reference is "right," a fixed earth or a fixed universe, is as meaningless as asking whether you stand on the earth or the earth stands on your feet. Only relative motions are "real," but the complexity of description required when the earth is taken as the preferred fixed frame is too great a price to pay.

The opposite is the case with respect to choosing between Euclidian space and the non-Euclidian spacetime of general relativity. It is possible to preserve Euclidian space and modify the laws of relativity accordingly—indeed, just such a proposal was advanced by Alfred North Whitehead—but here simplicity is on the side of non-Euclidian space. In the space-time of relativity, light continues to move in straight lines, rigid objects do not alter their shapes, and gravity becomes identical with inertia. It is only when we talk in a Euclidian language that gravity bends light, objects contract at fast relative speeds, and gravity and inertia appear as distinct forces.

Conventionalism is the term used for points of view that emphasize the extent to which mathematicians and scientists adopt basic axioms not because they are "true" but because they are the most convenient. Rudolf Carnap called it the "principle of tolerance," which he once expressed by saying, "Logic has no morals." One is free to adopt any set of axioms provided the system that follows is consistent and useful. One primary criterion of usefulness is simplicity. The inside-out model of the universe is rejected not because it is "untrue" but because an application of Occam's Razor—the law of parsimony—makes the Copernican model enormously simpler.

Abdelkader's geocosmos poses an extreme example of a choice between two conventions, one simple and the other insanely complicated. But on all levels of science Occam's Razor is a powerful tool. I will cite only one instance from thousands in the literature of psychic research. When parapsychologist Charles Honorton saw his friend Felicia Parise seemingly use psychokinesis to move a plastic pill bottle across a kitchen counter, the film of this great event showed her hands creeping slowly forward on each side of the bottle. The simplest explanation is that an "invisible" thread, stretched horizontally above the table from one hand to the other, propelled the bottle. The bottle even moved in little jumps, just as it would if friction resisted the pressure of an extremely fine, slightly elastic nylon thread. This conjecture gains support from the facts that Honorton did not know that invisible thread could be used in this manner to move light objects away from a person, that he did not examine Felicia's hands before the experiment, and that Felicia has never repeated the miracle.

Why do some parapsychologists, after simple tricks like this have been explained to them by magicians, refuse to thank the explainers or to alter their beliefs about the genuineness of the phenomena? Occam's Razor suggests the following hypothesis: They lack the courage to admit that, like the drunk, they had patted a pillar instead of a surrounding wall.

Addendum

Here is how geometrical inversion works for inverting the plane with respect to a circle. Exactly the same procedure inverts space with respect to a sphere.

Let o be the circle's center, r the radius, and p any point inside the circle. The inverse of p is p' outside the circle. The two points lie on a straight line with $(op) (op') = r^2$.

Given p, its inverse can be located by the simple procedure shown in the illustration. Draw a perpendicular from p to the circle's circumference at point x, then extend a tangent to x (a line perpendicular to r). It will intersect the horizontal line at p'. Reversing the construction locates p when p' is given.

The point at the center of the circle (or center of the earth) goes to infinity after inversion. This of course alters the topology as well as the metric of the universe, leading to such causal anomalies as the drill that goes through the center of the inverted cosmos to emerge on the sphere's opposite side. Philosophers of science disagree over whether causal anomalies of this sort prevent an inside-out universe from being empirically refutable. For a good discussion of this curious controversy, see "Quine on Space-Time," by J. J. C. Smart, in *The Philosophy of W. V. Quine,* edited by Lewis Hahn and Paul Schilpp (Open Court, 1986).

Inversion of the universe can be performed with respect to any sphere, a fact that prompted the following letter from Forrest Johnson, of Goleta, California. It appeared in the *Skeptical Inquirer,* Winter, 1989.

I was interested to read Martin Gardner's column about Abdelkader's inversion hypothesis (*SI,* Summer 1988), which holds that the earth is inside-out and the rest of the universe is within. However, I would like to suggest an alternative.

Suppose, not the earth, but the moon were inverted. The earth would orbit inside of the moon, and everything else would be within the earth's orbit. The same mathematics that support Abdelkader's inversion hypothesis would support my lunar inversion hypothesis. In fact, there is no scientific reason to prefer one to the other. Anyone who agrees with Abdelkader's hypothesis must agree that mine is equally plausible.

But—oops!—what about Mars? Could it be inverted? How about the sun? Or Alpha Centauri? Or some planet in a distant galaxy? The same model would support any of them as containing the universe. There is nothing special about the earth; the others are just as likely.

Suppose there are 10^{23} eligible bodies in the universe. Then the chance that we happen to be standing on the inside of the particular one that contains the rest is $1/10^{23}$, or pretty close to zero.

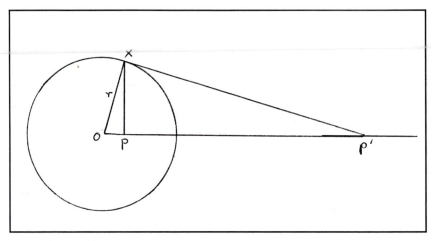

How to invert a circle . . .

Therefore, even if we accept Abdelkader's reasoning and agree that the universe is inverted, it still requires a leap of faith to believe that we are on the perimeter. We would, much more likely, be a tiny speck near the center of a vast and unknown world. A humbling thought!

The many-worlds interpretation of quantum mechanics is another theory that seems empircally nonfalsifiable, but such an extreme violation of simplicity that only a small minority of physicists are willing to defend it.

3 | Wilhelm Reich, the Rainmaker

Of the many fringe psychotherapies that flourished in the fifties, the two most bizarre were each founded by a paranoid egotist who had not the foggiest understanding of scientific method or even of the fields in which he claimed revolutionary discoveries. One was Scientology, the other was orgonomy.

Orgone energy—an energy no physicist outside orgonomy circles has detected—was "discovered" by Wilhelm Reich, who began his tragic career as an Austrian associate of Freud. After being expelled from the German Communist Party, and later from the International Psychoanalytic Association, Reich eventually settled in the United States, where he established a "laboratory" at Rangeley, Maine. Reich first discovered orgone energy in living things, hence its name, but he soon became convinced that it was a primeval force responsible for the evolution of the universe, for gravity, for life, and for the energy released in sexual orgasms. He announced that he had created living cells from inorganic matter and that cancer cells are actually protozoa that "have a tail and move in the manner of fish." Orgone energy, he insisted, made the sky blue and caused stars to twinkle, as if physicists hadn't long understood such phenomena.

Reich's main therapeutic tool was what he called an "orgone accumulator." It is a box about the size of a phone booth, its walls made of alternating layers of metal and organic material. (One is on display in St. Louis's National Museum of Quackery.) There are no electrical connections. You sit inside to soak up orgone energy that accumulates inside the box like heat in a greenhouse. The concentrated orgone is said to relieve symptoms of almost every illness from cancer to impotence. Smaller models, such as the shooter box, the orgone blanket, and the orgone funnel, apply orgone to ailing body parts.

Thousands of intelligent people with only a dim knowledge of science—including writers, artists, actors, educators, even philosophers—sat inside orgone boxes and believed they were enormously benefited. The comic Orson Bean sang the praises of orgonomy in his book *Me and the Orgone*.

"WR: Mysteries of the Organism" was a comic film about orgonomy by Yugoslav filmmaker Dusan Makavejev, who had earlier been enamored of Reich's ability to stir together psychoanalysis and Marxism.

Wilhelm Reich (1897–1956)

Unable to get published in mainstream journals, Reich came more and more to resemble a movie version of the mad scientist. He likened himself to such martyrs as Socrates, Bruno, Galileo, and Jesus. Soon he was discovering that orgone had a destructive side he called "DOR," an acronym for Deadly Orgone Energy. To dispel the DOR that accumulated in the atmosphere, Reich invented what he called a "cloudbuster." It consisted of long parallel pipes, their empty interiors "grounded" by hollow cables to a source of flowing water. Like a lightning rod, the machine was supposed to draw DOR from the sky. To his amazement, Reich found that his machine would also condense clouds and produce rain. "One may create clouds in the cloud-free sky in a certain manner by disturbing the evenness in the distribution of the atmospheric orgone energy. . . . The more clouds that are present and the heavier the clouds, the easier it is to induce growth of clouds and finally rain" (*Selected Writings,* p. 444).

This was topped by a still more sensational discovery. Reich observed that when his cloudbuster was operating it attracted EA's. EA stood for Energy Alpha, Reich's term for a UFO. (Reich was fond of acronyms, like HIG for Hoodlums in Government, EPPO for Emotional Plague Prevention Office, and dozens of others.) EA's are propelled by orgone motors that give off vast quantities of DOR. At first Reich thought this was an innocent by-product of spaceships, but soon became convinced that evil aliens were spying on him and intentionally damaging the area. Fortunately his cloudbuster drained the DOR from their motors, forcing the EA's to flee.

In 1954, when Reich banished his first EA, he recorded the great event in his notebook: "Tonight for the first time in the history of man, the war waged for ages by living beings from outer space upon this earth . . . was reciprocated . . . with positive results." The battle took place in Arizona. Here is how Reich's son Peter described it in *A Book of Dreams,* a touching biography of his father:

I was just about to go back downstairs when I saw it, hovering in the south. I watched it for a minute. It pulsated and glowed. Then I ran to get daddy. He was sitting in his work room at a long desk writing in one of his red ledger books. "Daddy, I spotted one. In the east. It looks pretty big." [Peter went to summon Reich's daughter, Eva, and her husband, Bill.]

Bill pulled out his binoculars. "Boy, it sure is something," he said, handing the glasses to Eva. She looked for a while and said, "I knew it would come."

Daddy took off his hat and pushed his hand through his long silvery hair. "I wish I knew if this was an attack or if they were just observing the Earth."

* * *

I moved the cloudbuster slowly from one side of the EA to the other. I let it draw on the right side for a while and then dipped it slowly like a baby's cradle on a yo yo and rubbed back and forth at the sky beneath it before coming back up to the other side. I let the cloudbuster orunize on either side. . . .

"Why it's gone!" Bill said. . . .

Daddy said, "That was very good Peeps, very good. You are a real good little soldier because you have discovered a new way to disable EA's. I am very proud of you."

Reich's last and craziest book, *Contact with Space,* was published posthumously in a limited edition and is now extremely rare. It tells of his efforts to save the world from the CORE (Cosmic Orgony Energy) men, Reich's term for the aliens from space. "On March 20, 1956, 10 P.M.," the book opens, "a thought of a very remote possibility entered my mind, which I fear will never leave me again. Am I a spaceman? Do I belong to a new race on earth, bred by men from outer space in embraces with earth women?" What inspired this thought? It was seeing the science-fiction film *The Day the Earth Stood Still,* about a spaceman who comes to Earth in a flying saucer to save us from self-destruction in a nuclear war. "All through the film," Reich says, "I had a distinct impression that it was a bit of *my story* which was depicted there, even the actor's expressions and looks reminded me and others of myself as I had appeared 15 to 20 years ago."

In 1956 the Food and Drug Administration, convinced that orgone boxes were damaging the health of gullible people by keeping them from needed medical care, ordered Reich to stop shipping them across state lines. Reich defied the injunction and was hauled off to court, where he served as his own attorney. The court proceedings sketch a tragic picture of a man seriously ill with delusions of grandeur and persecution. Sentenced to jail for two years and fined $10,000, Reich entered Lewisburg Federal Penitentiary persuaded that President Eisenhower, whom he greatly admired, knew of his genius and would pardon him. Reich died in prison of a heart attack, at the age of 60, a few weeks before he was to be released. To the end he believed his persecution was a conspiracy by a group of "red fascists" inside the FDA who were trying to steal for Russia the secret Y factor he claimed was necessary to operate another of his inventions, a motor that ran on orgone energy.

One might have thought that today's orgonomists (science cults never die, they just slowly fade after the death of their charismatic gurus) would confine themselves to Reich's youthful contributions to psychoanalysis, which are reasonably sane and still greatly admired by many psychiatrists, but no—most of them buy it all. Almost all of Reich's books, including some of the funniest (unconsciously funny, of course, because Reich had no sense of humor), are back in print by Farrar, Straus, and Giroux, and a raft of books have been written about him. The worst is by Colin Wilson, England's intrepid journalist of all things occult. The most reliable biography is *Fury on Earth* (1983) by Myron Sharaf, whose own wife had an affair with Reich. As Reich's third wife, Ilse Ollendorff, discloses in her candid biography, Reich was intensely jealous of her, while insisting on the Victorian freedom to have sexual romps of his own.

In 1967 the remnant faithful founded the semi-annual *Journal of Orgonomy,* and a year later, the American College of Orgonomy. In 1987 the new "college" moved its headquarters from Manhattan to Princeton, New Jersey. Patricia Humphrey, wife of conservative Republican Senator Gordon Humphrey from New Hampshire, was chairperson of a committee that raised $2.5 million for a college building and is now conducting a drive for an additional $3 million.

The most active rainmaker associated with the college is Dr. V. James DeMeo, Jr. He got his B.S. degree from Florida International University, Miami, in 1975, and his master's in 1979 from the University of Kansas, Lawrence. His thesis (available from Ann Arbor's University Microfilms, ID number 13-13336) is titled "Preliminary Analysis of Changes in Kansas Weather Coincidental to Experimental Operation with a Reichian Cloudbuster." His Ph.D. thesis (University of Kansas, 1986) is "On the Origin and Diffusion of Patrism: The Saharian Connection." Formerly an assistant professor of geology and geography at Illinois State University, Bloomington, he is now assistant professor of geography at the University of Northern Iowa, Cedar Falls.

DeMeo's cloudbuster, which he calls "Icarus," consists of ten parallel aluminum pipes, 3 inches in diameter and 18 feet long. The space inside the pipes is, as Reich specified, "grounded" by empty tubes to a source of nonstagnant water. When not in use, the lower ends of the tubes are stoppered and taken out of the water. The pipes can be raised, lowered, and swiveled by electrical controls to point at any spot in the sky. In an interview in Blooming-ton's *Daily Pantagraph* (August 9, 1983), DeMeo explained that water grounding was necessary because of a not-yet-understood property of water that relates it to air pressure and mag-netism: "For example, when you soak in a tub of hot water, the water draws tensions from your body." In analogous fashion, the water alters the atmos-phere's "tension parameter." To cause rain, the pipes are aimed not at the

An anti-aircraft gun? No. It's a "cloud-buster" manned by Reich and two assistants.

clouds but at nearby areas to relieve the "tensions" that prevent the clouds from releasing rain.

"Every phase of Reich's orgone theory was derived experimentally," DeMeo wrote in reply to angry letters in the *Pantagraph*. He accuses his critics of the same prejudice that persecuted Galileo and that provokes "otherwise calm and rational people into fits of irrational rage."

In a *National Enquirer* article that someone sent me undated, DeMeo put it this way: "The theory is simple enough. The atmosphere stagnates into deadly orgone and my machine simply conducts energy from the stag-nant area." He claimed thirteen rainmaking successes out of fifteen attempts. When the machine is on, birds tend to flock around it, and to fly away when it's off. Cumulus clouds of moderate size dissipate when the pipes of Icarus are pointed toward them, but they grow larger when the pipes are aimed to one side.

In 1987, at the Arid Lands Conference in El Paso, Texas, DeMeo gave a paper on "A Cloudbusting Expedition into the Southeast Drought Zone, August 1986." Funded by the American College of Orgonomy, DeMeo and his associate Robert Morris, a Reichian therapist, took two cloudbusters into Georgia and South Carolina to relieve a major dry spell. From August 6 through 12 they moved the machines from place to place, at thirteen different sites. DeMeo claims huge success in triggering rain. The cloud-busters operated poorly, however, in "areas where nuclear plants were located. . . . In those cases the orgone continuum around the cloudbuster became over-exercised, eliciting a mild to severe oranur reaction" that made everybody feel "uneasy." ORANUR was Reich's acronym for Orgonomic Anti-Nuclear Radiation.

DeMeo and Morris identify themselves as co-directors of Rainworks, and of the Orgone Biophysical Research Laboratory. DeMeo is tireless in traveling around the country giving profitable lectures and weekend workshops on orgone biophysics. He also makes and sells a variety of devices, such as the orgonotester ($1,500) and a pendulum that oscillates with orgone energy ($150). At the close of his El Paso lecture he thanked Fred Westphal for his help. Westphal is a philosopher at the University of Miami, Coral Gables, and the author of two philosophy textbooks published by Prentice-Hall.

There are rival Reichian groups. Courtney Baker, M.D., son of the founder of the American College of Orgonomy, heads the Institute for Orgonomic Science, which issues an annual periodical. Lois Wyvell, former editor of the college's journal, now publishes her own quarterly, *Offshoots of Orgonomy*. Jerome Eden, in Carrywood, Idaho, issues a newsletter, heavily UFO oriented, from his Center for Orgonomic Education. These and other splinter groups are sharply hostile toward one another, and toward Mary Higgins, administrator of the Reich Infant Trust Fund, which owns and operates the Reichian Museum, in Rangeley. Eva Reich has unsuccessfully sued the fund for access to her father's papers, and Higgins has repeatedly sued Reichian groups for copyright infringements. Lore, Reich's other daughter by his first wife, is an orthodox Freudian analyst in Pittsburgh, with no interest in orgonomy.

When Reich first observed that heat inside his orgone box rose above room temperature, he wrote to Einstein asking for a meeting to discuss this discovery. They met in 1941. Later Einstein wrote to Reich that the temperature does indeed rise, but there is a simpler explanation than concentrated orgone. Reich called this the "Einstein affair." Poor Einstein! In Reich's eyes he lacked the vision to see the discovery of orgone as ushering in a new Copernican Revolution, and one that would save our planet from the twin dangers of a nuclear holocaust and an attack by extraterrestrials.

H. G. Wells, who had a doctorate in biology, did not have Einstein's kindly patience in dealing with cranks. A. S. Neill, founder of the famous Summerhill School, was one of Reich's strongest supporters. When he sent Wells a copy of Reich's most famous book, *The Function of the Orgasm,* Wells replied:

Dear Neill,

You have sent me an awful gabble of competitive quacks. Reich misuses every other word. . . . There is not a gleam of fresh understanding in the whole bale. Please don't send me any more of this stuff.

Neill shot back:

Dear Wells,

I can't understand why you are so damned unpleasant about it. I considered you the man with the broadest mind in England and sincerely wanted light on a biological matter I wasn't capable of judging myself. Your Black Out letter might have been written by Colonel Blimp. I hoped you would give an opinion on bions and orgones, whether they were a new discovery or not, and all I got was a tirade against Reich. You apply the word "quack" to a man whom Freud considered brilliant, a man who has slaved for years in a lab, seeking truth.

I grant that I asked for it. I intruded. I apologise and . . . being a Scot . . . refund your postage. . . . But this is no quarrel, and I won't bother you again with Reich or anyone else.

Wells closed the exchange with:

Dear Neill,

No, I decline your stamps, but this business is quackery. You call me a Blimp, I call you a sucker. Bless you.

H. G. Wells

Addendum

James DeMeo is now research director of the Orgone Biophysical Research Laboratory, where he continues to be tireless in sponsoring workshops, selling Reichian literature and equipment, contributing to the *Journal of Orgonomy,* and writing angry replies to critics.

In 1989 DeMeo started a quarterly periodical called *Pulse of the Planet.* Its first issue (Spring) featured a lengthy "Response to Martin Gardner's Attack on Reich and Orgone Research in the *Skeptical Inquirer.*" This was reprinted in a freethinker's magazine, *The Truth Seeker* (Winter 1990). You can obtain a copy of the response by writing to DeMeo's Laboratory, P.O. Box 1395, El Cerrito, California 94530.

4 | Water With a Memory?

"Experimenter effect" has two meanings. Outside psychic research circles it refers to the way a strongly held mind-set can unconsciously bias an experimenter's work. Among parapsychologists it also refers to the supposed unconscious influence of an experimenter's PK (psychokinetic) powers on the research.

Putting aside the second meaning (if such an effect is real, it would throw doubt on all empirical findings since Galileo), a bizarre, almost comic instance of the experimenter effect came to light in July 1988. It involved a group of scientists at INSERM U200, a medical-research institute in a Paris suburb. Their findings were widely publicized (*Newsweek,* July 25, 1988; *Time,* August 8, 1988) not merely because they were so astounding, but because for the first time they seemed to provide strong empirical support for the fringe medicine of homeopathy.

The century's most notorious instance of an experimenter effect that sparked a vigorous scientific controversy also occurred in France. In 1903 René Prosper Blondlot, a respected French physicist, claimed to have discovered a new kind of radiation, which he called N-rays after the University of Nancy, where he worked. Scores of papers confirming the reality of N-rays had appeared in French journals before a skeptical American physicist, Robert Wood, visited Blondlot's laboratory and played a dirty trick on him. Wood secretly removed from Blondlot's apparatus a prism that was claimed to be essential to the observation of N-ray spectra. Blondlot went right on describing the lines he fancied he was seeing. After Wood reported this in the British science journal *Nature* (vol. 70, 1904, p. 530), N-rays vanished from physics, but poor old Blondlot never acknowledged his self-deception.

Last June, physicists and chemists around the world were incredulous over a paper in *Nature* (vol. 333, June 30, p. 816) titled "Human basophil degranulation triggered by very dilute antiserum against IgE." The report was signed by thirteen biologists—two from Israel, one from Italy, one from Toronto, and the others part of a team at INSERM (the Institut National de la Santé et la Recherche Médicale) headed by biochemist

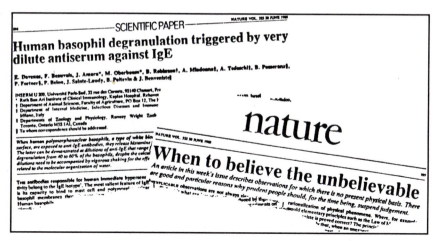

The French group's original report and *Nature*'s editorial calling it unbelievable.

Jacques Benveniste. The phrase "very dilute" in the title is a whopping understatement. As the editors of *Nature* pointed out in an unusual disclaimer accompanying the article, the dilution of the French group was so extreme that not a molecule of the antiserum was left in its solvent. The editors considered the results unbelievable, but said they were publishing the paper for two reasons: It purported to give an accurate account of work that had been widely trumpeted in France by popular articles, and it provided other scientists with an opportunity to confirm or falsify the extraordinary claims.

What were these claims? In essence the French researchers were convinced that, after all the molecules of a certain antibody were removed from distilled water, the water somehow "remembered" the antibody's chemical properties. Although such a claim violates fundamental laws of physics, it lies at the very heart of homeopathy, a medical pseudoscience that flourished in the United States in the nineteenth century and is now enjoying a modest revival. Homeopaths maintain that if a drug produces symptoms of a disease in a healthy person, inconceivably small quantities of that same drug will cure the disease. Moreover, the smaller the amount of the drug—including its total absence—the more potent its curative power.

Thousands of homeopathic drugs are listed in the cult's *materia medicas*—handbooks that vary widely from time to time and from country to country. If a drug is soluble—bee venom, for example—it is mixed with water or alcohol in repeated dilutions. The mixture must be shaken violently for about ten seconds after each dilution, otherwise the medicine won't work. If a drug is not soluble, it is ground into a fine powder and diluted by repeated mixing with powdered lactose (milk sugar). A moderate homeopathic dose, called "30c," is arrived at by first diluting the drug to a hundredth part and then repeating the process 30 times. As someone pointed out, it is like taking a grain of a substance and dissolving it in billions of spheres of water, each with the diameter of the solar system.

Benveniste claims that the antibody he used is still potent when dilutions are even more extreme—one part to 10^{120} parts of water! As science writer Malcolm Browne remarked in his *New York Times* account of the French claims (June 30, 1988), astronomers estimate the number of stars in the universe as a mere 10^{20}. Benveniste said the potency of his dilutions is comparable to swirling

Jacques Benveniste and Elizabeth Davenas, lead experimenters of the French group, in their lab. (Photo by James Randi)

your car key in the Seine, going some hundred miles downstream, taking a few drops of water out of the river, and then using them to start your car. It is easy to show mathematically that when such extreme dilutions are made of homeopathic drugs, as they are constantly, the chance of a single molecule remaining in the solvent or powder is vanishingly small.

Certain white blood cells, called "basophils," have granules that stain a reddish color when treated with a blue dye. Incubating these cells with a strong solution of an antibody causes them to lose those granules, a process known as "degranulation." When a solution of the antibody has been diluted to the point at which no molecules of the antibody remain in the distilled water, one would expect the cells to retain their red-staining granules. Not so. According to Benveniste, about half the basophils continued to degranulate when so treated.

How do homeopaths explain this supposed potency of infinitesimal doses, even when the dilution removes all molecules of a drug? They invoke mysterious vibrations, resonances, force fields, or radiations totally unknown to science. Benveniste suggests in his paper that antiserum molecules may somehow cause water molecules to rearrange their hydrogen atoms in some inexplicable fashion that mimics the action of the antibody even when it is no longer there. In other words, water can remember the properties of a missing substance.

This magic memory water is even weirder than polywater, a conjectured new type of water that caused an enormous flap among chemists in the 1960s. Boris Derjaguin, a Soviet chemist, announced that when water collects in hairlike capillary tubes it acquires all sorts of strange properties. John D. Bernal, a noted British physicist and historian of science (he was also a dedicated communist and a great admirer of Soviet science), hailed it as the "most important physical-chemical discovery of this century."

Because polywater, as it was called, could have great military uses, the Army, Navy, and other U.S. agencies began tossing out generous grants. A flood of papers about polywater popped up everywhere. Derjaguin even wrote a nontechnical article about the water for *Scientific American* (November 1970). *Nature* (224, 1969, p. 198) published a warning from an American scientist that research on polywater should proceed with extreme caution because it might polymerize the earth's oceans, destroy all life, and change the earth into a planet like Venus.

It turned out that the miraculous water was just ordinary water contaminated by dirty test tubes. Derjaguin himself threw in the towel by announcing that for ten years he had wasted his time studying nothing more than dirty water. Meanwhile millions of dollars had been squandered on polywater research. You can read all about this remarkable farce in *Polywater* (MIT Press, 1981), a fine book by Felix Franks. He faults government agencies for premature funding, technical journals for overpermissiveness, experimenters for repeated self-deception, and the mass media for irresponsible hype.

It is too early to know if Benveniste's homeopathic water will survive as long as polywater did, or if the French biochemist will eventually withdraw his paper. *Nature,* highly suspicious of so outrageous a claim, asked a team of unpaid volunteers to fly to Paris to devise and observe a replication of Benveniste's experiments in his own laboratory. (The visit and investigation were preconditions for publication of the original article.) Benveniste readily agreed, and even planned a celebration with champagne when the replication was over and his results were vindicated. The team consisted of John Maddox, editor of *Nature,* who has a background in physics; Walter Stewart, an organic chemist and a specialist in scientific fraud from the National Institutes of Health in Bethesda, Maryland; and the indomitable magician and psi detective James Randi.

Their blistering report in *Nature* (334, July 28) opens: "The remarkable claims made . . . by Dr. Jacques Benveniste and his associates are based chiefly on an extensive series of experiments which are statistically ill-controlled, from which no substantial effort has been made to exclude systematic error, including observer bias, and whose interpretation has been clouded by the exclusion of measurements in conflict with the [claims]. . . . The phenomenon described is not reproducible in the ordinary meaning of that word. We conclude that there is no substantial basis for the claim. . . . The hypothesis that water can be imprinted with the memory of past solutes is as unnecessary as it is fanciful."

The investigators were equally dismayed to learn that two of Benveniste's colleagues, Bernard Poitevin and P. Belon, were homeopathic physicians whose salaries at INSERM were paid by Laboratoires Boiron, a French firm that manufactures homeopathic remedies. The firm also paid the hotel bills for the *Nature* team. There is no need to belabor the point that, when research is funded by a corporation that stands to increase its profits if results go a certain way, the funding can have a corrupting influence on research. One thinks at once of the scientific hacks, paid handsomely by the tobacco industry, who repeatedly prove there is no connection between smoking and lung cancer.

The popular French magazine *Science et Vie* (Science and Life) in its August issue was disturbed by the fact that Benveniste had announced as early as May, at a national conference on homeopathy, that his paper would be appearing in *Nature*. On July 1 journalists in France received a thick press release about the forthcoming paper, and in July the French stock exchange did a brisk business in Boiron shares. *Science et Vie* wondered if French newspapers and television stations would give as much publicity to the debunking of Benveniste's work as they did to its promotion. If not, "water memory will remain an established fact for believers in homeopathy."

The key person in all the French experiments, as well as in their "confirmation" by a laboratory in Israel, was Dr. Elizabeth Davenas, a young woman in her twenties and a good friend of Poitevin, one of the two homeopathic doctors in the French group. She is the observer who looks through the microscope to count the red-staining granules that remain. Randi listed fifteen different pretexts on which she accepted "good" cases and rejected "bad" ones; Walter Stewart's list contained nineteen such items. It is not clear whether she is deceiving herself in a manner similar to Percival Lowell's famous self-deception when he peered through telescopes and drew pictures of intricate canals on Mars, or whether some cells actually lose color occasionally because of contaminants. On this point the *Nature* investigators write:

> In circumstances in which the avoidance of contamination would seem crucial, no thought seemed to have been given to the possibility of contamination by misplaced test-tube stoppers, the contamination of untended wells during

the pipetting process and general laboratory contamination (the experiments we witnessed were carried out at an open bench). We have no idea what would be the effect on basophil degranulation of the organic solvents and adhesives backing the scotch tape used to seal the polystyrene wells overnight, but neither does the laboratory.

The original *Nature* report was understandably greeted with loud hosannas by homeopaths around the world. Readers interested in the wild history of this once most popular of all alternative medicines can consult Chapter 16 of my *Fads and Fallacies* (Dover, 1952), or "Homeopathy: Is It Medicine?" by Stephen Barrett in the *Skeptical Inquirer* (12, Fall 1987; see also comments in the letters section of the 1988 Spring and Summer issues). Dr. Barrett is also the author of a hard-hitting paper in *Consumer Reports* (January 1987) about a yearlong investigation of homeopathy. His report concludes:

> Unless the laws of chemistry have gone awry, most homeopathic remedies are too diluted to have any physiological effect. . . . CU's [Consumers Union] medical consultants believe that any system of medicine embracing the use of such remedies involves a potential danger to patients whether the prescribers are M.D.'s, other licensed practitioners, or outright quacks. Ineffective drugs are dangerous drugs when used to treat serious or life-threatening disease. Moreover, even though homeopathic drugs are essentially nontoxic, self-medication can still be hazardous. Using them for a serious illness or undiagnosed pain instead of obtaining proper medical attention could prove harmful or even fatal.

I find in my files a sad clipping from the *New York Post* (July 25, 1954) about Jerold Winston, a Long Island boy, age 4, who died of leukemia. For sixteen months he had been treated only with a homeopathic remedy by his mother, the daughter of a homeopathic doctor. The parents were facing a possible manslaughter charge for child neglect. Who knows how many tragedies like this occur when gullible people rely solely on worthless medicines?

Homeopathy had almost died in the United States by 1960, though it continued to be popular in France, Germany, Russia, India, England, Mexico, Argentina, Brazil, and other countries. But in the New Age climate of the seventies and eighties it experienced a surprising upsurge among those who are attracted to holistic medicine, natural foods, herbal remedies, acupuncture, reincarnation, and the paranormal. There are now several hundred homeopathic doctors in the United States, about half with orthodox medical degrees. The others are mostly chiropractors, naturopaths, dentists, veterinarians, and nurses. This is a small number compared to some 14,000 such physicians in 1900, when more than twenty schools in the United States taught the art and there were more than one hundred homeopathic hospitals.

New books on homeopathy are appearing on general trade lists. Jeremy Tarcher, a publisher of New Age literature (including books on Spiritualism), has two homeopathic volumes in a recent catalog: *Everybody's Guide to Homeopathic Medicines,* by Stephen Cummings and Dana Ullman, and *Homeopathic Medicine at Home,* by Dr. Maesimund Panos and Jane Heimlich. Heimlich is the wife of Dr. Henry Heimlich, orginator of the famous "Heimlich maneuver," used to aid persons choking on food. In 1980 she was quoted in the *New York Times* (November 19) as saying she took great pride in converting her father, the dancing teacher Arthur Murray, to homeopathy.

The Complete Book of Homeopathy, by Michael Weiner and Kathleen Goss, was issued by Bantam Books in 1981. With all the media publicity about Benveniste, and the continuing growth of New Age nonsense, more such books are surely on the way. Nothing stimulates a fringe medical cult more than attacks by skeptics, or by "allopaths," the homeopathic term for orthodox doctors.

Cummings and Ullman, in their book on homeopathy, claim there are more than 6,000 homeopathic doctors in France today, and 18,000 pharmacies that sell their medicines. In India, they tell us, more than 70,000 doctors practice the art. (In an article in the January 1984 issue of *Fate* magazine, the nation's sleaziest occult periodical, Ullman upped this number to 200,000.) England's royal family, according to the Queen's physician, has been under homeopathic care for more than 150 years. Dozens of famous nineteenth-century American writers, political leaders, and businessmen patronized homeopathic physicians, including Washington Irving, who died under the care of a homeopathic family doctor. Ullman, who holds a master's degree in public health from the University of California, Berkeley, is the nation's top homeopathic journalist. He was arrested in California in 1976 for practicing medicine without a license.

How will homeopathic doctors and true believers react to *Nature*'s debunking? There is not the slightest doubt they will take their cues from Benveniste's angry reply, which ran in the same issue of *Nature* as the critique. His invective is unprecedented in a science journal. Members of the *Nature* team are branded "amateurs" who created "hysteria" in the French laboratory. Their investigation is called a "mockery of scientific inquiry." Benveniste likens it to the Salem witch-hunts and the McCarthy persecutions. He told the *Wall Street Journal* by phone (July 17, 1988) that the *Nature* report was a sinister plot to discredit him. In Paris he told *Le Monde* (July 27) that Walter Stewart was incompetent and the investigation was a "scientific comedy . . . conducted by a magician and a scientific district attorney who worked in the purest . . . Soviet ideology style" to install a "scientific gulag."

"During the whole week I was tempted to kick them out," he said to the French newspaper *Le Figaro* (July 27). "We never could imagine the extent to which these 'experts' were going to shuffle the cards." He attacked *Science et Vie* for calling him a "new Lysenko," adding "you should know that I am the most important researcher in the world and the one most in demand at colloquia."

It is obvious from Benveniste's fury that he learned absolutely nothing from *Nature*'s careful, restrained investigation. Its lessons had the same effect on his mind as a vanishing substance has on distilled water. All he can do now is squeal as loudly as he can, like a stuck pig, and hurl insults at his inquisitors.

Consider the egotism and folly of this man. He rushes into print with a claim so staggering that if true it would revolutionize physics and medicine, and guarantee him a Nobel prize. Yet he did this without troubling to learn the most elementary techniques for conducting truly double-blind tests or for supervising self-deceiving observers. When Randi mentioned N-rays to him, he said he had never heard of them! Does he remember, one wonders, the story of polywater?

A few scientists and science journalists criticized *Nature* for publishing the original article. Daniel Koshland, Jr., editor of *Science,* agreed that a responsible journal should "encourage heresy" but added that it also should "discourage fantasy." It is one thing, he told science writer Walter Sullivan (*New York Times,* July 17), to publish unorthodox work that may turn out to be wrong, but the French claim about water with a memory was too far on the fantasy side, like an account of the successful construction of a perpetual-motion machine.

Other scientists have faulted *Nature* both for publishing the French paper in the first place and for later investigating the claims. Arnold Relman, editor of the *New England Journal of Medicine,* said *Nature* should have required confirmation by an independent group of biochemists before running the article, and that it was not its function to serve as an investigative body. This view was shared by Henry Metzger, a colleague of Stewart at the NIH. He said he had urged this approach when he refereed the paper for *Nature.* Immunologist Avrion Mitchinson, at University College London, thought the French paper not worth publishing. "It is a whole load of crap," he declared, "a clear example of unconscious data selection." However, he did not believe it would do much harm. "Anyone who thinks the great ship of science can be damaged in such a way is greatly mistaken." (On such criticisms see "More Squabbling Over Unbelievable Result," in *Science,* 241, August 5, 1988, and "The Ghostbusters Report from Paris," in *New Scientist,* August 4, 1988.)

Nature's correspondence section (August 4) ran four letters from scientists who proposed conventional explanations for the French results. In the same issue the editors defend themselves in an editorial headed "When to Publish Pseudo-science." When one-fourth of French doctors prescribe homeopathic medicines, they argue, "there is plainly too much at stake for the issue to be dropped."

The editorial recalls an earlier publication in *Nature* (238, 1972, pp. 198-210) of the claim that, when the protein scotophobin is extracted from the brains of rats trained to run a maze and then injected into untrained rats, there is a transfer of maze-running ability. The paper was followed by a "devastating critique" by Stewart, and that ended the matter. "Is not a little of the 'circus atmosphere' inescapable on these occasions?" Why did *Nature* not withhold the French report until they made their investigation, then publish the two reports side by side? The editors have replied elsewhere that they did not do this because Benveniste had leaked information about his paper to the French press and, had they withheld his paper until after their investigation, he would have refused to allow *Nature* to print it.

INSERM has refused to take sides in the controversy. It did announce, however, that Benveniste's work would be subjected to its regular examination and a judgment made then. Benveniste took this to mean that INSERM was tossing him to the wolves. "*Nature* sends a magician to check my research," he declared, "and INSERM doesn't even protest. It's the limit!" I quote from Peter Coles's article, "Benveniste Controversy Rages in the French Press" (*Nature,* August 4). He also reveals that Boiron, a 51-percent shareholder in another firm, Laboratoires Homéopathiques de France, has purchased all remaining shares.

"Look," Randi said to the French group, "if I told you I keep a goat in the backyard of my house in Florida, and you happen to have a man nearby, you might ask him to look over my garden fence. He would report, 'That man keeps a goat.' But what would you do if I said, 'I keep a unicorn in my garden'?"

The point of course is that no extraordinary verification is needed to establish the existence of a goat in Randi's garden. But a unicorn? As the *Nature* authors write sadly at the close of their indictment, "We have no way of knowing whether the point was taken."

Addendum

Benveniste's effort to confirm homeopathy theory generated an enormous amount of publicity. For a list of major early newspaper and periodical references see the *Skeptical Inquirer,* Winter 1989, pages 145-146. A good later overview is Andrew Revkin's article "Dilutions of Grandeur," in *Discover,* January 1989. The title, independently thought of by several journalists, accurately reflects Benveniste's unalterable mind-set.

In 1989 Benveniste was suspended from INSERM until he submitted new plans for research and forbidden to discuss his homeopathy experiment with the media. I do not know what his present status is with INSERM, but I have been told that he is still working hard to replicate his earlier results.

A few science writers thought *Nature* behaved irresponsibly. The most vitriolic criticism came from *Nature*'s competitor, England's *New Scientist.* In an editorial of August 18, 1988, headed "Inhuman Nature," it blasted *Nature* for having "developed symptoms not unlike those often associated with rabies, madness and foaming at the mouth." Not only did *Nature* publish a paper without believing a word of it, but it then "set out to create an event more suited to the tabloid end of Fleet Street than the creator of volumes intended for posterity. The editor and his band of merry men descended upon Benveniste . . . card tricks in hand, ready to stitch up the unsuspecting scientist." *Nature* is accused of having engineered the whole thing as a PR campaign to boost circulation. The editorial writer hopes that the "aberration" will not be repeated.

Recently at an antique fair I picked up a copy of a homeopathic work titled *Lectures on Homeopathic Medicine,* by James Tyler Kent (Philadelphia: Boerick and Trefil, second edition 1911; the first edition was in 1904). Kent is identified as a professor at Hering Medical College, Chicago, and the author of other books on homeopathy. This book, 982 pages, is undiluted medical nonsense. Not a paragraph in it has a shred of empirical support. Hundreds of such homeopathic tomes were published around the world, when homeopathy was at its height of popularity, with very little agreement among the authors as to what substance, diluted of course, would cure what diseases or ailments.

Kent must have been eminent in his day because I found an entry on him in *Who Was Who in America.* His M.D. degree was given by the Eclectic Medical Institute, Cincinnati. He was a homeopathic physician in St. Louis from 1873 to 1888, and in Philadelphia from 1888 to 1900, after which he was affiliated with several homeopathic hospitals before he settled in Evanston, Illinois, where he died in 1916. "Allopathic" medicine was in a sorry state at the time. Ironically, Dr. Kent's patients probably did as well under the placebo effects of his worthless remedies as patients of the allopaths.

An interview with Walter Stewart, illustrated with photographs and stressing his debunking of Benveniste, appeared in *Omni,* February 1989. For background on the bizarre history of homeopathy, see the chapter on this in my old Dover paperback, *Fads and Fallacies in the Name of Science* (1952). Homeopathy continues to be fashionable in New Age circles and among addicts of alternative medicines, with new books on homeopathy appearing every year in the United States, England, France, and Germany.

5 | Gaiaism

Sherlock Holmes was Conan Doyle's greatest detective. Professor George Edward Challenger was his top science-fiction hero. Less well known than the professor's discovery of living dinosaurs (in *The Lost World*) is his discovery (in the short story "When the World Screamed") that the earth is a living organism. When Challenger drilled a hole eight miles deep, it punctured the earth's soft epidermis. All the world's volcanoes erupted while the injured earth howled with pain.

Although most of science-fiction's living worlds have been stars, many have been planets. The earliest seems to be in R. A. Kennedy's "The Tri-universe" (1922), where Mars divides by fission and its cells eat parts of other planets. Planets are eggs laid by Mother Sun in Jack Williamson's "Born of the Sun" (1934). Only Earth has hatched.

Among philosophers, pantheists tend to see the entire universe as a sentient Mind. If they are also panpsychics, they believe that everything is to some degree alive, including heavenly bodies. One of the most extreme panpsychics was the German philosopher-scientist Gustav Fechner. Here are some excerpts from William James's colorful tribute to Fechner in *A Pluralistic Universe:*

> All the things on which we externally depend for life—air, water, plant and animal food . . . are [the earth's] constituent parts. She is self-sufficing in a million respects in which we are not so. We depend on her for almost everything, she on us for but a small portion of her history. . . .
>
> The total earth's complexity far exceeds that of any organism, for she includes all our organisms. . . . As the total bearing of any animal is sedate and tranquil compared with the agitation of its blood corpuscles, so is the earth a sedate and tranquil being compared with the animals whom she supports. . . . A planet is a higher class of being than either man or animal; not only quantitatively greater, like a vaster and more awkward whale or elephant, but a being whose enormous size requires an altogether different plan of life. . . .
>
> What are our legs but crutches, by means of which, with restless efforts, we go hunting after the things we have not inside of ourselves? But the earth

is no such cripple; why should she who already possesses within herself the things we so painfully pursue, have limbs analogous to ours? Shall she mimic a small part of herself? What need has she of arms, with nothing to reach for? . . . of eyes or nose when she finds her way through space without either, and has the millions of eyes of all her animals to guide their movements on her surface, and all their noses to smell the flowers that grow? . . .

Think of her beauty—a shining ball, sky-blue and sun-lit over one half, the other bathed in starry night, reflecting the heavens from all her waters, myriads of lights and shadows in the folds of her mountains and windings of her valleys, she would be a spectacle of rainbow glory, could one only see her from afar. . . .

It was just such a spectacle seen from afar, photographed by astronauts who called it a "blue pearl in space," that inspired James E. Lovelock when he developed his Gaia hypothesis. In his two books about Gaia, Lovelock recognizes a dozen scientists who anticipated him. Why has he never mentioned Fechner, who more than any other thinker wrote eloquently in praise of a living earth?

Born in 1919, Lovelock is a British biochemist (he has a doctorate in medicine) who now lives in Cornwall, his Gaia research financed by income from his many inventions of scientific instruments. His first book, *Gaia* (1979), was followed almost ten years later by *The Ages of Gaia* (1988). Both center on the startling claim that Earth is a living organism— "the largest of living systems" known, an entity "endowed with faculties and powers far beyond those of its constituent parts."

Although Lovelock denies that Earth is a "sentient" organism—I assume he means one conscious of its existence—nevertheless his living earth is more than metaphor. "You may find it hard to swallow," he writes, "the notion that anything as large and apparently inanimate as the Earth is alive." Pages are devoted to the difficulty of defining "life," and to defending, along lines identical with Fechner's, the right to say the earth is truly living. Gaia (more commonly spelled Gaea or Ge) was the Greek goddess of Earth, a name suggested by Lovelock's fellow villager, novelist William Golding.

Are there other Gaias? Probably not in the solar system. Mars and Venus are surely dead—Lovelock does not buy Fechner's panpsychism— but perhaps living planets orbit other suns. If we colonize Mars, transforming it into a self-regulating planet, Mars will spring into life. Lovelock has even coauthored a science-fiction novel about this, *The Greening of Mars* (1984).

Lovelock's second major theme is that, instead of life and the earth evolving separately, with life adapting to environment as Darwin taught,

 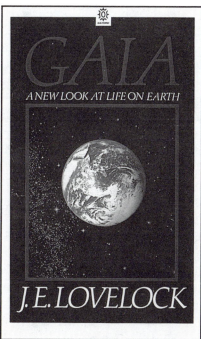

Gustav Theodore Fechner, and *Gaia,* the book that really got the ball rolling again.

as soon as life got beyond the early bacterial stage it lovelocked with Earth to form a system that henceforth evolved as a single entity. Life and its environment are in perpetual dynamic interaction. Earth regulates life, life regulates Earth. To dramatize this feedback, Lovelock constructed the Daisy-world, a simplified model of a planet whose main life-forms are daisies, some black, some white. They do more than just adapt to temperature. They control it. If sunlight is weak, black daisies increase, absorb more heat, and warm the earth. If sunlight is strong, white daisies increase, reflect light, and cool the earth.

Lovelock and his fellow colleagues are constantly finding instances of this kind of feedback, each new discovery taken as a confirmation of the Gaia hypothesis. Recently they published evidence that some species of plankton, floating in the ocean, produce a chemical that may influence world temperature by the way it affects the formation of clouds. (Research testing this interesting proposal—it found no evidence of any cloud-formation or global-temperature effect of a similar, man-made chemical, sulfur dioxide—was recently published in *Nature* [336:441, December 1, 1988] by Stephen E. Schwartz.)

There is new and legitimate scientific interest in considering the earth as a system of dynamic, mutually influencing interactions and feedbacks among living organisms and the oceans, atmosphere, and geosphere. Related to this is a worthy attempt to bring the knowledge of all the relevant sciences to bear on such issues and not be overly confined by rigid disciplinary boundaries. Lovelock's ideas may even have had an influence in this trend. Yet the *scientific* dispute about his ideas revolves around the controversial suggestion of *control.*

Stephen H. Schneider, a highly respected climatologist at the National Center for Atmospheric Research, credits Lovelock with a stimulating, even profound, concept but parts company with him on that point: "The realization that climate and life mutually influence each other is profound and provides an important counterpoint to the parochial view of the world as physical environment dominating life. . . . Nevertheless, the fact that climate and life 'grew up together' and mutually influenced each other . . . is not the same thing as to say that life somehow self-optimizes its own environment. . . . Few would have agreed that the influence of life is so effective and directed that it actually controls the environment for its own purposes. Indeed, that is the essence of the controversy surrounding Gaia: whether environmental self-control exists and whether it is in a sense a 'conscious' act of life processes. The former makes fascinating scientific debate, while the latter has strong religious implications." (See Schneider's detailed essay on Gaia in the *Encyclopaedia Britannica 1988 Yearbook of Science and Technology* and his shorter editorial in the journal *Climatic Change,* 8:1-4, 1986, which he edits.)

Lovelock's critics raise several other objections. Is it not a misuse of language to call the earth alive? As a poetic metaphor, okay, but to go beyond that generates confusion. If Earth is alive, why not a large ship? It too displays dynamic interaction between lifeless matter and hundreds of crew members. Another criticism is that scientists have known for centuries that life interacts with its environment. The outstanding instance is the way plants absorb carbon dioxide and produce the oxygen required by animals. This symbiosis of life and environment is so obvious, critics contend, that the Gaia hypothesis is like rediscovering the wheel.

Moreover, say the critics, Lovelock exaggerates the degree to which life influences environment. Take away seas, air, and soil, and life would perish. Take away life, and the earth would spin along very well, thank you, as if nothing had happened. In his first book, Lovelock suggests that plate tectonics may be "biologically driven." In his new book he writes: "It may be that the core of our planet is unchanged as the result of life, but it would be unwise to assume this." How life could influence the earth's core is as hard to imagine as its effect on continental drift.

Lovelock is of course opposed to atmospheric pollution and the destruction of forests, but he has annoyed many of his admirers by downplaying the dangers of nuclear radiation. He thinks the Laplanders were foolish to destroy their reindeer after the Chernobyl accident, because the loss of food did them more damage than eating mildly radioactive meat would have done. Gaia is not "some fragile and delicate damsel in danger from brutal mankind." Past changes of environment produced by glaciation, earthquakes, volcanic blowouts, and huge meteoric impacts "make total nuclear war seem, by comparison, as trivial as a summer breeze." Humanity may indeed commit suicide, but if so, Gaia won't care.

Lovelock in his home laboratory.

Although most scientists find Lovelock's vision charming—even scientifically provocative—they still think it distorts common speech and overblows the obvious. But the vision continues to catch on. More and more technical papers and popular articles are defending it; more and more conferences are debating it. A living planet called Gaia flourishes in Isaac Asimov's *Foundation and Earth*. Documentary films about Gaia have been produced. Gaia Books, a London house, has published *Gaia: An Atlas of Planetary Management* (1984), a large picture book edited and written by Norman Myers. Doubleday's edition here has sold more than 175,000 copies.

The appropriation of Gaia by New Agers into holism and ecology strikes most of Lovelock's associates as absurd. "The religious overtones of Gaia," said his leading collaborator, Boston University biologist Lynn Margulis, "make me sick." Lovelock himself was surprised by such overtones. He calls himself an agnostic who believes neither in a personal god nor an afterlife. He is down on teleology. The universe has no purpose; nor is Gaia in the least concerned with preserving humanity. Her self-regulation is automatic, as unconscious as the self-regulation of a tree or a termite colony.

To Gaia, we are "just another species, neither the owner nor the stewards of the planet." If we succeed in destroying ourselves, Gaia will turn without pity to other species to preserve life. Lovelock's first book closes with a surprising paean to whales. They have minds, he tells us, "far beyond our comprehension"—minds vast enough to include "the complete specification of a bicycle" but lacking the tools and knowledge needed to "turn such thought into hardware." Someday, he believes, we may harness whale mind-power the way we once harnessed horse muscle-power.

Lovelock is more tolerant of Gaia's religious side than are most of his associates. He has twice preached at the Cathedral of St. John the Divine, in Manhattan, where the dean is a Gaia buff and there is a church-sponsored Gaia workshop. "God and Gaia . . . are not separate," Lovelock declares in his new book, "but a single way of thought." He urges Catholics to look upon Mary as another name for Gaia, the true "Mother of us all." Although Lovelock denies that Gaia is a "surrogate God," he writes about her with the same awe and affection that Catholics write about Mary. Here again he is not far from Fechner, who likened the earth to a "guardian angel"—a living entity higher than human but lower than the ultimate God.

Like so many maverick scientists, Lovelock shares with cranks a bitterness toward the "establishment" for neglecting him. In his new book he faults its "tribal rules" and its "narrow-mindedness." Like medieval theologians, the mainstream scientists are "creatures of dogma" and the "scourge of heresies." Proud of his freedom to be "eccentric," Lovelock calls on other scientists to join him. They have "nothing to lose but their grants."

There is little evidence that the mystical aspects of Gaiaism are about to be warmly embraced by the establishment, but as a semireligious New Age cult Gaiaism is rapidly blossoming. There is even a Gaia hymn. I quote one stanza from "Britain's Whole Earth Guru," an article by Lawrence Joseph in the *New York Times Magazine* (November 23, 1986):

> Gaia is the one who gives us birth.
> She's the air, she's the sea, she's Mother Earth.
> She's the creatures that crawl and swim and fly.
> She's the growing grass, she's you and I.

Addendum

Lewis Thomas, the medical doctor and popular science writer, has become a surprisingly strong defender of Gaian mysticism. In a mini-essay "Beyond the Moon's Horizon—Our Home" (*New York Times Book Review*, July 15, 1989) he defines the Gaia hypothesis as "the new idea that the Earth itself is alive." (Far from new, this notion goes back to Plato's *Laws*. Giordano Bruno and Kepler held similar views.) To qualify as a living organism, Thomas writes, the only thing Earth lacks is the ability to re-

produce. But wait around! "Given enough time, and given our long survival as working parts of the giant creature. . . the Earth may be entering
the first stages of replication, scattering seeds of itself, perhaps in the form
of microorganisms. . . ."

> So the first moon walk brought forth two new possibilities of viewing our-
> selves and our home. First, the Gaia idea of a living Earth, not at all the
> mystical notion that it would have seemed a few years back (but still carry-
> ing the same idea of "oneness" that has long preoccupied the mystics among
> us), is now becoming the most practical, down-to-earth thought ever thought.
> And second is the idea of the Earth reproducing itself, and the possible role
> we might be playing, consciously or unconsciously, in the huge process.
> Finally, as something to think about, there is the strangest of all para-
> doxes: the notion that an organism so immense and complex, with so many
> interconnected and communicating central nervous systems at work, from
> crickets and fireflies to philosophers, should be itself mindless. I cannot be-
> lieve it.

It would take many pages to list important articles about Gaia that
have been published in the last few years. Here are a few that seem to
me of special interest:

"What Gaia Hath Wrought," by Francesca Lyman, in *Technology
Review,* July 1989.

"Gaia: Ecologists Embrace the Earth Goddess," by Rogelio Maduro,
in *21st Century,* September-October, 1989.

The Truth Seeker, March/April, 1989, is devoted entirely to articles
about Gaia,

"Gaia," by Tim Beardsley, in *Scientific American,* December, 1989.

As Beardsley points out, Lovelock has considerably modified his views
over the years. He now agrees with his critics that the earth, although
regulating itself in many ways by feedback from its life forms, does not
"optimize" the environment (occasionally it makes the environment worse),
nor does she have "foresight." What is left, then, Beardsley asks, "to
distinguish Gaia from a conventional view of evolution? . . . Is Gaia then
anything more than the simple persistence of life? If so, she has yet to
reveal herself. Her many lay followers, however, seem to be unwilling to
hear that the goddess of their temple is nowhere to be found."

These harsh words triggered a reply by Lynn Margulis and John Stolz
that ran in *Scientific American*'s March 1990 issue. They not only defend
the degree to which life regulates the physical earth, so essential to Lovelock's theory, but "We suspect that even plate-tectonic movements and ocean
salinity are biotically modulated." They call for research to test these conjectures.

It remains to be seen how long Gaia's broadening of the meaning of "alive"—what philosophers like to call a category mistake—will persist among its devotees. My guess is that it will soon fade, and Gaiaism will become a short-lived, eccentric phase in the history of what everybody calls ecology.

6 | Robert Gentry's Tiny Mystery

The most aggressive of the nation's "young earthers"—creationists who believe the earth and all its life were created six to ten thousand years ago—is Robert Vance Gentry. He was creationism's star witness at the 1981 creation/evolution trial in Little Rock, Arkansas, but his chief claim to fame is that, unlike other creationists, his research has been published in such mainline journals as *Science* and *Nature*. Jerry Falwell's museum at Liberty University has a dramatic exhibit of Gentry's claims. You'll even find him in *Who's Who in America*.

Born in Chattanooga, Tennessee, in 1933, Gentry obtained a master's degree in physics in 1956 at the University of Florida. Three years later he and his wife became converts to Seventh-Day Adventism as a result of watching George Vandeman's weekly telecast "It Is Written." Gentry has held posts as an engineer with private firms, taught at several colleges, and from 1966 to 1984 was a physicist at Columbia Union College, an Adventist school in Takoma, Maryland. For 13 years he had a contract with Oak Ridge National Laboratory that allowed him to use their costly equipment. It was not renewed after his participation in the Arkansas trial.

For the past several years Gentry has headed his own firm, Earth Science Associates, in Knoxville, Tennessee. The firm was originally funded by Elsworth McKee, an archconservative Adventist millionaire who owns and manages McKee Bakery, a company whose products have the trade name of "Little Debbies." It was McKee who paid for the printing of a book by Gentry, which we will discuss later.

Seventh-Day Adventists are fundamentalists who take every verse in the Bible to be accurate and divinely inspired, and who have almost the same reverence for the writings of their prophetess Ellen Gould White. Convinced that the idea of evolution was inspired by Satan, Gentry took it upon himself to find irrefutable evidence that the earth was created about 6,000 years ago in six 24-hour days. At first he thought he had found this evidence in the form of superheavy elements in the earth with half-lives too short to account for their presence. (A half-life is the time it takes half the atoms of a radioactive substance to disintegrate.) When this research proved flawed, Gentry turned his attention to polonium halos, "Po halos" for short.

Po halos are the cross-sections of concentric microscopic spheres found in the crystals, especially mica, of certain Precambrian granites, and in such substances as coal and zircon. When a tiny sphere is sliced in half, you see concentric rings, or halos. Everyone agrees that the halos are produced by radioactive decay of isotopes of polonium, element 84. What scientists have

Robert V. Gentry, aggressive "young earther."

called a "tiny mystery" arises from the fact that polonium isotopes have extremely short half-lives, ranging from a few microseconds to several months. If geologists are right in assuming it took millions of years for hot magma to cool and form granite, then the Po halos should have vanished long before the crystals formed. So how is it that the halos are there? It is Gentry's claim that their existence proves, beyond all doubt, that the granite crystallized almost instantly after God created the earth *ex nihilo*.

There is, of course, an enormous amount of hard evidence that the earth is billions of years old. As Frank Press, president of the National Academy of Sciences, compressed it in a letter to Gentry in 1987: "I cannot agree . . . that one small piece of data invalidates the vast body of evidence from geology, astronomy, biology, radiodating, the fossil record, genetics, and other fields that taken together irrefutably show that the age of the earth is about 4.5 billion years. . . ."

It is true that the halos are a tiny mystery, but all scientists who are not creationists, as well as many creationists, expect the mystery to be solved either by some overlooked aspect of nuclear physics or by some unusual geological process. Many conjectures have been made. Because there is no consensus, Gentry concludes that his work "stands like a Rock of Gibraltar" against the tide of evolution. He has issued a ringing challenge to his detractors. Synthesize a piece of granite with Po halos, he tells them, and he will admit defeat.

Geologists were quick to point out that to synthesize granite one would first have to produce magma and that would require heat and pressure far beyond any obtainable in a laboratory. Even if magma could be made, hundreds of thousands of years of slow cooling would be necessary to form crystals with Po halos. As one geologist put it, "Gentry has presented mainstream scientists with a totally unrealistic proposal, then faulted them for their silence."

How does Gentry escape from such proofs of an ancient earth as furnished by carbon dating, tree rings older than 6,000 years, evidence from polar ice caps, from limestone cave formations, from salt domes, and from a hundred other geological features, not to mention half a dozen techniques for estimating the ages of rocks, fossils, and human artifacts? Like Velikovsky, who supported his wild scenarios by invoking laws unknown to science, Gentry invokes what he calls three great "singularities"—occasions when God intervened to suspend the "uniformitarianism" of evolutionary theory.

The first great singularity was the six-day creation, about 6,000 years ago, of the entire Milky Way galaxy. How about the light reaching Earth from stars in the galaxy that are more than 6,000 light-years away? (The galaxy's radius is about 30,000 light-years.) This light, Gentry is persuaded, was created "on the way." And light from galaxies billions of light-years away? In 1987 astronomers observed the explosion of a supernova more than 150,000 light-years from Earth. This is not a problem for Gentry because he allows that other galaxies are much older than ours.

In Gentry's bizarre cosmology—he calls it the RSS model (Revolving Steady State)—the universe has spherical symmetry with a finite number of galaxies revolving around the universe's center. At the center, which he suggests is a few million light-years beyond the constellation of Orion, is nothing less than the Throne of the Almighty!

Why Orion? Because Ellen White, in one of her famous visions, saw the New Jerusalem descending to earth, at the Second Coming, through an "open space" in Orion. I had supposed that Adventists had long ago abandoned their quaint claim that God's Throne lies beyond an open space in Orion, but no. I recently came across a booklet by Vandeman, *Look! No Doomsday* (1970), that contains a chapter headed "Rescue from Orion."

The motion of our solar system can be measured relative to the microwave radiation that pervades space, a glow that astronomers believe to be left over from the big bang. Gentry considers this radiation to furnish an absolute reference frame for measuring motion. This of course would demolish relativity theory. Gentry actually believes that the microwave radiation has rendered relativity theory obsolete but that the world's top physicists are too stupid to realize it.

The second great singularity was the Fall of Man. The third was Noah's

Flood, which Gentry dates at about 4,300 years ago. This monstrous deluge produced all the earth's sedimentary rocks and all the fossils in those rocks. The dinosaurs are no longer with us because they were too big to go on Noah's ark. How does this scenario circumvent such evidence for an old earth as carbon dating and the other criteria mentioned above? Simple. Within each singularity God modified many physical laws. Radioactive decay, for example, was greatly speeded up. This generated enormous heat that caused intense volcanic activity and other upheavals, and presumably boiled away the flood waters. Naturally, the accelerated radioactive decay would account for false carbon-dating. Similar changes in physical laws explain the rapid formation of tree rings, striations in polar ice, the formations of limestone caverns, salt domes, coal beds, and so on. After the Flood, God kindly restored the laws we know and love today.

All this is detailed in Gentry's privately published *Creation's Tiny Mystery* (1986). The second edition, a 348-page paperback (1988), with 11 color plates of halos, can be obtained by sending $13.95 to the author's Earth Science Associates, Box 12067, Knoxville, TN 37912. The book includes a stirring account of the 1981 Arkansas trial, transcripts of testimony by Gentry and others, reactions of the media, a lengthy bibliography of Gentry's many published papers and letters, and an appendix that reprints major documents.

Gentry and his wife, Patricia Ann, live in Powell, a small town close to Knoxville and not far from where I live in North Carolina. In February 1989 I drove to Knoxville to meet with them. I was less interested in discussing Po halos, about which I know nothing, than in finding out how seriously Gentry takes Adventist doctrines. I was surprised to find him as ill-informed about his church's early history as he is about geology. He accepts Ellen White's visions and writings as inspired by the Holy Spirit, but he was not familiar with *The White Lie,* an explosive recent book by disenchanted Adventist minister Walter Rea. It contains detailed documentation of the extent to which White shamelessly plagiarized long passages from other writers, repeating many of them word for word. The Gentrys leafed through the copy I brought, but had little to say about it. I would be amazed to hear they have since tried to obtain a copy.

I was more astonished to learn that Gentry had never read *The New Geology,* by Adventist George McCready Price. As I emphasized in a chapter on Price in my book *The New Age,* this is *the* classic defense of a young earth and the Flood theory of fossils. Gentry seemed to know nothing about Price's clever arguments against uniformitarianism, although his own Flood theory is pristine Price. Nor was he aware that until the 1930s Adventist literature maintained that the Second Coming was sure to occur within the lifetimes of some who had witnessed the great meteoric shower of 1833.

Jesus said that "this generation" would witness his Second Coming, and Adventists took the phrase to mean, not the generation of his listeners, but the generation that would see various signs in the heavens, such as falling stars.

Gentry assured me that Adam and Eve had no navels and that trees in Eden had no rings, but he allowed that the couple were not bald even though hair seems as good evidence of past history as belly buttons. He believes that Eve was created from Adam's rib. When I said this struck me as demeaning to women—that the first mother would have been fabricated from a minor male bone—Gentry reminded me that a rib was one of the few bones that could be removed without damaging a person.

Gentry buys it all. Lot's wife turned to salt, Moses parted the Red Sea, Jesus walked on the waves and turned water to wine. Gentry was unconcerned about Jehovah's seeming cruelty in drowning all living babies. As he justified it: God could foresee that, had the little ones survived, they would have become evil adults. How about sinless dogs and cats? Well, that was a price that had to be paid. Why did God send lightning to destroy Moses' nephews when they failed to mix incense properly for a sacrifice? The ritual was so holy, Gentry explained, that violating it was a terrible crime. He had no objection to God telling Moses to kill all the men, women, and children of a conquered tribe, but was silent when I asked why God allowed Moses to keep all the virgin women as slaves. He had no comment when I told the story of Jephtha's sacrifice of his daughter. I had the impression I was bringing up parts of the Old Testament he had either not read or not thought much about.

Gentry's most vocal critic is J. Richard Wakefield, a Canadian amateur geologist. I recommend two of his papers: "Gentry's Tiny Mystery—Unsupported by Geology," in *Creation/Evolution,* 8 (1988):13-33, and "The Geology of Gentry's Tiny Mystery," in the *Journal of Geological Education,* 36 (1988):161-165. An unpublished article, "The Continuing Saga of the Po Halo 'Mystery' " (1988), is obtainable from Wakefield, 385 Main St., Beaverton, Ontario, Canada L0K 1A0. "Radioactive Halos: Geological Concerns," by creationist Kurt Wise, in the *Creation Research Society Quarterly,* 25 (March 1989): 171-180, is a vigorous attack, followed by Gentry's lengthy rebuttal.

What does the Adventist church think of Gentry's views? Not much. Robert Brown, a conservative Adventist at the church's Geoscience Research Institute, Loma Linda University, Loma Linda, California, told me that the church did its best to avoid criticizing Gentry until last year, when he demanded a confrontation. Its opinion was expressed in a strongly negative review of Gentry's book by five members of the institute, including Brown, in the institute's periodical *Origins,* 15 (1988):32-38.

The authors stress Gentry's inconsistency in assuming that God accelerated radioactive-decay rates for all elements except polonium, presumably to put Po halos in the rocks as evidence for a young earth. (Some halo-producing isotopes other than polonium have half-lives of thousands of millions of years.) They also point out not only that granite intrudes itself in older rocks that contain fossils but also that some fossil brachiopods are found within granite. As the authors put it, "One could hardly argue that God would place fossils in granite he was creating."

Adventist leaders long ago abandoned Price's young-earth view. They do not agree on exactly what to make of evolution, but the trend is toward accepting an ancient earth, while retaining the belief that all life was created six to ten thousand years ago, and that the fossils are (as Price argued) records of life destroyed by the big flood. However, the church is now aware, said Brown, that Price's self-taught geology bristles with blunders. It explains why the church has allowed his many books to go out of print.

Gentry clearly sees himself as ordained by the Lord, during these final days before He returns, to give the world positive proof of a young earth. Now that his own church has refused to endorse his Po halo evidence, it will be amusing to see how he carries on his divine mission. Stay tuned.

Addendum

Mystery in the Rocks, a 64-page paperback by Dennis Crews, was privately published in 1990 by Amazing Facts, POB 680, Frederick, Maryland. It is a vigorous defense of Gentry as a victim of establishment science, though it nowhere identifies him as a Seventh-Day Adventist. Until I read it I did not know that Gentry's views prevented him from getting a doctorate at Georgia Tech. The department rejected his plan to base his thesis on polonium halos.

Julian Goldsmith, a University of Chicago geophysicist, corrected my statement that magma cannot be produced in today's laboratories. There are now methods for producing heat and pressure much greater than those responsible for the formation of granite. However, there is no known way to allow for the slow cooling necessary to produce the crystals and texture of granite.

Let me clarify my assertion that the microwave radiation does not refute relativity theory. It is true that this radiation provides a reference frame against which the motions of stars can be measured. But this is no different from measuring the earth's motion relative to, say, the Andromeda nebula or the Milky Way Galaxy as a whole. In relativity theory, the principle of co-variance states that any inertial frame can be chosen as fixed. One may even assume the earth is neither moving nor rotating, with the entire cosmos (and its microwave radiation) moving and rotating relative to the earth. It is not a question of one being right and the other wrong, because only relative motions are "real." The tensor equations of relativity theory are unaltered by any choice of a fixed reference frame.

A paper offering an explanation of polonium halos, much too technical for me to have an opinion about it, is "Giant Radiation-Induced Color Halos in Quartz: Solution to a Riddle." Written by Leroy Odom and William Rink, geologists at Florida State University, it appeared in *Science,* October 6, 1989, pages 107–109.

The following letter from Robert F. Erickson, of Placerville, California, ran in *The Skeptical Inquirer,* Winter 1990:

> As an ex-Adventist (now an atheist), I appreciated Martin Gardner's article on Robert V. Gentry and his "Tiny Mystery." The author seems to have a pretty good grasp of not only Gentry's Adventist idiocy but the church's problem as well.
>
> Over almost a lifetime as a member of Adventism, I had found it loaded with all kinds of extremes, from those who some would call "Whiters" (ultra-conservative), to those with a more pragmatic (liberal) approach to the world of a soon-coming Christ. And, because of these variations in recent years, the church by its own admission is hemorrhaging and losing 50 percent of its members. . . . For a church that values education, it cannot enlighten its youth and expect them to remain in the ignorant stagnation of its inerrant, hopeless message of 1844, which is the foundation of its particular message!
>
> Gentry's arguments represent all the benightedness that Adventism produces in its extremism. He is a prime example of what true primitive Adventism is, and he, I betcha, has a true following of those "Whiters" who say *Amen!* to all his inerrant ramblings. To them Adventism is the remnant church, and only those that keep the seventh day will be saved! So evolution, which decries the Sabbath, is the epitome of Satanic thought in these days before Christ comes (to save the Sabbath keepers).
>
> There are now Adventists who look differently at the earth's age, as well as those who believe that modern humanity goes back 100,000 years. And because of this there is a split developing between them and the literal creationists that is tearing the church asunder. Gentry, in his obvious ignorance of his chosen faith, is the champion of those who would preserve the tradition and cornfield experience (their 1844 Sanctuary message) from which the church has developed.
>
> Adventism is in a crisis, for Christ has not come as they predicted 145 years ago. Men like Gentry are the result of this desperation, which I might add is not a new issue.

7 | Ira Einhorn: The Unicorn at Large

Strange as it may seem, radical political views, both left and right, often go hand in hand with beliefs in pseudoscience and the occult. In Philadelphia, throughout the sixties and seventies, the most prominent person to have his feet firmly planted both in the student leftist counterculture and in the rising New Age obsessions was Ira Einhorn. This is an account of how his life turned into a horror movie.*

Einhorn, or "the Unicorn," as he liked to call himself for obvious reasons, was born in Philadelphia in 1940 to working-class Jewish parents. When he graduated from the University of Pennsylvania with a degree in English, he was a large, muscular, slightly pudgy young man with pink cheeks, fierce blue eyes, a scruffy beard, and long dark hair that he often wore tied in a pony tail. He frequently broke into high-pitched giggling. During the sixties he was friendly with Abbie Hoffman, Jerry Rubin, Allen Ginsberg, Alan Watts, Baba Ram Dass, and other counterculture heros. He experimented with LSD and heroin. He was an active environmentalist. Bright, charismatic, gregarious, the Unicorn was a walking symbol of love, gentleness, compassion, and peace.

In 1964, Einhorn taught English for a year at Temple University, in Philadelphia, but his teaching style was too unconventional and the post was not renewed. In 1967 he sponsored the city's first Be-In. While emceeing the city's Earth Day in 1970, which he also organized, he startled U.S. Senator Ed Muskie, in front of television cameras, by kissing him on the mouth.

In 1971, Ira ran for mayor in the Philadelphia Democratic primary on the Planetary Transformation ticket and got 965 votes. Philadelphia newspapers loved him and covered his many lectures, calling him the city's "counterculture mayor," its "local guru," and its "oldest hippie."

---

*My account is based on Philadelphia newspaper clips, on Steven Levy's remarkably detailed book *The Unicorn's Secret: Murder in the Age of Aquarius* (Prentice Hall, 1988), and on a lengthy informative front-page article, "Blinded by the Light—the Einhorn-Maddux Murder Case," in the *Village Voice* (July 23, 1979).

Left, Ira Einshon, guru, at La Terrasse, the French restaurant on the Penn campus that was his hangout in the 1970s. He would lunch there with corporate executives, scientists, paranormal explorers, and friends and dazzle them with his intellect and energy. (Courtesy Bulletin/Temple Urban Archives)

Right, An independent filmmaker in the mid-1960s used Einhorn as an actor in a surrealistic short subject. Throughout the film, Ira wanders through Philadelphia carrying a female-shaped mannequin. (Copyright © 1980 by Christopher Speeth)

For years Einhorn ran an international information network of some 350 members, to whom he sent batches of material on psychic research and related topics. The network was funded, incredibly, by the Bell Telephone Company under a barter arrangement. Bell printed and mailed the releases, and Ira in turn helped Ma Bell handle the hippie community. At Penn's "Free University," he lectured on the virtues of psychedelic drugs.

In 1974, Doubleday Anchor published Einhorn's only book, *78-187880*. The title was the book's Library of Congress number. It is a wild work, filled with drivel about how the world will soon be transformed by New Age thinking. The book, bought and edited by Einhorn's good friend Bill Whitehead, was one of Doubleday's biggest commercial flops. Whitehead moved to Dutton, where he was conned by Einhorn into publishing a variety of worthless New Age books of which *Space-Time and Beyond* (1975), by Fred Wolfe, Bob Toben, and Jack Sarfatti, was the worst.

Of the many books about Israel's psychic charlatan Uri Geller, surely the most demented was Andrija Puharich's *Uri,* published in 1974 by Doubleday Anchor at Ira's insistence. (See my review in *Science: Good, Bad and Bogus.*) Einhorn and Puharich were buddies, both persuaded that Uri's spoon-bending powers would revolutionize physics. "Ira Einhorn's imagination helped to formulate this book," Puharich wrote on the acknowledgment page, "and to get it to the attention of publishers." Ira had earlier written the introduction to Puharich's *Beyond Telepathy* (Doubleday Anchor, 1962).

Here is how Ira evaluated Puharich's crazy book on Geller. I quote from Ira's "Uri and the Power of UFOs," in Arthur Rosenblum's oversized paperback *Unpopular Science* (Philadelphia: Running Press, 1974):

> Having spent much time with Uri Geller, and having seen him produce evidence again and again that his powers are genuine, I can only say that it behooves us to accept his explanation for his powers. He is a medium for an extraterrestrial civilization that has been monitoring earth for thousands of years. *Uri,* by Andrija Puharich, is the story of the development of those powers, and will be utterly convincing to anyone who is capable of reading with an open heart. I lived with Andrija while he was writing the book and was in constant dialogue with him about Uri's powers during that time. Still, the book blew my mind. . . . My editor at Doubleday, who is a close friend, and the agent who is working with the book, were so overwhelmed by *Uri* that they wondered if I would be connected with a fraud.

From Einhorn's other articles I single out "A Disturbing Critique," which ran in *CoEvolution Quarterly* (Winter 1977/78). Its theme: Russia has found a way to build Nikola Tesla's "magnifying transmitter." This device is said to use extremely low frequency (ELF) waves to transmit electrical power without wires. It can disrupt our radio communications, addle our brains, trigger weather disasters, cause massive power blackouts, transmit horrible diseases, and even translocate ships. By the late seventies, among some extreme right-wing groups, Tesla had become a cult figure. The Tesla Book Company (POB 1649, Greenville, TX 75401) still issues catalogs listing dozens of books and tapes extolling Tesla and warning of Soviet advances in psychotronic warfare. Research on Tesla's secrets was one of Puharich's obsessions. He currently sells wrist watches made to combat the deadly ELF radiation beamed to us by the evil Soviets.

In January 1977, Einhorn organized a "Mind Over Matter" conference at Penn, at which Puharich was a principal speaker. In the keynote address of a "Towards a Physics Consciousness" symposium at the Harvard Science Center (May 6-8, 1977), which he coordinated, Ira spoke about how far Russia was ahead of us in psi-warfare research. Our nation can be saved, he argued, only by a great spiritual awakening based on parapsychology, Eastern religions, and a "more accurate model of the universe."

Beneath Einhorn's flower-child exterior flowed dark undercurrents of narcissism, monstrous egotism, priapism, and sexual rage. "He wore women like jewelry," a friend commented. Although Ira demanded unlimited sexual freedom for himself, he was insanely jealous of similar freedom on the part of any girlfriend of the moment. In 1962 he came close to strangling a young Bennington student. "To kill what you love," he wrote in a notebook, "when you can't have it seems to me so natural that strangling —— last night seemed so right. . . . Insanity, thank goodness, is only temporary."

In 1966, he almost killed a Penn undergraduate by bashing her head with a Coke bottle. Later he wrote a poem about it. Titled "An Act of Violence," it contained these lines:

> Suddenly it happens.
> Bottle in hand, I strike
> Away at the head.
> In such violence there may be freedom.

Ira fancied himself a talented poet, but like all his other poems, this is on the lowest level of free-verse doggerel.

On September 11 or 12, 1977, the simmering rage in the Unicorn's brain exploded.

Helen Maddux, or Holly, as she was called, grew up in the East Texas town of Tyler, the daughter of a wealthy draftsman. She was blond, blue-eyed, beautiful, shy, frail, fey, and diabetic. A graduate of Bryn Mawr, with a degree in English, Holly was 25 when she and Ira met and fell in love. For five years they lived together, interrupted only by Holly's leaving for brief periods, desperately seeking her own "space," always to return. It was during their trip to Europe in 1977 that she decided to dump the Unicorn for good. Holly came home alone, settled on Fire Island, in New York, and began dating another man.

On September 11 or 12, 1977, Holly vanished. After a year of missed letters and phone calls, her parents hired a private investigator. Ira's pad was then a second-floor-rear apartment at 3411 Race Street, in the Powelton Village section of west Philly, near the Penn campus. It was the hippie center of the city, a "commune with traffic lights," someone called it. Ira slept on the floor surrounded by hundreds of books. First-floor residents told the detective about a foul odor that seemed to descend from Ira's screened-in back porch. The terrible smell lessened in the winter, returned in the spring.

On March 28, 1979, a homicide detective and six other men arrived with a search warrant. Ira said he had lost the key to a big padlock on the door to a back-porch closet. The hasp was snapped with a crowbar. In the closet was a black steamer trunk. Again Ira said he had no key.

The trunk was pried open with the crowbar. Inside, wrapped in plastic, was stuffed a decomposed, mummified body. It had been drained of blood, packed with styrofoam chips, and covered with newspapers whose dates matched the time of Holly's disappearance. The front and sides of the skull were fractured at a dozen places.

"It looks like Holly's body," said the detective.

"You found what you found," said Ira.

The Unicorn was released on $40,000 bail. A trivial cash bond of $4,000 was paid by Barbara Bronfman, ex-wife of Charles Bronfman of Montreal, a Seagram liquor heir. Barbara was and is a true believer in the paranormal, and to this day a loyal admirer of the Unicorn. Arlen Specter, a former Philadelphia D.A. (now a Republican senator), was Ira's lawyer. Einhorn steadfastly maintained he had been framed. By whom? Maybe the KGB, he said. Why? To discredit his knowledge of Russia's secret warfare devices based on Tesla's notebooks. Sensitive documents relating to these secrets, Ira insisted, had been locked in the trunk but were now missing.

During the eighteen months that the body mouldered in the trunk, Ira behaved as though nothing had happened. He told his friends and Holly's parents that he did not know where Holly was. He loved her deeply, he said, and longed to have her back. He ran a "Sun Day" in Philadelphia. After a bout of deep depression, in which he contemplated suicide, he began taking a dangerous drug called Ketamine. In 1978 he received $6,000 as a visiting fellow at the John F. Kennedy School of Government, at Harvard, where he taught a seminar titled "The Hierarchy Is Surrounded." In 1979, he attended a conference in England, and was the guest of the Yugoslavian government to arrange a celebration for Tesla.

On January 13, 1981, the day before his scheduled pre-trial hearing, Ira turned out to be in Europe. He was last seen in 1986, living near Trinity College, in Dublin, where he was studying German under the name of Ben Moore. His present whereabouts are unknown. "He betrayed everything I stood for," Jerry Rubin told a reporter.

While Ira was home on bail, he was visited by Martin Ebon, an occult journalist then writing a book on psi warfare. Ebon told Einhorn that I was interested in his case. To my surprise, the Unicorn sent me a two-page letter, hand-printed in blue ink. It is reproduced here.

I know that one should not publish a private letter without the sender's permission, but I doubt that the Unicorn will complain.

11/9/80
16 C
MORGAN HOUSE
7600 STENTON AV.
PHILA PA 19118

DEAR MARTIN GARDNER,

MARTIN EBON MENTIONED TO ME
THAT YOU HAD INQUIRED ABOUT MY CASE. THUS, I AM
HAVING SENT TO YOU, UNDER SEPARATE COVER, A PACKAGE
I SENT OUT AS A FUND RAISING EFFORT. PLEASE IGNORE
THE FUND RAISING LETTER + READ MY LAWYER'S LETTER
+ THE F.B.I. REPORT.

WE HAVE NOW RECEIVED THEIR FINAL SAY, IN
ANOTHER REPORT THAT TOTALLY DESTROYS THE CASE
AGAINST ME.

THEIR IS NO BLOOD OR HUMAN PROTEIN TO BE
FOUND ANYWHERE

THERE ARE NO BREAKDOWN PRODUCTS OF BLOOD
OR HUMAN PROTEIN.

THE F.B.I. COULD NOT EVEN IDENTIFY AS SIMI-
LAR THE SUBSTANCE FOUND IN THE TRUNK + SUB-
STANCES FOUND ON THE FLOOR BOARDS IN MY BACK
CLOSET.

WHOEVER DID IT BOTCHED THE JOB, FOR
NO JURY (IF IT GETS THAT FAR) WOULD BELIEVE
I CARRIED THE BODY BACK INTO MY APARTMENT
AFTER DRAINING IT OF BLOOD.

AN EXCERPT FROM A RECENT POEM
DESCRIBES MY PRESENT CONSTERNATION:

IRA EINHORN - SUSPECT;

(2)

HELEN HOLLY MADDOX - VICTIM;
MURDER

IS MY KOAN
OF THE MOMENT

WE HAVE A BODY
WITHOUT BLOOD

IN A TRUNK
WITHOUT BLOOD
OR HUMAN PROTEIN

DRIPPING SMELLY
OOZE
THAT IS NOT BLOOD
OR
HUMAN PROTEIN

CENTRAL CASTING
IN THIS CAPER
WHICH HAS PUT MY LIFE
AT STAKE
(READS) LIKE STANISLAW LEM

PEACE,
Ira Einhorn
215-242-2261

Addendum

The Unicorn is still a fugitive. *The Buffalo News* (June 4, 1989) reported that Barbara Bronfman, after reading Steven Levy's book about Einhorn, decided to cooperate with Philadelphia's district attorney. She said that Einhorn was then living in Stockholm. "But Mrs. Bronfman's boyfriend," said the *News*, "tipped off Einhorn and authorities found only empty rooms."

Here is a suggestion for capturing blue-eyed unicorns that I found under "Unicorn" in the *Reader's Encyclopedia*. The quotation is from a thirteenth-century bestiary:

> The unicorn has but one horn in the middle of its forehead. It is the only animal that ventures to attack the elephant; and so sharp is the nail of its foot, that with one blow it can rip the belly of the beast. Hunters can catch the unicorn only by placing a young virgin in his haunts. No sooner does he see the damsel than he runs towards her, and lies down at her feet, and so suffers himself to be captured by the hunters.

8 | The Great *Urantia Book* Mystery

No holy Bible offered to the Western world in the past few centuries is thicker, heavier, or stranger than *The Urantia Book*. This 2,097-page, 4.3-lb. volume purports to be written entirely by superhumans and channeled through an unknown earthling. To members of the Urantia movement, a steadily, quietly growing cult headquartered in Chicago, the book supposedly contains the earth's fifth revelation from God, superior to mainline Christianity and destined to transform the world.

In a way, the book is more amusing than the Book of Mormon, translated from hieroglyphics by Joseph Smith with the aid of a pair of magic spectacles called the Urim and the Thummim. It is almost as funny as the ravings of L. Ron Hubbard or Sun Moon, the channeled fiddle-faddle of Jane Roberts or J. Zebra Knight, or the work of such earlier mountebanks as Mary Baker Eddy and Madame Blavatsky. Indeed it may be the largest, most fantastic chunk of channeled moonshine ever to be bound in one volume.

The book's first two thirds concern cosmology and the history of Urantia (pronounced you-ran′-sha), the name for Earth. We live on the 606th planet in a system called Satania, which includes 619 imperfect, evolving worlds. Urantia's grand universe number is 5,342,482,337,666. Satania, with its headquarters at Jerusem, is in the constellation of Norlatiadek, part of the evolving universe of Nebadon. Nebadon in turn belongs to a superuniverse called Orvonton. Orvonton and six other superuniverses, each unfinished and still evolving, revolve around the central universe of Havona. At the core of Havona is the flat, timeless, motionless Isle of Paradise. This is the dwelling place of the Great I AM, the ultimate, eternal, infinite Deity. His triune nature (Father, Son, and Spirit) is symbolized on the Brotherhood's stationery by three concentric blue circles. Encircling the entire universe of inhabited galaxies are four uninhabited, elliptical rings of primordial matter in which millions of new galaxies are in the process of formation. Rings 1 and 3 revolve around the superuniverses in one direction. Rings 2 and 4 go the other way.

The Urantia Book swarms with a thousand curious words, but they lack the music of made-up names in the fantasies of Lord Dunsany or James Branch Cabell and the punning humor of *Finnegans Wake*. Below I AM are billions of lesser gods and angels, including a finite deity who is evolving toward becoming the Supreme Being of all evolving universes. Pages would be needed to list all their generic names. There are the Truth Revealers, the Mystery Monitors, the Universal Censors, the Divine Counselors, the Perfectors of Wisdom, the Ancient of Days, and a hundred others.

Technical Advisors include Supernaphim, Seconaphim, Tertiaphim, Omniaphim, Seraphim, Cherubim, and Sanobim. The Master Physical Controllers (some are machines) are the Power Directors, Mechanical Controllers, Energy Transformers, Energy Transmitters, Primary Associators, Secondary Associators, Frandalanks, and Chronoldeks. On Urantia's Advisory Council are Onagar, Masant, Onamonalonton, Orlandof, Porshsunta, Singlangton, Fantad, Orvonon, Adam, Eve, Enoch, Moses, Elijah, Machiventa Melchizedek, John the Baptist, and 1-2-3 the First.

Lucifer, who rebelled against his superiors 200,000 years ago, is now the deposed sovereign of Satania, named after Satan, his first lieutenant. Under Satan are lesser rebels, such as Caligastia and Beelzebub. All these rebels are now imprisoned in Satania. Some have repented. Those who never repent will eventually be annihilated.

Urantia's first two humans were not Adam and Eve. They were the black-eyed twins Andon and Fonta, children of beasts. The Garden of Eden was not established until almost a million years later. Adam and Eve were eight feet tall, had blue eyes, and bodies that shimmered with light. Their offspring founded what the book calls the "Violet race." Although Adam and Eve disobeyed higher authorities, there was no "fall of man." It is unthinkable that a loving God would allow us to suffer for the sins of Adam and Eve. The pair have since been "repersonalized" and live on Jerusem. Like the Koran and the Book of Mormon, *The Urantia Book* retells Old Testament yarns, but with many more corrections and embellishments.

Human minds are created at birth, but the soul does not develop until about age 6. When we die, our souls and their Thought Adjusters survive. Thought Adjusters are indwelling "fragments" of God. In due time we are reassembled on another world, the start of a long series of reconstitutions from world to world, universe to universe, until we finally reach Paradise. Guardian angels and indwelling Thought Adjusters help us along the way. The pilgrimage is not monotonous. There will be endless adventures and surprises.

The Urantia Book bristles with neologisms and bizarre proper names: mind-gravity circuit, absonity, reflectivity, trinitization, eventuation, final-

William S. Sadler (*left*) and his son, William S. Sadler, Jr. (*right*).

iters, agandonters, tabamantia, midwayers, grandfanda, everywhereness, ultimate quartan integration, and hundreds more. The authors of what cult members call "The Papers" have a curious compulsion to divide things into sevens. The Thought Adjusters, for instance, come in seven flavors: virgin, advanced, supreme, vanished, liberated, fused, and personalized. Here is a sample gem of prose:

> The triodity of actuality continues to function directly in the post-Havona epochs; Paradise gravity grasps the basic units of material existence, the spirit gravity of the Eternal Son operates directly upon the fundamental values of spirit existence, and the mind gravity of the Conjoint Actor unerringly clutches all vital meanings of intellectual existence.

The last third of the book fleshes out in incredible detail the life and teachings of Jesus. It seems that the Gospel writers, as well as Paul, Peter, and others, outrageously distorted this history, but now records supplied by the guardian angel of the Apostle Andrew have set matters straight. We learn that young Jesus was a skillful harpist and that he turned down a proposal of marriage by a wealthy young woman. Before he began preaching he toured the Roman world accompanied by two natives of India,

Gonod and Ganid.

The Man of Galilee was none other than Michael of Nebadon, number 611,121 among more than 700,000 Creator Sons of the Eternal Son, who is part of the absolute trinity. Michael created our entire universe. Coming to Urantia was his seventh and latest incarnation as one of his own lesser creatures.

Many of Jesus' miracles had what the *Urantia Book* considers natural explanations. Did Jesus turn water into wine at the wedding feast? He did not. This was done by higher powers. We are told that they "abrogated time, made the wine by natural laws, then exchanged the water for wine in what seemed to those present as an instantaneous magic trick. "No law of nature was modified, abrogated, or even transcended," the *Urantia Book* explains on page 1530.

Multiplying the loaves and fishes, says the *Urantia Book* (page 1702), was the only "nature miracle" that Jesus performed by "conscious planning." This, too, involved the abrogation of time, but was a "genuine supernatural ministration."

After Jesus healed a lunatic, a dog chased a herd of swine into the sea, giving rise to the legend that devils left the man to enter the pigs. Lazarus was the only person Jesus raised from the dead (the others were merely sleeping). Thanks to Lazarus's Personalized Adjuster, he was allowed to reenter his corpse. He lived to be 67, finally dying of the same disease that first killed him.

Although Jesus was crucified, his death was in no way a sacrificial blood atonement. Original sin is another of the Bible's grave errors. After Christ's death, entities rolled the stone from the sepulchre and disintegrated his body. When Jesus reappeared to his followers, it was in a reconstituted form. Eventually he will return to Urantia, but we have no inkling of when or where.

Why do I waste time on such a pretentious tome? Two reasons. One, the Urantia movement is gaining new recruits. More interestingly, the book's origin is a capital mystery. No one knows who wrote it.

The book was published in 1955 at the instigation of one of the strangest characters in our nation's religious history. He was William Samuel Sadler (1875-1969), surgeon, psychiatrist, and one-time ordained Seventh-Day Adventist minister who held prominent posts in Adventist hospitals. He was a close associate of the church's inspired prophetess Ellen Gould White. Because Adventists vigorously condemn Spiritualism and the occult, Sadler was impelled to write three books debunking such things: *The Truth About Spiritualism* (1923), *The Mind at Mischief: Tricks and Deceptions of the Subconscious and How to Cope with Them* (1929), and *Mental Mischief and Emotional Conflicts* (1947).

In an appendix to *The Mind at Mischief* Sadler writes that with two exceptions "all cases of psychic phenomena which have come under my observation have turned out to be those of auto-psychism." By this he means the influence of the subconscious. One phenomenon he could not debunk was the trance channeling of two persons. He does not name them, but one obviously was Mrs. White, and the other was a patient who channeled *The Urantia Book*. While in a deep trance, Sadler tells us, this man became a "clearing house for the coming and going of alleged extraplanetary personalities." Sad-

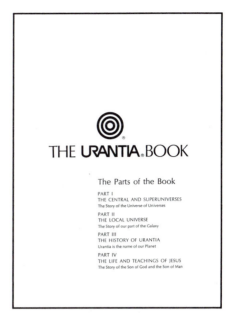

The cover of *The Urantia Book*.

ler goes on to say that "all the information imparted through this source has proved to be consistent within itself. . . . It is essentially Christian and is, on the whole, entirely harmonious with the known scientific facts and truths of this age." Who was this man? All we know is that in the early twenties Sadler started in Chicago a group of some 70 people called "The Forum" to study the new revelations. His son, William Sadler, Jr. (he died in 1963), was the Forum's first president and the author of two books about the Urantia papers. The movement's current headquarters is a three-floor brick mansion in Chicago that was the home of both Sadler senior and his son.

Harold Sherman, an Arkansas psychic, was a Forum member. In his 1976 paperback *How to Know What to Believe* he devotes a wild chapter to a conversation with the elder Sadler. Sadler said that the revelators were eager to answer questions. Forum members submitted 4,000. A few weeks later the trance channeler produced 472 handwritten pages that answered all 4,000 questions. More questions and answers followed until the revelations stopped—we are not told why—in the mid-thirties.

"The book is eventually to be published," Sadler told Sherman, "without any human personalities to be identified with it in any way and no authorship to be ascribed to it. Most of these higher beings have refused to use their own names and have only specified their *type* of being in the universe. There are only a few of us still living who were in touch with this phenomenon in the beginning, and when we die, the knowledge of it will die with us. Then the book will exist as a great spiritual mystery, and no human will know the manner in which it came about."

To this day the origin of the book remains a total enigma. Here is all the Urantia Foundation will say about it. I quote from their pamphlet "The Urantia Book: The Question of Origin":

> Who the human being was whose versatile Thought Adjuster aided in bringing the fifth epochal revelation to our world will never be known because the revelators asked the few people who knew to take a pledge of secrecy. They did not want any human beings to be mystically associated with *The Urantia Book*. It is amazing that the authors of the Urantia Papers tell us as much as they do. Upon reflection, you will recognize the persistent questions about the unrevealed "details" concerning the origin of the book as a psychological parallel to the reoccurring demand put to Jesus, "Show us a sign."
>
> Now let us turn to the human side of the story which may be interesting, but has no spiritual significance. In preparation for presenting the papers of the fifth epochal revelation and placing them in the custody of a responsible group of human beings, the revelators made contact with a small group of people in Chicago. The leaders of this group were asked by the revelators not only to refrain from revealing the identity of the individual associated with the presentation of the papers, but also not to discuss details related to the arrival of the papers. We will, therefore, never know just where or how the papers were received. Even these early leaders were puzzled; no human being knows just how this materialization was executed. The reason given for this request of secrecy is the revelators are determined that future generations shall have *The Urantia Book* wholly free from mortal connections.

In 1958 Sadler wrote: "While we are not at liberty to tell you even the little we know about the technique of the production of the Urantia papers, we are not forbidden to tell you how we did *not* get these documents." He then lists nine phenomena that he says were not involved: automatic (that is, subconscious) writing, talking, hearing, seeing, thinking, remembering, acting, personalization, and combined and associated psychic states.

Many Adventist doctrines, such as the denial of an eternal hell (the irredeemable wicked will ultimately be annihilated as though they had never existed), and the doctrine of soul-sleeping between death and resurrection, appear in the *Urantia Book*. Adventists regard Jesus as identical with the Bible's archangel Michael, who was the actual creator of the universe. The *Urantia Book* also makes Jesus and Michael equivalent. It calls Michael one of many thousands of Creator Sons, and the person who created our universe almost 400 billion years ago.

In describing the death of Jesus on the cross, the *Urantia Book* quotes him as saying to the good thief: "Verily, verily, I say to you today, you shall sometime be with me in Paradise." In the King James Bible a comma appears before the word *today,* not after, and there is no "sometime," thus implying that on that very day the thief will enter Paradise. Adventists insist that the comma was misplaced. In keeping with this view, *The Urantia Book* shifts the comma.

Now in its tenth printing, *The Urantia Book* can be obtained by sending $36.50 (this includes postage) to the Urantia Foundation, 533 Diversey Parkway, Chicago, IL 60614. (A French edition costs $40.65.) The cult also issues books, pamphlets, study aids, a quarterly journal, and a directory of study groups you can join. The *Concordex* (a 504-page index to the book) and *Paramony* (25,000 cross-references between *The Urantia Book* and the Bible) are available from the Jesusonian Foundation, 1790 Thirtieth Street, Boulder, CO 80301.

Dr. Sadler was the author of more than forty books on health, psychiatry, diet, and sex, many of them written in collaboration with his wife. They bear such titles as *Theory and Practice of Psychiatry* (1231 pages); *Modern Psychiatry* (896 pages); *Cause and Cure of Headaches, Backaches, and Constipation; Sex Life Before and After Marriage;* and *Race Decadence: An Examination of the Causes of Racial Degeneration in the United States.* You will find entries on him in early editions of *Who's Who in America* and in the ninth edition of *American Men of Science.*

Addendum

Since I wrote this column about Urantia, I managed to discover the person who channelled the *UB* (*Urantia Book*). Chapters 13 and 14 reprint later columns that report on this still active research.

The *UB* is precisely the mixture of Seventh-Day Adventist doctrines and Adventist heresies that one would expect from disenchanted Adventists who could not break completely away from Adventist dogmas. One major deviation from conservative Adventism is the *UB*'s full acceptance of evolution and the great antiquity of the earth. It is, however, an unorthodox evolution that proceeds by sudden jumps—mutations that at a single leap produce a new species. The first human beings, for example, the twins Andon and Fonta, result from such a mutation. They were reared and suckled by parents who were beasts.

The science in the *UB* is what one would expect from a well-read person, familiar with the science of his day, but not able to make any startling predictions about future science. Here and there are minor hits, but most of the book's speculations about science, especially about astronomy, are bizarre and wildly off the mark. There is no suggestion, for instance, that the universe, of which our galaxy is a part, is expanding. Particle physics in the *UB* has nothing in common with the great discoveries in this field made since the *UB* was written.

The *UB* is rich in specific details. The seraphim, for example, travel at 600,000 miles per second, much faster than light, thereby violating a main tenet of relativity theory. Three not-yet-discovered planets of our solar system, we are told, are beyond the orbit of Pluto. There are hundreds of other such scientific "facts" in the *UB* that are impossible, at least for now, to verify.

Dr. Sadler, who played such an essential role in the publication of the *UB*, was born in Spencer, Indiana, in 1875. While a teen-age student at Battle Creek College, Michigan, he worked in the kitchens of Dr. John Kellogg's Battle Creek Sanitarium. Later he became a salesman for the doctor's line of health foods. Kellogg picked Sadler to work for a group of medical missions he had established in Chicago. To learn techniques of evangelism, he sent young Salder to the fundamentalist Moody Bible Institute in Chicago. Afterward he was made secretary of the missions, including a Life Boat Mission on South State Street, the only one that was openly Seventh-Day Adventist. The missions operated a home for unwed mothers, found homes for unwanted babies, and did their best to persuade prostitutes to give up their trade by placing them in Christian homes.

In 1897, in Paris, Illinois, Sadler married Lena Celestia Kellogg, a neice of Dr. John Kellogg. I do not know when he or his wife, who had been raised a Seventh-Day Adventist, broke with the church. Sadler left the Chicago missions in 1901 to pursue a medical education, eventually getting an MD degree in 1906 at the American Medical Missionary College, Chicago. In 1910 he went abroad for further study at clinics in Leeds, England, and in Vienna where he attended classes by Sigmund Freud and Alfred Adler. He began private practice in Chicago, specializing in surgery, then about 1930 shifted to psychiatry. From 1918 until 1919 he was on the staff of Chicago's Columbus Hospital and was the hospital's consulting psychiatrist until 1940.

From 1937 until 1939 he was a psychiatric consultant of the W. K. Kellogg Foundation, in Battle Creek, and a professor of pastoral psychiatry at McCormick Theological Seminary, in Chicago, from 1930 until 1937. His first son Willis died in infancy. A second child, William Samuel Sadler, Jr., who was active in the Urantia movement, died in 1963. An adopted daughter, Emma Christensen, known as Christy, was the person who took down the Urantia revelations and typed them for her father's editing. Sadler died in 1969, age 94. For more details about his distinguished career, see the *National Cyclopedia of American Biography,* Volume 54. Not one of his many books mention his role in the Urantia cult.

The foregoing chapter is a much revised version of the column as it first appeared. I had many mistakes in that column. Irate believers in the *Urantia Book* were quick to point them out in angry letters. It was the passion in these letters that aroused my further interest in the Urantia movement and started me on a research project that has led to my preparing a book about the cult. A few of my discoveries are reported in this addendum and in two later chapters, but the full story of my findings will have to await the publication of my book.

9 | St. George Mivart and the Dragon of Creationism

No real beauty, no lasting goodness can, in my belief, result from anything which is not true.

—*St. George Mivart*

In the long, sad history of the war between science and Christianity, no episode is sadder than the career of St. George Jackson Mivart (1827-1900). It is a story that has been almost forgotten. It deserves retelling.

One of England's most distinguished zoologists, Mivart was born in London, where his father, a Low Church Anglican, owned the Mivart Hotel, on Brook Street. (Later it became Claridge's.) At the age of 16, Mivart was converted to Roman Catholicism. Until his death he remained loyal to his faith, never doubting a personal Triune God, an afterlife, the miracle of the Eucharist, or the superiority of Catholicism to all other religions. He had hoped to go to Oxford, but his conversion barred him from both Oxford and Cambridge.

It was Thomas Huxley who persuaded Mivart that evolution was as firmly established as Copernican astronomy—although the process by which it operated left room for debate. For years Mivart attended Huxley's lectures at the British Museum, and the two men became good friends. Later they had a falling out over disagreements about the process of evolution, but one of the finest tributes ever paid to Huxley was Mivart's "Reminiscences of Thomas Huxley," in the *Nineteenth Century* (December 1897). "I learned more from him in two years," Mivart wrote, "than I had acquired in any previous decade of biological study."

In 1871, Mivart published his most famous book, *The Genesis of Species.* Although he accepted the broad scenario of Darwin's *Origin of Species,* he argued convincingly that natural selection alone was insufficient to account for the rise of species. It had to be supplemented "by the concurrent action of some other natural law or laws, at present undiscovered." These were accurate and prophetic words. Like Darwin, Mivart was a Lamarckian, unaware of what would later become known about the role played by genes and their random mutations in the evolutionary process.

Darwin recognized the many gaps in the fossil record and the absence of known transitional forms, but he explained those blanks by stressing how rare conditions are for fossilization. Mivart believed the gaps were too large to be so explained. "These 'jumps' are considerable in comparison with the minute variations of 'Natural Selection,' " he wrote. In a dim way, Mivart

St. George Jackson Mivart, who sought to reconcile religion and science.

anticipated the punctuated-equilibrium theory advocated today by Stephen Jay Gould and his associates.

The biggest leap of all, Mivart argued in *Man and Apes* (1873), was the abrupt transition from apelike creatures to the first humans. Like most of today's Catholic philosophers, and like Mortimer Adler in his book *The Difference of Man and the Difference It Makes,* Mivart believed that the jump was too huge to be accounted for without a divine intervention that infused an immortal soul into the minds of the first men and women. "For my part," he wrote, "my reason *alone* convinces me that there is far more difference between the lowest savage and the highest ape than there is between the highest ape and a lump of granite."

Mivart was a skillful, prolific, widely read author of books and articles about anatomy, zoology, evolution, religion, and the philosophy of science. Among his some twenty other books, the following titles suggest the scope of his research and thinking: *The Common Frog; The Cat* (557 pages!); *Nature and Thought; A Philosophical Catechism; On Truth; The Origin of Human Reason; Birds; Essays and Criticisms; American Types of Animal Life; An Introduction to the Elements of Science;* and *The Groundwork of Science.* He also published, under the pseudonym of D'Arcy Drew, a novel of ideas titled *Henry Standon.* No book by Mivart is now in print.

The initial reaction to Mivart's views, among both Catholics and Anglicans, was favorable. Cardinal John Henry Newman, a friend of Mivart, thought highly of them. Pope Pius IX, in 1876, awarded Mivart a doctor of philosophy degree for his efforts to reconcile science and Catholic faith. On November 1, 1874, Lewis Carroll put this entry into his diary:

> Not being well, I stayed in all day, and during the day read the whole of [Sir George] Mivart's *Genesis of Species,* a most interesting and satisfactory book, showing, as it does, the insufficiency of "Natural Selection" *alone* to account for the universe, and its perfect compatibility with the creative and guiding power of God. The theory of "Correspobrence to Environment" is also brought into harmony with the Christian's belief.

In the sixth edition of *Origin of Species,* Darwin devoted many pages to Mivart's views on evolution and why he disagreed with them. At first, Darwin and Huxley treated Mivart with respect, but his continual attacks on their opinions soon turned both men against him. The church, too, became hostile. Why? Because Mivart kept insisting, over and over, that unless the church wholeheartedly accepted evolution as a fact, not just a theory that Catholics were permitted to believe, it would be repeating the same colossal mistake it had made in refusing to accept Galileo's Copernican astronomy. The Bible, Mivart argued, is not a guide for any kind of science. Nor can it be taken as accurate in its history.

Trying to persuade his church to accept evolution, and to broaden its approach to Scripture, became the dominant goal of Mivart's life. As he grew older, his views became more liberal. He began to denounce such entrenched doctrines as the everlasting punishment of the wicked. Three forceful articles titled "Happiness in Hell" (*Nineteenth Century,* December 1892, February and April 1893) were praised by liberal Anglicans, but roundly denounced by leading Catholics.

In "The Continuity of Catholicism" (*Nineteenth Century,* January 1900) Mivart outlined the major changes he believed were inevitable if his church were to continue to hold the allegiance of the educated: It must stop teaching that outside the church there is no salvation. It must accept evolution. It must abandon the doctrine of biblical inerrancy. Indeed, he wrote, educated Catholics had already ceased to accept the Genesis account of creation, the stories of Adam and Eve, Noah's flood, the Tower of Babel, Joshua's stopping of the earth's rotation, and hundreds of other biblical myths "no more worthy of respect than Jack and the Beanstalk."

Mivart soon was going even further in blasting cherished dogmas. Although the Bible is inspired in its theological and moral teachings, he wrote, informed Catholics of the future will have to abandon such primitive doctrines as the Virgin Birth, the Immaculate Conception, the physical resurrection of Jesus, and beliefs in witchcraft and demon possession. Such changes of opinion, he argued, had already taken place among liberal Catholics. In view of many past alterations of Catholic beliefs, Mivart did not consider these new changes to be serious breaches of church doctrine: "I am convinced that the great changes herein referred to are but preludes to far greater changes in the future—changes which will be most salutary."

In his last article before his death, "Scripture and Roman Catholicism" *(Nineteenth Century,* March 1900), Mivart continued to hammer home his message. He spoke of the "impassable gulf" that "yawns between science and Roman Catholic teaching." The church will decline, Mivart warned, if it continues to defend the doctrine of papal infallibility. Like the fatal garment of Nessus, that doctrine will "cling to her and eat away her substance till she is reduced to a mouldering and repulsive skeleton."

In a more hopeful mood, Mivart wrote elsewhere, "I do believe that a noble and true Catholicity is possibly developed in continuity with the Catholicity of the past, but it must be a continuous development like that of the butterfly from the grub." This new reformation is less likely to come from the Vatican, he believed, than from the pressure of enlightened Catholic opinion, a "slow, silent, indirect action" that in time will win the day.

Such strong indictments were too much for the church. Cardinal Herbert Vaughan, Archbishop of Westminster, demanded that Mivart sign a lengthy confession of faith. When Mivart refused, his *Nineteenth Century* articles were placed on the church's *Index* of forbidden writings, and Mivart was excommunicated. After his death two months later, from a heart attack, his body was denied Christian burial. The final ironic insult came four years later when his Catholic followers (often called "Mivartians" in England and "Mivart Men" in France) persuaded the church to transpose Mivart's body to sacred ground. He had been suffering from diabetes before he died, they said, and therefore was not in his right mind when he wrote his offensive articles!

Mivart's books on evolution are now dated and of only historical interest, but his quixotic, courageous efforts to liberalize his church have succeeded beyond anything he deemed possible. There is little in his writings about Catholic theology that is not now commonplace opinion among Catholic intellectuals even if such liberal views have not yet invaded the Vatican or filtered down to the masses of Catholics around the world. If there is a line in Mivart's attacks on church dogmas that Father Andrew Greeley, Hans Küng, Edward Schillebeeckx, and a hundred other liberal Catholic thinkers today cannot accept, I do not know what line it is. Even the Vatican's official position is that evolution may be taught in Catholic schools as a viable theory provided it does not deny that God injected human souls into the process when the time was ripe. Catholic theologians, philosophers, and scholars in their acceptance of evolution and modern biblical criticism are far ahead of today's know-nothing Protestant fundamentalists.

It is a scandal that Mivart's role in pioneering these changes has been so completely ignored. Only one book has been devoted to his career, *A Conscience in Conflict* (Columbia University Press, 1960), an excellent biography of Mivart by Jacob Gruber. Gruber sees Mivart as a tragic figure, a bit too vain and too sure of himself, who died rejected by both his church and by England's scientific establishment. Even the Catholic "modernists" who appeared on the scene in France and England around the turn of the century were not favorably impressed by his work. George Tyrell, a leading Jesuit modernist (he too was soon excommunicated), saw in Mivart no more than "a useful object lesson . . . on the necessity of keeping one's temper."

Like Galileo, Mivart fought his final battles alone. "Alone he reaped the galling punishment," Gruber writes in his epilogue. "Always he was alone." It is probably too early to expect the Catholic church to recognize Mivart's prescience. Surely it is not too early to gather his major articles on science and religion into a single volume.

10 | Relativism In Science

In recent decades there has been a growing trend among a small group of sociologists and humanities professors, even among a few scientists and philosophers, to deny that science moves closer and closer to objective "truth." This bizarre view is closely linked to an antirealist trend that has been stimulated by the paradoxes and mysteries of quantum mechanics. The properties of particles and quantum systems are, in a sense, not "real" until they are measured. The measurements can be made by apparatus, but the apparatus itself is a quantum system, so it too seems to be in an "indefinite" state until it has been observed by a person. Alas, the observer also is a quantum system. Is he indefinite until someone observes *him?* And how can we escape from this seemingly endless regress?

A few physicists, notably Eugene Wigner, argue that the quantum world, which of course is the entire universe, has no reality until observed by conscious minds. This view runs into grave difficulties over the question of how high on the evolutionary scale a mind has to be to make an object real. As Einstein, who was repelled by this kind of social solipsism, liked to ask: Is the moon nonexistent until a mouse observes it? And how about observation by a butterfly? Evolution seems to entail, for someone like Wigner, that reality is a matter of degree; that as life evolved on (at least) the earth, the universe slowly developed from some sort of featureless fog to the complicated mechanism it is today. And what would happen to the universe if all life became extinct? Would it fade back into the gloom?

If the universe has no reality without human observers, it is an easy step to suppose it is *we* who shape the structure of the outside world. If you and I are the creators of its laws, it follows easily that science should be regarded as similar to art, poetry, music, philosophy, and other products of human culture. Because folkways change in time and vary from culture to culture, and because science clearly is part of culture, one can look upon the history of science in the way one looks upon the history of fashions. Women's skirts are up in one decade, down in the next, then up again. The height of the skirt is a cultural preference. We cannot say a particular height is "true" and the others "false."

It is hard to believe that some intelligent people see the history of science not only as a series of cultural preferences but even write books about it. The Harvard astronomer Bruce Gregory, for example, recently produced a volume entitled *Inventing Reality: Physics as a Language* (Wiley, 1989). His wild theme is that physicists do not discover laws of nature. They invent them. Newton didn't discover the law of gravity. He invented it. J. J. Thompson didn't discover the electron. He made it up the way one makes up a tune. "The universe is made of stories," Gregory quotes the poet Muriel Rukeyser, "not of atoms."

Gregory's views are in the tradition of pragmatists who put human experience in the center of what is "real." They don't deny that there is an outside world with which we interact; but because we can know nothing about it except what we experience, they are unable to take seriously any talk about structures "out there" independent of human minds. Following in the footsteps of such pragmatists as Karl Pearson and Benjamin Lee Whorf, Gregory focuses on human language (including, of course, the language of mathematics) as the principal shaper of what scientists like to think is out there. "The stubbornly physical nature of the world we encounter every day is obvious," he writes. "The minute we begin to talk about this world, however, it somehow becomes transformed into another world, an interpreted world, a world delimited by language. . . ."

Since the world we talk about is the only one we can know, it follows that "as our vocabulary changes, so does the world." Again: "When we create a new way of talking about the world, we virtually create a new world." Books are real "not because of some mystical connection between language and the world, but because you can ask me to bring you a book and my action can fulfill your expectation."

Consider unicorns. Ordinary people would say they are unreal because there *are* no such animals. But Gregory claims that "unicorns are not 'real' because our community has no expectations about living or dead unicorns that can be fulfilled. . . ." Moreover, our language can even alter the past. When we stopped talking about unicorns, they ceased to be real. "History is not as immutable as we might think; language can apparently transform the past as readily as it shapes the present and the future." Shades of Orwell's *1984,* in which communist historians continually rewrite history!

It is a short step from such human-centered hubris to the belief of Shirley MacLaine and other New Agers that we have the power to create our own realities. There may be some sort of timeless world out there; but if so, as Kant maintained, its ultimate structure is forever beyond our grasp. "The laws of physics," Gregory bluntly puts it, "are *our* laws, not nature's." *We* are the gods who shape reality.

It is not surprising to learn that Gregory is a devotee of the early New Age cult of *est*. "I owe my appreciation of the immense power of the myth of 'is,' " he writes, "to Werner Erhard's relentless commitment to making a difference in my life. Absent his unremitting efforts to uncover the role of speaking in shaping experience, this book never would have been written."

Let's try to clear up some confusions involving subjectivity and relativism. First, the notion that science is always fallible is an ancient one, ably defended by the Greek skeptics; no scientist or philosopher today denies this. The very term *fallibilism* was coined by the American philosopher Charles Peirce to emphasize the way scientific statements differ from theorems in mathematics and formal logic. In logic and mathematics there are ironclad proofs inside formal systems. For example, you can prove the Pythagorean theorem within the system of Euclidian geometry—a proof that remains undamaged by the non-Euclidian structure of space-time. Given the axioms of Euclidian geometry, the theorem is true in all possible worlds. Science, on the other hand, has no infallible proofs.

Although all scientific statements are corrigible, it does not follow that they can't be placed in a continuum of probabilities that range from virtual certainty to almost certain falsehood. No one doubts, for instance, that the earth is shaped like a ball, goes around the sun, rotates, has a magnetic field, and has a moon that circles it. It is almost certain that the universe is billions of years old and that life on earth evolved over millions of years from simple to more complex forms. The big bang origin of the universe is not quite so certain. The inflationary model of the universe is still less certain. And so on. Science at present lacks any technique for applying precise probability values, or what Rudolf Carnap liked to call "degrees of confirmation," to its statements. That doesn't mean, however, that a scientist is not justified in saying that evolution has been strongly confirmed or that a flat earth has been strongly disconfirmed.

The title of Nancy Cartwright's book *How the Laws of Physics Lie* (Oxford University Press, 1983) seems to suggest that she agrees with Gregory, but on careful reading it turns out otherwise. What she does maintain— and who can disagree?—is that the phenomenological laws of physics (laws based on direct observations) have a much higher degree of confirmation than theories. We can be sure that all elephants have trunks because we can verify the statement by direct observation. Cartwright says she "believes" in the phenomenological laws, and also in such theoretical entities as electrons, even though their observation is indirect. If electrons don't make tracks in bubble chambers, she asks, what does? But when you turn to theoretical laws, such as the laws of relativity and quantum mechanics, she doesn't "believe" in them in the same way because they are too far from strong confirmation, and too subject to change. It is in this sense that science "lies."

Where does this leave us? Surely it does not leave us with a relativism in which competing scientific theories are "incommensurable"—that is, without standards by which they can be ranked. Science is like an expanding region with a solid core of truths that are very close to certainty. As you move outward from the core, assertions become progressively more tentative. In no way can one deny that science progresses in a manner quite different from the "progress" of music, art, or fashions in clothes.

Like almost all scientists, philosophers, and ordinary people, Peirce was a hard-nosed realist. Science, he wrote, is a method "by which our beliefs are determined by nothing human, but by some external permanency—by something upon which our thinking has no effect."

Here is how the eminent Harvard physicist Sheldon Glashow said the same thing in a mini-essay in the *New York Times* (October 22, 1989):

> We believe that the world is knowable, that there are simple rules governing the behavior of matter and the evolution of the universe. We affirm that there are eternal, objective, extrahistorical, socially neutral, external and universal truths and that the assemblage of these truths is what we call physical science. Natural laws can be discovered that are universal, invariable, inviolate, genderless and verifiable. They may be found by men or by women or by mixed collaborations of any obscene proportions. Any intelligent alien anywhere would have come upon the same logical system as we have to explain the structure of protons and the nature of supernovae. This statement I cannot prove, this statement I cannot justify. This is my faith.

It is important to understand that, when a theory becomes strongly confirmed by repeated observations and experiments, it can move across a fuzzy boundary to become recognized by the entire scientific community as a fact. That planets go around the sun was once the Copernican theory. Today it is a fact. That material objects are made of molecules was once a conjecture. Indeed, for many decades it was ridiculed by many physicists and chemists. Today it is a fact. In Darwin's day there was a theory of evolution. Today, only ignorant creationists refuse to call it a fact. It is also important to understand that so-called revolutions in science are not revolutions in the sense of overthrowing an earlier theory. They are benign refinements of earlier theories. Einstein didn't discard Newtonian physics. He added qualifications to Newtonian physics.

"The history of physics makes it hard to sustain the idea that we are getting closer to speaking 'nature's own language,'" Gregory naively writes. On the contrary, the history of physics makes it easy. Who, except academics smitten by relativism, can deny that science steadily improves its ability to explain and predict? Absolute truth may indeed be forever unobtainable, but if theories are not getting closer to accurate descriptions of the universe, why do they work so amazingly well? How is it we can build skyscrapers, hydrogen bombs, television sets, spacecraft, and other wonders of modern technology? Why is quantum mechanics able to predict with accuracies of many decimal places the outcomes of thousands of sophisticated experiments?

Surely it is insane to suppose that the enormous predictive power of science is nothing more than the power to predict the behavior of a world fabricated inside our tiny skulls. Of course all predictions are tested by human experience, but since everything we do is human experience, to say this is to say something obvious and trivial. Wigner wrote a now-famous essay on "The Unreasonable Effectiveness of Mathematics." To those who believe in a mathematically structured universe, independent of you and me, what could be more reasonable than the way mathematics fits the universe?

Nobody denies that science is a human tool, or that its history is influenced by cultural forces in all sorts of interesting ways. Nobody denies that scientists invent theories by creative acts similar to those of poets and artists. But once a theory is formulated, it is tested by a process that, in the long run, is singularly free of cultural biases. False theories are not shot down by a change of language, but by the universe.

James Trefil, in his stimulating book *Reading the Mind of God* (Scribner, 1989), recalls a lecture by a young sociologist on the history of the now-popular conjecture that dinosaurs were killed off by climatic changes that followed the impact of an extraterrestrial object striking the earth. She was good in describing the infighting among geologists, but she had no interest whatever in the evidence pro and con. From her perspective, her only task was to describe the conflict as if it were a battle between two rival art critics, with no mechanism for ever deciding who was right. A frustrated senior paleontologist in the audience finally burst out with the question, "Is it really news to sociologists that evidence counts?"

After all, Trefil concludes, "gravity pulls on the Bushman as well as on the European." Reading Shirley MacLaine, you might decide to create your own reality by jumping off a high building and soaring like Superman. Are we not assured by transcendental meditators that with training one can suspend gravity and levitate? Did not Jesus, that great super-psychic, walk on water? Last year a Russian psychic stood on a railroad track and tried to suspend the law of momentum (mass times velocity) by stopping a train. The poor man is no longer with us. Here is how Stephen Crane, in one of his short poems, reminded us that we are not the measure of all things:

A man said to the universe:
"Sir, I exist!"
"However," replied the universe,
"The fact has not created in me
A sense of obligation."

Addendum

Bruce Gregory took issue with my column in a letter published in *The Skeptical Inquirer* (Winter 1990):

Martin Gardner clearly had such a good time making me the bête noire of any rational person in the summer 1990 *Skeptical Inquirer* ("Relativism in Science") that I feel almost like the Grinch who stole Christmas for saying that I agree with much of what he says, and many of the points he seems to think he is making against my views were also made in my book.

Gardner concludes his argument against "relativism" by saying, "Nobody denies that science is a human tool, or that its history is influenced by cultural forces in all sorts of interesting ways. Nobody denies that scientists invent theories by creative acts similar to those of poets and artists. But once a theory is formulated, it is tested by a process that, in the long run, is singularly free of cultural bias. False theories are not shot down by a change in language, but by the universe." I heartily agree and say so at length in *Inventing Reality*. I would prefer not to use the word *false,* however, which I reserve for mathematical and logical proofs. I think the word *limited* is both more accurate and less perjorative.

I do *not* "see the history of science as a series of cultural preferences." I thought I made that clear in the extensive section where I approvingly quote Sam Ting's statement, "Science is one of the few areas of human life where the majority does *not* rule." Science is characterized by the progressive expansion of our ability to predict the behavior of the physical world. I do not believe that this progress, however, should be interpreted as some sort of asymptotic approach to grasping "nature's own language." After all, progress has come by way of major revisions in the way we think of nature (for example, from thinking of gravity as action at a distance, to gravity as a property of the geometry of space-time, to gravity as a manifestation of local gauge invariance).

Gardner accuses me of promulgating the "wild theme . . . that physicists do not discover the laws of nature. They invent them. Newton didn't discover the law of gravity. He invented it." But Gardner himself says, "Nobody denies that scientists invent theories by creative acts similar to those of poets and artists." So why is he so unhappy when I say the same thing? Perhaps he would have been less enraged had I said that what Newton *did* discover is that the law of gravity he invented is a useful way of describing the world, including among many other things, the motion of the planets. If Gardner wants to say that Newton invented a theory whose success demonstrated that he had discovered a law of nature, then Gardner will presumably have to add that this law of nature was repealed as a result of Einstein's work.

I think part of the problem may be that Gardner takes literally statements I use metaphorically. He quotes me talking about the mutability of history. Certainly he does not disagree that we, like the historians in Orwell's *1984*, continually rewrite history. Presumably Gardner is upset by my statement that the past is transformed by language. But this is simply a metaphorical way of pointing out that the past is only a present reality in the form of a collection of artifacts and the stories historians tell about those artifacts. The past, insofar as we are concerned, is transformed when new evidence leads historians to rewrite history.

Gardner becomes very exercised when I say, "The laws of physics are *our* laws not nature's." He concludes from this that I am saying, "*We* are the gods who shape reality." But his interpretation is nonsense. The laws of physics are our laws because, as Einstein says, they are "free creations of the human mind, and are not, however it may seem, uniquely determined by the external world." Of course we are not free to say whatever we like—not if we want what we say to lead to predictions that agree with experiments. Nature constrains, but does not dictate.

I do have a fundamental disagreement with Gardner, however. I do not find relativity and quantum mechanics to be "a benign refinement" of classical physics. I do not think that Einstein simply "added qualifications to Newtonian physics." Einstein fundamentally altered our views of the nature of space and time and shook a deep-seated belief that Newton had somehow discerned the mind of God when he invented mechanics. The *only* way in which Einstein's general relativity resembles Newton's theory of gravity is that the two theories make similar predictions under certain circumstances—conceptually and mathematically the theories are profoundly different. Quantum theory made even more fundamental changes in our view of the physical world, eliminating the hope that we could predict the behavior of individual atomic systems and forcing us to accept that some physical systems can never be truly "separated."

The view of language and reality I explore in the book is a product of the momentous impact that relativity and quantum mechanics have had on our understanding of the physical world. I share much of my view of this impact with Bohr, Heisenberg, and Einstein, as well as with almost every contemporary physicist. (I am not familiar with Shirley MacLaine's views on fundamental physics.)

Here is how I replied:

The basic disagreement between Gregory and me is that he is a pragmatist who defines truth as the passing of tests, whereas I, following Aristotle, define truth as correspondence with an external world. The very title of Gregory's book, *Inventing Reality,* implies that "reality" is a product of human experience rather than a structure "out there" toward which science moves closer and closer in its descriptions, even though it may never reach absolute accuracy.

Gregory writes that "insofar as we are concerned" history is transformed when historians revise their opinions. But this is trivial and obvious. It means no more than that historians change their minds. The deeper question, which Gregory evades, is whether there is a fixed, timeless past that is unaltered by changing opinions.

Gregory seems unaware that pragmatism has been on the skids for half a century, not so much because it is "wrong," but because it is too confusing a language. Look into any recent book on the philosophy of science, and you are unlikely to find a single reference to John Dewey. As to reasons for the decline, which I attribute mainly to Alfred Tarski's precise definition of semantic truth, see the chapter on "Why I Am Not a Pragmatist" in my *Whys of a Philosophical Scrivener.*

It goes without saying that Newton "invented" the law of gravity and Einstein "invented" relativity, in the sense that they thought of these conjectures and wrote them down. The deeper question, which Gregory ignores, is whether in devising conjectures, and having them strongly confirmed by testing, scientists "discover" facts and laws that slowly get closer to accurate descriptions of a structure "out there," not made by us. Astronomers may alter their opinions about the mass of Pluto, but that doesn't mean that Pluto keeps altering its mass. If science is not getting asymptotically closer to objective truth, there is no way to explain its steadily increasing predictive power.

It is a commonsense realism, assumed by almost all philosophers and scientists, and by all ordinary people, that Gregory is reluctant to affirm. If he did so, he would have called his book "Discovering Reality." In his letter, Gregory backs away from his more outrageous statements by calling them metaphors, but that is precisely the trouble. Such metaphors serve no useful purpose. We all know that science is fallible and keeps changing. Using metaphors that blur the distinction between what scientists say and what writers of stories say is to introduce nothing but confusion to the understanding of science.

Two other letters about the column ran in the Summer, 1991, issue of the magazine:

This letter addresses the article "Relativism in Science," by Martin Gardner (*SI,* Summer 1990), and Bruce Gregory's response (Winter 1991), accompanied by Gardner's reply.

Because I have not seen Gregory's book, I cannot defend it. I do, however, feel that *invention* is often a more satisfactory word than *discovery* when discussing science. I will try to defend this view.

Certainly, the *process* of uncovering natural laws is one of discovery. Also,

I have no quarrel with Gardner's framework: The outside world exists. Some theories are better than others. And investigators in different cultures (different worlds, for that matter) will eventually arrive at the same conclusions. I will argue, nonetheless, that the word *invention* is useful here.

In the discovery process, one looks at reality. Then a model is constructed and tried out. To the extent that the model explains relations between observations and (especially) has predictive value, *discovery* is occurring, i.e., a good representation of nature has been found. Most of us would subscribe to this approximation of doing science and would apply the word *discovery.*

If that is discovery, what shall we call the model-building step? Why not "invention"? The activity is surely similar to inventing a machine that accepts observations as input and generates predictions. We should expect the scientific-model builder to rely on the same ingenuity and creative juices as other inventors.

"Invention" fits especially well during the early stages of disciplines. One can picture early "astronomers" groping for ways to think about the heavens. Imagining figures in the night sky does not advance the science much, but it does help organize the data. (It helps me locate the North Star.) In my view this is doing science, albeit rudimentary. In any case, I doubt if anybody would want to call it "discovery."

A useful example can be found in approaches to the physical properties of gases. The thermodynamics model consists of the notion of entropy and the two very powerful laws of conservation and degradation of energy. Thermodynamics is often cited as one of the most powerful generalizations of classical physics.

More recently, the same relations were derived by treating a gas as a large collection of molecules in motion. By applying statistical mechanics and classical particle physics to the molecules, the "kinetic theory of gases" was born. This model was successively refined and eventually augmented by modern physics in this century. Most now prefer it as a representation of nature.

I leave it to the reader. What best describes the "thinking up" of these two models? I like "invention."

Gerald Lippey
Los Angeles, Calif.

The argument between Martin Gardner and Bruce Gregory is more semantics than substance. The use of the term *invention* in connection with natural phenomena can only be metaphorical. If a condition exists independent of humans it can be discovered but not invented; an invention is manufactured. America was discovered, not invented.

However, Gardner's reference to pragmatism and the philosophy of John Dewey as in decline is shocking. Dewey has not always been understood, and often misunderstood, but I have never read or heard anyone who understood Dewey say that his ideas are "on the skids." Pragmatism is the scientific method applied to philosophy and the best antidote to metaphysical and paranormal beliefs. It is a made-to-order and positive philosophy for skeptics. I do not mind the hair-splitters having their word games, but John Dewey stands for something that is too important to be trivialized by the wordsmiths.

Norman L. Edwards
Newton, Mass.

My reply:

Who could disagree with Norman Edwards and Gerald Lippey that scientists "invent" theories? The theories of course must be tested, and if they pass enough tests they become "discoveries." Newton invented his laws of gravity. It later turned out he had discovered them. Einstein invented relativity theory. It was soon apparent he had discovered that $e = mc^2$. If Lippey will read Gregory's book he will see why I stressed discovery as against invention.

As to the decline of Dewey, I think Edwards is half a century behind the times. That conjectures must pass empirical tests, and that all science is fallible, is not a Deweyan proposal but one that goes back to the Greek empiricists. Dewey's distinctive contribution was much more than this. He wanted to do away with a correspondence definition of truth (that goes back to Aristotle) and substitute the *defining* of truth as the passing of tests. Indeed, Dewey wanted to drop the word *truth* altogether and replace it with "warranted assertability." In proposing this he was following in the steps of William James, who in turn had misunderstood his friend and mentor Charles Peirce.

Dewey's effort to abandon "truth" was dealt a fatal blow by Alfred Tarski's work on "semantic truth," now accepted by almost every philosopher of science. Dewey was an influential writer on ethics, politics, and education, but his influence on the philosophy of science was minimal and is now close to zero. He had nothing to say about any of the deep problems with which such philosophers are concerned, such as the nature of induction, the role of simplicity, the philosophical implications of quantum mechanics, and a raft of others.

If Edwards doubts this decline of Dewey's influence, let him make the following simple test. Check the indices of fifty randomly selected books on the philosophy of science written since 1940. He will find either no mention of Dewey, or only a few scant references compared with lengthy discussions of the views of Bertrand Russell, Karl Popper, Hans Reichenbach, Rudolf Carnap, and many others. Russell was the most implacable foe of Dewey's idiosyncratic version of pragmatism, yet no one can accuse Russell of favoring metaphysics or of not understanding scientific method.

If pragmatism is taken in the broad sense of no more than the need for empirical testing of theories, then of course everyone is a pragmatist. But this trivializes the term in a way that ignores the heart of the revolution Dewey struggled so hard to achieve.

11 | The Old Finger-Lift Levitation

For centuries, throughout the world, it has been the custom of some children to amuse themselves with the following seemingly paranormal stunt. You may recall participating in such a feat yourself when you were young. The stunt can take numerous forms, but usually goes like this.

A heavy person, say an adult male, is seated on a chair or stool. We will call him the "subject." Two children stand behind him, and two on either side of his knees. One of the children in back puts an index finger under the subject's left armpit. The second child in back puts an index finger under the right armpit. The third child puts a finger under the subject's left knee, and the fourth puts his or her finger under the right knee.

An effort is made to lift the subject, but he is much too heavy. The lift is now repeated, but not until a ritual of some sort has been performed. This ritual can take many forms. Among American children, a common practice is for one child to put a hand palm down on the subject's head. A second child puts a hand on the first hand. This continues until all eight hands have formed a tower, with the proviso that no two hands belonging to the same person are in contact. Everyone presses down for a short time. After this is done, the four fingers are placed under the subject's knees and armpits. Someone counts from 1 to 3. On the count of 3, the lifters hold their breath and lift. Up goes the subject. Indeed, the lift seems so easy that there is a strong feeling on the part of lifters that the subject's weight has somehow miraculously decreased.

Although the stunt works as described, the lift is much easier if each lifter uses both hands. The two forefingers go side by side, palms down, the rest of the fingers closed in a fist. Since both arms now share in the lift, the weight of a 200-lb. person is divided eight ways, so each arm lifts a mere 25 pounds.

Years ago someone told me that the stunt is described by Samuel Pepys in his famous diary, but it was not until this year that I learned from physicist Donald W. Olson, at Southwest Texas State University, in San Marcos, and his wife Marilynn, who teaches English at the same university, where in the diary the trick is described. It occurs in Pepys's entry for July 31, 1665:

> This evening with Mr. Brisband, speaking of enchantments and spells, I telling him some of my charms; he told me this of his owne knowledge, at Bourdeaux, in France. The words these:
>
> > Voyci un Corps mort,
> > Royde come un Baston,
> > Froid comme Marbre,
> > Leger come un esprit,
> > Levons te au nom de Jesus Christ.
>
> He saw four little girles, very young ones, all kneeling, each of them, upon one knee; and one begun the first line, whispering in the eare of the next, and the second to the third, and the third to the fourth, and she to the first. Then the first begun the second line, and so round quite through, and, putting each one finger only to a boy that lay flat upon his back on the ground, as if he was dead; at the end of the words, they did with their four fingers raise this boy as high as they could reach, and he [Mr. Brisband] being there, and wondering at it, as also being afeard to see it, for they would have had him to have bore a part in saying the words, in the roome of one of the little girles that was so young that they could hardly make her learn to repeat the words, did, for feare there might be some sleight used in it by the boy, or that the boy might be light, call the cook of the house, a very lusty fellow, as Sir G. Carteret's cook, who is very big, and they did raise him in just the same manner. This is one of the strangest things I ever heard, but he tells it me of his owne knowledge, and I do heartily believe it to be true. I enquired of him whether they were Protestant or Catholique girles; and he told me they were Protestant, which made it the more strange to me.

James Randi provided the following translation of the verse recited by the French girls:

> Here is a dead body,
> Stiff as a stick,
> Cold as marble,
> Light as a spirit.
> We lift you in the name of Jesus Christ.

The Olsons also sent me pages from *The Lore and Language of Schoolchildren,* by Iona and Peter Opie (1959). After quoting from Pepys's diary, the Opies give another description of the feat by a correspondent who was at a school in Bath in the 1940s:

The queerest happening I know of I have on my own memory. Some of my form-mates one day resolved to try a trick they had heard of, in which one person sat in a chair, and several others (I think four) stood round, with some part of their hands pressed on the victim's head—I think it was their thumbs. The idea was to continue this in an atmosphere of intense concentration by all (no talking or giggles) for a few minutes, after which it was supposed that the person sitting, contrary to all the laws of nature, would actually become *lighter* and could be lifted by the others as easily as if she were a cushion. This experiment was watched with keen interest by the form, and seemed to have a curiously uncanny effect. Whether by self-hypnotism or not I do not know, but the lifters, with a few fingers only under arm-pits and knees, certainly lifted the seated one with ease and grace into the air, and put her down in the same manner. It was more like real magic than anything else I have seen.

The Opies continue:

We may add that when we were young we, too, practised this trick, three ways being known to us. In the first, the subject lay down and, if we recollect rightly, there were four raisers using one finger each; in the second, the subject was seated and there were two raisers using a finger of each hand; in the third, which was the most spectacular, the subject stood on a book with his heels and toes jutting over so that fingers could be placed underneath, and he went up vertically. In this last instance the child had to be smaller than the operators or they could not reach the top of his head to press upon. With us it was considered necessary for everyone taking part to hold his breath throughout the operation. One person counted to ten while all pressed downwards, then everyone swiftly changed to the lifting position.

David Brewster, in his *Letters on Natural Magic* (1862), gives a curiously different version of the lift:

One of the most remarkable and inexplicable experiments relative to the strength of the human frame, which you have yourself seen and admired, is that in which a heavy man is raised with the greatest facility, when he is lifted up the instant that his own lungs and those of the persons who raise him are inflated with air. This experiment was, I believe, first shown in England a few years ago by Major H., who saw it performed in a large party at Venice under the direction of an officer of the American Navy. As Major H. performed it more than once in my presence, I shall describe as nearly as possible the method which he prescribed. The heaviest person in the party lies down upon two chairs, his legs being supported by the one and his back by the other. Four persons, one at each leg, and one at each shoulder, then try to raise him, and they find his dead weight to be very great, from the difficulty they experience in supporting him. When he is replaced in the chair, each of the four persons takes hold of the body as before, and the person to be lifted gives two signals by clapping his hands. At the first signal he himself and the four lifters begin to draw a long and full breath, and when the inhalation is completed, or the lungs filled, the second signal is given, for raising the person from the chair. To his own surprise and that of his bearers, he rises with the greatest facility, as if he were no heavier than a feather. On several occasions I have observed that when one of the bearers performs his part ill, by making the inhalation out of time, the part of the body which he tries to raise is left as it were behind. As you have repeatedly seen this experiment, and have performed the part both of the load and of the bearer, you can testify how remarkable the effects appear to all parties, and how complete is the conviction, either that the load has been lightened, or the bearer strengthened by the prescribed process.

At Venice the experiment was performed in a much more imposing manner. The heaviest man in the party was raised and sustained upon the points of the fore-fingers of six persons. Major H. declared that the experiment would not succeed if the person lifted were placed upon a board, and the strength of the individuals applied to the board. He conceived it necessary that the bearers should communicate directly with the body to be raised. I have not had an opportunity of making any experiments relative to these curious facts; but whether the general effect is an illusion, or the result of known or of new principles, the subject merits a careful investigation.

Gaston Tissandier, in *Popular Scientific Recreations* (Paris, 1881), has the subject standing. Two lifters each put a finger under his shoes, two more under his bent elbows, and a fifth puts a finger under the chin. The illustration shown here is from an English translation of Tissandier's book.

I found still another description in *The Beautiful, the Wonderful, and the Wise,* edited by L. N. Chapin (rev. ed., Philadelphia, 1886):

A correspondent of the *Scientific American* gives the following, which is vouched for by plenty of good authorities: "I am glad to see the 'buzzing up' process again brought to notice. Fifty years ago the operation was to me a pastime, bewitching and unaccountable as now. It is not (?) animal magnetism; I know as much about that as anybody,—which is very little. I will explain the method of performing this most wonderful feat. A lies on his back on a floor, ground, or an open lounge. B and C (two are as good as four) place their forefingers under the shoulders and hips of A. They breathe in concert by finger signals from A. At the first inhalation B and C lift, but they don't lift; the least effort or grunt breaks the spell, and you begin anew. Thus A is breathed up, the breath lasting, if you are adroit, till you raise him as high as you can reach, when you must catch him, to prevent a fall. The head should be the high test, and then he will come down on his feet. He will feel that the gravitation is out of him; B and C lift only the clothing. He feels—have you ever dreamed of flying? That is it exactly. No need of a close or still room. It can be done out of doors, in a gale as well as in a closet. When you get

the knack of it,—and it has once cost me three hours to teach a class,—
any two of twelve or fifteen years can toss up a Daniel Lambert like a feather.
I do not know that any science can come out of it, but as an amusement,
it is the richest thing I ever knew.

I should explain the reference to Daniel Lambert. He was an Englishman
(1770-1809), world famous for his enormous bulk. He was 5 feet, 11 inches
tall, and weighed 739 pounds when he died. Lambert's name became a
popular synonym for immensity. London is the "Daniel Lambert of cities,"
wrote George Meredith, and Herbert Spencer once called a man a "Daniel
Lambert of Learning." His coffin measured 6 feet 4 inches by 4 feet 4
inches, and 2 feet 4 inches.

Why does the lift work? When four lifters are involved, the weight is
distributed four ways. If the subject weighs 200 pounds, each lifter has to
raise a mere 50 pounds—40 pounds if there are five lifters. At the first attempt,
lifters do not start hoisting at the same instant, and the subject's weight is
unevenly distributed. He will tilt to one side, putting a heavier burden on
certain lifters. The ritual, and the lift at the end of a count, ensures coordination
on the second try. The ritual also induces everyone to try harder.

Holding the breath may also contribute to the lift. Most people stop
breathing when they try to lift a heavy object. It has also been suggested
that if the lifters press down for a while on the subject's head, this may make
their arms feel lighter when they make the lift. (There is another old children's
stunt in which you stand in a doorway and press the backs of your hands
against the sides of the opening for a minute or two. When you step away,
your arms seem to float upward in the air of their own accord.)

It is hard to believe, but a few parapsychologists suspect something
paranormal is responsible for this old stunt. Thelma Moss, for example, in
The Probability of the Impossible (1975), takes this view. The British occult
journalist John Randall, in *Psychokinesis* (1982), writes: "No physicist has
ever given a 'normal' explanation of this phenomenon." In *The Story of
Psychic Science* (1930) the American psychic investigator Hereward Carrington
reports on experiments he made with the lift. He had five men perform
the levitation on a large platform that registered weight. According to
Carrington, the total weight before the lift was 712 pounds. During the lift
the scale registered a weight loss of 60 pounds. "I have no theory to offer
as to these observations," he writes, "which I cannot fully explain."

In recent years the lift has been routinely demonstrated by Uri Geller
in his stage shows. Uri invites on the stage the heaviest person he sees
in the audience, along with three others to assist. The first lift attempt
invariably fails. Before the second try, Uri's ritual is the usual stacking

Left, Finger lifting of the stone ball in Shivpuri, India.

Right, A man held up by five fingers. (From Tissandier's *Popular Scientific Recreations,* 1881.)

of hands on the subject's head. Colin Wilson, England's top journalist of the occult, tells of being lifted this way in his book *The Geller Phenomenon* (1976). The lifters were Uri, his old buddy Shipi, and two of his ladyfriends. The book's photos show four stages of this great event. The third photo graces the front cover of *When the Impossible Happens,* a volume in a series called *The Unexplained* (London, 1982). It is one of many predecessors of the current Time-Life series of shameful books promoting the paranormal.

The subject need not be a person. In Shivpuri, a village near Poona, in western India, there is a famous mausoleum containing the remains of Kamarali Darvesh, a Muslim saint. On the ground outside the entrance sits a large stone ball, 14 inches in diameter and weighing about 140 pounds. Any odd number of men, usually five or seven, stand around the ball and touch it with a forefinger at spots on the ball's equator or below. After they recite in unison "Kamarali Darvesh," an attendant gives the signal to lift. The ball slowly rises. Devout Muslims believe this to be a miracle of Allah's. (For a picture of the ball being raised, see the *SI,* Spring-Summer, 1978.)

Trying to explain to Muslim fundamentalists that with five lifters each man has to raise only 28 pounds, and with seven lifters, each hoists only

20 pounds, is as fruitless as trying to convince many top psychical researchers that levitations are not commonplace psychic phenomena.

Addendum

The following two letters are from the *Skeptical Inquirer's* Spring 1991 issue:

> Martin Gardner's interesting article about finger-lift levitation ("The Mysterious Finger-Lift Levitation," *SI,* Fall 1990) is spoiled by a needless and incorrect remark at the end. After describing how some Muslims visiting the tomb/shrine of Kamarali Darvesh near Poona take part in raising a large stone ball, Gardner next suggests that these Muslims are "Muslim fundamentalists" who would not be likely to accept a nonmiraculous explanation for the levitation. Unlike most of the other examples of levitation given in the article, the source of this story is not provided.
>
> Gardner does not seem to recognize that the overwhelming majority of so-called Muslim fundamentalists are in fact violently opposed to such "miraculous" displays, and indeed consider the entire phenomenon of saints' cults in the Muslim world to be a perversion of "true" Islamic practice. Like Gardner, these "Muslim fundamentalists" condemn levitatory displays as parlor tricks, and in the past have been very quick to dismiss other similar events as superstitious frauds.
>
> David Damrel
> Tucson, Ariz.

The Fallacy of the Monstrous "Merely" pops up more often than one might suspect. For example, of all the articles in this journal exposing the "backward masking" nonsense, none ever bothered to explain just how one "merely" plays a record or tape backward. I have had fairly sophisticated audio systems for 35 years, but haven't the faintest idea how to do what our satanically befuddled teens must be doing routinely.

Now, a latter-day hero, Martin Gardner, unveils the Mysterious Finger-Lift Levitation (*SI,* Fall 1990) by explaining that, for a 200-pound subject, ". . . each lifter has to raise a mere 50 pounds. . . ." The lifters in the text were often small children. Recalling my own springtime tussles with 40-pound bags of topsoil, perhaps someone could explain how one extended index finger is supposed to casually hoist "a mere 50 pounds."

Tony Pasquarello
Department of Philosophy
Ohio State University
Mansfield, Ohio

Mr. Pasquarello is right about 50 pounds being a strain on one extended finger. For this reason, if the person to be lifted is extremely heavy, more than one finger is usually involved. I mentioned the use of both hands, palm to palm, with the index fingers extended side by side. One hand can also be used with the first and second fingers extended, or all four fingers.

As the picture from Tissandier's book shows, the lift is frequently made by five people, one person placing a finger under the chin. This of course divides the weight five ways, and makes the lift easier.

When Uri Geller demonstrates the finger lift in his stage shows, he takes no chances. As one of the lifters he can make sure the first lifting attempt won't work by pretending he is lifting when he really isn't.

12 | Frank Tipler's Omega Point Theory

Frank Tipler is a professor of mathematical physics at Tulane University, New Orleans. He has edited a book of papers on relativity and coauthored *The Anthropic Cosmological Principle,* a 706-page work published by Oxford University Press in 1986. Among scientists he is best known for his vigorous opposition to the hopes of Carl Sagan and others that intelligent life flourishes elsewhere than on earth.

In recent years Tipler has been writing papers about what he calls his Omega Point Theory (OPT), research on which has been partly supported by the National Science Foundation. Here is his abstract of "The Omega Point as *Eschaton,*" a paper in *Zygon* (vol. 24, June 1989):

I present an outline of the Omega Point Theory, which is a model for an omnipresent, omniscient, omnipotent, evolving, personal God who is both transcendent to spacetime and immanent in it, and who exists necessarily. The model is a falsifiable physical theory deriving its key concepts not from any religious tradition but from modern physical cosmology and computer science; from scientific materialism rather than revelation. Four testable predictions of the model are given. The theory assumes that thinking is a purely physical process of the brain, and that personality dies with the brain. Nevertheless, I show that the Omega Point Theory suggests a future universal resurrection of the dead very similar to the one predicted in the Judeo-Christian-Islamic tradition. The notions of "grace" and the "beatific vision" appear naturally in the model.

If our universe is "open" it will expand forever. Eventually it will expire from the cold and all life will end. Tipler assumes that the universe is "closed" in the sense that space-time is positively curved by vast amounts of dark (invisible) matter. All closed universes will stop expanding and go the other way toward a big crunch. In most cases, this, too, would wipe out all life and all "memory" of the past. But there are special classes of closed universes (too technical to go into here) in which the recollapse leads to a special type of "crunch" that Tipler calls the Omega Point, borrowing the term from the unorthodox French paleontologist Teilhard de Chardin. At the Omega Point the temporal becomes eternal, and the entire cosmos is "engulfed" by total information about the universe's history.

This kind of universe, Tipler argues, necessarily exists. According to what he calls the Final Anthropic Principle, it is capable of sustaining life indefinitely. God, or the Omega Point—for Tipler the terms have the same meaning—is a "singularity" of space and time, in a region that traditional religions call "eternity." When this stage is reached, the universe will have become a "Person" who experiences all history in one blinding "now." Such a God will be omnipresent in occupying every part of the universe, omniscient in knowing all that can be known, and omnipotent in being able to do all that can be done.

Tipler prides himself on being an atheist in the sense that he is not a theist, nor is there as yet experimental evidence for his Omega Point god. Tipler has in effect joined the ranks of distinguished "process theologians"— Schelling, Alexander, Whitehead, Bergson, Hartshorne, and others—who see God as evolving as the universe evolves. Not until the end of history, at the Omega Point, does everything become a Personal Ultimate Reality. From our perspective, God is "forever growing in knowledge and power." From the Omega Point's perspective, God is the great I AM, "forever complete and unchanging."

> But all timelike and lightlike curves converge upon the Omega Point. In particular, all the light rays from all the people who died a thousand years ago, from all the people now living, and from all the people who will be living a thousand years from now, will intersect there. The light rays from those people who died a thousand years ago are not lost forever; rather, these rays will be intercepted by the Omega Point. To put it another way, these rays will be intercepted and intercepted again by the living beings who have engulfed the physical universe near the Omega Point. All the information which can be extracted from these rays will be extracted at the instant of the Omega Point, who will therefore experience the whole of time simultaneously just as we experience simultaneously the Andromeda Galaxy and a person in the room with us.

Tipler is a materialist in the sense that he follows Aristotle in regarding the "soul" as the body's "form"—the pattern of molecules in a brain. We are computers made of organic matter. Our "self" is no more than an enormously complex computer program. When we die we are truly dead, but our program is not lost. The Omega Point is capable of "resurrecting" every person who ever lived simply by giving that person's pattern a new, transcendent body. Here Tipler adopts the view known as "conditional immortality" or "soul sleeping." It was probably the view of St. Paul, and has been upheld by thinkers as diverse as Karl Barth and John Milton, as well as by such modern Christian sects as Seventh-Day Adventists and Jehovah's Witnesses.

Because the brain's pattern derives from a set of discrete genes, and because there are only a finite number of possible brain states, not only can God recreate all persons who ever lived, but also all who *could* have lived. Tipler finds this possibility enhanced by the Many Worlds Interpretation of quantum mechanics. In this view, which Tipler strongly favors, the universe is constantly branching into myriads of different histories in which all logically possible events occur and all logically possible universes and life forms exist. "Just as there is an infinity of actual paths which have led to the present state, so there is an infinity of really existing futures which evolve from the present state."

Because the universe gets hotter as it nears the Omega Point, where temperature goes to infinity, it will reach a stage at which life as we know it cannot survive. Our heirs, therefore, will have to be a markedly different species. Tipler believes that within a century, "certainly within a thousand years," we will be able to transfer our mind patterns to computers. Organic life will perish. Computers will be the new life forms. Because at the Omega Point all their programs, as well as all our programs, are preserved, the Omega Point will resurrect each of us provided it has sufficient "grace" to do so. "We shall, so to speak, live again in the mind of God." As Tipler puts it in a later paper, "We will be granted eternal life because it is probable that the Omega Point loves us!"

I should emphasize that this simulation of people that have lived in the past need not be limited to just repeating the past. Once a simulation of a person and his or her world has been formed in a computer of sufficient capacity, the simulated person can be allowed to develop further—to think and feel things that the long-dead original person being simulated never felt and thought. It is not even necessary for *any* of the past to be repeated. The Omega Point could simply begin the simulation with the brain memory of the dead person as it was at the instant of death (or, say, ten years before or twenty minutes before) implanted in the simulated body of the dead person, the body being as it was at age twenty (or any other age). This body and memory collection could be set in any simulated background environment the Omega Point wished: a simulated world indistinguishable from the long-extinct society and physical universe of the revived dead person; or even a world that never existed, but one as close as logically possible to the ideal *fantasy* world of the resurrected dead person. Furthermore, all possible combinations of resurrected dead can be placed in the same simulation and allowed to interact. For example, the reader could be placed in a simulation with *all* of his or her ancestors and descendants, each at whatever age (physical and mental, separately) the Omega Point pleases. The Omega Point itself could interact—speak, for instance—with His/Her simulated creatures, who could learn about Him/Her, about the world outside the simulation, and about other simulations, from Him/Her.

The simulated body could be one that has been vastly improved over the one we currently have; the laws of the simulated world could be modified to prevent a second physical death. Borrowing the terminology of Paul, we can call the simulated, improved and undying body a "spiritual body," for it will be of the same "stuff" as the human mind now is: a "thought inside a mind" (in Aristotelian language, "a form inside a form"; in computer language, a "virtual machine inside a machine"). The spiritual body is thus just the present body (with improvements!) at a higher level of implementation. With this phrasing, Paul's description is completely accurate: "So also is the resurrection of the dead. It is sown in corruption; it is raised in incorruption: It is sown in dishonor; it is raised in glory; it is sown in weakness; it is raised in power: It is sown a natural body; it is raised a spiritual body" (1 Cor. 15:42-44). Only as a spiritual body, only as a computer simulation, is resurrection possible without a second death: our current bodies, implemented in matter, could not possibly survive the extreme heat near the final singularity. Again, Paul's words are descriptive: ". . . flesh and blood cannot inherit the kingdom of God" (1 Cor. 15:50).

Nevertheless, it is appropriate to regard computer simulation resurrection as being a "resurrection of the flesh" (in the words of the Apostles' Creed). For a simulated person would observe herself to be as real, and as having a body as solid as the body we currently observe ourselves to have. There would be nothing "ghostly" about the simulated body, and nothing insubstantial about the simulated world in which the simulated body found itself. In the words of Tertullian, the simulated body would be ". . . this flesh, suffused with blood, built up with bones, interwoven with nerves, entwined with veins [a flesh] which . . . [is] . . . undoubtedly human."

In a later, unpublished paper, "Physics Near the Final State: God and the Resurrection of the Dead to Eternal Life," Tipler defends the possible existence of "realms that can be accurately described as Heaven and Purgatory." (Only the Omega Point knows if there is a Hell.) "A Christology can be developed in the Omega Point Theory, but it does not appear naturally in the model, and in any case the Christology depends on some unlikely possibilities in quantum cosmology."

Will there be sex in heaven? In the paper just cited, Tipler says this question is often asked by his students. The answer, he assures us, is yes. "Sex will be available to those who wish it. . . . A man like Aquinas who had no interest in sex will not experience it, but people who desire it will." However, all the difficulties that arise in our sex life now "will not exist for the resurrected humans, since the Omega Point can match people: the Omega Point should be able to calculate which amongst all possible people would be the best mate for a given person."

> To put it more dramatically (for unmarried males), it would be possible for each male to be matched not merely with the most beautiful woman in the world, not merely with the most beautiful woman who has ever lived, but to be matched with the most beautiful woman whose existence is logically possible! Because of the mutability of the appearance of the resurrection body, it would be easy to ensure that said male is also the most handsome (or desirable) man to this most beautiful woman (provided the man has spent sufficient time in Purgatory to correct personality defects).

As for "elbow room" in heaven, Tipler speculates:

> It would be possible for the Omega Point to simulate an entire visible universe for the personal use of each and every resurrected human! ("In my Father's house are many mansions. . . .") The required computer capacity is not measurably greater than that required to simulate all possible visible universes ($10^{10^{123}}$). Each private visible universe could also be simulated to contain 10^{10} separate planet Earths, each a copy of the present Earth, or the Earth as it was at a different time in the past. (There are about 10^{20} stars in the visible universe, so replacing a mere 10^{10} solar systems in a visible universe would be a minor modification.) This is more Earths than a single human could explore before exhausting his/her memory storage capacity of 10^{15} bits, to say nothing of the memories stored while visiting other humans in *their* private universes.

Thus does Tipler construct a colorful eschatology that he believes is based entirely on science. Theology has become a branch of physics. Tipler cites several ways his theory can be empirically tested, starting with observations to determine the universe's space-time curvature. If it turns out not to be closed, then the OPT will of course be falsified. So far, he concedes, because there is as yet no confirming evidence for the OPT "it is premature to accept it."

Although Jesus, the Bible, the Koran, and all other forms of revelation play no role in the OPT, Tipler (as we have seen) likes to invoke Paul— Saint Paul!—as a supporter of his vision. "The key concepts of the Judeo-Christian-Islamic traditions," he writes, "are now scientific concepts." Here is how Tipler concludes his 1989 paper:

> The hope of eternal worldly progress and the hope of individual survival beyond the grave turn out to be the same. Far from being polar opposites, these two hopes require each other; we cannot have one without the other. The

Omega Point is truly the God of Hope: "O death, where is thy sting? O grave, where is thy victory?" (1 Cor. 15:55).

I leave it to readers to decide whether they should opt for OPT as a new scientific religion superior to Scientology—one destined to elevate Tipler to the rank of a prophet greater than L. Ron Hubbard—or opt for the view that OPT is a wild fantasy generated by too much reading of science fiction.

Addendum

The following letter from Poul Anderson, the well-known science-fiction writer, appeared in the *Skeptical Inquirer* (Summer, 1991):

> With all due and considerable respect for Martin Gardner, I must say he seems rather unfair to Frank Tipler. Granted Tipler's Omega Point concept is imaginative, to say the least. Even an amateur like myself can raise some basic questions about the physics of it. These questions do not at present have definite answers, of course, but Tipler emphasizes throughout that his ideas are testable and that certain discoveries may well be made in the near future to falsify them.
>
> He is emphatically not setting himself up as the prophet of a new religion, à la L. Ron Hubbard. If anything, what he offers is fresh commentary on long-established faiths, especially Christianity, and it is worth noting that he first did so at a respectable conference on science and religion.
>
> In an era when basic principles of physics, e.g., causality, are being re-examined, we still need skepticism, but we can ill afford dogmatism. Personally, I look on Tipler's notion as a sort of high-powered playfulness, not altogether unlike some that Gardner himself has indulged in occasionally to the great pleasure of his readers.

My reply:

> In response to Poul Anderson's friendly letter, I gather he thinks Tipler is proposing his new religion in a spirit of fun, comparable to the entertaining resurrection motif in Philip José Farmer's *Riverworld* novels. My impression, based on Tipler's papers, letters, and phone conversations, is that he is quite serious in believing his conjectures to be superior to any of the world's great faiths, or to the speculations of philosophers.
>
> When I concluded that Tipler's views might become, like those of L. Ron Hubbard, the basis of a new science-fiction religious cult, that was intended as "high-powered playfulness."

I had a pleasant exchange of private letters with another noted science-fiction writer, Frederik Pohl. He chided me for suggesting, at the end of my column, that one could read too much SF. What I meant was that if one reads too much SF *uncritically,* it can have a baleful influence. Think of the SF fans who take seriously such common SF themes as UFOs, ESP, PK, and so on. I do believe that a few leading proponents of what is called "strong artificial intelligence" were unduly influenced by youthful reading of SF tales about robots. I think John Campbell, who edited *Astounding Science Fiction* and introduced Scientology to the world, read too much of L. Ron Hubbard, who in turn read too much of his own SF. I myself enjoy good SF, and have even written a few SF stories, but I hope I never confuse the wilder speculations of SF with science.

13 | Urantia, the *Titanic,* and a PPO, Part 1

Instead of devoting this chapter to a single topic, I will cover three unrelated topics on which I invite the help of anyone who may have information bearing on any of them. (I can be reached at 110 Glenbrook Drive, Hendersonville, NC 28739.)

First, some unusual new evidence has come to light about the origin of *The Urantia Book* (*UB*), the subject of Chapter 8. The *UB* is an enormous tome that purports to have been dictated by a group of superhuman intelligences. It is the Bible of a growing religious cult. The most interesting aspect of the *UB,* I wrote, is the mystery of who channeled it. Leaders of the group have resolutely refused to divulge the channeler's identity. All they will admit is that the channeler was a friend of a prominent Chicago psychiatrist and former Seventh-Day Adventist, Dr. William Sadler. The channeled material was given to Sadler, who edited it into what became the *UB.* Sadler is on record as saying that the identity of the channeler would forever remain unknown. Of all printed works said to be dictated by superpowers, the *UB* is the largest and the most detailed in its bizarre revelations and prophecies.

I am pleased to report that after many months of detective work I have learned the identity of the channeler. This was first disclosed to me by Iola Martin, an Adventist now living in Washington. It has since been confirmed by Mrs. Harold Sherman, of Arkansas. She and her husband had at one time been part of the Urantia movement's inner circle in Chicago.

The story begins with Dr. John Harvey Kellogg, a prominent Adventist surgeon who wrote many books on health and diet, and whose brother, William Kieth, started the Kellogg cornflake company in Battle Creek, Michigan. Kellogg eventually clashed with Ellen G. White, the Adventist prophetess whose visions and revelations from God became the basis of Adventist doctrines. In 1907 Kellogg was excommunicated by the church.

Sadler, too, was in his early years a devout Adventist. He began his career working for Kellogg, but later broke with the church to become a well-known Chicago psychiatrist and a prolific author. In his most popular book, *The Mind at Mischief,* he spoke of having known only two persons who channeled revelations in ways that he could not attribute to any sort of mental disorder. He does not name them, but clearly one was Mrs. White and the other was the man who channeled the *UB.*

The *Urantia Book*'s channeler was Wilfred Kellogg, whose relationship with the Battle Creek Kelloggs I will reveal in the next chapter. He was a founding trustee of the Urantia Foundation, a position held from January 1950 until his death on August 31, 1956. Mrs. Sherman tells me that Wilfred was a modest, quiet man, and the last person one would suspect of being capable of producing the *UB,* or, as believers would prefer to say, of having been chosen by the superpowers to be their conduit. Wilfred was business manager of Sadler's Chicago Institute of Research and Development, at 533 Diversey Parkway, Chicago. The building has long been the headquarters of the Urantia Foundation. Wilfred and Anna had one child, their daughter Ruth. She was born deaf, although I am told she did learn to speak. Later, Ruth and her baby died during childbirth somewhere on the West Coast.

The identity of the channeler, whose father was an Adventist minister, explains why the *UB* contains so much material that mirrors Adventist dogmas, such as the doctrine that the soul sleeps until the body's pattern is reconstituted on another world, and the ultimate annihilation of the wicked rather than their eternal torment in a mythical hell. Of course there are major differences in the two religions, especially in the *UB*'s acceptance of an old Urantia (the book's name for Earth) and the evolution of all life upon it. There are many amusing details that mesh with Adventist beliefs. Jesus and the archangel Michael, for example, are considered identical.

One of the strangest echoes of Adventism in the *UB* is a personage named Amadon. You can read all about him in the *UB*'s Paper 67. The great Lucifer rebellion of the Christian Bible is there described as taking place on Urantia some 150,000 years before Adam and Eve. For 300,000 years Urantia had been ruled by the evil Caligastia (the name suggests Caligula), a servant of Lucifer. When Caligastia decided to make himself absolute dictator, he was opposed by Van the Steadfast, chairman of the Supreme Council of Co-ordination.

Throughout Caligastia's seven-year rebellion, Van was supported by his loyal assistant Amadon, the human hero of the rebellion. He was not as intelligent as the superhuman Van, but he was unwavering in his devotion to God the Father and the Son Michael (Jesus). The rebellion ended in Caligastia's expulsion. The Amadonites were a "noble band" that supported

Amadon; their descendants, along with the rival Nodites, flourished until the establishment of Eden. Sustained by the Tree of Life, Amadon continued to serve Van for more than 150,000 years, until the arrival of Adam and Eve.

Now for the curious coincidence. George Washington Amadon (1832-1913) was a prominent Adventist editor and publishing executive, no doubt descended from the noble Amadonites. It was he who interviewed John Harvey Kellogg about his heretical opinions just 34 days before the doctor was kicked out of the church in 1907. Most of this lengthy interview was published in the April and June 1990 issues of *Spectrum,* an unofficial Adventist journal. It is a fascinating interrogation because it reveals that the church was then fully aware of Ellen G. White's continual plagiarisms, but was not disclosing this to church members. These plagiarisms and the church's suppression of the truth about them was one of the main reasons for J. H. Kellogg's disenchantment with Mrs. White.

I would welcome hearing from anyone who can supply information about Wilfred Kellogg. When and where was he born? Did he attend college and, if so, where? How heavily were his revelations edited by Sadler? It will be interesting to see if Urantia leaders (the group recently split into two rival organizations) will now admit that the *UB* came from the mind of an ex-Adventist.

*   *   *

In 1986 Prometheus Books published my book *The Wreck of the Titanic Foretold?* The theme is that, contrary to what many believers in precognition have argued (notably Ian Stevenson, a parapsychologist best known for his research on reincarnation), there is no good reason to believe that the *Titanic*'s disaster had been paranormally anticipated. My book focused on Morgan Robertson's prophetic novel *Futility* (later retitled *The Wreck of the Titan*), first published in 1898, fourteen years before the *Titanic* sank.

Robertson's sea tales were enormously popular in his day. Even after his death in 1915 there were large advertisements for his books in popular magazines—for instance, the entire back cover of *Scientific American,* April 8, 1916. Today Robertson is remembered mainly for the striking parallels between the sinking of the *Titanic* in April 1912 and the fate of his 1898 book's imaginary liner, the *Titan,* which also sank in April after striking an iceberg in the North Atlantic.

"She was the largest craft afloat and the greatest of the works of man," was how Robertson described the *Titan* in his novel's opening sentence. The structural resemblance of the *Titan* to the *Titanic* is remarkable, but no correspondence has been more impressive to occult writers than the name of Robertson's fictional ship.

New evidence has come to light suggesting that this similarity of names may not be so titanic after all. Everett Bleiler, in his marvelous reference work *Science Fiction: The Early Years* (Kent State University Press, 1990) reports his discovery of an obscure novel by William Young Winthrop. Nothing is known about Winthrop except that he was born in 1852 and lived in Woodmont, Connecticut. Titled *A 20th Century Cinderella or $20,000 Reward,* Winthrop's novel was published in 1902 by the Abbey Press, a New York vanity house. Bleiler summarizes the plot, calling the book "a very long amateurish novel" and a "silly bore." I mention the novel here only because it refers to a gigantic ocean liner called the *Titanic* that had been built by England's White Star company sometime before 1920, the year in which Winthrop's science-fiction story takes place.

Now the actual *Titanic* was also a White Star liner, although not built until a decade after Winthrop's novel was published! This could be another coincidence (believers in precognition will no doubt consider it another paranormal prophecy even though the fictional *Titanic* does not sink), but does it not suggest the following? It seems to me entirely possible that the White Star company, as early as 1898, when Robertson wrote his novel, had announced plans to construct the world's largest ocean liner and to call it the *Titanic.*

Perhaps someone in England with access to newspapers and periodicals of the late 1890s, or access to old White Star records, can find evidence to support this conjecture. Winthrop may, of course, have read Robertson's earlier novel and slightly modified the name of its ship, but Robertson had not named the steamship company that built his *Titan.* Was it to avoid giving White Star unearned bad publicity?

*   *   *

The January 1991 issue of England's *Journal of the Society for Psychical Research* carries an article titled "A Permanent Paranormal Object?" translated from a German journal of parapsychology. Written by Bernhard Wälti, it describes two tiny frames, one made of paper, the other of aluminum foil, that are said to have been paranormally linked by a Swiss psychic, Silvio Meyer. Each frame is square shaped and about one inch on each side. Meyer claims that he cut the paper frame from notepaper and the aluminum frame from some metal foil that had been wrapped around a sandwich. First he sliced the paper frame, slid the foil frame through the slot, then held the cut between his thumb and finger for ten minutes. The cut miraculously welded, leaving no trace.

According to the article's author, the links were examined at the Swiss Federated Laboratories for Materials Testing and Research, at St. Gallen, by technicians (not named) who were unable to determine how this PPO could have been produced normally without using machinery to which Meyer is said to have no access. PPO is John Beloff's acronym for a Permanent Paranormal Object. Beloff edits the *Journal of the SPR,* and is England's best-known parapsychologist. He has long been searching for a genuine PPO, which he likens to the Holy Grail. We are told that the linkage still exists and can be examined by any scientist.

Does anyone have a theory about how Meyer could have linked the two little frames without making use, or having a friend who made use, of machinery for making paper or tinfoil? Can any reader in Switzerland check on what the laboratory at St. Gallen made of the linkage? Was it actually examined by scientists, or by some subordinate in the laboratory?

Beloff is certainly right in contending that if a PPO can be found that no one is able to duplicate by normal methods, it would constitute the best evidence yet for psychokinesis. For a short time bent spoons and Polaroid "thought photographs" were considered PPOs by many parapsychologists. Who now can take such artifacts seriously, aside from such gullible souls as Rhode Island's Sen. Claiborne Pell?

14 | Urantia, the *Titanic,* and a PPO, Part 2

In my Spring 1991 column (the previous chapter) I asked readers for help on three research projects: Information about Wilfred C. Kellogg, who channeled the *Urantia Book* (*UB*); data about the year the White Star Company decided to name its liner the *Titanic*; and speculations on how Silvio Meyer, a Swiss psychic, could have paranormally linked two tiny frames, one of paper, the other of aluminum foil.

Readers were most generous in responding. Four Illinois correspondents—James Ott, of Elmhurst; Don Pearlman, Skokie; Charles Stats, Oak Park; Robert Michaelson, Evanston—and Greg Bart, of Los Angeles, sent copies of the obituaries of Wilfred Kellogg and his wife Anna, from the *Chicago Tribune* and other Chicago papers. The obits were brief, giving little more than the deceased man's name, address, and the name of the funeral parlor that serviced both deaths. Wilfred lived at 2752 Hampden Court, a half-block from the Urantia Foundation's headquarters at 533 Diversey. The building where he and his wife Anna lived has since been replaced by a high-rise condominium.

Dr. John Kellogg, of Battle Creek, Michigan, had a half-brother, Smith Moses Kellogg, who died November 26, 1927, in Battle Creek. His obit lists among his survivors two daughters, Lena Celestia, who married Dr. William Sadler, and Anna Bell, who married Wilfred Kellogg.

Dr. Sadler, a prominent Chicago psychiatrist, edited the revelations that purportedly came from superhumans and which make up the *UB*, the massive "Bible" of the Urantia cult. Dr. Sadler also arranged for its publication. It was Mrs. Sadler who first became persuaded that the channeling of her brother-in-law Wilfred was the genuine revelation of a new religion superior to Christianity. Dr. Sadler was soon in enthusiastic agreement. He repeatedly said that the channeler's identity would never be disclosed, and leaders of the Urantia movement have maintained strict silence on this ever since. A former Seventh-Day Adventist minister and associate of Dr. John Kellogg,

Sadler stated in his popular book *Mind at Mischief* that only twice in his career had he encountered trance channeling by persons he could not accuse of deception: one was the undisclosed *UB* channeler, the other Mrs. Ellen Gould White, the inspired prophetess of the Adventist church.

With the aid of Ken Reveill, and death certificates from the Chicago funeral parlor, the immediate ancestors of Wilfred and his wife have now surfaced. Wilfred Custer Kellogg was born in Berkshire, Vt., the son of Rev. Charles Leonidis Sobeski Kellogg, a Seventh-Day Adventist minister. Charles's father, Edward Kellogg, was also an Adventist minister. His uncle, Moses Eastman Kellogg, was an Adventist editor in Battle Creek, and author of *The Supremacy of Peter,* published by the church in 1897.

Wilfred's mother was Emma Kellogg, born in Tyrone, Michigan, February 7, 1850, the daughter of John Preston Kellogg by his second wife. John Preston was an Adventist who begat Smith Moses Kellogg, half-brother of W. K. Kellogg and Dr. John Kellogg. All three brothers left the Adventist church later in life. Smith Moses was the father of Lena and Anna. Thus Wilfred and his wife Anna had the same grandfather and were first cousins.

It is believed that when Wilfred and Anna, then living in Battle Creek, decided to marry, they were prevented by a state law against first-cousin marriages. They moved to LaGrange, Illinois, where it seems that for a time they shared a house with Dr. Sadler and Lena before all four came to Chicago.

The mystery of why so much Adventist doctrine is in the *UB* is now clear. Sadler was a former Adventist minister, Wilfred was the son of an Adventist minister, and their wives were sisters who had been brought up in the church. It is not yet known whether Wilfred had any formal education beyond grade school. It is said that he channeled the *UB* both orally and by writing. When he spoke the messages while in trance, Dr. Sadler's adopted daughter took them down, then typed them for reading by Dr. Sadler at Sunday afternoon meetings of what was called the Forum. Sadler, by the way, has an interesting discussion of trance states on pages 392–94 of his 896-page *Modern Psychiatry.*

Gary Vey, of Simsbury, Connecticut, wrote to point out that Urantia, the *UB*'s name for the earth, becomes Urania when you remove the T. Urania was one of the nine muses of Greek mythology who were daughters of Zeus. She was the muse of astronomy, commonly depicted with one arm on the spherical earth, her other hand pointing to the heavens. Frequently she wears a crown of stars. Urania was also taken by the Greeks as a personification of the love that unites the earth and universe, making her name even more appropriate for the Urantia revelation.

Dr. Anthony Garrett, of the University of Glasgow, and C. D. Allen,

Stoke-on-Trent, England, convinced me that the White Star Company could not have made plans for a ship to be called the *Titanic* before Morgan Robertson chose the name *Titan* for the huge liner, in his prophetic novel of 1898, that sank when it struck an iceberg in the North Atlantic.

However, some unusual new light on the story came in a letter from Mrs. Brenda Bright, of Croton-on-Hudson, New York. She sent a copy of a page from a book I had not seen, *Titanic: Destination Disaster,* by John P. Eaton and Charles Haas (Norton, 1987). The authors reproduce in its entirety the following news story that appeared in the September 17, 1892, issue of the *New York Times.* This was six years before Robertson's 1898 novel was published.

> London, Sept. 16—The White Star Company has commissioned the great Belfast shipbuilders Harland and Wolff to build an Atlantic steamer that will beat the record in size and speed.
>
> She has already been named *Gigantic,* and will be 700 feet long, 65 feet 7½ inches beam and 45,000 horsepower. It is calculated that she will steam 22 knots an hour, with a maximum speed of 27 knots. She will have three screws, two fitted like *Majestic*'s, and the third in the centre. She is to be ready for sea in March, 1894.

The figures given for the planned liner are very close to those Robertson used for his imaginary *Titan.* The *Gigantic* was to be 700 feet long, with 45,000 horsepower, a speed of 22 to 27 knots, and three propellers. The *Titan* was 800 feet long, 40,000 horsepower (changed to 75,000 in the book's second printing), a speed of 25 knots when it struck the iceberg, and with three propellers.

The *Gigantic* was never built. At the time Robertson wrote his novel the White Star had built the *Oceanic* (1871), the *Britannic* (1874), the *Teutonic* (1889), and the *Majestic* (1889). The company always added "ic" to the names of its liners. After Robertson's novel was published it would build a second *Oceanic,* a *Celtic, Cedric, Baltic, Adriatic, Olympic,* and *Titanic.*

It seems clear now what happened. Knowing of plans for the *Gigantic,* Robertson modeled his ship on this proposed mammoth liner. After the use of such names as as *Oceanic, Teutonic, Majestic,* and *Gigantic,* what appropriate name is left for a giant liner except *Titanic?* Not wishing to identify his doomed *Titan* with the White Star line, Robertson dropped "ic" from the names. The White Star's later choice of *Titanic* for its 1910 ship was almost inevitable. The company was surely aware of Robertson's *Titan,* but perhaps did not mind adopting a similar name because it was firmly persuaded that its *Titanic* was absolutely unsinkable.

Two readers, first John Geohegan, of Albuquerque, New Mexico, then P. M. deLaubenfels, Corvallis, Oregon, explained how easy it would have been for Silvio Meyer to link his two little frames. Cut a piece of paper into tiny pieces, boil them in water, then beat the mixture with a blender to make a viscous liquid. Pour the liquid over wire mesh and press it flat. When it dries, and is smoothed with the back of a spoon, it is indistinguishable from the original paper. By cutting a slot in the screen, and inserting a foil frame, the puddle can be formed around one side of the foil frame. The dried paper is then cut into a frame that is linked with the foil. For more details, see my note "How to Make a P.P.O.," in the July 1991 issue of England's *Journal of the Society for Psychical Research,*" edited by the well-known parapsychologist John Beloff. "P.P.O" is Beloff's term for Permanent Paranormal Object. He has long hoped that such an object could be created by a psychic that would defy any normal explanation and therefore provide positive proof of the reality of psi powers.

Beloff should have been suspicious of Silvio's linkage because the paper frame in his P.P.O. bore no watermark or printing. It would have been just as easy for Silvio to slice and "heal" a frame cut from a printed page or from currency. The fact that he used only blank paper should have given the game away, and it would have saved Beloff from the embarrassment of trumpeting a fake P.P.O. in what purports to be a scientific journal. Silvio is the spoon bender of Switzerland, and Bernhard Wälti, who wrote the paper about Silvio's P.P.O., is a parapsychologist too gullible to comprehend that Silvio is no more than a magician.

15 | Cal Thomas on the Big Bang and Forrest Mims

Our local newspaper carries a column by Cal Thomas, a tall, handsome fundamentalist of extreme right-wing political views. When Jerry Falwell's Moral Majority was in full swing, Thomas was his vice president in charge of communications. He began his career in radio news, but is now best known for his widely syndicated column, and for his frequent appearances on television talk-shows.

On January 10 of this year, Thomas's column was headed "Big Bang Theory Explodes." It has been decades since I have encountered so much scientific ignorance compressed in so small a space.

Astronomers have recently discovered superclusters of galaxies, surrounding monstrous voids and sometimes forming giant "sheets," that are hard to explain by current theories of galaxy formation. It is assumed that a vast amount of invisible or "dark" matter is involved, but the nature of such matter has yet to be identified. In no way do these large-scale structures discredit the big bang. They just mean that cosmologists have more work to do in understanding the bang and how galaxies evolve.

To Thomas, however, the big-bang theory "has gone bust" and this proves that modern science is a tissue of shaky theories put forth by scientists to rationalize their secular-humanist bias. "Those who inquired after other possible origins of the universe," Thomas writes, "including the theory that a God might have created it all, often have been denounced and their ideas expelled by court order on grounds that they are not 'scientific.' "

Thomas brings up Einstein's "cosmological constant"—a conjecture Einstein made when he favored a closed, steady-state model of the universe. To prevent gravity from collapsing a static universe, Einstein suggested that matter might contain a weak repulsive force. As soon as it became known that the universe is not static, but expanding, Einstein called his conjecture "the greatest blunder of my life." To Thomas, this shows how Einstein distorted his equations to fit his beliefs. Balderdash. At the time, the conjecture was a reasonable one. Thomas is probably unaware that the cosmological constant is now making a comeback among several cosmologists.

Thomas sees today's scientists as dominated by "extreme hubris," constantly altering their theories, but always dogmatically defending whatever is currently fashionable. "Maybe scientists should eat a little humble pie and consider what God . . . said to Job: 'Where were you when I laid the foundations of the earth?' "

Scientists have no more hubris than anyone else, and certainly less than fundamentalists who commit the sin of willful ignorance. Science is a vast, complex, cooperative, often bumbling enterprise that has built into it a marvelous power of self-correction in the light of fresh data. It cannot reach final, absolute truth, but it continually moves closer to it. Otherwise, how explain the incredible power of science to make predictions and build technologies? If there isn't a mathematically structured world "out there," toward which scientific assertions to some degree correspond, it is impossible to account for our ability to build skyscrapers, television sets, and atom bombs. It is impossible to explain why, if you bury a steel cube where no one can see it for years, then dig it up, it still has six faces and eight corners.

Cal Thomas is not content with exploding the big bang and making cosmologists seem like simpletons. He goes on to cite a recent flap concerning *Scientific American* that involves a free-lance writer named Forrest Mims III. To Thomas, this incident is another glaring example of the scientific community's prejudice against religion.

Mims, age 47, is a self-educated engineer with a degree from Texas A&M and a home in the village of Seguin, Texas. He says he has written seventy books (only three are listed in *Books in Print*) and five hundred magazine articles, mostly about electronics and computers. Long an admirer of C. L. (Red) Stong, who for many years wrote *Scientific American*'s Amateur Scientist column, Mims approached the magazine in 1989 in the hope of continuing the column after Stong's successor, Jearl Walker, gave notice that he would shortly have to stop writing it. Jonathan Piel, the magazine's editor, and others on the staff were favorably impressed by Mims's proposals. But when Mims visited the magazine to discuss the possibility of becoming a permanent contributor, to Piel's astonishment it became apparent that Mims did not believe in evolution.

Although he prefers to call himself an evangelical, Mims is a Southern Baptist fundamentalist. He is not a "young earther" who thinks the universe was created about ten thousand years ago. He allows that individual species were created at intervals over long periods of time, the "days" of Genesis not to be taken as 24-hour time-spans. Adam and Eve had no navels, Mims told me over the phone, for the simple reason that they had no parents. He was not sure whether Eve had hair and had not realized that hair bears as much evidence of past events as belly buttons. (Hair is dead tissue that grows from its roots, like teeth and fingernails, in small increments. If God could provide Adam and Eve with hair, teeth, and nails that had no past history, he could just as easily give them navels with no past history.) He admitted being puzzled over the question of whether the first trees had rings.

Cal Thomas quotes Mims as saying, "Insect paleontologists are totally frustrated by the complete lack of any fossil evidence that links insects to anything else." Indeed, Mims told me, it was his study of insects caught in amber that first made him doubt evolution.

Since *Scientific American* decided not to buy columns from Mims, he has been tirelessly appearing on television and radio talk-shows and giving press interviews charging unjust discrimination for his religious views. The *New York Times* (October 24, 1990) headlined its account: "Hire a Creationist? A Nonbeliever in Darwin? Not a Proud Science Journal."

Piel agreed to publish three of Mims's columns as part of a legal settlement of this situation. At least two *Scientific American* editors thought Mims should have been made a permanent writer of the column in spite of his naive views about evolution. According to the *Washington Post* (November 1, 1990), the Texas affiliate of the American Civil Liberties Union supports Mims's claim, likening the action of the magazine to the blacklisting of leftists in the 1950s.

"*Scientific American*'s editor is living in the dark ages," Mims told the *Post*. "He's practicing what was practiced at the time of the Inquisition, judging people for their beliefs and not what they can do." The *Wall Street Journal* (October 22, 1990) wrote: "The dispute raises explosive constitutional issues. On one side is an individual's right to practice his religion; on the other is a publication's right to decide whom it will employ."

Mims secretly recorded a 30-minute phone conversation with Piel from which a long excerpt was published in *Harper's Magazine* (March 1991). "I'm sure that you're a man of honor . . . ," Piel said. "There's no question that on their own merits the columns are fabulous. . . . That's just not an issue. It's the public relations nightmare that is keeping me awake."

No one doubts Mims's ability to write about home experiments without smuggling in opinions on evolution and the Bible. But I agree with Piel that the PR nightmare was sufficient grounds for not hiring Mims as a contributing editor. It was not Mims's religion. I know from having been a contributing editor of *Scientific American* for twenty-five years that it does not discriminate against anyone on the basis of sex, color, or creed. There have been practicing Catholics and Jews on staff, and conservative

Protestants. I myself am a philosophical theist.

From a PR standpoint, having a creationist write regularly for the magazine would become increasingly embarrassing. Creationists are fond of boasting about how many of them hold responsible positions in the scientific community. You can be sure that their magazines and books and lawyers would soon be trumpeting the fact that Mims was a contributing columnist for *Scientific American.*

Let's make two thought experiments. Suppose a medical journal considered having someone write a column about nutrition and then discovered that the person was a naturopath who did not believe that germs cause disease. Would the journal have the freedom not to publish that writer? Suppose *Sky and Telescope* planned on assigning someone to write a column on how to make or buy home telescopes and then found out that the columnist believed the sun went around the earth. Such a person could be well informed about telescopes, but would the magazine be justified in not giving the writer the assignment to avoid facing ridicule for having as a contributor someone who did not accept Copernican astronomy?

It is true that believers in an earth-centered universe are rare these days, but the fact of evolution is as strongly supported by thousands of pieces of evidence as the Copernican theory. When a conjecture becomes this strongly confirmed it is called a fact. There is, of course, dispute over the *process* of evolution, but no dispute over its fact by anyone with an elementary understanding of historical geology and the life sciences. "If he [Mims] believes in creationism," said Robert Park, a University of Maryland physicist, "he has established that he doesn't have credibility to write about science." Mims was not abandoned for his religious views but for the embarrassment his scientific ignorance would have caused the magazine.

Mims is now editor of *Science Probe!*, subtitled "The Amateur Scientist's Journal." It is a new, slickly produced quarterly, which Mims co-founded with the publisher Larry Steckler, head of Gernsback Publications. As of the time I write, only two issues have so far appeared. The lead article in the first issue was by Dennis Flanagan, a former editor of *Scientific American,* who wrote about his memories of C. L. Stong.

Although nothing so far in this handsome magazine reflects creationist views, a regular column on science fairs is written by David R. McQueen, a member of the staff who is an active creationist. If *Science Probe!* gets off the ground, it will be interesting to see if Mims ever has the courage to run an article on, say, how amateur scientists can build equipment for testing (by any of several different techniques) the ages of fossils and human artifacts. Or will he, like a good creationist, carefully avoid any topic that might provide support for a theory that fundamentalists believe to be the work of Satan?

Science loses little time acknowledging errors. Look how quickly Einstein admitted his blunder. Look how quickly the revolutions of relativity and quantum theory took over physics. Look how quickly the claims of N-rays, polywater, and cold fusion were shot down. Compare this with the centuries it took the Vatican to admit its blunder about Galileo. It is unlikely that either Cal Thomas or Forrest Mims will ever go back to college—fundamentalist colleges like Jerry Falwell's excepted—to take Geology 101 and change their minds about evolution.

Addendum

In addition to the references on the Mims controversy cited in this chapter, here are two more of special interest. The February 18, 1991, issue of *The Scientist* contained an essay on the controversy by Arthur L. Caplan, a University of Minnesota philosopher, who supported *Scientific American*'s decision not to hire Mims. Mims defended himself in the same issue. The two essays sparked many letters from scientists and journalists, seven of which were published in the April 29, 1991, issue. Terry Eastland's article, "*Scientific American* on Trial," ran in the *American Spectator,* February 1991.

Mims's response to my column, which ran in the *Skeptical Inquirer* (Winter 1982) is given below, along with my rejoinder:

> Shortly before I went on a cruise to measure the ozonesphere during last summer's solar eclipse, I read the articles by Robert Felt and Martin Gardner in the Summer 1991 *Skeptical Inquirer* about the withdrawal of my assignment as a columnist for *Scientific American.*
>
> Felt based his report on personal interviews and a review of the correspondence. His piece is reasonably objective and among the few that reports that editors at *Scientific American* asked me questions about abortion and my Christian faith in addition to Jonathan Piel's single question about Darwinian evolution.
>
> Gardner's piece has many errors, and after two days at sea I looked for a quiet place to compose a response. As usual, the ship's casino was virtually empty, it's sole occupant being a plump old gentleman wearing a red bow tie seated before an expensive 386 laptop perched on a gaming table.
>
> "Are you here to gamble?" he asked.
>
> "No," I explained, "just looking for a quiet place to work."
>
> "That's too bad," he sighed as he introduced himself. He was Register X. Array, the famous professor of skeptical statistics. An outspoken opponent of gambling, Professor Array was on the cruise to study the ultimate gamblers: eclipse chasers. He regaled me with tales of eclipse chasers who had seen only a single eclipse out of a dozen attempts, and he had fully expected the casino

would be jammed during the entire cruise.

"I wasn't sufficiently skeptical," he sighed. "I didn't realize eclipse chasers spend all their time attending lectures and watching stars."

The professor then said he regretted what had happened to me at *Scientific American;* I was only slightly surprised by this, for several other passengers had expressed similar sentiments. But I was embarrassed when he asked me if I had read Gardner's piece in the *Skeptical Inquirer.*

"I hope you were able to separate the fact from the fiction!" I blurted out.

"What do you mean?" he asked.

"Well," I responded, "he said I live in a village, which isn't even true, and then he attempted to portray me as the village idiot. He didn't even get my age right!"

The professor suggested that I cool down and then asked me to be more specific.

"Gardner claimed I said Eve had no hair since she was the product of instant creation," I responded. "That's fiction; I said nothing of the kind!"

The portly professor chuckled and said, "Well, I don't have any hair, and I'm certainly not the product of instant creation! Martin writes both fact and fiction; apparently he did a little of both in your case."

"To say the least," I agreed. "Since he advised me to take a geology course, I should advise him to take a course in ethical journalism!"

Array then asked if I told Gardner that Adam and Eve had no navels. I told him yes, but in the context of the old riddle about the only difference between Adam and Eve and everyone else. The professor rolled his eyes and mumbled something about Gardner taking navels very seriously. He then asked if I discussed science with Gardner during our two-hour conversation.

"Repeatedly," I answered. "But each time I mentioned fossils, ozone, biology, or *any* science topic, he recoiled and said, 'Don't talk about science!' "

"That's definitely Martin," sighed the professor.

"There's more," I added. "Gardner said, 'Science is almost a religion.' When I asked to whom I should send tithes at *Scientific American,* he ordered, 'Don't quote me on that!' "

The professor smiled and asked to see my palmtop computer. "Mind if I type you a note?" he asked. Before I could answer, he began poking at the keys with two stubby fingers. Half a minute later he said, "Promise you won't read this until the cruise is over. Now how about showing me the instruments you brought along?"

Thanks to Professor Array and a spectacular eclipse, I forgot about Gardner's column and enjoyed the remainder of the cruise. A few weeks later, I was in a library working on a paper about the eclipse when I noticed the professor's file in the directory of my computer. I punched in PROARRAY.RX, and this message flashed on the screen:

> For relief from an attack of the Martin Gardner bug, take *Scientific American,* call 235/5/132, and find Martin's secret mantra. Henceforth your only symptom will be a chuckle each time you see his name. Your closet-creationist friend, R. X. Array.

It was time for a break, so I found a librarian who led me to the bound copies of *Scientific American*.

"This is what you're looking for," she said, handing me volume 235 before vanishing down an aisle. I placed the book on a table, and it fell open at Martin Gardner's "Mathematical Games" column on page 132 of issue number 5. The column included an account of a sensuous dance by the famous Dr. Matrix's Eurasian daughter, Iva, wearing only a pentagonal mirror in her navel. Professor Array was right about Gardner and navels.

Finally I arrived at the point where Iva gave Gardner his secret mantra: *Ohwa-taboo-biam*. In the column, Gardner figured out its meaning after a couple of cocktails. The only trip I needed was the one down in the elevator. By the time it reached the third Floor, I was laughing so hard that the librarian, who was on the elevator, politely held a finger to her lips. As she exited at the second floor, she turned and whispered, "It's impossible to take Martin Gardner seriously after you learn his secret mantra!"

Stunned, I tried to read her pentagonal nametag, but it was so shiny it dazzled my eyes. Just before the doors closed, she giggled and handed me a folded card which read: *Wewhula-flastl-afbest.* Indeed! As I left the library her message cycled through my mind: *Wewhula-flastl-afbest . . . Wewhula-flastl-afbest . . . Wewhula-flastl-afbest. . . .*

My reply:

I am pleased to see Mims confirming the fact that he told me Adam and Eve had no navels. It makes sense because he has since assured me that Adam was created from the dust of the earth, as described in Genesis, and that Eve was fashioned from Adam's rib.

I apologize for two terrible errors: I called Seguin, Texas, a village when apparently it is a town, and I gave Mims's age as 47 when, he tells me, it was 46 at the time. The *Washington Post* (November 1, 1990), in its account of the Mims fracas, gave his age as 47.

There is a false statement in Mims's letter. He says I wrote in my *Skeptical Inquirer* column that he told me Eve was bald. I said nothing of the kind. What I said was, "He [Mims] was not sure whether Eve had hair." After Mims told me Eve had no navel, I asked if she had hair. Mims did not answer. I asked this because hair, like fingernails and many other parts of the human body, bears evidence (like tree rings) of past events. If Eve was created all at once, many parts of her body, aside from a navel, would record past events that never happened.

Mims may consider all this a joke at which he laughs last. To me, even funnier is the fact that a handsome new science magazine, *Science Probe!* is being edited by Mims, a Christian evangelical who believes that our earliest ancestors had no parents.

16 | The Sad Story of Professor Haldane

We all know how intense religious beliefs can prevent intelligent persons from accepting well-confirmed scientific theories. The church officials who persecuted Galileo provide the classic instance. There was no reason to doubt that the earth went around the sun or that there were mountains on the moon, but Roman scientists would not even look through Galileo's telescopes.

After Darwin, when evidence for evolution became as overwhelming as evidence for Copernican astronomy, strong belief in the historical accuracy of Genesis made it impossible for most conservative Christians to accept evolution. Even today, millions of fundamentalists commit the sin of willful ignorance by refusing to learn elementary geology and biology.

A vast literature covers ways in which religious convictions can distort thinking about science. Much less attention has been paid to how political ideologies can have similar influence. The two outstanding instances of all time are furnished by the ideologies of Nazism and Communism. During Hitler's reign of terror, German anthropology became a pseudoscience. Under Stalin, Marxist ideology distorted almost every science. Even Einstein's relativity theory was attacked, not as Jewish science (as it was in Germany), but as "bourgeois idealism." In both countries it finally became obvious that disregarding relativity would be fatal to physics, especially in efforts to construct an atom bomb, whose energy is measured by Einstein's famous formula.

In Russia the major instance of how a science can be crippled by political dogma was the abandonment of modern genetics for the crackpot Lamarckian views of plant-breeder Trofim D. Lysenko. Genetics in the Soviet Union is still struggling to recover from Stalin's merciless purging of his top biologists.

Did any respected Western biologist defend Lysenko? Yes, and though almost beyond belief, it was England's most admired geneticist, J. B. S. Haldane. There is no sadder example of how political dogmas can corrupt the mind of a distinguished scientist.

John Burdon Sanderson Haldane was a tall, tweedy, bald, bear of a man, with shaggy eyebrows, blue eyes, and a clipped mustache. He was born at Oxford in 1892, the son of a Scottish physiologist. His sister Naomi Mitchison became an admired novelist. JBS, as he was known, took his degree in classics at Oxford. After fighting valiantly in the First World War, he became an instructor in biochemistry at Cambridge.

Cambridge expelled him in 1925 when he was named co-respondent in a messy divorce suit involving Charlotte Franken. After various notables, including Bertrand Russell and G. K. Chesterton, came to his defense, the ouster was rescinded. He and Charlotte married. After a year at the University of California, JBS became a professor at London University.

Haldane's immense contributions to genetics and evolutionary theory brought him many medals and honorary degrees. In 1937 France declared him a chevalier in the Legion of Honor. His dozens of books made him England's most widely read popularizer of science. "On Being the Right Size," from his collection *Possible Worlds,* became his most reprinted essay. "My own suspicion is that the universe is not only queerer than we suppose, but queerer than we *can* suppose"—a sentence at the close of that book's title essay—became his most quoted remark.

In the mid-thirties Haldane discovered Karl Marx, and in 1942 he joined the Communist Party. For the next seven years he was chairman of the editorial board of London's *Daily Worker.* He wrote hundreds of articles, mostly about science, for that publication and for New York's *Daily Worker.* His political quips were so outrageous that he became one of England's comic eccentrics. What would JBS say next? Lenin, he solemnly declared, had cured his constipation. "I had it for about fifteen years until I read Lenin and other writers, who showed me what was wrong with our society and how to cure it. Since then I have needed no magnesia."

Charlotte was as dedicated to Stalin as her husband, although her disenchantment preceded his. In Paris, where the Party sent her during the Spanish Civil War, she fell in love with Arnold Reid, an American Communist who was an editor of *New Masses.* Reid died in action in the war, having enlisted in the Lincoln Brigade. After leaving the Party, Charlotte became bitter about how Reid had been exploited.

For years Charlotte wanted to divorce Haldane, but as she tells it in her autobiography *Truth Will Out,* the Party refused to allow it. She was told: "The Party would not for one instant tolerate a divorce between two comrades whose partnership, in addition to the usefulness of their individual services, was of immense propaganda value to it." Charlotte finally obtained her divorce in 1945.

It was obvious to all biologists outside the USSR and its influence that Lysenko was a classic example of a sincere but hopelessly ignorant crank. "Lysenko's writings . . . are the merest drivel," said H. J. Muller, a Nobel winner for his work in genetics. S. C. Hartland, another top geneticist, called Lysenko "blazingly ignorant of the elementary principles of plant physiology and genetics." Talking to him, said Hartland, was like discussing the differential calculus with a man who did not know how to multiply. Not only did Lysenko totally reject Mendelian genetics, he did not even believe that genes existed!

But Stalin, who knew nothing about science, liked Lysenko. In 1948, at a Moscow meeting of the Lenin Academy of Agricultural Sciences, Lysenko made a famous speech (Stalin helped write it) in which he announced that the Party had approved his work. When he ended by shouting "Glory to the great friend and protagonist of science, our leader and teacher, Comrade Stalin!" everyone obediently stood up and cheered.

Honor upon honor was heaped upon Lysenko. He was given the Order of Lenin and was made a vice-president of the Supreme Soviet. All over Russia laboratories were closed. Biologists who had disagreed openly with Lysenko lost their jobs. Many were sent to die in labor camps.

In the fall of 1948, when the Lysenko controversy was at its height, the BBC invited four distinguished biologists to debate Lysenkoism. Haldane was one of them, and the only one to defend Lysenko. His speech was a masterpiece of tap-dancing evasion and obfuscation. John Langdon-Davies, in his witty little book *Russia Puts the Clock Back* (1949), devotes a chapter to Haldane's shameful fence-sitting. It is from that chapter that I take what follows.

"I disagree with a lot of Lysenko's theories," JBS began, "but I agree with him on some fundamental points." One of Lysenko's startling claims was that he had altered the hereditary nature of wheat so it would withstand severe winter frosts. "This is a very revolutionary discovery if true," said Haldane. "Naturally I cannot form any serious opinion of this claim until I have seen a full account." Repeatedly he spoke of withholding judgment until he had read a translation of all 500 pages of a verbatim report by the Academy. However, summaries had earlier been published which made clear that existing genetic laboratories throughout the Soviet Union were to be abolished, and all scientists fired who favored what the report called the "pseudoscience" of Mendelian genetics. When the translation of all 500 pages finally appeared, Haldane remained silent.

"I find it very hard to believe," Haldane said in his BBC speech, "that the Soviet Government would back him [Lysenko] were he false." We may not like the Soviet Union, Haldane continued, "but after their achievements in the war we really cannot say that they are idle theorists." If the claim of "vernalizing" wheat is valid, he went on, "we shall have to listen seriously to what Lysenko has to say about heredity." Earlier experiments had already demolished Lysenko's vernalization theory, but Haldane was careful not to bring them up. Soon it was apparent even in Russia that efforts to vernalize wheat were a total failure.

Haldane could not believe that the laboratories of eminent Soviet biologists were being dismantled. "If, as I am told, Dr. Dubinin's laboratory in Moscow has been closed down, I am very sorry to hear it." Earlier that year the Academy of Sciences had announced that Dubinin's laboratory was to be "abolished as unscientific and useless." All Haldane could say was that if true he was sorry! That London has no courses in plant breeding, he said, is a serious matter "which we might well put right before we start telling Moscow what it ought to do."

In his speech Haldane seemed not to know, as all biologists outside of Russia knew, that Vavilov, the Soviet Union's greatest biologist, had been exiled to Siberia and accused of being an American spy. "You have been told," Haldane said, "that Vavilov died in prison." JBS had heard differently. He "appears to have died in Magadan in the Arctic in 1942 while breeding frost-resistant plants." Either Haldane did not know or would not say that Magadan was a notorious slave-labor camp. "It has been hinted," he said, "that the Soviet Academy bowed to political dictation" when it put its imprimatur on Lysenko's theories. "It is also possible that they bowed to facts."

So unshakable was Haldane's Stalinist faith, and so obedient was he to Party discipline, that he could not see, or was unable to say, that Lysenko was a fanatical Savonorola as scientifically illiterate as Comrade Stalin. In an essay "J. B. S.," in *Pluto's Republic,* Peter Medawar recalls coversations in which Haldane insisted that Beria, whom Stalin executed, was in the pay of Americans. He told Medawar that the Czech political leaders hanged by the Russians "got the punishment they deserved." At no time did Haldane condemn Stalin's great purges that sent millions of innocent people to their deaths.

Eventually the evil nature of Stalinism partially soaked through Haldane's skull. He left the Party furtively, some time in the late forties, without explaining why. Fifteen years later he said it was because Stalin had "interfered" with science. He continued until 1950 to write, however, for the U.S. *Daily Worker.* Seven years later he resigned from London University, giving as his reasons the continued presence of American troops in England.

Haldane never called Lysenko a crank. In an obituary that he wrote himself he said, "I am often asked what I think of Lysenko. In my opinion, Lysenko is a very fine biologist and some of his ideas are right." Some also are wrong, he added, and it was unfortunate that Stalin gave him powers to suppress valuable work by others. To the end, JBS remained a convinced Marxist and a friend of the Soviet Union.

Haldane and his second wife Helen Spurway, a research assistant, moved to India in 1957 where they established a laboratory in Calcutta. "One of my reasons for settling in India," he said, "was to avoid wearing socks." He became an Indian citizen, a stricter vegetarian, adopted Indian garb, and occasionally fasted like Gandhi to protest one thing or another. In 1964, at his home in Bhubaneswar, age 72, he died of cancer.

J. B. S. Haldane

Shortly before dying, when he did not know his cancer was incurable, he wrote for *The New Statesman* a long poem that was widely reprinted, praised, and condemned as frivolous. Its title, "Cancer's a Funny Thing," is taken from a poem by W. H. Auden.

I wish I had the voice of Homer
To sing of rectal carcinoma,
Which kills a lot more chaps, in fact,
Than were bumped off when Troy was sacked.

I noticed I was passing blood
(Only a few drops, not a flood).
So pausing on my homeward way
   From Tallahassee to Bombay
I asked a doctor, now my friend,
To peer into my hinder end,
To prove or to disprove the rumour
That I had a malignant tumour.
They pumped in BaSO₄
Till I could really stand no more,
And, when sufficient had been pressed in,
They photographed my large intestine.
In order to decide the issue
They next scraped out some bits of tissue.

(Before they did so, some good pal
Had knox ed me out with pentothal,
Whose action is extremely quick,
And does not leave me feeling sick.)
The microscope returned the answer
That I had certainly got cancer.
So I was wheeled into the theatre
Where holes were made to make me better.
One set is in my perineum
Where I can feel, but can't yet see 'em.
Another made me like a kipper
Or female prey of Jack the Ripper.
Through this incision, I don't doubt,
The neoplasm was taken out,
Along with colon, and lymph nodes
Where cancer cells might find abodes.
A third much smaller hole is meant
To function as a ventral vent:
So now I am like two-faced Janus
The only god who sees his anus.
I'll swear, without the risk of perjury,
It was a snappy bit of surgery.
My rectum is a serious loss to me,
But I've a very neat colostomy,
    And hope, as soon as I am able,
To make it keep a fixed time-table.
So do not wait for aches and pains
To have a surgeon mend your drains;
If he says 'cancer' you're a dunce,
Unless you have it out at once,
For if you wait it's sure to swell,
And may have progeny as well.
My final word, before I'm done,
Is 'Cancer can be rather fun.'
Thanks to the nurses and Nye Bevan
The NHS is quite like heaven
Provided one confronts the tumour
With a sufficient sense of humour.
I know that cancer often kills,
But so do cars and sleeping pills;
And it can hurt one till one sweats,

Haldane as a Hindu, with his caste mark.

So can bad teeth and unpaid debts.
A spot of laughter, I am sure,
Often accelerates one's cure;
So let us patients do our bit
To help the surgeons make us fit.

Had Haldane been less politically blind, he could have added, after the couplet about cars and sleeping pills:

Not to mention, now we know,
The millions killed by Uncle Joe.

Reviews

17 | "The Last Temptation of Christ"

My wife and I, out of unashamed curiosity, recently attended a showing in Asheville of "The Last Temptation of Christ." There were no protesters, but a policewoman inspected my wife's pocketbook, and two policemen stood in the lobby. The theater was almost empty. About twenty persons sat in eerie silence through the film, except for an occasional giggle from a girl behind us.

The movie was more boring than we expected. The Moroccan scenery was superb, but the dialogue was banal, the acting mediocre, and the story devoid of theological ideas above the level of a sermon by Oral Roberts. There were the familiar frontal nude scenes, the wigglings of the sex act, extreme violence accompanied by blood spattering—all the ingredients that movie moguls find so essential in dragging viewers away from the boob tube. Jesus came through as a tormented, guilt-ridden psychotic who suffered from seizures and paranoid delusions both visual and auditory—a '60s hippie with a Messiah complex.

The movie offends everybody. Conservative Christians and fundamentalists are rightly furious over its blasphemies and bizarre departures from the Gospels. Liberal Christians and non-Christians are equally miffed by the miracles. Thank goodness the virgin birth is not depicted. (Paul mentions it briefly in the film despite a total silence about it in his New Testament letters.) The bodily resurrection of Jesus is also not shown, though its coming is implied. A smelly Lazarus, emerging from mummy-like wrappings, looks and talks as if he would have preferred staying dead, and is no doubt relieved when Saul (before his conversion and change of name) stabs him back to eternity. After the wine-to-water bit, Jesus grins like Dan Quayle (whom he somewhat resembles) after delivering a one-line zinger.

This appeared in the *Times-News,* of Hendersonville, North Carolina, October 30, 1988, and is reprinted with permission.

The most outrageous miracle is Jesus reaching into his chest and pulling out his heart. It looks exactly like a videotape of a Philippine psychic surgeon extracting a bloody tumor from a patient's belly without slicing the skin. Blood is everywhere in the film. It flows in the streets from slaughtered lambs, it gushes out of an apple (from the forbidden tree?) when Jesus bites it. The wine of the last supper—women are present to placate Christian feminists—turns to actual blood.

The most interesting character is the little guardian angel with a British accent who rescues Jesus from the cross and leads him into connubial bliss with Mary Magdalene. The former hooker, pregnant with Jesus' first child, is slain either by God or Satan. This allows Jesus to live the rest of his life in happy bigamy with Lazarus's sisters Mary and Martha. The little angel turns out to be one of Satan's many disguises. Earlier ones include a cobra who speaks with the voice of Mary Magdalene, a lion with the New York street accents of Judas, and a roaring but mute pillar of fire. Judas, who is Jesus' dearest friend and most loyal disciple, persuades his master to crawl back to Golgotha to fulfill his mission of becoming the ultimate sacrificial lamb.

We do not know whether Jesus' married life, which extends to a serene old age, was real but later expunged from the past, or whether he is simply hallucinating on the cross. Apparently the latter was intended. I prefer the former on the grounds that it couldn't have been much of a temptation if it was no more than the dream of a dying man who could not possibly escape from the cross without divine or Satanic intervention.

The picture is monumental in absurdities. How could Jesus have cast out demons, given eyes to the sightless, restored a severed ear, raised a man from the dead, and still had doubts about his divinity? And why would anyone take seriously the preaching of a man so devoid of charisma that the best he can do is mumble pantheistic platitudes such as "Everything's a part of God"? Jimmy Swaggart could have preached rings around him. My vote for the script's most vapid line is Jesus, on his way to Calvary, telling his mother, "I'm sorry I was such a bad son."

It is hard to believe that Martin Scorsese had much in mind beyond yielding to the temptation of making a picture that he hoped would arouse enough rage to generate enormous publicity, create a blockbuster, maybe even win some prizes. He insists that for decades he has agonized over what to make of his Catholic upbringing, but it seems to me the agony has stimulated minimal study and thought. "I am a devout Catholic," he said in an interview (*Commonweal,* Sept. 9). "Maybe I'm not a good Catholic, maybe I'm not even a practicing Catholic." This strikes me as like a man who lives a few blocks from his old mother but has not seen or telephoned her in thirty years. Nevertheless, he would like to read to you a lengthy ode he has just written to express his great and abiding love for her.

Like the forgettable novel on which it is based, Scorsese's picture is all shlock, sham, and scam. It is worth seeing for its unintended sarcasm and laughs. If it prods some tepid Christians into asking themselves, perhaps for the first time, exactly what they believe about Jesus, it might even do some good.

18 | Pseudoscience in the Nineteenth Century

How can good science be distinguished from bad? Philosophers of science call this the "demarcation problem." Like most problems about distinguishing parts of spectra, sharp definitions are impossible, but from hazy borders it doesn't follow that distinctions between extremes are useless. Twilight doesn't invalidate the contrast between day and night. The fact that top scientists disagree about many things doesn't mean that terms like pseudoscience, crank, and charlatan have no place in the history of science.

Naturally it takes knowledge to make sound judgments. Nineteenth-century Americans were mostly poor and untutored, and even the few who made it to college learned almost nothing about science. It is hardly surprising that the age, like earlier ages, swarmed with scientific claims easily recognized now as absurd. Arthur Wrobel, who teaches American literature at the University of Kentucky, is to be cheered for editing *Pseudoscience and Society in Nineteenth-Century America* (University Press of Kentucky, 1987). The book is a long overdue study of the period's bogus science, an anthology whose nine contributors range in fascinating, sometimes frightening, detail over most of the outrageous theories that bamboozled millions of our ancestors.

One might imagine that fringe scientists would be indifferent to social and political trends, but a surprising thing about the nineteenth century is that the opposite was true. It was a time of great millennial hopes. For conservative Christians hope lay in the return of Jesus, but for more enlightened Christians the Second Coming had become a symbol of humanity's march—onward Christian soldiers!—toward liberty and justice. When Unitarian Julia Ward Howe opened her great hymn with "Mine eyes have seen the glory of the coming of the Lord," she was not speaking of the

This review appeared in *The New York Review of Books,* March 17, 1988, and is reprinted with permission.

literal return of Christ but of the widespread expectation that the Civil War would hasten fulfillment of the American Dream. Abolition of slavery was only part of a larger complex of causes that included women's rights, temperance, health, better treatment of criminals and the insane, elimination of poverty, and more compassionate government. All these humanitarian ideals found their way into the rhetoric of the fringe sciences.

Influences went also in the other direction. Reformers were as eager to rebel against mainline science, especially medical science, as they were to challenge the government. Many political radicals embraced one or more pseudosciences. Robert Owen, the Welshman who founded the socialist community at New Harmony, Indiana, in the 1820s, and his son, like another socialist, Upton Sinclair, in this century, became ardent spiritualists. This intermixing of social forces with fringe science makes Wrobel's book much more than just a compendium of strange beliefs. His book is of special interest to historians of the period whether their concern is with science, literature, religion, or politics.

Robert Collyer, a now-forgotten mesmerist and phrenologist, is the subject of a contribution to Wrobel's book by Taylor Stoehr, a professor of English. Stoehr sees Collyer as a prototype of the mad scientists who figure so prominently in the fiction of Hawthorne and Poe. Indeed, so many writers of the period were influenced by pseudoscience—Chapter 80 of *Moby Dick* is devoted entirely to a satirical phrenological analysis of the white whale—that one of the book's persuasive themes is that knowledge of fringe science is essential to understanding the century's literature.

Collyer came to America in 1836 from England to become a traveling mesmerist. On the platform he would put his brother Fred into a trance. Then after Fred clairvoyantly diagnosed the ailments of spectators, Collyer would heal them with hypnosis. He also practiced painless dentistry, extracting teeth from dazed patients, their trances intensified by booze and opium.

Collyer claimed he was the first to unite mesmerism and phrenology. When he massaged the bump for "mirthfulness," the mesmerized subject would burst into laughter. Fingering the bump for "tune" made the subject sing, and similarly for the other traits. Mesmerized patients were believed to have enhanced psychic powers. In England no less a scientist than Alfred Russel Wallace became a firm believer in what Collyer called "psychography"—a blend of mesmerism, phrenology, and ESP. In his 1899 book *The Wonderful Century,* Wallace tells of touching the outlined regions of a model head and seeing his mesmerized subject instantly make correct responses.

Phrenology spread from its Austrian founders Franz Gall and Johann Spurzheim, and their Edinburgh disciple, the barrister George Combe, throughout the U.S. and fell into the hands of traveling mountebanks like

Collyer. Orson Fowler and his brother Lorenzo were the most famous. Sometimes they would have themselves blindfolded. Orson would skull-read a group of strangers. Then when the same persons were randomly presented to Lorenzo, he would deliver identical readings. One suspects that simple conjuring methods—ranging from trick blindfolds to peeking down the side of the nose—were essential for these dramatic "proofs" of phrenology's claims.*

The Fowlers later teamed up with a businessman to form Fowler and Wells, a Manhattan firm that booked hundreds of cranium readers around the country's cities and hamlets. It quickly mushroomed into a vast publishing enterprise from which streamed hundreds of books on phrenology, hydropathy, and other fringe sciences. England's prestigious *Phrenological Journal* lasted only about two decades, but Fowler and Wells's *American Phrenological Journal* flourished from 1838 to 1911. Fowler and Wells published the first two editions of *Leaves of Grass*. So smitten was Walt Whitman by the wonders of phrenology that he scattered its phrases throughout his poetry—"O adhesiveness—O pulse of my life"—and proudly reproduced in his book a chart of his own head displaying the prominence of various admirable bumps.

It has been said that anyone foolish enough to believe in phrenology should have his head examined, and of course that is exactly what millions of people of all classes did in Europe, England, and America. Couples consulted phrenologists to decide if they should marry. Corporations demanded head examinations of prospective employees. New regions of the cranium were added until the count passed 150, with bumps for such traits as love of pets and desire to see ancient places. It is hard to believe, but phrenology even influenced American art, and Charles Thomas Walters, who teaches and writes on art, has a chapter to prove it. *Phrenology Applied to Painting and Sculpture* was one of George Combe's most popular monographs.

Combe studied the heads of leading Renaissance painters to determine how their character influenced their work. Michelangelo's skull, he concluded, shows traits that made his work less graceful than Raphael's. To analyze Raphael, he actually had the artist's tomb opened and plaster casts made of Raphael's skull. Several American sculptors of the day, nota-

---

*See the chapter on dermo-optical perception in my *Science: Good, Bad and Bogus* (Prometheus, 1981). In his autobiography Mark Twain tells of visiting Orson Fowler in disguise and being told, after a head reading, that he had no sense of humor. Three months later he returned under his own name. The humor cavity had vanished, replaced by what Fowler said was "the loftiest bump for humor he had ever encountered." Twain may have made this up, but in any case it shows how easy it is to invent traps for charlatans.

bly Thomas Crawford and Hiram Powers, put head-bumps on their statues to correspond with the character of their subjects. Crawford's bust of Beethoven, now at the New England Conservatory of Music, shows a prominent "tune" bump in the forehead. Powers's most famous statue, *The Greek Slave,* shows the woman's forehead to be high in sprituality.

Electricity, newly discovered and utterly mysterious, seemed to underlie mesmerism, and did it not also carry information throughout the nervous system? It is easy to understand how it would be looked upon as a potent healing force. An amusing chapter by John Greenway, a professor of English, surveys the century's infatuation with electric therapy. Publications bristled with stirring ads for electric belts, rings, garters, corsets, brushes (for both hair and teeth), even an electric cigarette. Greenway reproduces a marvelous Sears Roebuck ad for the "most powerful" electric belt made. It had detachable pouches for carrying a strong current to the genitals of both men and women. The current was said to stimulate potency as well as to relieve genital ailments. A New York quack cured syphilis by seating a male patient with his back against a metal plate and his scrotum suspended in whirling water. Plate and water were wired to a power source, making it hard to comprehend how the poor fellow escaped electrocution. As with all crank remedies, the placebo effect generated many testimonials of miraculous electrical healings.

Hydrotherapy, crisply covered by the historian Marshall Legan, goes back to ancient times, but the nineteenth-century craze was kicked off by Vincent Priessnitz, an uneducated Austrian farmer whose institute in Gräfenberg became an international success. Only cold water was used. The therapy involved baths, the winding of wet sheets around the body, enemas, douches, and water dripping on ailing parts of the body. Hydropathic physicians popped up everywhere. Institutes were founded. Fowler and Wells took over the *Water-Cure Journal.* Many who spent weeks, months, sometimes years in the fashionable cold-water spas that proliferated around the nation were unquestionably invigorated. It was more than the placebo effect. Alcohol, tea, coffee, tobacco, and spices were forbidden. Food was served cold. There were gyms for exercise and wooded areas through which to stroll. No doubt many felt healthier. The movement came to a crest about 1850, leaving a legacy in the form of whirlpool baths and the fondness for drinking natural spring water.

The life of Andrew Jackson Davis, America's first famous psychic, is the subject of the historian Robert Delp's article. Known as the seer of Poughkeepsie, Davis started out as a devotee of Emanuel Swedenborg, the Swedish mystic whose wild religious fantasies were inexpicably admired by thinkers such as Emerson and the elder Henry James. When Davis was twenty, and in a trance, Swedenborg's spirit dictated *Nature's Divine Revelations: The Principles of Nature,* the first of Davis's many heavy tomes. The Poughkeepsie Seer claimed extraordinary powers of clairvoyance. Believers paid him to gaze into their bodies, diagnose diseased organs, and prescribe weird remedies. His visions produced detailed accounts of intelligent humanoids on Mercury, Venus, Mars, Jupiter, and Saturn.

Delp's opinion of Davis is curiously sympathetic. He says nothing about the seer's blindfold performances (which leave little doubt that he was in part a charlatan), nothing about his spying on extraterrestrials, or the childishness of his metaphysics. Instead, Davis is praised for emphasizing the harmony of body and mind (a central notion of his masterwork, *The Great Harmonia*), for his "ready wit and perceptive understanding," for his support of humanitarian reforms, and for his attacks on mediums who produced physical manifestations. Instead of seeing Davis as a clever crank, Delp finds his life "characterized by extraordinary personal growth and maturity," and one that "epitomized the spirit of his age." On the contrary, Davis's primitive occultism and crude psychic demonstrations were aberrations. Even in its heyday spiritualism had a smaller following than Christian Science or Seventh-Day Adventism, not to mention the all-pervasive fundamentalism of mainline churches.

Harold Aspiz, another English professor, has written the book's drollest chapter—a survey of offbeat speculations about sex. Conservative preachers recommended strict monogamy, but cult leaders like George Rapp, who ran an Adventist colony at Harmony before Robert Owen took over the town, recommended total celibacy (the sect soon disappeared). The Fowler brothers had strong opinions about sex. They argued that electrical energy was released during orgasm, and that the longer a man conserved this energy, the more vigorous would be his copulation, and the finer his offspring. Women were said to become sexually aroused only when they passionately wanted a child, and for this reason husbands were urged never to force lovemaking.

Eugenics was favored by large numbers of pseudoscientists as a way to weed out undesirables and strengthen the nation. John Humphrey Noyes, a socialist and eugenicist who ran the Oneida community in central New York, distinguished between the phrenological traits of propagativeness and amativeness. Members of the colony could engage in as much amative play as they liked, with anybody, provided they blocked pregnancy with *coitus reservatus.* Alice Stockham, in a system she called Karezza, also campaigned for prolonged copulation without climax. Ezra Pound, Aspiz tells us, along with his "heavy burden of pseudoscientific baggage," also believed that conserving semen increased mental powers, in turn boosting a nation's racial destiny.

George Hendrick, another professor of English, gives a colorful account of Washington Irving's illnesses and their treatment by a homeopath. After water cures, bleeding, and leeching failed him, he turned to homeopathy, the century's chief rival to orthodox medicine. Its shibboleth was "like cures like." If a drug produced symptoms of a disease, then that drug in infinitesimal amounts—the more minute the dose the greater its potency—would cure the disease. Thousands of compounds were tested and listed in the cult's many *materia medicas,* all innocuous because of their extreme dilution, often to just a few molecules, sometimes to none at all. Homeopathy began its downward slide when orthodox medicine developed statistical techniques for evaluating remedies, but old cults seldom die completely. Homeopathy is now making a comeback among New Age junkies.

Robert Fuller, a professor of religion, skillfully sketches the history of mesmerism. The founder, Franz Mesmer, was a German occultist (surprising that so many of the nation's pseudosciences were European imports) who believed that a force called "animal magnetism" flowed from the mesmerist's hands into the subject's brain. Like Wilhelm Reich, whose orgone therapy was one of the funnier follies of the present century, Mesmer was convinced he had discovered the fundamental energy of the universe. Fuller sees mesmerism as America's first popular psychology, one that played a role in the emergence of experimental psychology as a discipline distinct from moral philosophy and in Freud's infatuation with the unconscious.

Wrobel, in his introduction, afterword, and a chapter on phrenology, rightly makes much of the fact that pseudoscience was far from confined to the poor and ignorant. "I look upon phrenology as the guide to philosophy and handmaiden of Christianity," declared the noted educator Horace Mann. Horace Greeley wanted all railroad engineers to have their skulls examined for the sake of safety. In England, George Eliot had her head shaved twice for more accurate analysis. Among educated people, enthusiasm for fringe science was largely confined to persons outside the scientific community. Their respect for science was unbounded, but their classical education provided them with little comprehension of the need for extraordinary evidence to support extraordinary claims.

The list of notables who took water cures and who shared Irving's faith in homeopathy is very long indeed. Spiritualism won its most distinguished converts in England and Europe; they included several leading physicists and astronomers, and writers as famous as Yeats, Conan Doyle, and Elizabeth Browning. In America James Fenimore Cooper, Harriet Beecher Stowe, William Cullen Bryant, and scores of political leaders became believers.

Homeopathy and hydropathy seemed to have firmer empirical support than orthodox medicine. In the first half of the century mainline medicine was more like astrology than science, favoring remedies that Wrobel summarizes as "blistering, puking, purging, cupping, bleeding, and poisonous doses of mercury and arsenic." At least the effects of electric currents, homeopathic doses, and cold water were harmless. All true, but when Wrobel says of fringe scientists that "by nineteenth-century standards their empiricism was beyond reproach," I must demur.

Although standards of science then were far lower than they are today, especially in medicine, the century was not without scientists who saw clearly how shaky the fringe claims were. Benjamin Franklin ridiculed the notion that mesmerism was anything more than psychological suggestion. Physician Oliver Wendell Holmes wrote blistering and accurate attacks on homeopathy and hydropathy. There were plenty of orthodox scientists around who had a good grasp of scientific methods, but like mainline scientists today they preferred not to squander valuable time opposing what they saw as nonsense. It is not easy to find establishment scientists of the period who tumbled for fringe claims.

It seems to me that Wrobel also overdoes the extent to which fringe scientists were right. It doesn't credit phrenology with much to say that it pioneered measurements of the cranium (as if physical anthropologists would not soon have gotten around to it), or that parts of the brain have specialized functions. Nor am I impressed by statements that a few homeopathic drugs later proved useful. Of thousands of homeopathic remedies, it would have been remarkable if all were worthless; moreover, they really were worthless in their extreme dilutions. I see the merits of pseudoscience less in its trivial anticipations of later science than in the way it encourages the pursuit of all leads no matter how bizarre, and in the fact that the refutation of false claims not only enlightens everybody; it often opens new paths to significant discoveries.

No anthology can cover everything, but perhaps it is worthwhile to mention some American pseudosciences not covered in the book: ignorant attacks on evolution and on the inferiority of non-Caucasians, physiognomy (reading character from facial features: William James took it with great seriousness), above all osteopathy and chiropractic. Osteopaths have since abandoned the crazy doctrines of Andrew Still, their founder, and half of today's chiropractors are now little more than physical therapists, but in the past century both groups attributed all diseases to imaginary "subluxations" of the vertebrae—a medical delusion as unsupported by evidence as homeopathy. Spiritualism, on the other hand, seems to me more a fringe religion than pseudoscience. It claimed empirical support, but no less so than Christian Science or Theosophy.

None of the book's writers considers the question of whether Americans today are more or less gullible than their forebears. My own opinion is that the gullibility of the public today makes citizens of the nineteenth century look like hard-nosed skeptics. A larger fraction of Americans now go to college, science has made astounding strides, popular books and magazines about science abound, and big newspapers have first-class science editors. The result? Almost every newspaper runs a daily horoscope, and astrology books, like books about crank and sometimes harmful diets, far outsell books on reputable science. A Gallup survey in 1986 found that 52 percent of American teen-agers believe in astrology and 67 percent in angels. A 1974 poll by the Center for Policy Research in New York reported that 48 percent of American adults are certain that Satan exists and 20 percent more think his existence probable. Electric belts are out but crystal power is in. Time-Life is vigorously promoting a set of lurid volumes about paranormal powers. Mesmerism now stimulates memories of past lives and the recall of being abducted by aliens from outer space. The most preposterous book ever written about UFO abductions, *Intruders,* by Budd Hopkins, was published by Random House with full-page ads in the *New York Times Book Review.* Acupuncture charts show paths of energy-flow as nonexistent as the paths of similar flow on chiropractic charts. *The Hite Report* and treatises on the "G-spot" are as comic as any sex manual of the past century. Spiritualism is back in full force in the form of trance channeling. Shirley MacLaine has become richer and more influential—she is certainly prettier—than Madame Blavatsky ever was.

There is an amusing error on page 226. We are told that in 1933 J. B. Rhine, the father of experimental parapsychology, earned the first doctorate in psychical research ever given by an American university. Dr. Rhine obtained his Ph.D. in 1925, at the University of Chicago, with a thesis in botany titled "Translocation of Fats as Such in Germinating Fatty Seeds." If fatty seeds are taken as symbolic of fat-headed delusions, in part translocated from the nineteenth century, they are germinating as never before throughout the land.

Addendum

The following letter from Julian Winson, of Washington, D.C.'s National Center for Homeopathy, along with my reply, ran in the *New York Review of Books* (June 2, 1988):

In his review ["Bumps on the Head," *NYR,* March 17] Martin Gardner states the following (in reference to homeopathy):

> Homeopathy began its downward slide when orthodox medicine developed statistical techniques for evaluating remedies, but old cults seldom die completely. Homeopathy is now making a comeback among New Age junkies.

I beg to differ with Mr. Gardner's opinions (and they are opinions!). I suggest that such invective does not belong in such a fine publication as yours.

Mr. Gardner obviously has never read either *Divided Legacy* by Harris L. Coulter, or *Homeopathy: The Rise and Fall of a Medical Heresy* by Martin Kauffman. Both books outline the history of the homeopathic movement in this country, and neither one gives credit to "statistical techniques" for the decline of homeopathy.

If Mr. Gardner thinks that "New Age junkies" are bringing back homeopathy, I wonder if that epithet refers to the English Royal Family (who support and use homeopathy), to the orthodox medical schools in France (who are mandated to teach a course in homeopathy), to the staffs of over 400 teaching hospitals in India who use homeopathy, or to the members of the American Institute of Homeopathy, the oldest medical society in this country, whose members have graduated from the finest orthodox medical schools in this country, and who have turned to homeopathy because they have found its therapy more effective than orthodox methods.

Mr. Gardner might find it curious that *Portraits of Homoepathic Medicines* by Catherine R. Coulter was mentioned as "best book of the year" by Martin Seymour-Smith, the literary critic of *The Independent* in Great Britain.

Mr. Gardner should confine himself to reviewing things he knows about.

My reply:

The slightest criticism of any fringe medicine is sure to generate angry letters from the true believers. There is no popular pseudoscience that has not produced seemingly impressive books and periodicals. That England's Royal Family sometimes uses homeopathic remedies no more impresses me than learning that William Gladstone was a hardshell fundamentalist, or that Canada's longtime prime minister, W. L. Mackenzie King was a practicing spiritualist, or that Ronald Reagan believes in astrology, the Second Coming, and supply-side economics. The popularity of homeopathy in India, where a hundred pseudosciences bloom, is a strong count against it.

If readers are interested in what the medical profession thinks of homeopathy, just ask your family physician or check the January 1987 issue of *Consumer Reports*. CU gives the results of a year-long investigation of homeopathy by Stephen Barrett, M.D. The report concludes:

Unless the laws of chemistry have gone awry, most homeopathic remedies are too diluted to have any physiological effect. . . . CU's medical consultants believe that any system of medicine embracing the use of such remedies involves a potential danger to patients whether the prescribers are M.D.'s, other licensed practitioners, or outright quacks. Ineffective drugs are dangerous drugs when used to treat serious or life-threatening disease. Moreover, even though homeopathic drugs are essentially nontoxic, self-medication can still be hazardous. Using them for a serious illness or undiagnosed pain instead of obtaining proper medical attention could prove harmful or even fatal.

19 | Astrology and the Reagans, Part 1

President Reagan, asked at his May 17, 1988, press conference if he believed in astrology, replied: "I've not tied my life to it, but I won't answer the question the other way because I don't know enough about it to say is there something to it or not." In the unkind sense that there are few topics outside of show business about which Reagan knows enough to have sound opinions, his answer may have been truthful, but in any ordinary interpretation his reply was deceptive. There is ample documentation for the President's long-standing enthusiasm for astrology.

Reagan's autobiography, *Where's the Rest of Me?*, written with Richard Hubler, was published in 1965 by Elsevier-Dutton when Reagan was running for governor of California. (The title is the question he asked in his favorite movie, *King's Row,* when he awoke in a hospital to discover that one of his legs had been amputated.) "One of our good friends is Carroll Righter," he declares in a passage on astrology, "who has a syndicated column on astrology. Every morning Nancy and I turn to see what he has to say about people of our respective birth signs."

Reagan had just been offered a lucrative chance to do a nightclub act in Las Vegas. His horoscope read: "This is a day to listen to the advice of experts." Reagan cut out the horoscope, took it to his studio bosses, and asked: "Are you guys experts?" They assured him they were. Reagan accepted their advice, and opened in Vegas at the Last Frontier.

> I . . . put together several minutes of (hopefully) funny monologue. . . . [I got laughs talking] about typecasting, my yen to be a "ricky-tick" floor show fellow, and my background of benefits in which I always introduced other acts because I couldn't sing or dance myself.
>
> We had a wonderfully successful two weeks, with a sellout every night and offers from the Waldorf in New York and top clubs from Miami to Chicago.

This review appeared in the *New York Review of Books* (June 30, 1988) and is here reprinted with permission.

Until his death in 1988, Righter was the nation's most famous astrologer. *Time* put him on its cover (March 21, 1969) for a six-page feature on "Astrology and the New Cult of the Occult." Formerly a Philadelphia lawyer, Righter moved to Los Angeles where for almost half a century he was the top astrologer for hundreds of Hollywood stars. Among his clients *Time* listed Marlene Dietrich, Susan Hayward, Robert Cummings, Tyrone Power, Van Johnson, Ronald Coleman, Peter Lawford, and Ronald Reagan. Asked if he used astrology to run California, Reagan gave one of his typically coy responses. He was no more interested in astrology, he said, than the "average man."

The President has repeatedly denied that the stars had anything to do with his scheduling his 1967 inauguration as governor at the bizarre time of ten minutes past midnight,[1] but both Righter and Sybil Leek, an astrologer who likes to call herself a "witch," took credit for setting the time. Leek told an interviewer in 1982 that she was one of four astrologers Reagan had consulted for the most propitious moment to begin his term. "He really believes in astrology," she added. "It guides his life."

Henry Gris, a former UPI bureau chief in Hollywood and one of Righter's best friends, told the *National Enquirer* (May 24, 1988) that Righter informed him in confidence that Reagan frequently called him from the White House. "Carroll told me before his death that the Reagans also conferred with him on recent personal crises in their lives, including checking with him before each of four operations on the President to make sure the surgery dates were favorable."

Edward Helin, an instructor at the Carroll Righter Foundation, told the *Enquirer* he was present on several occasions when calls from the White House came in. Righter would initially answer by saying "Mr. Reagan" or "Mr. President" or "Mrs. Reagan." As the conversation continued he would address them by their birth signs—"Mr. Aquarius" or "Mrs. Cancer." When Reagan phoned to ask which of three dates, A, B, or C, was most favorable for making "a major political decision," Gris says he overheard Carroll say: "The C choice will work best for you, Mr. President."

Gris was quoted in the *Enquirer* as saying that while Reagan was still married to Jane Wyman he began seeking Righter's advice, but when I telephoned Gris to check the accuracy of the *Enquirer*'s quotations he told me it was the other way around. It was Nancy who became "fanatical" about astrology before she and Ron were married, Righter had told him, and it was she who introduced Ron to Righter. Aside from this, Gris confirmed all the other statements the *Enquirer* attributed to him. When Ron and Nancy decided to marry, Righter selected their wedding date, according to Gris. After the President was shot, Gris said, Righter received a "panic call" from Nancy, seeking assurance that Ron would recover. Reagan became paranoid about personal contacts, according to Gris, "so Nancy began making all the calls."

A few months before he was elected president, Reagan was interviewed by Angela Dunn for the Los Angeles Times Syndicate. Her article ran in numerous papers, including *The Washington Post* (July 13, 1980). "I believe you'll find," Reagan said, "that 80 percent of the people in New York's Hall of Fame are Aquarians." (Born February 6, 1911, Reagan is an Aquarian.) He cited Lincoln, Franklin Roosevelt, Adlai Stevenson, and George Washington as Aquarians. He missed (Miss Dunn pointed out) on Washington—a Pisces.

Warren Hinckle, in his *San Francisco Chronicle* column "Hinckle's Journal" (July 19, 1980), reported his conversation with Alice Braemer, for many years an aide to Jeane Dixon, America's best-known psychic. In the Sixties and Seventies, Braemer told Hinckle, Reagan consulted regularly with Dixon during his visits to Washington. The meetings were held secretly in the Mayflower Hotel and were carefully "covered up" so Democrats couldn't poke fun at the governor. No picture of the two together was permitted. President Nixon, she said, was less prudent. Nixon allowed himself to be photographed several times with Dixon until his aide Haldeman forbade further pictures for fear of gossip about a "Nixon-Dixon" alliance. "She lost Nixon," said Braemer, "but she's got Reagan."

Hinckle phoned Dixon. All she would admit was that Reagan "had been a very good friend . . . for ages and ages." The seer added that she had seen Reagan often over the years to "read" for him, though she never charged a fee. "I'm not considered one of his advisers," she said cryptically, "but I advise him."

Joyce Jillson, a former Hollywood starlet turned syndicated astrologer for the *Chicago Tribune* and the New York *Daily News* told the *Los Angeles Herald Examiner* in 1980 that she had been paid $1,200 by Reagan aides to work up horoscopes on eight prospective candidates for vice-president. It was a rush order, she said, so Reagan could take the results with him to study during a vacation in Mexico. Her charts showed that George Bush, a Gemini, would be the best running mate. Lyn Nofziger, Reagan's communications director, called Jillson a liar. Jillson assured Hinckle it was true—"all $1,200 worth."

We now know that the Reagans became disenchanted with Jeane Dixon. She claims that she told Reagan he would some day be president, but Reagan has a different memory. "Jeane Dixon . . . was all for me in one part of her mind," he told the *Los Angeles Times* reporter Angela Dunn in 1980. "She was always gung-ho for me to be president—but in that foretelling part of her mind, she said back in '68, 'I don't see you as president. I see you here at an official desk in California.' " Whether this failed prophecy (among hundreds of other wild misses by Dixon over the years) had anything to do with the Reagans' break with Jeane is not known. We do know they shifted their allegiance to the San Francisco astrologer Joan Quigley. One of her loyal clients, Merv Griffin (he and Nancy have the same birth date, July 6), had introduced her to Nancy.

Astrology had an obscure origin several thousands of years ago in Babylonia. It spread to Greece during the Hellenistic period when it became popular with the masses, though not with leading thinkers except for those in the Stoic school. The astronomer Ptolemy (in those days astronomy was fused with astrology) wrote the first great book on the topic. Greek astrology became even more popular among the Romans. Before Rome fell, dozens of treatises on the "science" were written, and every rich family had its personal astrologer. As in Greece, it was ridiculed by many intellectuals. Cicero, in his debunking book *On Divination,* calls astrology "incredible lunacy," adding that some mental aberrations called for stronger words than "stupidity."

Astrology also spread from Babylonia into Egypt, China, and India. Chinese astrology, the basis of Japanese astrology, has little in common with Western stargazing, and Hindu astrology differs from both Chinese and Western versions. This is puzzling to believers. It is hard to argue that Western astrology must be true because it has such a long tradition behind it, because Chinese and Indian astrology have equally long traditions. If one is right, the others are wrong. In modern India astrology is practiced to a far greater extent than anywhere else.

Chinese astrology is based on a lunar cycle of sixty years, broken into five periods of twelve years each. To each year is assigned an animal, the cyclical order said to correspond with the order in which twelve animals bade farewell to the Buddha when he left Earth. One of the animals is also assigned to each month and to each two-hour period of the day. These signs are coordinated with five elements influenced by the five planets known to the ancients—Mercury-water, Venus-metal, Mars-fire, Jupiter-wood, and Saturn-earth—and with the male influence of the sun (yang) and the female influence of the moon (yin). Reagan is a metal pig, Jimmy Carter is a wood rat. Some years are especially dreaded such as the Fire Horse year of 1967 in which terrible things happened. Nineteen eighty-eight is the year of the Earth Dragon in which good things will occur.[2]

There are strong condemnations of astrology in the Old Testament, and it is easy to understand why Christian theologians, stressing both free will and God's providence, would not look kindly on the fatalism implied by classical astrology. Saint Augustine set the precedent with a strong attack on astrology (*The City of God*, Book V) which reads as if it were written by a modern skeptic. Among numerous objections is one that Cicero had also cited—the fact that fraternal twins, born within seconds of each other, have widely different personalities and destinies. The time of conception would seem to be much more significant than the arbitrary moment of birth, and some ancient astrologers actually preferred it to the birth date, but because it is almost impossible to pin down, astrologers understandably ignore it. Even birth dates are seldom known precisely, and for that reason astrologers are content to accept them to the nearest hour. Here are Augustine's words:

> How comes it that they have never been able to assign any cause why, in the life of twins, in their actions, in the events which befall them, in their professions, arts, honours, and other things pertaining to human life, also in their very death, there is often so great a difference, that, as far as these things are concerned, many entire strangers are more like them than they are like each other, though separated at birth by the smallest interval of time, but at conception generated by the same act of copulation, and at the same moment?

The saint has similar remarks about the "lying divinations and impious absurdities of the astrologers" in his *Confessions* (Book VII, Chapter VI). Some "dotards" are so smitten by the constellations, he writes, that they even cast horoscopes for their household pets.[3] He goes on to tell what first convinced him that astrology was "empty and ridiculous." Ferminius, a well-to-do friend, had been born at precisely the same instant as one of his father's slaves. Ferminius "ran his course through the prosperous paths of this world, was increased in wealth, and elevated to honors; whereas that slave, the yoke of his condition being unrelaxed, continued to serve his masters."

That the sun influences weather (the seasons for instance), Augustine did not deny, and he knew that tides were correlated with phases of the moon. But when astrology is applied to human affairs, any accuracy must be ascribed, he argued, to demons—a view still held by conservative Catholics and Protestant fundamentalists. Although Church leaders throughout the Middle Ages condemned astrology, it was so enormously popular among the credulous that the Church tended to ignore it. Occasionally, when claims became extreme, the pope took action. A classic instance is provided by Cecco d'Ascoli, a famous Italian poet, philosopher, and stargazer. Cecco's horoscopes correlated star patterns with the Deluge of Noah, the destruction of Sodom and Gomorrah, and other biblical catastrophes.

His horoscope for Jesus accounted for his birth in a stable, his poverty, and his wisdom. Libra, ascending in the tenth degree, made his crucifixion inevitable. Although Cecco's following was enormous, the Inquisition burned him at the stake.

Astrology was the object of violent controversy during the Renaissance, but it began to lose ground among the educated during the Age of Enlightenment. Modern astronomy demolished all claims that gravity, or any other known force from the sun, moon, and planets, could influence human life. The prestige of astronomy was so strong that during the nineteenth century American astrology almost died. (The leading pseudoscience then was phrenology.) Divination by the stars began to rise again during the Depression, when Evangeline Adams was the nation's top astrologer; then astrology revived as part of the occult revolution of the Sixties.

There are now far more professional astrologers in America than astronomers, and it is hard to find a newspaper or women's magazine without a horoscope column. A 1984 Gallup poll showed that the number of teen-agers who say they believe in astrology had risen from 40 percent in 1971 to 55 percent. Among teens who claim to believe in astrology, those from well-educated families outnumber those from the untutored classes, and whites outnumber blacks. The old stereotype of superstitious blacks is mocked by recent surveys. On all aspects of the paranormal, black teens are much more skeptical than whites. Several polls have shown that among adults, women who believe in astrology outnumber men by almost two to one.

The largest single group of professionals in the United States today who believe in astrology are actors, with dancers and people in the fashion business close behind. Among recent writers, the true believers included William Butler Yeats, the British poet Louis MacNeice, and the leftist playwright Clifford Odets. Believers do not seem in the least interested in hearing about the dozens of careful empirical studies made during the last few years that have established a total lack of correlation between star patterns and anything that relates to a person's character or future.[4]

Why do so many bright people insist that astrology "works" or have ambivalent feelings about it? The main reason is that horoscopes are so ambiguous that everyone can manage to apply them to himself. When predictions fail, a hundred excuses are at hand. The notion that physical forces radiate from heavenly bodies and influence human affairs has long ago been abandoned by leading astrologers. The correlations are now explained as patterns of what Jung called "synchronicity"—a paranormal harmony that links every part of the universe with every other part. Astrologers are not in the least disturbed by the fact that the wobbling of the earth's axis causes its path to "precess" westward through the zodiac so that during the last two thousand years the earth's path has shifted by one full constellation. Mrs. Reagan thinks she is a Cancer. Actually, the sun was in Gemini when she was born. Reagan is not really an Aquarian. He's a Capricorn. A few radicals called "sidereal astrologers" have tried to revise their "science" to take into account this steady drift of the sun's path, but no one has paid attention to them. Most astrologers now regard the zodiac's sun signs as no more than symbols of a mysterious synchronicity that bears no relation to astronomical facts.

Nor are astrology buffs troubled by sharp disagreements among astrologers over the best way to prepare charts. No two newspaper horoscopes published on the same day are alike, and if you ask ten astrologers to prepare a chart based on the day, time, and place of your birth you'll get ten different readings. Every astrologer is convinced that he or she has the true technique and that most competitors are either incompetent or outright charlatans. Many believe they have psychic powers that augment their readings. Jeane Dixon, for example, has stated that when she prepares a horoscope she meditates, using her "psi" abilities to absorb the influence of a tenth planet that astronomers haven't yet discovered. The ancients, of course, knew nothing about Uranus, Neptune, or Pluto, but that hasn't bothered astrologers in the least. As new planets were found, they simply added their influences to charts that became increasingly complex.

About the books by Joan Quigley herself, there is almost nothing to say except that they resemble tens of thousands of astrology books that have been published around the world in the last few decades. At the moment, about a thousand such books are in print in the United States alone. Miss Quigley's books are out of print, deservedly so because there is not a fresh idea or a memorable pararaph in any of them. A typical sentence: "The adolescent girl with Moon in Libra loves clothes and has a wonderful sense of style." The only passage of interest I encountered was in the introduction to *Astrology for Parents of Children and Teenagers* (Prentice-Hall, 1971):

> Many astrologers believe in reincarnation—that your child comes to you with a character that has developed over a series of past lives. This doctrine helps explain why some children are born more advanced than others. For instance, consider Mozart. . . .

That was written in 1971. Today, when the doctrine of reincarnation has become so pervasive among New Agers such as Shirley MacLaine and her followers, I suspect a poll would find that "almost all" astrologers and their most dedicated followers believe in reincarnation.

This suggests an interesting question to ask the President. Does he or Mrs. Reagan, or both, believe in reincarnation? If so, it would conflict with his professed Protestant evangelical faith, but no more so than astrology does, and we all know that contradictory notions of all sorts can bounce around harmlessly inside Reagan's head.

The question I most eagerly await hearing is one directed to the vice-president. What does *he* think of astrology? Bush once called Reaganomics "voodoo economics," but as soon as he became vice-president he changed his mind. George Will, a staunch friend of both Reagans, recently called astrology "rubbish." Will Mr. Bush have the courage to express an equally forthright opinion? My guess is that he will say something like: "Personally I have no interest in astrology, but I respect the right of anyone to blah blah. . . ."

Notes

1. It is possible when an astrologer recommends a date or time to Reagan he immediately thinks of good political reasons for it, or that he has a date in mind and astrology seems to confirm it. This would persuade him that astrology was not the primary basis for his decision, allowing him to say, as he did recently, that he has never based any policy decision "in my mind" on astrological forecasts.

2. Those who want to learn Chinese astrology can consult *Suzanne White's Book of Chinese Chance,* a Literary Guild alternate when M. Evans published it in 1976, and now a Crest paperback. She followed it in 1986 with her 684-page *New Astrology* (St. Martin's), subtitled "A Unique Synthesis of the World's Two Great Astrological Systems: The Chinese and the Western." We can look forward to an even weightier tome in which she harmonizes Western and Chinese stargazing with Hindu and Muslim traditions.

3. *Cat Astrology,* by Mary Daniels, was published in 1976 by Morrow, and is still available as an Avon paperback. "If your cat is an Aries she's power-hungry; and likely to chase bulldogs," reads an advertisement. "Gemini cats are just plain hungry and enjoy relaxing. Now you can discover your cat's sign . . . and help make both your lives happier." Morrow was not directing this ad at ignoramuses. It appeared in the *New York Times Book Review* (June 13, 1976).

4. For a recent impeccably controlled experiment that refutes astrology see "A Double-Blind Test of Astrology," by Shawn Carlson, in *Nature,* Vol. 318 (December 5, 1985), pp. 419–425. Carlson is a research physicist at the University of California, Berkeley. For an excellent overview of similar disconfirmations, see Geoffrey Dean's two-part report, "Does Astrology Need to Be True?" in the *Skeptical Inquirer,* Vol. 11 (Winter 1986–1987), pp. 166–184, and (Spring 1987), pp. 257–273.

20 | Astrology and the Reagans, Part 2

When I wrote the preceding chapter, Donald Regan's *For the Record: From Wall Street to Washington* (Harcourt Brace, 1988) had not been published. Had it been I would have included it among the books mentioned. The superstitions of the Reagans were known to many politicians and journalists inside the Beltway, but it was Regan's revelations that brought their faith in astrology to public attention. Regan did not name Joan Quigley, but he made clear his disgust with the fact that "virtually every major move and decision the Reagans made during my time as White House Chief of Staff was cleared in advance with a woman in San Francisco who drew up horoscopes to make certain that the planets were in a favorable alignment for the enterprise."

Here are a few more excerpts from Regan's book:

> Deaver told me that he had been dealing with astrological input for a long time. Mrs. Reagan's dependence on the occult went back at least as far as her husband's governorship, when she had depended on the advice of the famous Jeane Dixon. Subsequently she had lost confidence in Dixon's powers. But the First Lady seemed to have absolute faith in the clairvoyant talents of the woman in San Francisco.
>
> Apparently Deaver had ceased to think that there was anything remarkable about this long-established floating seance; Mike is a born chamberlain, and to him it was simply one of many little problems in the life of a servant of the great.
>
> "Humor her," Deaver advised. "At least this astrologer is not as kooky as the last one."

*   *   *

> Although I never met this seer—Mrs. Reagan passed along her prognostications to me after conferring with her on the telephone—she had become such a factor in my work, and in the highest affairs of the nation, that at one point I kept a color-coded calendar on my desk (numerals highlighted

in green ink for "good" days, red for "bad" days, yellow for "iffy" days) as an aid to remembering when it was propitious to move the President of the United States from one place to another, or schedule him to speak in public, or commence negotiations with a foreign power.

*   *   *

Before we parted, [George Bush] raised a question about the President's schedule. I told him it was in the hands of an astrologer in San Francisco. Bush listened to the history of my dealings with Mrs. Reagan on this question with surprise and consternation on his features. When I was finished, he uttered what was a strong expletive for George Bush.

"Good God," he said, "I had no idea."

He did not ask if the President knew about the Friend. I understood his reluctance perfectly, because this was a question I myself had never asked.

The flap over astrology in the White House prompted candid comments by both conservative and liberal newspaper columnists. George Will, who considers himself a personal friend of Nancy and a great admirer of her husband, had this to say on David Brinkley's "This Week" television show: "I wouldn't put it in the newspaper. I think it's transparent rubbish. . . ." Sam Donaldson suggested that horoscopes belong on the comic page, but Will disagreed. Comics, he said, "make no truth claim." Elsewhere he wrote: "The reported resort to astrology in the White House has occasioned much merriment. It is not funny. Astrological gibberish, which means astrology generally, has no place in a newspaper, let alone government . . . astrology is a fraud. The idea that it gets a hearing in government is dismaying."

"Astrology is the sheerest hokum," wrote James Kilpatrick. "This is the sawdust baloney of the carnival midway." Ellen Goodman: "A serious public debate over the validity of astrology? A serious believer in the White House? Two of them? Give me a break. What stifled my laughter is that the image fits. Reagan has always exhibited a fey indifference toward science. . . . It has been clear for a long time that the president is averse to science."

David Greenberg: "The spectacle of astrology in the White House . . . is so appalling that it defies understanding and provides grounds for great fright . . . it isn't funny. It's plain scary."

Robert Maynard: "Ronald Reagan, according to his once-trusted aide Michael Deaver, is a deep believer in the paranormal who will read 'whatever he gets his hands on' dealing with the occult. . . . Now that Donald T. Regan has decided to take revenge on the Reagans by exposing their reliance on astrology for scheduling decisions, the [largely unnoticed] Deaver disclosures assume new meaning. Taken together with the Regan revelations, they show a president for whom superstition is a significant aspect of his belief system."

Mary McGrory: "Certain things about the last seven years become clearer when reviewed through the horoscope. For example, astrologer Joyce Jillson, who says she was a White House consultant, tells us . . . that presidential press conferences were timed to coincide with the full moon. This explains the mad misstatements of fact that so often occurred during those rare sessions."

Michael Deaver, former aide to Reagan and a good friend, said in a radio interview: "I'm convinced that if you emptied his [Reagan's] pockets on any given day you'd find about five good luck charms."

My favorite comment was a letter from Mel Mandell that appeared in the *New York Times* (May 15, 1988): "The report that important decisions in the White House were based on astrological advice is most disturbing. The results could undermine faith in astrology."

Jack Anderson reported that the Soviet consulate in San Francisco probably tapped the unsecured phone lines used by Nancy for discussing national policy with Joan. If true, this would have given the Soviets considerable inside knowledge of Reagan's geopolitical plans.

Regan's exposure of Nancy's naive faith in astrology triggered two related books. In *My Turn,* Nancy did her best to downplay her astrological obsession. Joan was so furious over what she considered severe distortions and evasions in Nancy's book that in 1990 she published *"What Did Joan Say?": My Seven Years as White House Astrologer to Nancy and Ronald Reagan* (Birch Lane Press):

> I was responsible for timing all press conferences, most speeches, the State of the Union addresses, the takeoffs and landings of Air Force One. I picked the time of Ronald Reagan's debate with Carter and the two debates with Walter Mondale; all extended trips abroad as well as the shorter trips and one-day excursions, the announcement that Reagan would run for a second term, briefings for all the summits except Moscow, although I selected the time to begin the Moscow trip. I timed congressional arm-twisting, the second Inaugural Oath of Office, the announcement of Anthony Kennedy's Supreme Court nomination. I delayed President Reagan's first operation for cancer from July 10, 1985, to July 13, and chose the time for Nancy's mastectomy.

The incident that angered Joan more than anything else was a forty-minute phone call from Nancy urging her not to talk to the media. "What will I do if someone asks me about sensitive matters?" Joan asked. "Lie if you have to," replied Nancy. "If you have to, lie." Nancy never phoned again. After seven years of being constantly in touch, Nancy's last word to Joan was "lie."

Quigley's book is almost as damaging to Nancy as the later unauthorized biography by Kitty Kelley. It is also a self-serving book in which Joan portrays herself as one of the greatest and most "scientific" astrologers of all time. She even uses computers to draw up horoscopes, and of course she takes into consideration the important influences of those planets discovered long after Western astrology got underway. "Astrology," she informs us, "is God's way of letting us read His overall plan for our lives."

Like most believers in astrology (Nancy and Ronald included?) Joan believes in reincarnation. She is confident that the friendship between Reagan and Gorbachev is the continuation of a friendship between the two men in their past lives! She claims it was she who persuaded Nancy to persuade Ronald that he had to abandon his notion of the Soviet Union as an "evil empire." Nancy agreed, but said it might be hard to convince Ron, who could be very "stubborn" about changing his views. The title of Joan's book comes from a question Reagan asked Nancy during the Irangate scandal. Wanting to know when the bad publicity would end, he asked, "What does Joan say?" There is not the slightest doubt that Reagan knew and approved of Nancy's dependence on Joan.

The funniest statement in Joan's preposterous book is on page 18 where she says that Albert Einstein was a believer in astrology! How the book's editor allowed this to stand beats me. It is like saying that Einstein believed the earth is flat.

The other day, in a local supermarket, I picked up a brochure in which Joyce Jillson offers to send you a personal astrological forecast for "only $1 (plus 95 cents for computer processing and postage)." For an additional unspecified "nominal fee" you can get a "personal monthly prediction and transmitting planets chart." The brochure features a photograph of Joyce standing beside George Bush, personally inscribed to her from Bush. Among quotations from newspapers is one from the *Miami Herald* saying: "Jillson spent a lot of time at the White House after the assassination attempt," and another from *USA Today*: "Things didn't go smoothly with the first two ladies, Jillson explained, because Raisa Gorbachev's birth date is unknown and consequently no guiding horoscope could be cast for her." Joan Quigley had earlier said the same thing in her book. Jillson's astrology column is syndicated in more than 100 newspapers in the U.S. and Canada. Will the time ever come, I wonder, when a courageous newspaper will drop its horoscope on the grounds that it insults intelligent readers, not to mention fundamentalists who consider astrology the work of Satan?

Joan Quigley, for seven years the astrologer who guided events in the presidency of Ronald Reagan.

To the credit of the *New York Times* it has never had an astrology column. Not so the *Washington Post.* Not only does it run a daily horoscope, but on January 1, 1988, it devoted a color cover and three pages of its Weekend section to "Modern Astrology: The '88 Forecast." What in the world prompted this prestigious newspaper to devote thousands of words to such crap? Answer: the author was Carl Kramer, an editor of the *Post's* "Weekend" section, who has long been an amateur astrologer!

21 | Hans Moravec's *Mind Children*

Hans Moravec, who heads the Mobile Robot Laboratory at Carnegie Mellon University in Pittsburgh, has written a bizarre little book: *Mind Children: The Future of Robot and Human Intelligence* (Harvard University Press, 1988). The book opens by predicting that human life is on the verge of replacing itself with intelligent machines. "Our genes have finally outsmarted themselves." For a while, he continues, we will benefit from the labors of our robots, "but sooner or later, like natural children, they will seek their own fortunes while we, their aged parents, silently fade away."

There are two ways to view computers. One is to see them as essentially the same as lifeless, unthinking adding machines except enormously faster and able to twiddle far more complicated information. The other view, held mainly by workers in artificial intelligence (AI), is to see human-like qualities emerging as computers grow more powerful, and to foresee the day when they will become living entities capable of simulating every human function, including emotions, consciousness, and free will.

The second view assumes that our brain is nothing more than a computer made of organic molecules, and everything we call the "self" is in essence a mathematical pattern. If this is true there is no reason, Moravec argues, why a mind cannot be transferred to a computer and live as long as the pattern is preserved. "Your suddenly abandoned body goes into a spasm and dies." You open your eyes to find yourself in a "shiny new body of the style, color, and material of your choice."

I have elsewhere called this the Tin Woodman conjecture. As all Oz buffs know, the Tin Woodman was once an ordinary "meat person." An evil witch enchanted his axe, and as parts of his body were chopped off, they were replaced by tin until he was entirely made of tin. This notion that minds can be preserved by transfer to machines is now popular among

This review appeared in the Raleigh *News and Observer* and is reprinted with permission.

"strong AI" enthusiasts. Few seem aware of the role it has played in the history of theology, where it is known as "conditional immortality"—the view (perhaps held by St. Paul) that the soul is a pattern preserved only because God remembers it and eventually will give it a new body.

Moravec is skillful in sketching the growth of AI from crude devices to today's supercomputers which, in his words, "think (weakly) . . . see (dimly) . . . grasp (clumsily) . . . explore (haltingly)." There is a frightening discussion of computer "viruses" that can be planted deep inside a program (or can arise by spontaneous hardware mutation) where they hide as "time bombs" until they explode and destroy the computer's memory. There are crisp discussions of recent advances in computer science and robotics, of John Conway's famous computer game Life, of how evolution fabricates genes for "selfish altruism," of the paradoxes of quantum mechanics, of fantastic schemes by which our robot descendants can avoid the "heat death" of an expanding cosmos.

All this makes for stimulating reading, but the book's central ideas are pure Isaac Asimov. Moravec imagines robots of the far future using ultradense matter at the centers of collapsed stars to make computers trillions of times more powerful than today's machines. He sees robot supercivilizations spreading outward from millions of suns to coalesce and transform the universe into one monstrous brain. Robot archaeologists, armed with "wonder-instruments" for probing atomic structure, may some day be able to reconstruct "long-dead people . . . in near-perfect detail at any stage of their life. . . . It might be fun to resurrect all the past inhabitants of the earth this way. . . . Resurrecting one small planet should be child's play long before our civilization has colonized even its first galaxy."

How soon does Moravec think robots will be as bright as we are? Within forty years! This is, of course, the ultimate in AI hubris, comparable to Billy Graham's conviction that the Second Coming is just around the corner. It is a hoary theme, pre-dating science fiction in such books as Samuel Butler's *Erewhon*. My favorite novel about computers self-replicating and taking over the world is Lord Dunsany's *The Last Revolution*. There is, however, one big difference between Moravec's wild fantasies and those of Butler and Dunsany. Butler and Dunsany did not take their scenarios seriously.

22 | Colin Wilson Invades an *Oxford Companion*

Israel Rosenfield's review of *The Oxford Companion to the Mind* [NYR, September 29] is a splendid commentary on the book's articles about linguistics and the structure and function of the brain. As Rosenfield points out, most of the book's articles on the paranormal admirably reflect the skepticism of an overwhelming majority of psychologists, but readers should be alerted to two articles in this area that should never have been commissioned. Indeed, their inclusion reveals a singular lack of judgment on the part of the book's two editors.

I refer to the entries "Astrology" and "Paranormal Phenomena and the Unconscious." Both are by Colin Wilson, England's leading journalist of the occult, and a firm believer in ghosts, poltergeists, levitations, dowsing, PK (psychokinesis), ESP, and every other aspect of the psychic scene. After dismissing classical astrology as pseudoscience, in his four-column entry on astrology, Wilson goes on to defend what he calls "astrobiology"—the view that positions of the sun, moon, and planets strongly influence human personality and behavior. He praises the studies of Michel Gauquelin, which correlate a person's choice of profession with the positions of planets at the time of birth. Wilson is persuaded that this correlation is mediated by the earth's magnetic field. He believes that dowsing is successful because arm muscles "react to weak changes in terrestrial magnetism caused by underground water."

Although dozens of recent studies have exploded the myth that a full moon causally influences psychotic behavior, Wilson cites none of those studies. Instead, he refers to research purporting to show that the "electrical potential between the head and chest is greater in mental patients than in normal people, and increases at the full moon." Someone in Tokyo,

This letter appeared in the *New York Review of Books* (February 16, 1989), and is reprinted with permission.

Wilson adds, has correlated sunspot activity with the rate at which "albumin curdles in the blood," and the rate at which it curdles "before dawn, as the blood responds to the rising sun."

These and other "medical facts," Wilson asserts, provide a foundation for astrobiology, though he admits it is not yet clear how terrestrial magnetism can "influence a human being to the extent of predisposing him to one profession or another." He is convinced that our ancient ancestors, back to Cro-Magnon man, had a knowledge of astrobiology that later degenerated into traditional astrology.

Wilson's five-column article on the paranormal and the unconscious is comparable rubbish. He defends the view that the unconscious is the source of PK—the mind's ability to levitate tables and generate the poltergeist phenomena of haunted houses. As evidence for PK he cites the little miracles performed by Nina Kulagina, the Uri Geller of the Soviet Union, and the fact that Felicia Parise, a friend of American parapsychologist Charles Honorton, once moved a plastic pill bottle across her kitchen counter. Honorton's videotape of this great event suggests that she had an invisible thread stretched between her hands as they inched forward on both sides of the bottle. She has never repeated the trick. Wilson mentions the theory of British physicist John Taylor that PK forces are electromagnetic, but he fails to say that Taylor later repudiated both this conjecture and the reality of PK.

Wilson believes that psi powers reside in the right side of the brain, and that the self is actually a "ladder of selves" with our consciousness at the bottom rung. The higher selves possess awesome paranormal powers that are becoming stronger as the race evolves. He ties all this to the philosophy of Edmund Husserl, and recommends that all parapsychologists take a course in Husserlian philosophy.

Why the editors would have asked England's wildest occultist to write two lengthy articles for an otherwise praiseworthy encyclopedia passes all comprehension. As one reviewer put it, "This is like letting a creationist write an appreciation of Darwin for a scientific review volume on evolution."

Addendum

The best description of Colin Wilson I can think of is one I picked up from H. L. Mencken: "a geyser of pishposh." The following letter, followed by my rejoinder, appeared in the *New York Review of Books* (June 15, 1989):

I have just seen Martin Gardner's attack [Letters, *NYR,* February 16] on my two articles in *The Oxford Companion to the Mind,* which, with his usual level of polemical courtesy, he dismisses as "rubbish." He also refers to me as "England's leading journalist of the occult, and a firm believer in ghosts, poltergeists, levitations. . . ."

It might surprise Mr. Gardner to know that I am not particularly interested in "the occult." In 1969, I was commissioned by Random House to write a book on the subject, and I started out from a position of total skepticism convinced that it would turn out to be mostly fraud and wishful thinking. However, I did something that Mr. Gardner would not dream of doing: I actually studied the facts. At that stage, I still rejected ghosts, poltergeists and the rest, and tended to believe that most paranormal phenomena—for example—telepathy—are simply due to "unknown powers" of the unconscious mind. Twenty years of studying the evidence has convinced me that ghosts and poltergeists cannot be dismissed as delusions. Yet, oddly enough, I don't give a damn one way or the other. It wouldn't worry me in the least—although it would greatly surprise me—if Mr. Gardner turned out to be completely correct in his across-the-board skepticism.

For the record, I should state that Mr. Gardner and I were once friends. This ceased when I directed a few extremely mild criticisms in my book on Wilhelm Reich, at his attitude of rigid scientific dogmatism. Mr. Gardner very promptly and angrily broke off the relation and has periodically continued to attack me in his books.

It seems to me a pity that two fairly balanced and reasonable people should not be able to agree—or agree to disagree—about whether paranormal phenomena are entirely fraudulent and nonsensical. Unfortunately, Mr. Gardner has no interest in rational discussion. I think I could describe his attitude as sticking both fingers in his ears, tightly closing his eyes and screaming over and over again: "I don't believe, I don't believe!"

Personally, I don't give a damn whether he believes or not. The facts are there to prove that his attitude is narrow and dogmatic.

What strikes me as so interesting is that when Mr. Gardner—and his colleagues of CSICOP—begin to denounce the "Yahoos of the paranormal," they manage to generate an atmosphere of such intense hysteria, reminiscent of a medieval Inquisitor denouncing heresy, or Hitler fulminating against the Jews. They seem unaware that the heresy-hunting mentality is the reverse of the open-minded curiosity that has led to all the great scientific discoveries.

My reply:

Colin's coy claim that he is not particularly interested in the occult is impossible to swallow. When his 608-page book *The Occult* outsold any of his earlier volumes, he quickly followed it with a 667-page tome, *Mysteries,* packed with more of the same garbage. He edited a twenty-volume set, *A New Library of the Supernatural,* which includes two crazy books by himself: *Mysterious*

Powers and *The Geller Phenomenon*. The latter book extolls the spoon-bending talents of the Israeli mountebank Uri Geller. Wilson's *Poltergeist!* is an impassioned defense of the reality of ghosts.

More recently Colin has churned out a dozen or so more books promoting pseudoscience and the occult. They include *The Psychic Detectives* (on paranormal crime detection), *Frankenstein's Castle, Rudolf Steiner* (the anthroposophist), *G. I. Gurdjieff, Life Force, The Laurel and Hardy Theory of Consciousness,* and *The Encyclopedia of Unsolved Mysteries.* "Forty-two amazing true cases," says the last book's jacket, "of psychic powers."

The man is obviously obsessed by the occult, with an ignorance of science exceeded only by his ego and a compulsion to believe in all things paranormal. Here is how I described him at the end of chapter twenty-nine, "Colin Wilson Prowls Again," in my *Order and Surprise*:

> The former boy wonder, tall and handsome in his turtleneck sweater, has now decayed into one of those amiable eccentrics for which the land of Conan Doyle is noted. They prowl comically about the lunatic fringes of science, looking for ever more sensational wonders and scribbling ever more boring books about them for shameless publishers to feed to hungry readers as long as the boom in occultism lasts.

Colin says that he and I are "two fairly balanced and reasonable people." Sorry, old bean. That applies to only one of us.

23 | Linus Pauling and Vitamin C

Linus Pauling: A Man and His Science (Paragon House, 1989) is the first book-length biography of an American scientist who is hailed, by Isaac Asimov in his foreward, as "the greatest chemist of the 20th century." It is also the first book by Anthony Serafini, a philosopher at Centenary College in Hackettstown, N.J., and an excellent book it is.

Linus Pauling is a brilliant theoretician, fond of making bold intuitive leaps, then relying on experimenters to confirm them. His finest achievement was applying quantum mechanics to the way atoms bind to form molecules. This led to his great discovery of the alpha-helix, the backbone of all protein molecules. His pioneer work on sickle-cell anemia won him a Nobel Prize in chemistry.

But to many Linus Pauling is associated with something as common as Vitamin C. More than twenty years ago, he and his wife Ava Helen began taking large doses of the vitamin (ascorbic acid) and found that they felt better and seemed to have fewer colds. In 1970 Dr. Pauling's book "Vitamin C and the Common Cold" triggered a craze that has yet to subside. Today Americans buy more ascorbic acid than any other food supplement.

Dr. Pauling soon convinced himself that vitamin C also cures cancer. Research supporting this claim was reported in "Cancer and Vitamin C," a book Dr. Pauling cowrote, and later in his popular *How to Live Longer and Feel Better.* His controversial views were enthusiastically welcomed by health-food freaks, untrained dieticians, periodicals such as *Prevention,* and of course by companies that manufacture vitamin C pills.

Tests of cancer patients by Dr. Pauling's followers invariably support his claims. Tests by others, notably at the Mayo Clinic, provide no support. Dr. Pauling always finds "flaws" in his detractors' tests, and accuses the medical establishment of unethical prejudice. It in turn accuses him

This review appeared in *The News and Observer,* Raleigh, North Carolina, September 17, 1989, and is reprinted with permission.

of dabbling in areas outside his competence. Mr. Serafini wonders if Dr. Pauling's tireless crusade is not colored by memories of his pharmacist father, in Condon, Oregon, who sold 25-cent bottles of "Dr. Pfunder's Oregon Blood Purifier." We learn the grim fact that Dr. Pauling's wife, after a decade of daily megadoses of ascorbic acid, died of stomach cancer.

Before his enthusiasm for vitamin C, Dr. Pauling's obsession was with the evils of nuclear war. A physician friend who had saved his life when he was sick with Bright's disease was a Communist Party member. Did the doctor influence his patient to turn from New Deal liberalism to fellow-traveling with the Soviets? Urged on by the strong convictions of his wife—we are told that she almost assaulted Lawrence Spivak on "Meet the Press"—the two joined almost every communist front on the American scene. In his book *No More Wars!* Dr. Pauling condemned all wars except those of liberation. Were he and his wife merely naive democratic socialists? This is impossible to believe when we learn that Ava once called Norman Thomas—a prominent American Socialist—a "bourgeois reactionary."

Dr. Pauling's blindness to Stalin's paranoia naturally brought him under fierce attack during the McCarthy madness. He refused to tell any committee that he was not then or ever had been a Communist, though he readily said as much to the press. He defended the Rosenbergs and the Hollywood 10. The State Department repeatedly denied him a passport, but relented when he flew to Stockholm in 1962 to receive the Nobel Peace prize. An editorial in *Life* was headed "A Weird Insult from Norway."

His fury at being labeled a fellow-traveler prompted numerous libel suits. A $400,000 lawsuit against a Washington paper and a half-million-dollar action against the New York *Daily News* were, like others, settled out of court. Only one went to trial—a million-dollar claim against William F. Buckley's *National Review*. Serafini devotes a colorful chapter to this 10-year battle that ended with Mr. Buckley's legal victory.

Pauling the man emerges here as a genius with an enormous ego, ruthless in self-promotion, dogmatic, combative, cooperative only with those who will praise him. He was often accused of stealing the ideas of others, or using them without giving proper credit. He once added a fourth name to a paper so it would be referenced "by Linus Pauling, et al.," rather than with all four names.

Pauling's battles with distinguished colleagues were bitter and often damaging to careers. After he started the Linus Pauling Institute, in Menlo Park, California, he abruptly fired his co-founder, Arthur Robinson. Was he annoyed more by Robinson's conservative opinions or by his research with mice, which suggested that megadoses of vitamin C might actually *cause* cancer? This time it was Linus Pauling who was taken to court—

he was penalized more than half a million for breach of contract.

Now in his 89th year, 6 feet tall, with pink cheeks, bushy eyebrows, and balding white hair under a dark beret, Linus Pauling is still going strong —as cantankerous and infuriating as when he failed to graduate from high school because he refused to take a course in civics. His work on vitamin C still has a chance of being his final triumph, but only a slim one. More likely, as Anthony Serafini writes, it will be a once-great man's Waterloo.

24 | John Beloff Seeks the Holy Grail

John Beloff's new book (*The Relentless Question: Reflections on the Paranormal,* McFarland, 1990) opens with an autobiographical essay, followed by fifteen papers and lectures updated with notes, and a bibliography of his books and articles. It is a splendid, candid, well-written introduction to one of the most curious minds in modern parapsychology.

I say "curious" because none of Beloff's experiments has ever indicated the reality of psychic phenomena, yet he is absolutely incapable of attributing this to his impeccable honesty and experimental skill. He has never had a psychic experience. His parents, he tells us, were nonreligious Russian Jews who settled in London. Neither believed in the paranormal. As a teenager, Beloff lost his faith in God and has been an atheist ever since. (He doesn't mention it, but this supports the view that for many parapsychologists, belief in psi has become a substitute for religious faith.) His four siblings also do not share his belief in psi. Moreover, he reveals, "Neither my wife nor our children nor any of my many nephews and nieces were ever troubled by my 'relentless question.' " By "relentless question" he means: Are there paranormal phenomena?

One would expect that under these circumstances a person would have serious doubts about the paranormal. On the contrary, Beloff is not only convinced of the reality of ESP (extrasensory perception), PK (psychokinesis), and precognition; he also accepts the reality of such "extreme phenomena" as levitations, poltergeists, miraculous healings, materializations of human forms by mediums, and just about everything else on the psi scene. He is so trusting of the competence of psi researchers and the honesty of their subjects that only the booms of enormous smoking cannons will convince him that anyone has dissembled.

Beloff was born near London in 1920. After obtaining a bachelor's degree in psychology, he taught for a year in the United States at the University of Illinois. He and his wife, also a psychologist, then took posts

This review appeared in *Free Inquiry,* Winter 1990-91, and is reprinted with permission.

at Queens University, in Belfast, where they also obtained their doctorates. His first experiment was an effort in 1961 to demonstrate PK influence on beta particles randomly emitted from radioactive sources. The null results, he writes, were a "presage of things to come." It was the beginning of his reputation as what he calls a "negative or psi-inhibiting experimenter." He wonders whether he is "tone deaf" to psi, and whether this personality defect is what dogs his investigations.

In 1962 his first book, *The Existence of Mind,* was a vigorous attack on Gilbert Ryle's *Concept of Mind,* a book defending the view of most psychologists that mind is no more than the function of a complicated material brain, with no "ghost in the machine." Beloff defends a sharp dualism—it is a recurring theme in his papers. Although mind and matter interact, they are widely separate domains. Because psi phenomena transcend space, time, and matter, Beloff does not think they will ever be "explained." They have less affinity to physics, he is convinced, than to "magic, sorcery, and witchcraft." The currently fashionable effort of some parapsychologists to base psi on quantum mechanics leaves Beloff cold. Although an atheist, he admits that he is open to the possibility that there is some sort of "universal cosmic intelligence" which, although uncaring about human history, nevertheless may be responsible for the extreme manifestations of psi.

> Jung, who had a better nose for the paranormal than Freud, was driven to extend the personal unconscious and introduce a collective unconscious. But even the collective unconscious may be inadequate. The parapsychologist may need to come to terms with something in the nature of a cosmic mind conceived as being at once a universal data bank and a reservoir of power which suitably endowed individuals can occasionally draw upon in order to achieve some paranormal goal. Perhaps it is just such a cosmic mind that the great mystics, from all ages and from all faiths, have been alluding to when they claim to be in direct communion with the godhead.

Since 1962 Beloff has been a psychologist at the University of Edinburgh. After a terminally ill Arthur Koestler and his healthy younger wife joined one another in a suicide pact, their will named their friend Beloff as one of the executors. He was instrumental in establishing the Koestler Chair of Parapsychology at his university, and in appointing the American Robert Morris to occupy it.

Although for years Beloff's graduate students were getting doctorates in parapsychology and going on to successful careers, Beloff's own research continued to be fruitless. Pavel Stepanek, a Czech psychic, was tested with positive results by many parapsychologists, but when Beloff tested him in

1964, the results were negative. In 1965 Beloff and John Smythies, now at the University of Alabama, sought evidence for psi among brain-damaged subjects. "No luck here either," Beloff writes. He and Smythies later collaborated on *The Case for Dualism,* published in 1989.

Beloff was president of the Society for Psychical Research (1974–1976), and twice president of the Parapsychological Association (1972 and 1982). He retired from the University of Edinburgh in 1985, though he continues as editor of the *Journal of the SPR.*

"Can it be," he asks himself, "that I no longer dared to doubt?" He was badly shaken, he confesses, by two revelations of dishonesty: the discovery that Walter J. Levy, a rising young American parapsychologist in the laboratory of J. B. Rhine, had cheated on experiments with animal psi, and the proof by Betty Markwick that S. G. Soal, England's top psi researcher, had shamelessly fudged data. A third blow was the revelation that a "remarkable medium" Beloff had discovered on the Isle of Wight was a charlatan. Through the help of a sister and friends, "I realized this just in time to prevent my making a fool of myself."

In spite of such "bitter pills," Beloff has never doubted the wildest forms of psi. Although he admits he is not certain about strong phenomena, over and over again he lambasts all skeptics who express doubts. "I have come to realize," he admits, "that my own ignorance of conjuring techniques may have misled me," yet his self-admiration is sufficient to justify continual attacks on the conjectures of knowledgeable magicians about methods used by psychics to produce extreme results.

Let me cite some instances. Ted Serios is a Chicago psychic who once claimed the power to project images from his mind onto the film of a Polaroid camera. "Knowing all we know now about the conditions under which Ted Serios was tested," Beloff writes, "can we say categorically that we refuse to believe in psychic photography? . . . It is, of course, most unfortunate that [Serios] lost his ability, just when the controversies surrounding him reached a peak." Beloff does not tell his readers that this loss occurred immediately after the American monthly magazine *Popular Photography* explained how easily Ted could have produced his thought pictures by using a tiny optical device readily available in novelty stores. It would be charitable to assume that Beloff has never read this exposé.

What about Uri Geller, the Israeli magician who created such a flap a few years ago with his paranormal spoon bending? "Dare we rule out the numerous accounts of teleportations that have been reported in connection with Geller?" Geller's most famous teleportations were of himself. He claims that while walking a street in Manhattan he was suddenly teleported to the back porch of Andrija Puharich's house in Ossining, New

York. In his book *Uri,* Puharich also tells of an occasion when Uri teleported himself from Ossining to Rio de Janeiro, then returned with a thousand cruzeiro note. "I find myself still undecided," Beloff naively writes, "as to whether [Geller] was ever anything other than a charlatan and an entertainer or whether he used his knowledge of stage magic to gain the wealth and fame he so ardently desired and which his modest psi ability would not have enabled him to do so."

Psychic surgery? "Given only the agreed facts about the career of the late Arigo, have we the right to affirm that there is nothing at all in psychic surgery?" Arigo, the most famous of Brazil's psychic surgeons, performed his paranormal operations by following instructions that a dead German doctor whispered into his left ear.

Throughout his career Beloff has been haunted by reports of humans being lifted into the air. "A *siddhi,* such as levitation, is a natural concomitant of a certain advanced stage of Yoga." He is enormously impressed by the fact that Saint Teresa, the most famous of Catholic flying nuns, was "greatly embarrassed when her nuns caught her levitating." The many levitations of St. Joseph of Cupertino—the "flying friar" who often floated above treetops, sometimes carrying a fellow monk with him—Beloff regards as "the best attested miracles associated with any religious figure in history."

E. Cobham Brewer's *Dictionary of Miracles* (1884) contains thousands of documented Catholic miracles so stupendous that one cannot help wondering why they no longer occur. See especially the levitation miracles listed in the book's first section under the heading "Lifted Up." One would suppose that only a glance through this book would convince Beloff of the wisdom of a famous paragraph by David Hume in the chapter on miracles in his *Enquiry Concerning Human Understanding:*

But suppose, that all the historians who treat of England, should agree, that, on the first of January 1600, Queen Elizabeth died; that both before and after her death she was seen by her physicians and the whole court, as is usual with persons of her rank; that her successor was acknowledged and proclaimed by the parliament; and that, after being interred a month, she again appeared, resumed the throne, and governed England for three years. I must confess that I should be surprised at the concurrence of so many odd circumstances, but should not have the least inclination to believe so miraculous an event. I should not doubt of her pretended death, and of those other public cir-cumstances that followed it; I should only assert it to have been pretended, and that it neither was, nor possibly could be real. You would in vain object to me the difficulty, and almost impossibility of deceiving the world in an affair of such consequence; the wisdom and solid judgment of that renowned queen; with the little or no advantage which she could reap from so poor an artifice. All this might astonish me; but I would still reply, that the knavery and folly of men are such common phenomena, that I should rather believe the most extraordinary events to arise from their concurrence, than admit of so signal a violation of the laws of nature.

Beloff has no doubts about the powers of the great spiritualist mediums of the past, even though he concedes that at times they must have cheated. "A readiness to cheat," he warns, "should never be taken as a sign that the medium lacked genuine psychic ability." Again: "There may be something inherent in the psychodynamics of producing strong phenomena that predisposes one to cheat." He readily admits that Eusapia Palladino, the notorious fat little Italian medium, was a charlatan. "When things were not going well, she lapsed into her old habit of cheating."

Such a stance makes it difficult for magicians to persuade Beloff of anything. If they succeed in convincing him that a psychic once cheated, the most he will admit is that he or she cheats *sometimes*. When not caught cheating, a psychic's miracles are presumed genuine. Many pages in Beloff's book defend Palladino, as well as the powers of such known mountebanks as the Boston medium Margery, Eva C., and the American entertainer Bert Reese, who specialized in what magicians call "billet reading."

An amusing illustration of Beloff's colossal ignorance of conjuring methods is his statement that on occasion a psychic with exceptional PK ability will "move an object other than the one on which they are concentrating." Beloff seems never to have heard about the art of misdirection. A favorite ploy of Geller's is to misdirect attention to his hands by strenuous efforts to make a key bend, while one of his secret aides surreptitiously deforms another object that has been placed to one side.

The book's final chapter, on extreme phenomena, is the book's funniest. Beloff cites five cases that he insists no skeptic can explain. First, the case of Louise Coirin, a French woman whose left breast was totally destroyed by cancer. After placing on it a clod of earth from a saint's tomb, the entire breast, including the nipple, regenerated. Beloff is not in the least troubled by the fact that the only source for this miracle is a 1745 three-volume work by Carré de Montgeron, a French nobleman who did time in the Bastille because his writings offended the king.

Beloff's second example is Joseph of Cupertino, the third is Margery, and the fourth is Indrid Indridason, an Icelandic medium who died in 1912, age twenty-nine. He produced all the usual absurd phenomena—raps, levitations, floating luminous forms, strong breezes, voices from the Great Beyond, ectoplasm that formed human bodies, and what Beloff calls "unaccountable odors." Why the departed would stoop to such trivial pranks, and always in near darkness, is something that believers have never made clear. What most impresses Beloff is that on three occasions Indridason's left arm vanished. Beloff unwittingly gives the game away when he adds that investigators were never allowed to undress the medium after his arm dematerialized, and that we do not even know if he wore a coat on these occasions!

Beloff's fifth example is the medium Helen Duncan, of Dundee, Scotland, who died in 1956. He describes her as gross in appearance, uncouth in language, and often caught in fraud. He fails to mention that Harry Price wrote a book in 1931 titled *Regurgitation and the Duncan Mediumship* in which he gave convincing evidence that Duncan swallowed much of her paraphernalia, then regurgitated it when the lights were out. However, Beloff says he has talked to persons who saw her produce ghostly forms of people they recognized, and who vanished by sinking into the floor. One housewife said that when she embraced her dead husband she could feel the arthritic knobs on his fingers. Another identified her dead mother by two moles on her face. Helen was tried for witchcraft in 1944, and sentenced to nine months in prison.

Beloff is scornful of skeptics, like the philosopher Antony Flew, who scoff at such reports. *Flewism* is Beloff's derisive term for such scoffing. Let me propose another term, *Beloffism*. It is the gullible tendency to believe even the most preposterous psychic miracles. Beloff admits that the dearth of powerful mediums today puzzles him. All they do now is talk in funny voices. The best he can come up with are the Chinese clairvoyant children who are said to be able to read messages tucked in their armpits.

The most amusing aspect of this final chapter is Beloff's hope that someday a psychic will produce what he calls a PPO, or Permanent Paranormal Object. As an example of a PPO of the past, he cites the wooden rings that Margery would cause to link together. "Unfortunately, with the perversity that is typical of extreme phenomena, Margery's linkages regularly (but paranormally) became unlinked."

It is typical of PPO's that they never last long enough for scientists to inspect them and show how they can be duplicated. Beloff does not mention an inside-out tennis ball that occult journalist Lyall Watson, in his book *Lifetide,* says a psychic girl in Venice produced for him. Watson fails to disclose what happened to this marvelous artifact. The American parapsychologist Stanley Krippner reported that a European psychic once magnetized some matches in his presence, but he didn't bother to take one away with him to be examined for an interior wire. Beloff writes that he once gave one of his students two black leather rings to give to the Indian psychic Sai Baba, but Sai Baba refused to link them. However,

Beloff adds, Sai Baba did produce for a lady an apple attached to the branches and leaves of a tamarind tree. She tried to preserve this PPO in formaldehyde. Alas, the apple became detached from the branch so she threw it away.

In the January 1991 issue of the *Journal of the SPR,* Beloff published an English translation of an article that appeared two years earlier in a German journal of parapsychology. It shows a photograph of two tiny square frames, each about an inch on the side, one made of paper, the other of aluminum foil. They are interlocked. The Swiss psychic Silvio Meyer, who claims to have linked them paranormally, says he cut the paper frame from a sheet of notepaper, and the aluminum frame from the metal foil in which a sandwich was wrapped. First he sliced the paper frame on one side, slid the foil frame through the slot, then held the cut between his thumb and finger for ten minutes. The cut miraculously welded together. The author of the article claims that several laboratory technicians have been unable to determine how this splendid PPO could have been produced normally without using technical equipment, to which Silvio is said to have had no access. The object still exists, we are told, and can be examined by any scientist. It remains to be seen if anyone can come up with an explanation of how Silvio could have faked it.

Beloff is gloomy about the prospect that any psi experiment will soon be performed that can be regularly repeated on demand. However, if a PPO is created, "the onus lies with the skeptic to show, if he can, that the object in question is a normal artifact." Such an object would be irrefutable proof of the paranormal. "I feel that we would be failing in our duty if we did not continue to pursue the goal—or should I say the grail?—of *conclusive* evidence."

This, with its italics, is the book's final sentence. To Sir John Galahad Beloff I can only say, "Lotsa luck!"

Addendum

A much shorter version of this review appeared in the London *Times Literary Supplement* (August 3–9, 1990). I made the mistake of saying that Arthur Koestler had "persuaded his healthier and younger wife to join him in a suicide pact." Several readers wrote to say that this was not true. One such letter, from Harold Harris, was published in the *TLS.* He said that Koestler's wife Cynthia had decided to join her husband "at the last moment when she added a brief note to his suicide note, saying 'I cannot live without Arthur.' "

The following letter from John Beloff was published in *Free Inquiry* (Spring 1991):

I do not know whether to feel flattered at having my book of essays reviewed so prominently in your esteemed journal by so distinguished a critic as Martin Gardner or to yield to irritation at being exposed to ridicule as a gullible Sir Galahad.

It is obvious that my "relentless question" does not bother my reviewer in the least. He has been mercifully spared the heart-searchings and torment that have pursued me. I am still trying to decide whether there are any genuine paranormal phenomena, but I fully expect to die in this state of uncertainty.

But, if I have sometimes been too uncritical of paranormal claims, Gardner, it seems to me, has a no less touching faith in the omnicompetence of conjurors. Of course I read that article he cites form *Popular Photography* which purported to expose the *modus operandi* that Serios employed. But the reason why it failed to impress those who had actually worked with Serios is that, despite Eisenbud's persistent entreaties, no one came forward to show how it could have been used in the conditions in which Serios had to operate.

Gardner again betrays his faith in conjuring when he comes to disucss the case of Palladino. The question for us is whether she could have outwitted even her sharpest investigators. On p. 160 of my book I quote Everard Feilding, a man skilled in conjuring and of a severely critical disposition. Allow me to repeat here his words:

> I realize as an appreciable fact of life, that, from an empty cabinet I have seen hands and heads come forth, that from behind the curtain of that empty cabinet I have been seized by living fingers, the existence and position of the very nails of which could be felt. I have seen this extraordinary woman sitting visible outside the curtain, held hand and foot by my colleagues, immobile except for the occasional straining of a limb, while some entity within the curtain has over and over again pressed my hand in a position clearly beyond her reach. I refuse to entertain the possibility of a doubt that we were the victims of a hallucination. I appreciate exactly the fact that ninety-nine people out of a hundred will refuse to entertain the possibility of doubt that it was anything else. And, remembering my own belief a very short time ago, I shall not be able to complain, though I shall unquestionably be annoyed when I find that to be the case.

This says it all. Feilding was genuinely open-minded and genuinely willing to change his mind. He recognized the ludicrous nature of the phenomena he describes but refused to fall back on scoffing. The case of Palladino raises another question we should ponder. Although physical mediumship has, it seems, disappeared, conjuring continues to make progress. Where, then, is the conjuror who could operate under the constraints to which she had to submit and yet produce comparable effects?

Gardner quotes at length, for my edification, from Hume's essay on miracles, forgetting that, in my book, I repeatedly allude to and quote from this source. Indeed, I have the greatest reverence for David Hume, a fearless freethinker. But I cannot accept his *a priori* attitude to miracles for the reasons I discuss. The "knavery and folly of men" does not suffice to exonerate us from asking in any particular case that we find hard to believe: What is the counter-explanation? The reviewer makes me appear more credulous than I am by omitting to mention that, in all the miracles that I discuss, I always try to consider every conceivable counter-explanation that I can think of.

The evidence for psi phenomena at the present time based on laboratory research is less spectacular than the cases drawn from spiritualist or religious sources but is, in other ways, still more convincing. It is not wounded pride that induces me to write this letter but concern that the *a priori* skepticism displayed by so many supporters of the Committee for the Scientific Investigation of Claims of the Paranormal, like your reveiwer, is making it more difficult for parapsychologists to obtain the funding they need if the questions they raise are ever to be answered in a rational manner.

I did not reply to this letter, which of course strongly underscores Beloff's willingness to take seriously almost any paranormal claim. I will comment here only on his statement that no conjuror has been able to duplicate Serios's thoughtography under conditions imposed when Serios had this power. What conditions? At the time Serios was producing his Polaroid pictures, not one investigator was aware of the possibility that he could be palming an optical device in and out of the black paper cylinder he called his "gismo."

James Randi has produced identical pictures, using such a device, under conditions much *stronger* than any imposed on Serios. Serios took hours to produce a few pictures, and for only one or a few investigators who were totally ignorant of techniques of misdirection. Randi has produced Polaroid pictures exactly like those of Serios, in just a few minutes, and on well-lit stages in front of hundreds. Now that the method is well known, naturally Randi cannot produce the pictures under new conditions imposed by those who know the secret—conditions never imposed by investigators who had no inkling of what Serios could have been secretly doing.

A definitive explanation of how Silvio produced his two linked frames is given in this book's Chapter 14.

Essays

25 | Speaking in Tongues

Among Protestants and Catholics in the United States a long-standing rift has been widening between those who promote "tongues speaking" as a miraculous gift of God and those who are appalled by the practice. The controversy grew increasingly bitter in the wake of the Jim and Tammy Bakker scandal. The Bakkers belonged to the Assemblies of God, a Pentecostal denomination convinced that speaking in tongues is essential for a full Christian life. After Bakker's downfall, his television empire was temporarily taken over by Jerry Falwell, an independent Baptist fundamentalist who once likened tongues speaking to the belly rumblings of someone who had eaten too much pizza. (No wonder so many Pentecostals call him Jerry *Foul*well.)

Exactly what *is* tongues speaking? It is a stream of unintelligible sounds spoken in a state of religious exaltation. Psychologists call it glossolalia, and it has a long and varied history. Early Hebrew prophets known as the Nebiim (1 Samuel 10:5) were given to wild dancing and glossolalia. In ancient Greece and Rome, oracles, soothsayers, and devotees of the mystery religions often gurgled gibberish while in ecstatic trances. The Maulawiya, or Whirling Dervishes of Islamic Sufism, accompany their ecstatic dancing with glossolalia. The more extreme Rifa'iya, or Howling Dervishes, not only howl in tongues but also lash themselves with whips, cut themselves with knives, walk on fire, eat glass, and play with serpents, convinced that Allah will protect them. Anthropologists have encountered glossolalia in the religious rites of many primitive tribes.

Christian glossolalia arose among the faithful soon after the death of Jesus. In Mark 16:17–18, a risen Christ tells his disciples: "And these signs shall follow them that believe: In my name shall they cast out devils; they shall speak with new tongues; they shall take up serpents; and if they drink any deadly thing, it shall not hurt them; they shall lay hands on the sick, and they shall recover."

This essay appeared in *Free Inquiry* (Spring 1989), and is reprinted with permission.

Fundamentalists believe that Jesus was referring prophetically to the "gifts" of the Holy Spirit given to the disciples on the Jewish feast day of Pentecost, as described in the second book of Acts. There was first a "rushing mighty wind." When "cloven tongues like as of fire" descended on them, "they were all filled with the Holy Ghost, and began to speak with other tongues. . . ."

"Other tongues" does not here mean what St. Paul later called the Unknown Tongue. It clearly refers to the disciples preaching in languages they did not know. "Behold," said their listeners, "are not all these which speak, Galileans? And how hear we every man in our own tongue?" Psychologists call this xenoglossy or xenoglossolalia. Some Biblical scholars take the passage to mean that the disciples preached in their native language while listeners *heard* it in *their* native tongues—a miraculous phenomenon known as heteroglossy or heteroglossolalia.

The Unknown Tongue, a supernatural language understood only by God and the angels, is first mentioned in Paul's 1 Corinthians, a letter written to the faithful in Corinth. In Chapter Twelve he lists different gifts of the Holy Spirit, including healing, speaking in "divers kinds of tongues," and the ability to interpret what was said. In Chapter Fourteen he exhorts the Corinthians not to overdo glossolalia. "For he that speaketh in an unknown tongue speaketh not unto men, but unto God: for no man understandeth him." Although glossolalia does the speaker good, Paul goes on to say, it does no good to others. It is like talking to empty air.

Here is how Edgar Goodspeed translates a famous passage in Paul's letter: "Thank God, I speak in ecstasy more than any of you. But in public worship I would rather say five words with my understanding so as to instruct others also than ten thousand words in an ecstasy."[1] To quote a better known verse, 1 Corinthians 13:1 (this from the King James Bible): "Though I speak with the tongues of men and of angels, and have not charity, I am become as sounding brass, or a tinkling cymbal."

Although widely practiced by first-century Christians, glossolalia gradually faded except for a brief revival during the second century among the frenzied followers of Montanus of Phyrigia and his two prophetesses, Priscilla and Maximilla. Montanism was an adventist movement centered on the imminent return of Jesus; when the Lord failed to appear, the sect soon evaporated. In the fourth century Saint Augustine taught that glossolalia was given only to the early church, then withdrawn. This became the official view of the Catholic church and of the Protestant Reformers. There is no evidence that Luther or Calvin even tried to speak in tongues, although the practice surfaced here and there in the seventeenth century, mainly in France among the Protestant Camisards and the *convulsion-*

naires of the Catholic Jansenists, and in England among the Ranters.

In the eighteenth century, glossolalia was revived by the Methodists, and was soon flourishing within such fringe sects as the Quakers, Shakers, Irvingites, and Mormons. After 1900 a variety of churches sprang up in the United States among the rural poor and unlettered, on fire with tongues and faith healing. They grew into the denominations now called Pentecostal. Today there are about thirty-five of them, the largest of which is the Assemblies of God. The Pentecostal denominations are the fastest growing branch of Christianity, not only here but throughout the world, especially in Africa, Korea, and Latin America.

In the 1960s an astonishing thing happened. Glossolalia suddenly invaded the Catholic, Episcopal, and mainline Protestant denominations. These charismatics are dignified, quiet glossolalists, mostly middle-class whites with strongly conservative political opinions; they are often called neo-Pentecostal to distinguish them from the "classical" Pentecostals. Doctrinally they remain loyal to their churches, varying widely in beliefs that range from hardshell fundamentalism to liberalism. They are loosely organized, with their own periodicals and with centers in such unlikely academic spots as Notre Dame and the University of Michigan.

Accurate statistics are hard to come by, but it has been estimated that in the United States there are about five million charismatics (a term that includes both neo- and classical Pentecostals), of which half a million may be Catholic. Worldwide, the number of charismatics could be near two hundred million. Many Catholic leaders are disturbed by this seeping of glossolalia into their church. In the past, the Vatican has regarded tongues speaking as an uncouth manifestation of demon possession. In view of charismatic growth among Catholics in Spain, France, and Latin America (curiously, the movement has had no success in Ireland), the Vatican has muted its opposition. What the pope thinks about it is anybody's guess.

All Pentecostals are fundamentalists who believe the Bible is inerrant, but the word *fundamentalist* is increasingly being applied only to those who, like Falwell, think the gift of glossolalia was withdrawn after apostolic times. "Evangelical" is another blanket adjective. It refers to any Christian who places great stress on the born-again experience. Although charismatics admit that tongues speaking is not essential for salvation—only conversion is—they believe that to lead the richest possible Christian life a believer should earnestly seek a second baptism by the Holy Spirit. It is this baptism that confers—though not necessarily right away—the ability to glossolate.

Four of today's best-known televangelists—Oral Roberts, Jim Bakker, Jimmy Swaggart, and Pat Robertson—are zealous Pentecostals who speak in tongues, as do their wives and most of their children. You seldom hear them glossolate on the tube, because they recognized long ago that it frightens the uninitiated, but in private they practice it frequently. Brother Roberts and his wife Evelyn pray in tongues every day, as do many of the students at Oral Roberts University.

In his three-volume work *The Holy Spirit in the Now,* Oral argues that glossolalia is a prayer language readily available to every born-again believer:

> As you continue thanking and praising the Lord in your natural language, you will feel the Holy Spirit coming up in your spirit. Now all you have to do is let the prayer language come out . . . you may think that you are making up words. But you are not. You are allowing the Holy Spirit to form the words.[2]

Unlike most charismatics, Oral urges every tongues speaker to ask God immediately for an interpretation. In Pentecostal churches the gift of interpretation is usually possessed by someone other than the speaker. During a church service someone may stand up, jabber unintelligibly for several minutes, then sit down. Someone with the gift of interpretation will then rise to explain the prayer.

What does the Unknown Tongue sound like? Many Pentecostals, especially older members of the classical churches, believe they are speaking a natural language, unknown to them but spoken somewhere on earth. Linguists agree that this is not the case. Glossolalia has no discernible grammatical structure. The tongues have nothing in common except a vague overall resemblance to the sounds and cadences of a natural language. It may sound something like "Alarathon ahialee tharnee ekbathaton," or "Kla-atu barada nikto." To outsiders the syllables seem bizarre, comic, and a bit scary, but to the speaker the experience is joyful and invigorating. It is also, as sociologists point out, a ritual that binds the faithful in a kind of secret society, a fellowship of illuminati from which the uninitiated are excluded.

In her autobiography, *I Gotta Be Me,* Tammy Bakker recalls her first experience in glossolalia. She was a young girl, newly converted, when she responded to an altar call. "Slowly, slowly, slowly . . . I disappeared and the Lord filled me with his Holy Spirit. For hours I lay on the floor and spoke in an unknown language. I wasn't aware of anyone else. I was walking with Jesus."[3]

Jimmy Swaggart, as he recalls in his autobiography, *To Cross a River,* was eight years old when he responded to an altar call by a visiting Houston evangelist named Thelma Wiggins. He recalls it this way:

Kneeling at the altar, praying as usual, I became aware of what seemed to be a brilliant shaft of light descending from heaven and focusing on me. Moments later I was speaking in tongues.

For days afterwards, I spoke very little English. In fact, one day mamma sent me to the post office to get a three cent stamp. I placed a nickel down on the counter but instead of telling the clerk I wanted a stamp I began speaking in tongues.

"Son, I can't understand the language you're speaking," the tense little man behind the counter said.

I had been praying about half the day in tongues and didn't think anything about it, but it sure frightened the postal clerk.[4]

Pat Robertson writes about his initiation in *Shout It From the Housetops*: "I felt waves of love flow over me as I began to give praise to Jesus. . . . It was in this moment that I became aware my speech was garbled. I was speaking in another language. Something deep within me had been given a voice, and the Holy Spirit had supplied the words. . . . It sounded like some kind of African dialect."[5]

Later in the book Pat tells how his wife Dede first glossolated. One night Pat retired early. About midnight he was awakened by the sound of Dede praying:

[She was] kneeling at the foot of our bed, speaking in the most beautiful language I had ever heard. It sounded like French—but I knew it was tongues. . . . I slipped out from under the covers and knelt on the floor beside her. . . . Softly I joined her, praying in tongues as the Spirit gave utterance. . . . Finally the tongues ceased, and we knelt in silence, drinking in the indescribable beauty of that holy moment.[6]

When Pat Boone, the best known Pentecostal in show business, was baptized by the Spirit, he sang in tongues. In his life story, *A New Song,* he says it started with a single tone, then suddenly "a beautiful melody came out, and words began to float in on the melody! . . . How can I describe such a thing? It was an uplifting, inspiring, joyful experience—the most profound of my life. I had a deep sense of knowing that I was singing a new song to God."[7]

Although tongues speaking has now moved out of primitive farm communities into affluent and sedate churches, you can still find Pentecostal congregations in small towns, or in the mean streets of big city slums, where scenes of bedlam occur—believers gyrating wildly to steady clapping, dancing in the Spirit, howling in tongues, perspiring, sometimes collapsing on the floor when they are "slain by the Lord." No wonder they were once called "holy rollers." In the Appalachian mountains and in other regions of poverty and ignorance, Pentecostal groups still practice the more obscure gifts of surviving snake bites and poison.

Rituals involving snakes and poison are an embarrassment to enlightened charismatics, but Oral Roberts has a clever way of rejecting them. The word *serpent,* he explains, refers to human enemies from whom God provides protection. As for poison, the Bible simply means that believers won't die if they drink poison *accidentally.* Several southern states have laws against handling rattlers and gulping diluted strychnine, but the laws are often violated and every year or so some poor soul dies as a result.

Psychologists who have studied the personalities of tongues speakers have found no more evidence of mental illness than in the general population; on the contrary, charismatics seem happier and better adjusted than most. Psychologist John Kildahl, in a 1971 study sponsored by the National Institute of Mental Health, cited five elements characteristic of charismatics prior to their first experience with tongues: a "magnetic" relationship with a group leader, a sense of personal distress, an "intense emotional atmosphere," a supporting group, and a strong belief in the religious importance of tongues speaking.

The "glossolalists are able to develop a deeply trusting and submissive relationship to the authority figure who introduces them to the practice," Kildahl stated. "Without this complete turning oneself over to the leader, there can be no beginning to speak in tongues."[8] This role of the "shepherd," as the leader (always a man) is called in some neo-Pentecostal circles, has been criticized for its authoritarianism and occasional damage to the unstable "sheep" in his fold.

Psychologists find that glossolalists are less inhibited in displaying their emotions than most people. The autobiographies of Roberts, the Bakkers, Swaggart, and Robertson drip with episodes of weeping. Tammy sobs on almost every page of her book, and her husband, someone recently said, cries if the breakfast toast burns. Swaggart constantly works up crocodile tears while he sings, waves the Good Book, begs for money, or asks forgiveness for his sins.[9] Tongues speakers are also inclined to hear God speak directly to them and to see visions. Oral has described several visions of Jesus and angels, and in 1986 revealed that Satan had invaded his bedroom and tried to strangle him. When Robertson bought his first television station, his devout mother had a vision of large bank notes floating down from heaven into her son's hands. Tammy's visions are marvelous. In one of them Jesus wore a helmet and brandished a sword.

Noncharismatic Christians vary in their attitudes toward glossolalia. Liberal Protestants seldom talk about it; most have never even heard it.

Popular non-Pentecostal preachers such as Norman Vincent Peale and Robert Schuller also avoid comment on glossolalia for fear of being divisive. The Baptist Billy Graham, in a section on tongues in *The Holy Spirit,* perches on a fence. He has never spoken in tongues, but he allows that he knows no biblical authority for thinking the gift was withdrawn. Maybe it's still God-inspired. Maybe not. Like Paul, he warns against its misuse, pointing out how easily it can be counterfeited.

William Samarin, professor of linguistics in the anthropology department at the University of Toronto, grew up in a tongues-speaking Russian sect in Los Angeles called the Molokan Spiritualism Jumpers. His 1972 book *Tongues of Men and Angels* reports that 53 percent of the glossolalists he studied said it was easier to speak the Unknown Tongue than to speak in ordinary language. You don't have to think—just let the words flow. One minister said he could "go on forever; it's just like drumming."[10] Indeed, Samarin suggests, it is closer to improvisational jazz than to language.

Samarin, who now attends an Anglican church, rejects the view that tongues speaking has a supernatural origin, but he is not opposed to it if it is regarded as a "linguistic symbol of the sacred"—a form of prayer that can be a joyful, faith-strengthening experience for those who practice it. Unlike some other investigators, he does not believe it requires an altered state of consciousness. Although some glossolalists may undergo trancelike states, most do not. It is, Samarin is convinced, a learned behavior that can be mastered by anyone willing to drop his or her inhibitions and give it a try. It may be crude at first, but it quickly improves with practice.

Tongues speakers who lose their Pentecostal faith invariably retain the ability to glossolate. Some have said they enjoy glossolating during orgasms. Sid Caesar and other comics are experts in rattling off gibberish that sounds exactly like German, Japanese, or some other foreign tongue. I myself, while researching this article, began to practice tongues speaking and now can babble it fluently. "Drawk cabda erfi esnes nonton." And I can assure Brother Falwell it's been months since I ate a pizza.

Addendum

> . . . aposteriorious tongues this is nat language at any since of the world.
>
> —James Joyce, *Finnegans Wake*

After writing this article I came across a little known reference to tongues speaking in the Testament of Job, an Old Testament apocryphal book believed to have been written in the first century B.C. It tells how Job's three daughters, after wrapping themselves with magic cords, burst into ecstatic speaking in the tongue of angels. Although not in the King James Bible, this book was highly respected by the tongues-speaking Montanists.

Jimmy Swaggart, writing on tongues in his magazine *The Evangelist* (November 1987), said that anyone baptized by the Holy Spirit will speak in tongues, but that not everyone who glossolates has been so baptized. Those in the second category are inspired by Satan, the "master counterfeiter." The fact that counterfeit tongues exist, writes Jimmy, testifies to the genuine article. "Satan's counterfeit of speaking with other tongues is a sign that the genuine article is scriptural, valid, and for the Church today, otherwise Satan would not be using it to cause difficulties and problems." As for backsliders who continue to glossolate, "they will die and go to hell just as any other unsaved individual."

People continue to die handling snakes and drinking poison. Last week, as I write, the newspaper in the North Carolina town where I live, reported (July 17, 1991) that Jimmy Ray Williams, Jr., age 28, died a few hours after handling a rattlesnake in a small Holiness Church near Newport, Tennessee. Jimmy's father and another man had died eight years earlier during a church service in the same county.

For two good references on this abominable practice, see "They Shall Take Up Serpents," by Lisa Alther, in the *New York Times Magazine* (June 6, 1976), and "The Holy Ghost People," by Michael Watterlond, in *Science 81* (May 1981).

In *Don't Call Me Brother* (Prometheus, 1989, page 254), backslider Austin Miles recalls an incident when a young man took his girlfriend to a Pentecostal church and was firmly persuaded that the glossolalia he heard came straight from the Almighty. He was equally impressed by Sister Anita Kenyon's "interpretations."

"That's a bunch of garbage," said the girlfriend. "Watch, I can mumble anything and Mrs. Kenyon will interpret it." During a quiet moment she yelled out, "Abba coca cola coca cola ruma babba." Sure enough, Sister Kenyon stood up and interpreted the babbling. The boyfriend was devastated.

The Word of God community, in Ann Arbor, Michigan, is the oldest and most influential of the Catholic charismatic movement in the U.S. According to a story in the *Chicago Tribune* (June 28, 1991) a sharp split has developed between its two principal founders, Ralph Martin and Steve Clark. Martin suddenly decided that the authoritarian practices of the movement, as embodied in its training courses, had caused great harm to individuals. The courses taught strict obedience to community leaders, and submission of wives to husbands. Martin apologized for such practices, saying they had been especially harmful to women, and had fostered an atmosphere of elitism.

Clark, who founded the international charismatic Sword of the Spirit in 1982, has rejected these criticisms. There is no suggestion, however, that any leader of the movement has abandoned belief in tongues.

Because no two tongues speakers babble the same words, any string of nonsense syllables is indistinguishable from true glossolalia. My first example, "Alarathon. . . ." is a rune recited by the old witch in Lord Dunsany's novel *The Curse of the Wise Woman.* "Kla-atu . . . ," is the phrase that activates the robot Gort in the famous science-fiction movie "The Day the World Stood Still." And the chapter's next-to-last sentence can be spelled backward to determine its meaning.

Notes

1. From Edgar J. Goodspeed's translation of the New Testament in *The Complete Bible: An American Translation* (Chicago: University of Chicago Press, 1939).

2. Oral Roberts, *The Holy Spirit in the Now* (Tulsa: Oral Roberts University, 1981), vol. 2, p. 57.

3. Tammy Bakker, *I Gotta Be Me* (Green Forest, Ark.: New Leaf Press, 1978), p. 32.

4. Jimmy Swaggart, *To Cross a River* (Baton Rouge, La.: Jimmy Swaggart Ministries, 1984), pp. 33–34.

5. Pat Robertson, *Shout It from the Housetops* (South Plainfield, N.J.: Bridge Publishing, 1972), pp. 63–64.

6. Ibid., p. 95.

7. Pat Boone, *A New Song* (Carol Stream, Ill.: Creation House, 1970), p. 127.

8. Quoted in Edward B. Fiske, "Study of Speaking in Tongues Issued: Participants Not Different Emotionally, It Finds," the *New York Times,* May 2, 1971, p. 88.

9. Jimmy's most spectacular fit of sobbing on television occurred early in 1988 after he had been caught consorting with a hooker. It never occurs to Jimmy that his besetting sin is not sexual but the sin of willful ignorance. When Paul advised Timothy to study, he didn't mean study the Bible, because the Bible did not then exist and the gospels had not even been written. Everything Jimmy knows about science, history, and religious doctrines other than his own can be written on the back of a postage stamp.

10. William Samarin, *Tongues of Men and Angels* (New York: Macmillan, 1972).

26 | Is Realism a Dirty Word?

Every now and then a philosopher is smitten with incredible hubris. "Man is the measure of all things" was how Protagoras vaguely put it. For some metaphysicians, mostly in Germany, hubris mounted to such heights that they imagined the very existence of the universe depended on human minds. Only our shifting perceptions are real. If we cease to exist, presumably the universe would dissolve into structureless fog, perhaps cease to exist altogether, perhaps never to have existed. Laws of science and mathematics, the structures of fields and their particles, are not "out there." They are free creations of the human spirit.

Instead of seeing our brains as feeble, short-lived ensembles of atoms dancing to universal rules, this curious view sees our brains as actually inventing physical laws—in a sense, constructing the universe. J. J. Thomson did not discover the electron. He invented it. Einstein did not discover the laws of relativity, he fabricated them. The fact that such fabrications are so successful in explaining past observations and predicting future ones strikes a cultural solipsist as uncanny, inscrutable magic. "The Unreasonable Effectiveness of Mathematics" was the title of Eugene Wigner's best-known essay.

Now there is nothing unusual about philosophers holding such opinions because no view is so bizarre that some metaphysician hasn't defended it. The astonishing thing is that in recent years a few working physicists have abandoned the realism of Newton and Einstein. "The purpose of this article is to refute the fallacy that reality exists outside of us," writes British physicist Paul Davies in his contribution to *The Encyclopedia of Delusions*. The theme of astrophysicist Bruce Gregory's *Inventing Reality: Physics as a Language* is accurately described on the book's flap: "Physicists do not discover *the* physical world, they invent *a* physical world . . . as the poet Muriel Rukeyser puts it, 'The universe is made of stories, not of atoms.' "

For decades, John Wheeler has been telling us that sentient life exists

This appeared as a guest editorial in the *American Journal of Physics* (March 1989), and is reprinted with permission.

nowhere in the universe except on little old Earth; that if the universe had not been structured so as to allow itself to be observed by us, it would have only the palest sort of reality. "Quantum mechanics," he asserts, "demolishes the view that the universe exists out there." Frank Wilczek, reviewing a recent book honoring Wheeler (*Science,* 28 October 1988) diplomatically comments on this remark: "The importance of Wheeler's technical contributions to physics gives his statements a weight that, coming from another source, they would not have."

It is a short step from Wheeler's social solipsism to the notion that science is not a progressively better understanding of eternal laws, but a cultural creation like music and art. Competing scientific theories are "incommensurable," varying from place to place and time to time like fashions in clothes. You can no more say one is true and the others false than you can say one nation's traffic laws are superior to those of another. It is a view held mainly by social scientists, unable to escape from cultural relativism, who look for support to historian Thomas Kuhn and philosopher Paul Feyerabend.

Physicists influenced by New Age nonsense, and by what they fancy certain Eastern religions say, find the strongest support for antirealism in the "measurement problem" of quantum mechanics. A particle's property seems not to be out there until the particle interacts with a measuring apparatus that collapses its wave packet and allows the property to become "definite." Because all material things, including measuring devices, are ensembles of particles, it seems to follow that they too are not there until someone observes them.

"To be is to be perceived," said George Berkeley, but the canny Irish bishop generously restored the external world by allowing God to observe it. Cultural solipsists, unwilling to call on God, are left with what Wheeler calls a "participatory universe"—one whose reality depends on our cooperation in experiencing it.

Does it follow from the fact that an electron is not there until observed that the universe is not there until observed? It does not. There is nothing new about the fact that many things that seem to be out there are not. The image in a mirror is not behind the mirror, as baby chimps suppose. No two persons in front of a looking glass see the same reflection. A mirror does not look like anything in an empty room. It does not follow that a well-defined structure of room, mirror, and bouncing light rays is not there. A rainbow is observer dependent. No two people see the same bow. No arc of colors is out there. It does not follow that a well-defined structure of Sun, sunlight, and raindrops is not there. Moreover, neither rainbow nor mirror images require human observation. Unmanned cameras photograph them admirably.

It is true that an electron is somehow—no one knows exactly how—not there until measured even though the measurer can be a mindless machine. It does not follow that the macroscopic records of measuring instruments are not there, as Wigner and some parapsychologists maintain, until a human mind sees them. It does not follow that quantum fields, interacting in enormously complex ways, are not there. Because the sound of a falling tree is a sensation in your brain, it does not follow that the tree and the compression waves are inside your brain. Quantum mechanics raises not a single fresh metaphysical problem. It has nothing to say about such ancient unanswerable questions as whether the universe was created or exploded all by itself, whether it would go on running if all minds vanished, or why quantum fields exist rather than nothing.

If you are compelled to think, for emotional reasons or because some guru said so, that you are essential to the universe, that the Moon would not be there without minds to see it (the mind of a mouse? Einstein liked to ask), you are welcome to such self-centered insanity. Don't imagine that it follows from quantum mechanics.

Realism is not a dirty word. If you wonder why all scientists, philosophers, and ordinary people, with rare exceptions, have been and are unabashed realists, let me tell you why. No scientific conjecture has been more overwhelmingly confirmed. No hypothesis offers a simpler explanation of why the Andromeda galaxy spirals in every photograph, why all electrons are identical, why the laws of physics are the same in Tokyo as in London or on Mars, why they were there before life evolved and will be there if all life perishes, why all persons can close their eyes and feel eight corners, six faces, and twelve edges on a cube, and why your bedroom looks the same as it did yesterday when you wake up in the morning.

Addendum

Art Hobson, in *Physics and Society* (July 1989), referred to my editorial on realism and accused me of failing to understand how odd quantum mechanics is. This prompted my following letter, and Hobson's reply, in the periodical's October 1989, issue:

> Holy smoke! Whatever gave you the notion that I don't think quantum mechanics is weird? I won a prize a few years ago for an article in *Discover* titled "Quantum Weirdness" (reprinted in my *Order and Surprise*), and I have written about the mystery of the EPR (which suggests an interconnectedness

on a superluminal level) in half a dozen places. I agree with Feynman that QM is crazy, and I certainly regard it as a much more fundamental break with classical physics than relativity theory.

You have totally missed the point of my editorial. It is that quantum weirdness does not justify a leap to the views of Wheeler and Wigner that the reality and mathematical structure of the external world is mind-dependent. The Schroedinger equation, as you know, changes in a completely deterministic way. It is only when measurement occurs that chance enters the picture, but it does not follow from this fact that the external world does not exist and have a structure independent of observation. It is *this* metaphysical solipsism my editorial attacked, and I would guess that 99 percent of working physicists agree with me. I even received a letter from Glashow saying he couldn't comprehend how anyone could find fault with my editorial, just as I have nothing in *your* comment to oppose.

Please, don't accuse me again of views I don't hold!

Hobson's response:

The quotation marks around "not odd at all" in reference to Gardner's article were meant to indicate the article's general attitude toward quantum theory, rather than an actual quotation from the article. The quotation marks were thus misleading, and I apologize for that.

On the other hand, the drift that I get from carefully re-reading this particular essay of Gardner's is still that quantum theory is not odd at all. Maybe I am reading too much into such statements as (and here I do quote) "Quantum mechanics raises not a single fresh metaphysical problem." At any rate, I thank Gardner for the above clarification of his views.

My second letter about this, and Hobson's response, ran in the January, 1990, issue:

Thanks for running my letter.

When relativity was new, many physicists who had little background in philosophy wrote carelessly about how relativity theory introduced fresh insights into metaphysical questions—how it supported determinism, abandoned the correspondence theory of truth, led to all sorts of relativisms, etc., but it soon turned out that relativity raised no fresh metaphysical problems. The same thing is happening all over again with QM, perhaps starting with the claim (Eddington, Compton, etc.) that QM supports free will. My own view, which I am prepared to defend, is that the nature of science and metaphysics (as Carnap said, there is no bridge between these two continents) is such that science cannot solve *any* metaphysical problem, let alone raise new ones.

When I say that QM has not raised a single fresh metaphysical problem, we must have a common understanding of two key words: "fresh" and "metaphysical."

By fresh I mean new. By metaphysics I mean problems that by defini-tion are beyond the reach of empirical physics. This is how the word is used by all modern philosophers of science: Russell, Carnap, Popper, Reichenbach, Hempel, to mention a few. In Carnap's often-used phrase, metaphysics has no "cognitive content."

"Philosophy of Science" is a different matter altogether. Carnap rejected all metaphysics as meaningless, but he wrote a book (on which I collaborated) called *Introduction to the Philosophy of Science.* Now obviously relativity and QM have made significant contributions to the philosophy of science. As I stressed in my *Relativity Explosion,* it was relativity theory that made clear that determining the structure of spacetime was an *empirical* question (in contrast to Kant's views). And QM did indeed make clear that physical laws can rest on a basic indeterminism.

None of this raises a fresh metaphysical problem. For example, the ques-tion of whether the future is completely determined by the present, or whether elements of pure chance underlie "being" is one of the oldest questions in philosophy. It was constantly debated by the ancients and the medievals. The Greek atomists injected randomness into the basic structure of the universe by introducing a random "swerving" of particles on a level too small to be seen. Lucretius has a beautiful metaphor for this. He speaks of a flock of sheep moving about at random on a hill. But to a distant viewer, they appear as a white spot that is motionless. Jumping to recent times, Charles Peirce, America's greatest philosopher, firmly believed (before QM) that pure chance was an element in the evolution of the cosmos. He called his view "tychism." It had a major influence on William James. Note also that this old metaphys-ical question is far from settled today. Many QM experts, Bohm for exam-ple, believe (with Einstein) that QM is incomplete and that when a deeper level is discovered, determinism will be restored. And if one accepts (I don't) the many-worlds interpretation of QM, strict determinism *is* restored. Thus, the indeterminism of QM is certainly not a "fresh metaphysical question."

Consider another ancient metaphysical debate. Did the universe have an infinite past, or was it created by a transcendent deity, or did it pop into exis-tence, all by itself, from nothing? Again, this was endlessly debated by the ancients and medievals. QM has shed *no* light on this question. There is speculation that the universe started with a random quantum fluctuation in the false vacuum, but this vacuum has nothing to do with metaphsyical "nothing." The fluctuation presupposes quantum fields and laws, and laws of probability. So the question is simply pushed down to a deeper level, but the problem of why there is something rather than nothing is as opaque as ever.

Finally, take the question of whether the tree exists when no one ob-serves it. QM has indeed introduced a tinge of solipsism into the measure-ment problem, which is far from completely understood, but it certainly hasn't introduced a "fresh metaphysical question." One of Wigner's famous essays, in which he wonders about the persistence of a tree when no one sees it, never mentions Bishop Berkeley!

Hobson:

OK, I can agree that quantum mechanics raises no metaphysical problems that have not been raised at some point in the history of human thought. But most of us tend to frame the question in the more limited context of the history of scientific thought (i.e. not Bishop Berkeley) since Copernicus (i.e. not Lucretius, either). Relative to post-Copernican scientific thought, quantum mechanics does indeed raise fresh questions about determinism versus free will, the existence of a purely objective reality, and other matters. Quantum mechanics, or any other scientific theory, should not be expected to answer such metaphysical ("beyond physics") questions, but it does throw them into a fresh perspective, and I think this fresh perspective is important.

I have no argument with Hobson's comments.

27 | Recent Blunders of Oral Roberts

Media coverage of Jim Bakker's trial and conviction has obscured news about the near collapse of another Pentecostal empire—one older and seemingly more secure than Bakker's. In September 1989, Oral Roberts announced that he was closing his City of Faith, a glittering complex containing a medical school, hospital, and research center. Burdened with a $25 million debt, he is also selling the palatial homes in which he and his faith-healing son Richard live, and three other houses on the nine-acre family estate adjoining Oral Roberts University (ORU). Two California vacation homes owned by Oral and Richard, valued at more than $1 million, were sold earlier this year.

It was almost thirty years ago that God said to Oral, "Build Me a university." The Almighty spoke again in 1977: "You must build a new and different medical center for Me. Build it exactly as I have given you the vision." The one thing Tulsa didn't need, Oral was told by the city's political leaders and doctors, was another big hospital. But Oral had to obey his Master. It was while raising money for the medical complex that he had his most spectacular vision:

> I felt an overwhelming holy presence all around me. When I opened my eyes, there He stood . . . some 900 feet tall, looking at me. . . . He stood a full 300 feet taller than the 600-foot-tall City of Faith. There I was face to face with Jesus Christ, the Son of the Living God. I have only seen Jesus once before, but here I was face to face with the King of Kings. He stared at me without saying a word; Oh! I will never forget those eyes! And then, He reached down, put His hands under the City of Faith, lifted it, and said to me, "See how easy it is for Me to lift it!"

Millions of dollars poured in. Posters went up around Tulsa showing the City of Faith behind a warning sign: "Begin 900-foot Jesus Crossing."

This blast at Oral first ran in the *Times-News*, of Hendersonville, North Carolina (October 21, 1989), and was reprinted in *Free Inquiry* (Winter 1989/90). Used here with permissions.

More millions followed when Oral announced that his doctors were on the verge of discovering a cure for cancer. In 1984 Oral noticed an angel in the corner of the room, "so tall his head touched the ceiling." Tiny figures of angels were offered in return for donations.

The empire started to crumble in the mid-1980s. Of the hospital's 777 beds—for Oral, 777 is a symbol of Jesus—only a small fraction were ever filled. The highest occupancy rate was an average of 148 beds in 1984. Rising televangelists were diverting huge chunks of loot from Oral's faithful. In 1985 he closed his dental school and gave his law school to Pat Robertson's CBN University.

Oral made his greatest public relations blunder in 1987 when he said that God told him he would be "called home" unless he quickly raised $8 million. Just before the deadline, Satan sneaked into Oral's bedroom and tried to strangle him, but his wife rushed in and banished the fiend. Bumper stickers in Tulsa said "Send Oral to Heaven in '87." Roberts climbed his Prayer Tower to fast and pray. A Florida man, the owner of a dog-race-track, saved Oral's life with a check for $1.3 million.

But the downhill slide continued. Oral blundered again by telling the world he had often restored life to persons who had died at revival meetings. "I had to go back in the crowd and raise the dead person so I could go ahead with the service." Richard, who by then had become his father's clone, assured the press that there were "dozens and dozens and dozens of documented instances" of faith healers raising the dead.

God next told Oral he had to snare $14 million for a new healing center. Construction began, and the father, son, and Holy Ghost began pleading for funds. Soon God was telling Oral to raise $1 billion more for an ORU endowment. The Lord told Oral he would either die or be raptured before the Second Coming, but that he would return with Jesus to help rule the earth during the millennium. "Watch what happens to ORU when I get back," Oral said.

I was born and raised in Tulsa, and have been a bemused Oral-watcher all my life. I find him and his singing son funnier than clowns, though in some ways more tragic than Jim and Tammy. Oral may be an ignorant, self-centered, deluded country bumpkin with a totally closed mind, but in my opinion he is not, like Bakker and Jimmy Swaggart, a hypocrite. I think he really sees what he sees, and hears what he hears. His hallucinations are too absurd to be lies. Poor Richard is doing the best he can to take over the fading ministry, but his "prayer partners" no longer respond eagerly to the gimmicks he and his father are forever concocting to pry cash from elderly women on Social Security. How can they ever top the "God will call me home" gimmick?

Oral Roberts

It is to the old man's credit that he has not yet publicly blamed his woes on the devil, nor did he say that God ordered him to shut down the City of Faith. Is that because Oral would have had to admit that the Lord had made a mistake in telling him to build the City, or, God forbid, because when Oral thought he heard God speak he was only listening to himself?

Jokes about Roberts are always floating around Oklahoma. The latest tells of a small earthquake that toppled the giant praying hands in front of his 61-story hospital. While huge cranes were making fruitless efforts to get the 60-foot bronze hands back in place, a Tulsan stepped forward and said he could do the job for 25 cents. Incredulous, Richard handed over a quarter. The man tossed it toward the hands, which instantly jumped upright and smacked together to capture the coin.

Alas, in the wake of the Bakker and Swaggart scandals, not enough quarters are being tossed Oral's way. For once in his life the 71-year-old evangelist doesn't, in the words of his credo, "expect a miracle." His dream of establishing a "Mayo Clinic of the Southwest" has dissolved, but ORU and a retirement village remain. Richard will continue to perform his skillful impersonation of his father, with the Holy Spirit giving him the "word of knowledge" about the ills of his television-watching flock, allowing him

The cover of Richard's autobiography.

to assure them that they are being "healed right now." Richard and his father may be forced to endure a life-style more in keeping with Jesus' strong attacks on conspicuous waste (Richard's closet covers 432 square feet), but you can be sure that they will not stop praying daily in the Unknown Tongue or waiting to be raptured before the Battle of Armageddon begins.

28 | Fatherly Advice to Tammy Faye Bakker

I have never met Tammy Faye Bakker, nor do I know anyone who knows her, so my impressions of the real Tammy are based mainly on her autobiography, *I Gotta Be Me,* as told to Cliff Dudley (New Leaf Press, 1978), and on media accounts of her shenanigans.

Tammy comes through her memoirs as a naive, whimsical, miserably educated woman who genuinely believes all the Pentecostal doctrines to which she and Jim were converted in their youth. She weeps on almost every page. She speaks in tongues. She has vivid dreams in which Jesus and angels tell her what to do.

Over the decades, as we all know, Jim and Tammy persuaded themselves that God wanted them to become wealthy. He wanted them to adopt a life-style of conspicuous waste. Oral Roberts likes to tell about the time he flipped open his Bible and saw the passage, "Beloved, I wish above all things that thou mayst prosper. . . ." (3 John: 2). This revelation hit him like a thunderbolt. God doesn't intend his faithful to be poor! For fifty years Oral has proclaimed this doctrine of "seed faith." The more money you give to God's work, especially to Oral's ministry, the more loot you'll get back. Like Oral, Jimmy Swaggart, and Pat Robertson, Jim and Tammy convinced themselves that they deserved every dollar they received. They still think so.

It is not easy to understand how televangelists rationalize their riches in light of the fact that Jesus thundered against conspicuous consumption and status symbols. He told a rich young man he couldn't be a disciple until he sold all his possessions and gave the money to the poor. He urged his listeners not to put their trust in things that can rust or become moth-eaten and stolen. He told them not to think about the clothes they wore. One of his parables has a rich man in hell begging for drops of water. It is easier, he said, for a camel to go through a needle's eye than for

My advice to Tammy appeared in *Free Inquiry* (Summer 1990), and is reprinted with permission.

a rich man to enter heaven. I recall a cartoon by Art Young, in the old *Masses* magazine, that showed a preacher instructing his wealthy flock. On a blackboard was a picture of a camel being put through a meat grinder, and the resulting particles being pushed through the eye of a large needle.

Now that the Bakker ministry has collapsed as a result of incredible folly and greed, what should poor Tammy do? Here is my fatherly advice.

First, stop believing that every time you think God speaks to you in the spirit it is really God talking. Has it never occurred to you it could be the voice of Satan? Or that you were talking to yourself?

Second, consider the possibility that what happened to you and Jim may be God telling both of you to stop preaching. There is no way, sister Tammy, you can revive a dead ministry. No one wants to listen to you anymore, except a handful of simple-minded followers. The more you try to revive your ministry, the more pitiable you appear.

Third, give up thinking God wants you to look like a hooker. Have you heard the one-liner about the time someone washed your face and discovered you were Jimmy Hoffa? Actually under your paint you are still a comely woman. Go on a diet. Start exercising. Pay an expert to teach you how to apply make-up with skill and taste.

Fourth, divorce Jim. Regardless of whether he serves his full prison term, the bum isn't worth waiting for. His preaching days, like yours, are kaput. But don't worry about him. When he finally leaves the slammer, he'll make a fortune with a ghost-written book about the evils of prison life. You should have no trouble marrying again, perhaps to a wealthy born-again businessman. A career in films may open up for you.

Fifth, latch on to a top music agent and start recording country and gospel songs. All you need is one hit record to make the country-music scene. Your voice could be worse, and (as you know) technicians can do wonders these days in the way they modify voices electronically. A Tammy Faye who gave up preaching would be invited on endless talk shows. Americans love to welcome sinners back into show biz. Publicity from the television movie about you and Jim has been priceless. In no time at all you could be making almost as much money as you made as a religious huckster.

Your first gospel recording should not be a new hymn, but one of the golden oldies. How about "The Old Rugged Cross"? It's hard to understand why a modern rendition of this greatest of all evangelical hymns has never made it to the top ten. As a video, with sound and visual effects similar to those for the crucifixion scenes Jim staged in Heritage Village, complete with earthquake noises and the blood of Jesus, you'll have a sure blockbuster on your hands.

And never forget, dear Tammy: God loves you!

A young Tammy Faye before the you-know-what hit the fan.

Addendum

Although I doubt if Tammy Faye ever saw my article of advice, she seems to have taken almost all of my advice. On April 8, 1991, according to a wire service story, she gave a singing concert in Wichita, Kansas. "I'm not a Barbara Mandrell," she told the reporter. "Or I'm not a Dolly Parton. All I am is a Tammy Bakker and I hope that's okay."

"Her childish voice ranged from mousy to exuberant," the report said, "as she giggled and laughed her way through the news conference."

I saw no accounts of the concert, so I don't know how successful it was.

In August 1991, when Tammy appeared in the Charlotte federal courthouse for Jim's resentencing to eighteen years, everybody was awed by how beautiful she looked. She had lost 23 pounds, had a soft, natural makeup, a tasteful wig, and clothes from an elegant shop. The *National*

Enquirer (September 10, 1991) said she had consulted a beauty expert for a totally new look, had begun dieting and exercising, and had plans for her own TV show backed by a group of wealthy businessmen. Tammy had looked over old photos, said the *Enquirer*, and decided she "looked like Bozo the clown." The tabloid reported her saying, "I don't need Jim the way I once thought I did. I have plans of my own."

Both the *National Enquirer* and the *Globe*, in their January 28, 1992, issues reported that Tammy has decided to dump Jim for his old friend Roe Messner. Roe is a wealthy contractor who helped build Jim's Heritage USA theme park, and the man who secretly funneled hush money to Jessica Hahn. He and Ruth, his wife of 36 years, have separated. She blames Tammy for the break-up. If the two tabloids are to be trusted, it was Roe who paid for Tammy's recent plastic surgery that has given her her new sexy look. At her Wichita concert, mentioned above, Tammy sang "Over the Rainbow," dedicating the song to Roe.

According to the *Globe*, Tammy and Roe have been meeting in sleazy Tulsa motels and elsewhere. Both have asked their spouses for a divorce. Jim and Ruth are said to be devastated, and close to coming apart at the seams.

Do Jim and Tammy still believe the primitive Pentecostal doctrines? My guess is yes, although Ted Koppel, after interviewing the couple on "Nightline," put it succinctly: "He's a con man and she's a con woman."

One thing Tammy hasn't yet gotten over is her habit of giggling and sobbing. More fatherly advice, dear Tammy: Try to control those sobs and giggles. You're a big girl now. And God still loves you.

29 | Aleister Crowley, the Beast 666

Early in 1990 an editor at Dover Publications asked me to write a fore-word for a reprinting of *Magick in Theory and Practice,* by the notorious British occultist Aleister Crowley. First published in 1976, Dover's edition had been one of their best sellers.

I was somewhat taken aback by this request because Dover was well aware that I considered Crowley to be a mountebank, and had said so in my Dover book *Fads and Fallacies in the Name of Science.* Of course I would be delighted to write a foreword, I told the editor, provided Dover would allow me to blast the book. The editor thought this an amusing idea. He told me to go ahead. Such a foreword, we both realized, would be something of a first in the history of book publishing.

Unfortunately, my blast was so strong that when the top brass at Dover read it, it aroused considerable controversy. Because the book was profit-able, there was a strong urge to reprint. On the other hand, would it be good public relations to publish a book with a foreword telling the reader he was a fool to buy it? There were three alternatives: Reprint with my foreword, reprint without a foreword, or drop the book from Dover's list.

At first the decision was to reprint with my foreword and see how well the book would do. I had already been sent galleys when word came in August that the decision had been changed. Dover had decided to aban-don the book. Although a new edition would bring in lots of money, it was just too damaging to the reputation of a house that for many decades has been a leading publisher of distinguished books on science. I like to think that my foreword had something to do with Dover's admirable decision.

Would that other publishers could acquire the guts and altruism to follow Dover's lead. Each year hundreds of books are printed about astrol-ogy, the paranormal, fake reducing diets, harmful alternative medicines, UFOs, and other wonders—books that strengthen the public's growing scientific illiteracy and feed its insatiable hunger for New Age miracles. Publishers and editors know that such books are trash, but simple greed overcomes their distaste.

Here is the foreword that will not appear in any edition (two others remain on the market) of Crowley's crazy book on black magic.

*   *   *

Over the decades I have written dozens of forewords, but this is the first for a book so totally without merit that it did not deserve even its first printing. Why, then, has it sold so well in its Dover edition? The answer lies in today's idiotic interest in witchcraft and Satanism, in turn a part of the occult or New Age Revolution. Gilbert Chesterton once said that when persons stop believing in God, they don't believe in nothing —they believe in anything. Starved for the miracles of their lost faiths, and illiterate with respect to science, they buy anything they think might initiate them into the mysteries of genuine sorcery.

Aleister Crowley, one of our century's most preposterous mounte-banks, was born in England in 1875 to parents who were devout Plymouth Brethren. His wealthy father, a brewer of ale, left him a fortune that enabled him to wander around the world without doing any useful work, and to pay for the printing of his worthless books. Like many of today's New Agers, Crowley's life was one long rebellion against the fundamentalist beliefs of his mother, father, and a hated uncle. "Crowleyanity" was the ugly term he gave to a religious cult he tried unsuccessfully to establish. Every act his parents considered sinful was an act he felt compelled to make. "Crowley was just a boy who got mad at his parents," was how Thomas Sugrue put it in reviewing John Symonds' standard biography of Crowley, "and decided to spite them by spitting on the floor."

Like L. Ron Hubbard, the psychotic founder of Scientology who in his early years went through a phase of intense preoccupation with witchcraft, Crowley was a man of enormous ego, concerned only with promoting himself regardless of how severely he injured others. His crazy antics and bisexual shenanigans earned him the title of "The Wickedest Man in the World," but the phrase he most liked to apply to himself was "The Great Beast 666." One of his foolish conceits was that he was none other than the infernal Beast described in the Bible's Apocalypse (Chapter 13), and to whom the number 666 is attached. There were other curious titles he gave himself from time to time, such as Brother Perdurabo of the Golden Dawn,[1] the Master Therion, Prince Chioa Khan, Count Vladimir Svareff, the Prophet Bahomet, and the Laird of Boleskin.

Crowley was a lifelong womanizer and male chauvinist pig. (It was not until his later years that he began to seek homosexual encounters.) Many of his seemingly endless series of concubines were prostitutes hooked on drugs and occultism. The women who found him attractive were invariably masochistic and mentally unstable. As a student at Cambridge, he said that abstinence from sex for forty-eight hours was impossible, and he complained of having "to waste uncounted priceless hours in chasing what ought to have been brought to the back door every morning with the milk." Each mistress of the moment was called his "Scarlet Woman," another image from the Book of Revelation. Using a heated dagger, he branded one mistress between her breasts with a cross inside three concentric circles.

"I rave; and I rape and I rip and I rend," is a line from his phallic "Hymn to Pan" that opens this book. It is Pan who speaks, but it just as well could be the satyr Crowley. He liked to call his amorous romps "sex magic" because they were so often combined with occult rituals and animal sacrifices. Both of his wives went insane, and five mistresses were suicides. Scores of his concubines ended in the gutter as alcoholics, drug addicts, or in mental institutions. The Beast had two front teeth filed to needle points so he could give women the "Serpent's Kiss" on the wrist or throat and draw blood like a vampire. Among his children, many illegitimate, was a daughter he named Nuit Ma Ahathoor Hecate Sappho Jezebel Lilith. The neglected baby died of typhoid in Rangoon after Crowley had thrown away the mother.

It is impossible to say to what extent Crowley believed the nonsense he wrote about black magic, or to what extent it was just part of his act. Like Madame Blavatsky and other occult charlatans, he was a compulsive liar. He claimed that he once called up Beelzebub and forty-nine other demons, along with a plague of beetles. On another occasion, in a London flat, he conjured up 316 devils who danced wildly around the room. A lady invited him to tea, only later to be assured by Crowley that she had entertained his astral body while he was home asleep. He insisted he had the power to make himself invisible, though when a judge once asked him to prove it, he refused. He reported seeing a former friend, who had become a Buddhist monk, floating in the air and being blown about by the wind. He claimed to be in touch with "Secret Chiefs" of the Spirit world, including Aiwass, his Guardian Angel. They told him what to do, and supplied him with prophecies.

The high noon of Crowley's mad career was the founding of his notorious Abbey of Thelema, in Cefalu, Italy. Fancying himself an artist, he personally decorated the walls with grotesque pornographic murals. The abbey quickly became a retreat for the taking of hard drugs, and for sexual orgies based on bizarre rites written and directed by the Beast. "Do what thou wilt shall be the whole of the law," was the abbey's central motto. (Crowley had stolen it from Rabelais.) Initiates carried a razor blade to slash their arm each time they said "I." Crowley, of course, was the abbey's only "I." Guests came from everywhere, including Elizabeth Fox, an American movie actress, and Norman Mudd, a troubled mathematician from South Africa who later drowned himself. Scandals at the abbey were the constant delight of British tabloids.

In 1923 Mussolini closed down the abbey and expelled Crowley from Italy. France also later deported him. After his fortune finally ran out, he settled in a boarding house in the seaside town of Hastings, where his declining years were spent in poverty and depression. All his life he had abused alcohol and drugs. Toward the close, he was taking enough heroin to kill a dozen men.

His last act of foolishness was suing the British writer Nina Hamnett and her publisher over her autobiography *Laughing Torso* in which she wrote about the scandals and deaths associated with the Abbey of Thelema. The judge made the following memorable remarks before the jury decided in Nina's favor:

> I have been over forty years engaged in the administration of the law. I thought that I knew of every conceivable form of wickedness. I thought that everything which was vicious and bad had been produced at one time or another before me. I have learned in this case that we can always learn something more if we live long enough. I have never heard such dreadful, horrible, blasphemous and abominable stuff as that which has been produced by the man who describes himself to you as the greatest living poet. Does the jury still want the case to go on?

Crowley died in 1947, age 72, in Hastings. The supreme humiliation was that the media had forgotten him. His reputation had been that of a man who worshipped Satan, but it was more accurately said that he worshipped no one except himself. Yet in spite of his vanity, his posturing, his cruelty, his monumental falsehoods, and the monotonous drivel of his books, he had a few admirable qualities. He was charming and intelligent, he played a good game of chess, and he was a passionate and expert mountain climber and big-game hunter. He liked to brag that England had produced two great poets, "for one must not forget Shakespeare." Many of his poems were outright porn, though occasionally his mediocre verse contained alliterative passages that compare favorably with Swinburne. None of his novels or short stories are worth reading. I don't know if this is true but I read somewhere that Alice Meynell, a Catholic poet and critic, had high praise for fifty hymns that Crowley had written to the Virgin Mary. When she found out who the poet was, she fainted.

Crowley's love poem "La Citana," from his book *Olla,* strikes me as one of his best:

Your hair was full of roses in the dewfall as we danced,
The sorceress enchanting and the paladin entranced,
In the starlight as we wove us in a web of silk and steel
Immemorial as the marble in the halls of Boabdil,
In the pleasuance of the roses with the fountains and the yews
Where the snowy Sierra soothed us with the breezes of the dews!
In the starlight as we trembled from a laugh to a caress,
And the God came warm upon us in our pagan allegresse.
Was the Baile de la Bona too seductive? Did you feel
Through the silence and the softness all the tension of the steel?
For your hair was full of roses, and my flesh was full of thorns,
And the midnight came upon us worth a million crazy morns.
Ah! My Gypsy, my Gitana, my Saliya! were you fain
For the dance to turn to earnest?—O the sunny land of Spain!
My Gitana, my Saliya! more delicious than a dove!
With your hair aflame with roses and your lips alight with love!
Shall I see you, shall I kiss you once again? I wander far
From the sunny land of summer to the icy Polar Star.
I shall find you, I shall have you! I am coming back again
From the filth and fog to seek you in the sunny land of Spain.
I shall find you, my Gitana, my Saliya! as of old
With your hair aflame with roses and your body gay with gold.
I shall find you, I shall have you, in the summer and the south
With our passion in your body and our love upon your mouth—
With our wonder and our worship be the world aflame anew!
My Gitana, my Saliya! I am coming back to you!

Somerset Maugham's forgotten pot-boiler *The Magician* (1908) was based on Crowley. The two first met in Paris. "I took an immediate dislike to him," Maugham recalls in an introduction to a late edition of his novel, "but he interested and amused me. He was a great talker and he talked uncommonly well. . . . He was a fake, but not entirely a fake. . . . He was a liar and unbecomingly boastful, but the odd thing was that he had actually done some of the things he boasted of."

Maugham called his black magician Oliver Haddo, turning him into a repulsive fat man with supernormal powers which, Maugham continues, "Crowley, though he claimed them, certainly never possessed. Crowley, however, recognized himself in the creature of my invention . . . and wrote a full page review of the novel in *Vanity Fair,* which he signed 'Oliver Haddo.' I did not read it, and wish now that I had. I dare say it was a pretty piece of vituperation, but probably, like his poems, intolerably verbose."

"Backmasking," a whimsical technique practiced by some hard rock groups, is the inclusion in songs of phrases that can be understood only when the recording is played backward. An example is the Led Zeppelin's "Stairway to Heaven," of which guitarist Jimmy Page was a co-composer. One of its many backward passages, "Here's to my sweet Satan," was produced by singer Robert Plant's slurring of the forward line "There's still time to change." Page has long been obsessed by Crowley. He owns what may be the world's largest collection of Crowley memorabilia, and he even bought Crowley's old mansion in Boleskine, Scotland, near Loch Ness. Page's occult bookstore in London, "The Equinox," is named after one of Crowley's journals.

A listing of Crowley's books fills two and one-half columns in *Books in Print.* You'll find those dreary volumes on sale in most New Age stores —stirring testimony to the adolescent gullibility of their customers. A picture of the Great Beast, along with the faces of Poe and Lewis Carroll, grace the cover of the Beatles' famous album *Sergeant Pepper's Lonely Hearts Club Band.*

Turn now to pages 417-20 of this book where you will find Crowley's absurd exercises for training one's mind to think backward. One exercise is to watch film projected in reverse, and to listen to phonograph records turning the wrong way. The object of this training is to learn how to project one's memory back to prior incarnations. Crowley's infatuation with doing things backward derived from the reversed movements and backward recitations of Latin phrases and the Lord's Prayer in forms of the Black Mass—a blasphemous parody of the Eucharist.[2] One of Crowley's favorite publicity stunts—he was an incurable exhibitionist—was to enter an expensive restaurant in a black robe, his head shaved except for a strip of hair down the middle, and eat his dinner backward, starting with the dessert and ending with soup.

A few words now about the book you hold. Tricks of the stage conjurors actually work. You can watch a magician pluck live doves from the air, or vanish an elephant, and have not the faintest idea where the birds came from or where the beast went. But if you draw a pentagram on the floor, slit the throat of a black cat, recite the required incantations, and call on Satan to appear, you'll find that he doesn't. That, of course, is the trouble with real magic. It doesn't work.

Some notion of how far Crowley was willing to go in shocking readers can be gained from page 95, in a chapter on the importance of blood sacrifices. After extolling the merits of sacrificing lambs and rams, he writes: "For the highest spiritual working one must accordingly choose that victim which contains the greatest and purest force. A male child of perfect innocence and high intelligence is the most satisfactory and suitable victim."

To this incredible statement Crowley appends an even more incredible footnote saying that between 1912 and 1928 he (Frater Perdurabo) performed just such a sacrifice "on an average about 150 times every year." There is, of course, not a shred of truth in this boast—it would make Crowley the greatest serial murderer of all time—nor in most of the events described in his autobiographical writings.

Only gullible believers-in-anything, such as England's occult journalist Colin Wilson (in 1987 he published an entire book about Crowley),[3] are capable of taking seriously what Crowley wrote about himself or in believing that the man possessed genuine supernormal powers. *Magick* has a certain historical interest in that it is Crowley's most notorious book, and a book whose continued sales today tell us something about the extent to which interest in the occult and witchcraft has invaded sections of our culture. But if you bought this book in the hope of learning how to practice witchcraft, you are a bigger fool than Wilson. From first to last, *Magick* is unadulterated balderdash, the product of a diseased and evil mind.

Notes

1. The Hermetic Order of the Golden Dawn was England's most prestigious secret occult organization. Active members included many noted writers, such as William Butler Yeats, Arthur Machen, and Charles Williams. Yeats and Crowley quarreled violently. According to Crowley, Yeats refused to advance Crowley to a higher grade because he (Crowley) was a greater poet.

2. According to an Associated Press release in the *Chicago Tribune* (April 13, 1990), a Milwaukee judge ruled Deborah Kazuck, 27, insane for trying to kill a man with an axe. She reportedly planned to dismember the man's body, drain his blood, and eat his kidneys in a Satanic ritual that would resurrect Jack the Ripper, England's nineteenth-century serial killer. The victim testified that when he was attacked, Deborah kept chanting "red rum," which is "murder" backward. Thanks to correspondent Trekcib Mot for sending me this clipping.

3. Wilson earlier devoted a lurid chapter to Crowley in his book *The Occult,* and Crowley is a central character in Wilson's novel *The Sex Diary of Gerard Sorme.* Biographies of Crowley rely heavily on the two volumes of his *Confessions.* Although laced with fabrications, these two books are fascinating reading.

30 | How to Test Your PK

For decades parapsychologists have been saying that every person has latent ESP powers that can be developed by proper training, but when it comes to PK (psychokinesis) they are of divided opinion. In my view, there is not the slightest doubt that PK, like ESP, can be developed by training. Moreover, every one of us—man, woman, or child—can demonstrate PK almost at once by performing any number of extremely simple experiments.

In many cases, PK merely supplements and magnifies normal muscular movements. Water witching is the most familiar example. Although the muscles of a dowser's arms and hands actually turn the dowsing rod, the movement is triggered by a sudden burst of PK, in turn prompted by the dowser's remote viewing of water streams below the soil, or whatever mineral one is trying to locate. The movement of a planchette is another example of arm muscles unconsciously being influenced by the effect of PK on the planchette. Table tipping is still another instance.

Israeli psychic Uri Geller has taught us all how to bend metal spoons. Just hold both ends of a spoon firmly in your fists and keep saying to yourself that it will bend. Apply mild pressure. PK quickly takes over, and the spoon bends as if made of wax.

A striking demonstration of PK is the old parlor game of levitation said to be described in Samuel Pepys's *Diary*. Parapsychologist Thelma Moss, in her popular book *The Probability of the Impossible,* devotes several pages to what she calls an experiment in levitation that any group of five people can perform.

Have a heavy person sit in a chair. Four people stand around him or her, two with an extended index finger under the subject's armpits and two with an extended finger under the subject's knees. Try as they will, they cannot lift the subject. Now everyone concentrates, saying to themselves "Lift! Lift!" On the count of ten, the four simultaneously raise their

This article appeared in the *Physics Teacher* (April 1990), and the addendum ran in the same periodical (May 1990). Both are reprinted with permission.

fingers. Up goes the heavy person, as if he or she were a dummy stuffed with straw! [For more on this levitation, see Chapter 11.]

Psychic motors that operate by PK take numerous forms. Here is one version that is easy to make. With a pair of pliers, push the head of a needle into a large cork so the needle points straight up when the cork is stood on end. Take a fresh new dollar bill and very accurately fold it in half both ways to make two perpendicular creases that intersect at the bill's center. Balance the unfolded bill on the needle (the folds form "mountain folds" when you look down on the bill), its point at the intersection of the two creases.

Sit by this miniature "motor" with your head as close as possible to the bill without touching it. Concentrate on making the bill rotate. After a few seconds, or maybe a few minutes, the bill will slowly rotate. Be patient! Sometimes you may have to wait five or ten minutes. With a little practice, you can start the bill turning instantly and make it go in whatever direction you choose.

A fresh chicken egg is another object you can rotate by PK. This must be practiced over a bed because there is danger of the egg dropping to the floor. Place a table knife with a wide flat blade on the bed. Put the egg on its side (not its end) on top of the tip of the knife. Grasp the knife's handle with your left hand, while you hold a second table knife by its handle in your right hand. Put the blade's tip flat on top of the egg. Holding both knives firmly by their handles, lift the egg off the bed so it is held in the air firmly between the two blades, one below the egg, one on top. In a few seconds, while you concentrate on turning the egg, it will slowly begin to rotate. As in the dollar-bill motor experiment, with practice you can make the egg turn clockwise or anticlockwise.

A playing card can also be made to rotate by PK. Bend the card so that it is very slightly convex on its back side, the axis of bend running lengthwise along the middle of the card. Don't fold it; just give it an extremely slight curvature. Now hold the card between two diagonally opposite corners, back of card up. The tip of your forefinger should be at one corner and the tip of your thumb at the other corner. Support the card with the least possible amount of pressure—just enough to keep the card from dropping to the floor. Stare at the back of the card and mentally order it to turn over. The card will slowly rotate until its face is uppermost.

Here's another easy demonstration of PK's power over muscles. Clasp your hands, then extend your two index fingers. The tips should be about an inch apart. In your mind, order the fingertips to come together, but at the same time try to keep them an inch apart. No matter how hard you try, if you strongly will the tips to close, they will slowly move toward each other until they touch.

Now for the most dramatic test of all. Tie a finger ring to the end of a piece of string. Rest your elbow on the table and hold the string's free end so that the ring hangs vertically inside a tall glass. Mentally choose any number from 1 through 10. Concentrate on the ring. Soon it will start swinging like a pendulum until it strikes the side of the glass. Suppose you thought of the number 7. The ring will strike the glass just seven times and then stop swinging!

The next time you are sitting near the rear of a bus, or in a theater or church, concentrate as hard as you can on the back of the head of anyone sitting in front of you. Strongly urge the person to turn his or her head and look. Within a minute or so the person's head is likely to turn, and he or she will look directly at you without knowing why.

These are only a few of many easy ways to test and improve your PK ability. Keep practicing these experiments for a year or two, and you will be surprised at what wonders you can accomplish. If you are gifted at birth with strong psychic powers, maybe you will be able to suspend a ping-pong ball in the air like the famous Russian psychic Nina Kulagina, or move a plastic pill bottle across a kitchen counter like Felicia Parise, the friend and subject of parapsychologist Charles Honorton. Maybe you will even develop the talent to project thought pictures onto camera film like the famous Chicago psychic Ted Serios!

Addendum

I hope no reader took seriously the April Fool hoax that I wrote for last month's issue. None of the experiments described operates by PK (psychokinesis). Indeed, there is no evidence whatsoever that PK exists. All supposed demonstrations of its reality are flawed; not one is replicable by experimental psychologists. If there were such a force, a group of psychics, standing around a tiny sphere suspended by magnetic fields inside a vacuum, would be able to make the sphere rotate. That all such experiments have failed is one of the greatest unpublicized scandals of modern parapsychology.

Most spoons, unless made of heavy silver, are easily bent in the hands. So easy, in fact, that persons who don't know this—and most people don't —imagine that PK is assisting the bending when they apply pressure at the ends. Uri Geller's more impressive cutlery-bending feats are based on trickery familiar to magicians.

The old parlor stunt of lifting a heavy person with fingers under the armpits and knees wass explained in Chapter 11, but I will summarize here. On the first try, there is no coordination of the lifting. The body is thrown off balance and the lift becomes difficult. But after counting to ten (or any similar ritual), everybody lifts at exactly the same moment, and also tries a little harder. A person weighing 200 pounds has his or her weight distributed over four fingers, so each person has only to exert a lift of 50 pounds—40 if a fifth finger is under the subject's chin. When Geller

Fig. 1—Proof of precognition

demonstrates the lift in one of his magic shows, he is always one of the lifters. During the practice lift he pretends to be exerting all his strength, while actually exerting none. This guarantees a failure.

What causes the creased dollar bill to rotate on the needle's point? Air currents. It is impossible to eliminate them in a room because of thermal currents produced by the rising of heated air, by movements of people in the room, by currents coming under doors from other rooms, and so on. If your head is close to the bill, additional currents are produced by your breathing and by heat from your body. There is no way to control the direction of rotation. However, air currents can vary and cause the bill to stop and start going the other way. If you are trying to change the rotation with your mind, you may imagine that you are causing the change.

The chicken egg between the knife blades turns because it is impossible to keep both hands completely still. This imperceptible jiggling starts the egg rotating. Once it starts, inertia keeps it going the same way while the jiggling continues.

Extended forefingers, when your hands are clasped, are a strain on finger muscles. As the muscles tire, the fingers tend to move together without any conscious effort on your part.

The horizontally held playing card, which rotates while opposite corners are held lightly between the tips of a finger and thumb, is best understood if you take a piece of stiff wire about four inches long and give it a slight bend. Hold the ends between thumb and finger, the wire forming a slightly circular arc with its convex side upward. Lighten pressure on the ends, and the wire will turn 180 degrees. Why? Because at the start its center of gravity is higher than its ends. The unstable wire rotates to bring its center of gravity to the lowest possible point. The card turns for the same reason. The slight crimp in the card (it should be so slight as to be almost invisible) raises its center of gravity just enough so that, as you relax pressure on opposite corners, the card slowly turns face up.

The effect is startling and sure to mystify your students and friends.

Unconscious arm movements start the ring swinging on a string, just as they also cause the movements of a planchette over an Ouija board or the turning of a dowsing rod. For many people, an expectation that the ring will strike the side of the glass a specified number of times, from 1 through 10, is sufficient to stop the swinging after the number has been chimed. Novelty shops used to sell a "sex indicator" based on the same principle. A small wooden ball, at the end of a string or chain, is held over someone's hand. If the person is a man, the ball starts swinging back and forth along a vertical plane. Over a woman's hand, it swings in a small ellipse.

Persons sitting ahead of you in a church, theater, or bus frequently turn to look around. So, if you stare at the back of someone's head and are sufficently patient, he or she will often turn and look back, giving you the strong impression that somehow they sensed you were staring at them. If they fail to do this, you will quickly forget you even looked at them. If they happen to turn, you will be sure to remember it.

Now let me prove to you that I have the power of precognition. Circle any of the digits in the matrix shown in Fig. 1, then cross out its row and column. Circle any digit not crossed out and again draw lines through its row and column. Circle the digit that remains. Add the three freely selected digits to obtain the sum n. Count to the nth word of this article. I predict that you will get the "last" word.

31 | The Smith-Blackburn ESP Hoax

One of the most difficult notions for psychic investigators to get through their heads is that the deceptions of magicians rest on peculiar principles that must be thoroughly understood if one intends to investigate psychic miracles. As all conjurers know, intelligent persons are extremely easy to deceive; if they are trained in science they are even less likely to penetrate the deceptions of skilled mountebanks. Electrons and microbes don't cheat. Psychic miracle-workers do. Over and over again in the history of psychic research, scientists have assumed they were capable of detecting fraud without troubling to learn even the simplest of magic techniques. As a result, they have repeatedly played the roles of gullible fools.

This is as true today as in the past. Ted Serios, for example, the Chicago bellhop who pretended he could project photographs from his mind onto Polaroid film, completely convinced two psychiatrists, Jule Eisenbud and Ian Stevenson, that his feats were genuine. Joseph Gaither Pratt, John Beloff, and many other eminent parapsychologists were similarly taken in. To this day Eisenbud, Stevenson, and Beloff have been unable to accept the exposure of Ted's methods that were published in *Popular Photography* (October 1967). On the contrary, Eisenbud recently issued a new edition of his book about Serios. He has accused the magicians responsible for exposing Ted of setting psychic research back fifty years by causing Ted to lose his powers!

Nina Kulagina, in Russia, using magnets and invisible thread in ways familiar to magicians, made dupes of scores of psychic investigators. Charles Honorton still refuses to believe that his friend Felicia Parise used invisible thread to move a plastic bottle across her kitchen counter. Dozens of parapsychologists around the world were for a time convinced that Uri Geller was able to bend spoons and keys by psychokinesis. Science writer Charles Panati, totally ignorant of magic, edited *The Geller Papers*—a

This article appeared in the *Skeptic,* a British journal, September-October 1991, and is reprinted with permission.

collection of embarrassing articles defending Uri's psychic powers.

During the heyday of Spiritualism, thousands of mediums around the world were levitating tables, making luminous trumpets float, exuding ectoplasm through the mouth and nose, and producing unearthly music, strange odors, and photographs of the dead. Some of the best minds in science and literature—writer Arthur Conan Doyle and physicist Oliver Lodge, to mention two—accepted all these wonders without taking the time to learn even the most rudimentary elements of deception. Hundreds of other examples could be cited of intelligent investigators who were hornswoggled by the simplest of conjuring tricks. Let me focus on one outstanding example from the nineteenth century that is not as well known as it should be.

The story begins in 1882 when journalist Douglas Blackburn, editor of a weekly journal in the seaside resort of Brighton, became a friend of George A. Smith. Smith, age 19, was then performing a stage act as a hypnotist. The two young men decided to team up and develop a mind-reading act in which Blackburn would send messages telepathically to Smith.

To publicize their act, Blackburn wrote about it in his journal *The Brightonian.* One of his articles was reprinted in the August 26, 1882, issue of *Light,* a Spiritualist magazine. Here is how Blackburn described what they did:

> The way Mr. Smith conducts his experiments is this: He places himself *en rapport* with myself by taking my hands: and a strong concentration of will and mental vision on my part has enabled him to read my thoughts with an accuracy that approaches the miraculous. Not only can he, with slight hesitation, read numbers, words and even whole sentences which I alone have seen, but the sympathy between us has developed to such a degree that he rarely fails to experience the taste of any liquid or solid I choose to imagine. He has named, described, or discovered small articles he has never seen when they have been concealed by me in the most unusual places, and on two occasions, he has successfully described portions of a scene which I either imagined or actually saw.

The letter caught the eye of Edmund Gurney (1847–1888), one of the distinguished founders in 1882 of England's Society for Psychical Research (SPR). Gurney later wrote numerous books on psychic phenomena, of which his two-volume *Phantasms of the Living* (1886) was the most notable. Written with the help of friends Frederic Myers and Frank Podmore, it became the classic account of persons who claim to see spirit forms of friends and relatives shortly after they die. Myers (1843–1901), the man who coined the word "telepathy," was another founder and active member of the SPR. His two-volume *Human Personality and Its Survival of Bod-*

ily Death (posthumously issued in 1903) was his magnum opus.

Smith and Blackburn joined the SPR, and Smith even became Gurney's private secretary and research assistant, a post he held until Gurney died. Smith brought to London from Brighton a number of young men who demonstrated telepathy after Smith hypnotized them. These experiments were supervised and reported in the SPR's journal by Mrs. Henry Sidgwick, wife of the Cambridge philosopher who had been the SPR's first president.

Not until after Myers, Gurney, and Podmore died did Blackburn publish three remarkable articles in which he explained how he and Smith secretly signaled to each other. His "Confessions of a Famous Medium," in *John Bull,* a popular magazine (December 8, 1908), was followed by a more detailed "Confessions of a Telepathist" in London's *Daily News* (September 1, 1911). This article should be carefully read and pondered by every person who wishes to investigate psychic wonders, or to evaluate reports of such investigations by others. Here is the article in full:

> For nearly 30 years the telepathic experiments conducted by Mr. G. A. Smith and myself have been accepted and cited as the basic evidences of the truth of Thought Transference.
>
> Your correspondent "Inquirer" is one of many who have pointed to them as a conclusive reply to modern skeptics. The weight attached to those experiments was given by their publication in the first volume of the proceedings of the Society for Psychical Research, vouched for by Messrs. F. W. H. Myers, Edmund Gurney, Frank Podmore, and later and inferentially by Professor Henry Sidgwick, Professor Romanes, and others of equal intellectual eminence. They were the first scientifically conducted and attested experiments in Thought Transference, and later were imitated and reproduced by "sensitives" all the world over.
>
> I am the sole survivor of that group of experimentalists, and as no harm can be done to anyone, but possible good to the cause of truth, I, with mingled feelings of regret and satisfaction, now declare that the whole of those alleged experiments were bogus, and originated in the honest desire of two youths to show how easily men of scientific mind and training could be deceived when seeking for evidence in support of a theory they were wishful to establish.
>
> And here let me say that I make this avowal in no boastful spirit. Within three months of our acquaintance with the leading members of the Society for Psychical Research, Mr. Smith and myself heartily regretted that these personally charming and scientifically distinguished men should have been victimized, but it was too late to recant. We did the next best thing. We stood aside and watched with amazement the astounding spread of the fire we had in a spirit of mischief ignited.
>
> The genesis of the matter was in this wise. In the late [eighteen-]seventies and early eighties a wave of so-called occultism passed over England. Public

interest became absorbed in the varied alleged phenomena of Spritualism, Mesmerism, and thought-reading. The profession of the various branches abounded, and Brighton, where I was editing a weekly journal, became a happy hunting ground for mediums of every kind. I had started an exposure campaign, and had been rather successful. My great score was being the first to detect the secret of Irving Bishop's thought-reading. In 1882 I encountered Mr. G. A. Smith, a youth of 19, whom I found giving a mesmeric entertainment. Scenting a fraud, I proceeded to investigate, made his acquaintance, and very soon realized that I had discovered a genius in his time. He has since been well known as a powerful hypnotist. He was also the most ingenious conjurer I have met outside the profession. He had the versatility of an Edison in devising new tricks and improving on old ones. We entered into a compact to "show up" some of the then flourishing professors of occultism, and began by practicing thought-reading. Within a month we were astonishing Brighton at bazaars and kindred charity entertainments, and enjoyed a great vogue. One of our exhibitions was described very fully and enthusiastically in "Light," the spiritualistic paper, and on the strength of that the Messrs. Myers, Gurney, and Podmore called on us and asked for a private demonstration. As we had made a strict rule never to take payments for our exhibitions, we were accepted by the society as private unpaid demonstrators, and as such remained during the long series of séances.

It is but right to explain that at this period neither of us knew or realized the scientific standing and earnest motive of the gentlemen who had approached us. We saw in them only a superior type of the spiritualistic cranks by whom we were daily pestered. Our first private séance was accepted so unhesitatingly and the lack of reasonable precautions on the part of the "investigators" was so marked, that Smith and I were genuinely amused, and felt it our duty to show how utterly incompetent were these "scientific investigators." Our plan was to bamboozle them thoroughly, then let the world know the value of scientific research. It was the vanity of a schoolboy who catches a master tripping.

A description of the codes and methods of communications invented and employed by us to establish telepathic rapport would need more space than could be spared. Suffice it that, thanks to the ingenuity of Smith, they became marvellously complete. They grew with the demands upon them.

Starting with a crude set of signals produced by the jingling of pince nez, sleeve-links, long and short breathings, and even blowing, they developed to a degree little short of marvellous. To this day no conjurer has succeeded in approaching our great feat, by which Smith, scientifically blindfolded, deafened, and muffled in two blankets, reproduced in detail an irregular figure drawn by Mr. Myers, and seen only by him and me.

The value of a contribution such as this should not lie so much in describing the machinery as in pointing out how and where these investigators failed, so that future investigators may avoid their mistakes.

I say boldly that Messrs. Myers and Gurney were too anxious to get corroboration of their theories to hold the balance impartially. Again and again they gave the benefit of the doubt to experiments that were failures. They allowed us to impose our own conditions, accepted without demur our explantions of failure, and, in short, exhibited a complaisance and confidence which, however complimentary to us, was scarcely consonant with a strict investigation on behalf of the public.

That this same slackness characterized their investigations with other sensitives I am satisfied, for I witnessed many, and the published reports confirmed the suspicion. It is also worthy of note that other sensitives broke down or showed weakness on exactly the same points that Smith and I failed —namely, in visualizing an article difficult to describe in words signalled by a code. A regular figure or familiar object was nearly always seen by the percipient, but when a splotch of ink, or a grotesque irregular figure, had to be transferred from one brain to the other, the result was always failure. We, owing to a very ingenious diagram code, got nearer than anybody, but our limitations were great.

Smith and I, by constant practice, became so sympathetic that we frequently brought off startling hits, which were nothing but flukes. The part that fortuitous accident plays in this business can only be believed by those who have become expert in the art of watching for and seizing an opportunity. When these hits were made, the delight of the investigators caused them to throw off their caution and accept practically anything we offered.

I am aware it may be reasonably objected that the existence of a false coin does not prove the non-existence of a good one. My suggestion as the result of years of observation is that the majority of investigators and reporters in psychical research lack that accurate observation and absence of bias which are essential to rigorous and reliable investigation. In fine, I gravely doubt not the bona fides, but the capacity, of the witnesses. I could fill columns telling how, in the course of my later investigations on behalf of the Society for Psychical Research, I have detected persons of otherwise unimpeachable rectitude touching up and redressing the weak points in their narratives of telepathic experiences.

Mr. Frank Podmore, perhaps the most level-headed of the researchers —and to the end a skeptic—aptly puts it: "It is not the friend whom we know whose eyes must be closed and his ears muffled, but the 'Mr. Hyde,' whose lurking presence in each of us we are only now beginning to suspect."

I am convinced that this propensity to deceive is more general among "persons of character" than is supposed. I have known the wife of a Bishop, when faced with a discrepancy in time of a story of a death in India and the appearance of the wraith in England, [to] deliberately amend her circumstantial story by many hours to fit the altered circumstances. This touching up process in the telepathic stories I have met again and again, and I say, with full regard to the weight of words, that among the hundreds of stories I have investigated I have not met one that had not a weak link which should prevent its being accepted as scientifically established. Coincidences that at first sight appear good cases of telepathic rapport occur to many of us. I have experienced several, but I should hesitate to present them as perfect evidence.

At the risk of giving offense to some, I feel bound to say that in the vast majority of cases that I have investigated the principals are either biased in favor of belief in the supernatural or not persons whom I should regard as accurate observers and capable of estimating the rigid mathematical form of evidence. What one desires to believe requires little corroboration. I shall doubtless raise a storm of protest when I assert that the principal cause of belief in psychic phenomena is the inability of the average man to observe accurately and estimate the value of evidence, plus a bias in favor of the phenomena being real. It is an amazing fact that I have never yet, after hundreds of tests, found a man who could accurately describe ten minutes afterwards a series of simple acts which I performed in his presence. The reports of those trained and conscientious observers, Messrs. Myers and Gurney, contain many absolute inaccuracies. For example, in describing one of my 'experiments,' they say emphatically, "In no case did B. touch S., even in the slightest manner." I touched him eight times, that being the only way in which our code was then worked.

In conclusion, I ask thoughtful persons to consider this proposition: If two youths, with a week's preparation, could deceive trained and careful observers like Messrs. Myers, Gurney, Podmore, Sidgwick, and Romanes, under the most stringent conditions their ingenuity could devise, what are the chances of succeeding inquirers being more successful against "sensitives" who have had the advantage of more years' experience than Smith and I had weeks? Further, I would emphasize the fact that records of telepathic rapport in almost every instance depend upon the statement of one person, usually strongly disposed to belief in the occclt.

Smith and Blackburn's most convincing demonstration took place when Smith was securely blindfolded, his ears stuffed with cotton and putty, and his entire body and the chair he sat in covered by blankets. Myers drew a complicated figure of randomly tangled lines. Blackburn was successful in sending it telepathically to Smith.

When Blackburn wrote his two confessions he was living in South Africa and under the impression that his former friend was no longer living. Actually, Smith not only was alive but he was still employed by the SPR. In an interview in the *Daily News* on September 4 he denied that he and Blackburn had ever used trickery, and that the feat described above was genuine telepathy. However, Blackburn followed with a third article, in the *Daily News* of September 5, in which he gave a detailed account of how the miracle was accomplished. It is hard to believe, but so strong was the mind-set of most SPR members that they believed Smith and accused Blackburn of lying! I know of no parapsychologist today who doubts Blackburn's detailed explanation. Here is an excerpt:

Blackburn began his reply to Smith by writing:

Why does Smith deny my statement? That we had a code is proved because we gave exhibitions of thought reading at Brighton prior to our experiments with the members of the Society for Psychical Research, and no public exhibition without a code is possible.

If I had been aware of Smith's existence, I should not have opened up the subject, for I am aware that Smith spent many of the years that elapsed since our acquaintance in the close association of the leading members of the Society for Psychical Research in a fiduciary capacity. I am also aware that that position was the legitimate reward for his services in connection with our telepathic experiments. I am sorry that I should have unintentionally forced him into having to defend the position he has so long occupied.

If Smith could see, why did he always fail on irregular things? Because our code didn't cover irregular or grotesque things.

We failed so often on the irregular things that the committee abandoned them in the tests.

I have not had access to the original newspaper article. The quotation above is taken from Joseph Rinn's *Sixty Years of Psychical Research* (1950). The following excerpts from the rest of the article are from C. E. M. Hansel's *ESP: A Scientific Evaluation* (1966, revised edition 1980):

The committee had realised the possibility of conveying by signals a description of a regular figure or any object capable of being described in words . . . but the more irregular and indescribable. . . . the greater and wider were the discrepancies between the original and the copy. . . . I had a signal, which I gave Smith when the drawing was impossible. We made a pretence of trying hard, but after a time would give up. . . . As a matter of fact the committee were beginning to have grave doubts when the "great triumph" I shall now describe saved our reputations. . . .

The conditions of the trick were these: Smith sat at a table. His eyes were padded with wool and, I think, a pair of folded kid gloves, and bandaged with a thick, dark cloth. His ears were filled with a layer of cotton-wool, then pellets of putty. His entire body and the chair on which he sat were enveloped in two very heavy blankets. I remember, when he emerged triumphant, he was wet with perspiration, and the paper on which he had successfully drawn the figure was so moist that it broke during the examination by the delighted observers. Beneath his feet and surrounding his chair were thick, soft rugs, rightly intended to deaden and prevent signals by feet shuffles—a nice precaution. . . . At the farther side of . . . a very large dining-room, Mr. Myers showed me, with every precaution, the drawing that I was to transmit to the brain beneath the blankets. It was a tangle of heavy black lines, interlaced, some curved, some straight, the sort of thing an infant playing with a pen or pencil might produce. . . . I took it, fixed my gaze on it, pacing the room meanwhile . . . but always keeping out of touching distance of Smith. These preliminaries occupied perhaps ten minutes, for we made a point of never hurrying. I drew and redrew the figure many times, openly in the presence of the observers, in order, as I explained and they allowed, to fix it in my brain. I also drew it secretly on a cigarette paper. By this time I was fairly expert at palming, and had no difficulty while pacing the room collecting "rapports" in transferring the cigarette paper to the tube of the brass protector on the pencil I was using. I conveyed to Smith the agreed signal that I was ready by stumbling against the edge of the thick rug near his chair.

Next instant he exclaimed "I have it." His right hand came from beneath the blanket, saying, according to the arrangement, "Where's my pencil?" Immediately I placed mine on the table. He took it and a long and anxious pause ensued. . . .

Smith had concealed up his waistcoat one of those luminous painted slates which in the dense darkness gave sufficient light to show the figure when the almost transparent cigarette paper was laid flat on the slate. He pushed up the bandage from one eye and copied the figure with extraordinary accuracy. It occupied over five mintues. During that time I was sitting exhausted with the mental effort quite ten feet away.

Presently Smith threw back the blanket, and excitedly pushing back the eye bandage produced the drawing, which was done on a piece of notepaper and very nearly on the same scale as the original. It was a splendid copy.

Had Myers and Gurney known something about conjuring, they would never have allowed Blackburn to give his pencil to Smith.

Both Gurney and Myers were intimate friends of the American philosopher, psychologist, and psychic investigator William James. According to Ralph Barton Perry, one of James's biographers, Gurney was the dearest of his friends among the SPR. In a letter to his wife, James described Gurney as "one of the first-rate minds of our time . . . a magnificent Adonis, six feet four in height, with an extremely handsome face, voice, and general air of distinction about him." James called Gurney's book on music, *The Power of Sound* (1880), "the best work on aesthetics ever published." He praised Gurney's "metaphysical power," and said there was a "very unusual sort of affinity between my mind and his. . . . I eagerly devoured every word he wrote." *Phantasms of the Living* was for James "an amazingly patient and thorough piece of work. . . . I should not at all wonder if it were the beginning of a new chapter in natural history." For James's equally great admiration of Myers, see his tribute to Myers in his *Memories and Studies*.

Unlike his wife, James's younger sister Alice was skeptical of her brother's psychic enthusiasms, and had a low opinion of both Myers and Gurney. In letters to William she called Myers an "idiot," and described Gurney as "weak" and "effeminate"—a man who had been persuaded by Myers to marry an ignorant woman far beneath him. Curiously, Myers insisted on accompanying his friend on his honeymoon in Switzerland even though Gurney's wife Kate strongly objected. Kate, Alice wrote, chattered constantly on all subjects with "extreme infelicity." She was ignored and constantly snubbed by her husband who quickly regretted marrying her.

Gurney killed himself in 1888, in a hotel at Brighton, by inhaling chloroform. Trevor Hall in *The Strange Case of Edmund Gurney* (1964) conjectures that Gurney's mounting depression was caused not so much by his unhappy marriage as by a realization, many years before Blackburn confessed, of how thoroughly he had been flimflammed by Smith, his trusted friend.

32 | William James and Mrs. Piper

> I should be willing now to stake as much money on Mrs. Piper's honesty as on that of anyone I know, and am quite satisfied to leave my reputation for wisdom or folly, so far as human nature is concerned, to stand or fall by this declaration.
>
> —William James (*Proceedings of the Society for Psychical Research,* Vol. 6, 1889/90, p. 654)

William James (1842–1910), considered by many to be America's most distinguished philosopher, psychologist, and pioneer psychic investigator, was a Platonist in the following sense. He believed that the world open to our experience and scientific probing is only a small fraction of a much vaster realm about which we know nothing. Our universe, he liked to say, is a tiny island in a vast Mother Sea. Such a vision may lead to a healthy acceptance of strange phenomena as worthy of investigation. It can also lead, as in James's case, to a careless acceptance of anomalies without first making a strenuous effort to be sure such phenomena exist.

James's Platonism helps explain his lifelong fascination with mediums. His father, Henry James, Sr., was a spiritualist who wrote a book about Emanuel Swedenborg, the famous Swedish trance medium. Although not in any sense a Christian, William James believed in an afterlife, which he defended with a clever model of the brain in his little book *Human Immortality.* He was a founder and life member of the ASPR (American Society for Psychical Research). Many of his best friends, notably the British psychic investigators Frederic Myers and Edmund Gurney, were spiritualists.

James was never able to persuade himself that mediums channeled voices from the dead, though he always remained open to this possibility. He was, however, firmly convinced that some mediums had paranormal powers, even though their "controls" were perhaps what he called "counter-

---

This essay was serialized in *Free Inquiry,* Spring and Summer 1992, and is reprinted with permission.

feit" personalities conjured up by a medium's subconscious mind.

Mrs. Piper is still considered the most famous, most trustworthy, direct-voice medium who ever lived. No one ever caught her in fraud. Unlike other famous mediums of the time, she never produced physical phenomena such as levitated tables, floating trumpets, luminous ectoplasm from her nose, rappings, cold breezes, spirit photographs, unearthly music, strange odors, or other wonders which, for reasons spiritualists were never able to explain, took place in near total darkness. To James's credit he was strongly skeptical of such manifestations and did not hesitate to brand as charlatans such mediums as Madam Blavatsky and Eusapia Palladino.[1]

Mrs. Piper simply went into trances, during which discarnates took over her vocal chords or seized her hand, which would rapidly write what the spirits dictated. After a trance she insisted she recalled nothing of what had transpired. On one occasion James asked the control to order her (like a hypnotist commanding a mesmerized subject) to remember everything, but the ploy did not work. We shall see later why such claimed amnesia is of great advantage to a medium.

Leonora Evelina Simonds (1859-1950) was born in Nashua, New Hampshire. She never finished high school. When twenty-two she married William J. Piper, identified in some references as a Boston store clerk and in others as a Boston tailor. (It would be surprising if his middle name were James.) For a while the Pipers lived with William's parents. William's father was an ardent spiritualist. Later William and Leonora moved to Pinckney Street, in Boston's Beacon Hill section, where they raised two daughters, Minerva and Alta. Alta wrote *The Life and Work of Mrs. Piper* in 1929. Both daughters became professional musicians. I do not know when or where either died.

Mrs. Piper was tall, stout, and handsome, with blue eyes and brown hair; she was good-natured, self-possessed, matronly, modest, and shrewd. In his *History of Spiritualism* Conan Doyle says that a head injury preceded her discovery that she could contact the dead. Alta Piper, in her biography of her mother, describes the injury as a mysterious sharp blow over her right ear that occurred when Leonora was eight, followed by a voice that said, "Aunt Sara, not dead, but with you still." Later Leonora learned of her aunt's death.

In 1884 an ice sled struck Leonora, injuring her internally. Soon there-after she developed an ovarian tumor, which was later removed along with her fallopian tubes. Her spiritualist father-in-law persuaded her to seek advice about the tumor from J. E. Cocke, a blind medium and healer who liked to develop mediumship in others. On her second visit she fell into a trance. After awakening she was told that a young Indian girl with the improbable name of Chlorine had spoken through her. Mrs. Piper was soon giving her own private séances, charging each client (as she liked to call a sitter) a dollar per sitting. This would have been a considerable sum in today's currency. In later years the fee was raised to $20. The Society of Psychical Research (SPR) in England eventually provided her with a trust income sufficient to support her and her two daughters.

James's mother-in-law was so impressed after attending a Piper séance (the control told her where to find a lost bank book) that she recommended the medium to William. James began attending and soon encouraged a raft of relatives and friends to take part in Mrs. Piper's sittings. Alice, James's wife, was quickly convinced that Mrs. Piper was indeed channeling voices from the dead. As one of James's biographers puts it, Alice was "credulous" where William was merely "curious."

After her fame spread abroad, Mrs. Piper made three trips to England under the auspices of the SPR. During an 1889–1890 visit, she and her daughters stayed in Frederic Myers's home, and later in the homes of physicist Oliver Lodge and other SPR members. Her next two trips were supervised by the SPR. In England her two most famous converts, who became absolutely convinced she was channeling discarnates, were Myers and Lodge.

In America her most eminent convert was James Hyslop, a professor of logic and ethics at Columbia University, a man as gullible and ignorant of magic as Doyle. Through Mrs. Piper he conversed with his mother, brother, and uncles. He wrote in *Life After Death,* one of his many worthless books:

> I regard the existence of discarnate spirits as scientifically proved, and I no longer refer to the sceptic as having any right to speak on the subject. Any man who does not accept the existence of discarnate spirits and the proof of it is either ignorant or a moral coward. I give him short shrift, and do not propose any longer to argue with him.

Mrs. Piper liked to begin a séance by asking for a personal possession of either the sitter or the spirit the client wished to contact. It could be a watch, ring, necktie, lock of hair, sweater, and so on. (Getting the right vibes from such an object is known in the trade as "psychometry.") In his autobiography Lodge says that it took Mrs. Piper a long time to move in and out of a trance, "going through contortions which were sometimes painful to watch." James speaks of the "great muscular unrest" that preceded her trance. Her pupils dilated, she moaned and sobbed, her eyes rolled upward, and her ears wiggled violently in a way James says she could not move them when awake. How did James know? Mrs. Piper said so. Later, her transitions between the trance state and awake became much calmer, although curiously it always took her longer to emerge from the state than to go into it. In these later years her breathing became slower during a trance, and she snored throughout. She claimed to feel a snapping in her head when the trance ended. Sitters would witness weeping, disjointed mutterings, and exclamations of pleasure, pain, and sometimes disgust; her eyes would be open and staring, and saliva would drool from her lips.

Alta Piper writes that when her mother came out of a trance she always saw people in the room as small and black, and often greeted a sitter with "Oh! How black you are!" Alta adds that her mother "always resumes the conversation at that point where it was broken off before the sitting began."

James and others tried to hypnotize Mrs. Piper, but she never went beyond a light sleep, her body limp and unlike her trance condition. During one trance she ignored a small cut James made on her left wrist. It did not bleed, Alta tells us, but when her mother awoke it "bled freely," leaving a permanent scar. When a lighted match was pressed on her arm, her control said it "felt cool." She remained undisturbed when a needle was pushed into her hand and when a French investigator stuck a feather up her nose. On the other hand, she reacted if the doorbell rang. On one occasion her control tested a medicine he advised a sitter to take by having Mrs. Piper dip her finger into the liquid then put her finger to her forehead, after which he declared that the medicine had been properly prepared. When a piece of onion was put in her mouth, she smacked her lips and the control said he could taste it.

Mrs. Piper's voice, like the voices of today's trance channelers, always altered when different controls took over. Males spoke like males, children like children. Irishmen had Irish brogues. Frenchmen and Italians had French and Italian accents. Lodge had no doubt he conversed with his dead sister Anne because he recognized her "well remembered voice."

When Mrs. Piper later lived in Arlington Heights, near Boston, her séances were held in an upstairs room she called her Red Room because its wallpaper and furnishings were red. A clock in the darkened room was kept illuminated. One skeptic dared suggest that this was so she could know when to end a séance, since she preferred that it not go beyond an hour.

After Chlorine, Mrs. Piper's earliest controls included Martin Luther, Commodore Cornelius Vanderbilt, Longfellow, George Washington, Lincoln, Loretta Pachini (a young Italian), J. Sebastian Bach, and Sarah Siddons (an English actress). After they stopped coming, the next and most famous of all her controls was an eighteenth-century French physician named Dr. Phinuit (pronounced Fih-*nuee*), who had died of leprosy. Phinuit had a deep, gruff voice. Oddly, Phinuit sounds very much like the French physician Dr. Albert G. Finnett (pronounced *Finee*), the control of the blind medium who launched Mrs. Piper on her career.

Dr. Phinuit said he came from Metz, but strenuous efforts to find evidence of a doctor by that name who lived in Metz were fruitless even though the doctor gave his birth and death dates. Phinuit spoke English with a stage French accent, but was unable to speak French even though Mrs. Piper said she had studied French for two years. Nor could Phinuit understand James when he spoke in French, or recognize the names of French drugs. Later he said he had lived so long in Marseilles, in an English speaking colony, that he had lost all knowledge of French except for such phrases as *bonjour* and *au revoir!*

The next major control, who continued for a time in parallel with Phinuit, was known as G. P., the initials of George Pelham. The name was a pseudonym used by the ASPR to conceal the identity of George Pellew, a young lawyer by training but a writer by profession. He wrote a dissertation on Jane Austen and published two books, *In Castle and Gable* and *Women of the Commonwealth.* Pellew died in 1882 at age thirty-two in New York City after falling off a horse. A month later he turned up as one of Mrs. Piper's favorite controls.

Pellew had been a good friend of Richard Hodgson, a British psychic investigator who came to Boston in 1887 to serve as secretary of the ASPR and editor of its journal. He died in 1909 of heart failure while playing handball. Hodgson and Pellew became friends, often arguing about life after death, in which Hodgson believed but Pellew did not. When Pellew began coming through Mrs. Piper, Hodgson was at first so suspicious that he hired a detective to shadow Mr. and Mrs. Piper for several weeks to make sure they were not secretly researching "evidential" information about his friend. But when Mrs. Piper put Hodgson in touch with the spirit of a former girlfriend in Australia (Hodgson came from Melbourne) who informed him for the first time of her death, Hodgson abandoned all doubts.

Early in her career Mrs. Piper channeled only voices, but gradually the voices gave way to automatic writing. During her voice period the séances were either not recorded or notes were taken by stenographers, but of course the automatic writing provided its own record of what the controls said. Unfortunately records were seldom kept of what the sitters said.

During a trance Mrs. Piper would turn her head to one side, on a pillow, while her right hand rapidly scribbled messages. The writing was often illegible and subject to different interpretations. Frequently she pressed so hard that a pencil would break. At other times her hand would violently sweep the writing paper off the table. For a while Mrs. Piper spoke and wrote at the same time. On at least two known occasions, three sitters received simultaneous communications, a vocal one from Phinuit, a written one from G. P. through one hand, and another written by a deceased sister of the sitter through the other hand. Writing with both hands was not hard to do because Mrs. Piper was ambidextrous. She was normally left-handed, but wrote and sewed with her right, and could handle a fork equally well with either hand.

One time Mrs. Piper pressed a sheet to her forehead and wrote on it in mirror-reversed script. (Try this and you will be surprised at how easily it can be done with paper on your forehead.) Mrs. Piper's right hand did more than write while she was in a trance. It also functioned as a strange kind of telephone to the controls. If sitters wanted to ask a question, they held the hand close to their mouth and spoke into it with a loud voice.

In 1896 the controls became a group called the Imperators. They had earlier been the controls of William Stainton Moses, a famous British medium. They were immortals on a higher plane who had such names as Imperator, Rector, Director, and Mentor, and who talked constantly about God, heaven, and the angels. In 1905 this group (someone suggested it should have been called the Imposters) gave way to the dead Richard Hodgson. However, Rector would appear first, then locate Hodgson in the spirit world and bring him to Mrs. Piper. At the end of a séance he would return to pronounce a benediction.

James had known Hodgson well. The spirit of Hodgson did his best to persuade James it was actually he, but James never budged from the fence. Whenever he asked Hodgson for details about the other side, Hodgson either driveled nonsense or refused to answer. After Hodgson vanished, there were many other controls, including the dead Frederic Myers and Edmund Gurney.

At about this time England's SPR began experimenting with what it called "cross correspondence." The idea was to have Mrs. Piper and several other mediums in distant localities seek simultaneous messages from the same discarnate. The messages were then checked for correlations. Doyle gives some examples in his history of spiritualism that would impress nobody except himself. For example, Mrs. Piper would get a message with the word *violet* in it. Another medium would channel a message that referred to "violet buds." (For a detailed analysis of these correspondences, see the book by Amy Tanner discussed in my epilogue.)

Every psychic investigator of Mrs. Piper was impressed by her simplicity and honesty. It never occurred to them that no charlatan ever achieves great success by acting like a charlatan. No professional spy acts like a spy. No card cheat behaves at the table like a card cheat. No successful con artist acts like a con artist. No fake psychic ever gives the impression of being anything but honest.

What convinced so many intelligent persons that the dead actually spoke through Mrs. Piper? It was the astonishing amount of information she provided that she seemed to have no normal way of acquiring. Even James was persuaded that she got this information by paranormal means, although he doubted it came from discarnates. A common conjecture of the time was that Mrs. Piper was telepathic and clairvoyant, picking up data from the minds of sitters, or from the minds of others far away, or from a clairvoyant viewing of letters, tombstones, and so on. It was even suggested that her controls had such ESP. James did not buy this theory. He was inclined to believe that she was tapping into some part of the transcendent Mother Sea. Using diagrams and playing cards, he once gave Mrs. Piper tests for telepathy and clairvoyance, all of which she totally failed.

How can a hard-nose skeptic like myself account for the seeming flood of accurate data that constantly flowed from Mrs. Piper's controls?

A reading of verbatim records of Mrs. Piper's séances shows that her controls did an enormous amount of what was then called "fishing" and today is called "cold reading." First a vague statement is made, followed by more precise statements depending on a sitter's reactions. Mrs. Piper liked to hold a client's hand throughout the sitting, or even to place the hand against her forehead. This made it easy to detect muscular reactions even when a sitter remained silent.

During a trance Mrs. Piper's eyes were often only half-closed, so it was also easy for her to observe how a sitter responded to fishing. If a reaction, often a spoken one, is unfavorable, the medium at once takes off on a different tack. If the reaction is favorable, the medium knows he or she is on the right track. Many tests have shown that victims of skillful cold reading are never aware of how they subtly guide what the cold reader is saying. Afterward they will vigorously deny they made statements indicating whether the medium was right or wrong, and are astounded when they listen to a recording.

Dr. Phinuit had a habit of babbling on and on, making inane conversation while he shamelessly fished. If he made an outright mistake, he followed with silly excuses. Often when asked a question he could not answer, he would profess deafness and leave. His ignorance of science and literature was monumental, yet he was well informed about hats and clothing! Frequently a client would get nothing from Mrs. Piper, James wrote, but "tiresome twaddle" and "unknown names and trivial talk."[2] To any skeptic, this indicated either that the client was carefully uncooperative during a cold reading, that Mrs. Piper had no advance information, or both.

When you read books about Mrs. Piper by believers, such as the anthology *William James on Psychical Research,* edited by Gardner Murphy and Robert

Ballou, you will learn only about her hits—nothing about her abundant misses. On one occasion Mrs. Piper told James that a certain ring had been stolen, but it was later found in James's house. On three occasions Phinuit tried to guess the contents of a sealed envelope in James's possession. All three were failures even though Phinuit contacted Hannah Wild, the very person who wrote James the letter! In a typical séance hundreds of statements would be made, and there were thousands of séances. By chance alone one would expect some fantastic lucky guesses. The verbatim records reveal a weird mixture of hits and misses. Believers of course forget the misses—"selective amnesia," it has been called—and remember only the hits.

On many occasions a Piper control would *pretend* to be fishing to give the impression that something was partly but not fully known. This is a common dodge of mediums, as well as magicians who perform what in the trade is called a "mental act." For example, when a control tried to give the name of Mrs. James's father, which everyone in the area knew to be Gibbens, the control first tried "Niblin," then "Giblin," before finally getting it right. The name of Herman, a child of James who, as everyone knew, died the previous year, was first spelled "Herrin."

On another occasion James's deceased father thanked William for bringing out a certain book. "What book?" James asked. His father could do no better than spell L-i, the first two letters of the title. The book was *Literary Remains of the Late Henry James,* a collection of his father's papers. Of course the title would have been well known to Mrs. Piper, but James was actually persuaded that she could not be faking her partial guess. Why? Because had she known the complete title she would surely have given it! Phinuit's stumbling, spelling, and otherwise "imperfect ways of bringing out his facts," James wrote, "is a great drawback with most sitters, and yet it is habitual with him." I am reminded of how Merv Griffin, introducing Uri Geller on his television talk show, said the thing that convinced him Geller was not a magician was that magician's tricks always work, whereas Uri's paranormal feats sometimes fail!

Although true believers were overwhelmed by the accuracy of information coming through Mrs. Piper, skeptics had exactly the opposite reaction. According to Joseph Rinn in his *Sixty Years of Psychic Research,* Hodgson constantly lied in reporting on how members of the Pellew family reacted to what George Pellew said through Mrs. Piper. Hodgson repeatedly spoke of how they confirmed what George's spirit was saying, but exactly the opposite was the case. George's mother called the data "utter drivel." In 1921 Rinn came upon a series of letters written by George's brother Charles when he was a professor of chemistry at Columbia University. (In 1923 Charles succeeded to his British father's title and became Viscount Exmoouth and a member of the House of Lords.) The letters had been written to Edward Clodd, author of an anti-spiritualist book called *The Question: If a Man Die, Shall He Live Again?*—published in London in 1917. The letters were later printed in an annual of London's Rationalist Press Association. Here is the full text of one of Charles's letters, sent to Clodd in 1918:

> I must apologize for delaying so long in answering your letter of inquiry about Mrs. Piper, but I have been engaged in some extremely important professional work, necessitating some weeks' stay in Washington, and have only just got a chance to clear up my correspondence.
>
> My brother G. P. died very suddenly, by accident, some twenty-five years ago. He was an exceedingly clever fellow, of remarkable literary ability, and had written one or two good books, had taken the prize at Harvard for an essay which, together with his class O.K., is still passed down by the staff of their English Department as indicating the "high-water mark" of student ability.
>
> At his funeral, one friend, a famous novelist (Mr. Howells) begged father and myself to have his poems collected and published, saying that he considered two of them as among the very finest sonnets in the English language. A very well-known historian and essayist (John Fiske) told me to be sure and print some essays of his on philosophy, which he assured us were well worth preserving, in permanent form.
>
> The poems were gradually sorted out from various papers and scrapbooks, and a collection of them was published a few months later. We could not, however, put our hands on his philosophical papers, though we heard from various friends who believed they must still be in existence.
>
> A few weeks after George's death, word came to us from some very excitable friends of his in Boston that they had been in communication with his spirit, through the medium Mrs. Piper. One of the first questions asked of him, so we were told, was, "Where are those philosophical notes of yours?" Back came the answer, "At Katonah," this being the name of our country place, not far from New York City. "Whereabouts at Katonah?" "In a tin box, in the corner cupboard in my bedroom," came the reply.
>
> As I remember the story, it was one of his friends, possibly a cousin, who immediately started for Katonah and went to the bedroom, in the corner cupboard, and found the tin dispatch box—*empty.*
>
> The papers themselves, as I only found some twenty years later, when of course their value was entirely gone, were at the time in the possession of one of G. P.'s friends, to whom he had given them before his death.
>
> This was the closest that Mrs. Piper ever came, so far as I know, to saying anything that might conceivably have come from my brother, although for weeks and months, and even years, we were continually bombarded with like reports of interviews of all sorts and conditions of people with him under the auspices of the Psychical Research Society.
>
> After this had been going on for at least fifteen years, my people showed me, one New Year's, a letter they had just received from Hodgson. He reminded

them that ever since G. P.'s death his society had been sending them repeatedly the bulletins and reports of the Piper sittings where G. P. was involved and that, undoubtedly, my parents had long been convinced, as was every other intelligent and unprejudiced reader, that they had at least been able to prove, without question, the existence of G. P.'s own self in the other kingdom, etc., and that, while of course the mere question of a few dollars was not of any importance to any of them, he did hope that my father and mother would become regular members of the Psychical Research Society, and have their names published as such, to show their acceptance of the accuracy of the conversations with my brother.

To which Mrs. Pellew, George's mother, replied briefly, and, it seems to me, not without a very considerable amount of intelligence and good, sound common sense. It was to the effect "that they had been receiving, for years past, numerous communications from the society concerning supposed interviews of various people with my brother, and some of these they had read more or less carefully. Everybody, however, who had ever met G. P. in life had always been impressed by the fact that his keen, clear, brilliant intellect was unfortunately kept down by a weak body. And that nothing could possibly convince her, who knew G. P. so well, that, when that wonderful mind and spirit of his was freed from the trammels of the flesh, it could under any conceivable circumstances, have given vent to such utter drivel and initially as purported, in those communications, to have been uttered by him," and they did not join the society.

For my own part, I was telling this story once, before a meeting just addressed by one of Mrs. Piper's most ardent believers, and was informed that I evidently had not, myself, carefully read the reports in question—which was the case. So, next day, I went to the public library and getting hold of some of the *Transactions* of the Psychical Research Society, I hunted round in them to find some characteristic interview with my brother. I soon found one. An old friend, so I gathered, or certainly an acquaintance, was at last put in touch with him, per Mrs. Piper, and began to identify him. "You hear what I say, George?"—"Yes."—"You are sure you understand me?"—"Yes, go ahead."—"Well, George, listen to this carefully: '*Pater hemon.*' "—"Pat?"— "Do you understand, George? '*Pater, hemon ho en toise ouranois.*' "—"Pat— what is that? I don't quite catch it." I chuckled. Whoever it was answering that fellow, whether Mrs. Piper or Phenuit or anyone else, it was *not George*.

George was a good scholar, and had been at St. Paul's School, Concord, N.H., for at least five years, and had, every Monday morning of his school term, to recite, and hear his classmates recite, the Lord's Prayer in Greek.

Unless I'm very much mistaken, it was some old friend of his who was trying him with the first words, knowing that if George was there he would recognize them *instantly,* as I did some ten or fifteen years later, just seeing them in print this way.

The most curious evidence, to my mind, of the absolute unreliability of any statement of the believers in the Mrs. Piper cult happened to me in connection with these same philosophy papers I spoke about.

I had supposed the Piper nuisance had faded away, not having heard of it for a year or two, when, having run over to Washington to see my people, I was shown a curious letter from Hodgson. It was something to this effect: "Of course they all knew and regretted that my parents so persistently refused to recognize the truth of those wonderful interviews with George, but that now they had some evidence which was convincing—absolute, positive proof. My people knew John Fiske, what a clever, keen mind he had, what a close friend of George he was, and what a hardheaded, practical, unemotional sort of fellow—well, he had at last been persuaded to see Mrs. Piper—much against his wishes—sure that it would amount to nothing—and yet, after a sitting with her, he had come out *absolutely convinced* that he had been talking with his dear old friend George. He had even asked him some questions about points in Revolutionary history, which George had either discovered or was going to discuss with his, George's, ancestors, who had been prominent in that period, etc. And really, when John Fiske was so absolutely and completely convinced of the truth of the interview, my own people ought to reconsider their position in the matter."

I told my father to reserve judgment, and a few days afterward returned to New York.

Within a week or two, happening to be at the Century Club at one of their monthly gatherings, I saw big, jolly, burly John Fiske walk into the reading room. I at once hailed him (I had met him only a few times): "How are you, Mr. Fiske? Do you remember me, Charles Pellew? By the way, I hear you've been having a talk recently with my brother George." Fiske stopped—gasped, "Good heavens—your brother George—why, he's been dead for twenty years!" "That's all right," said I; "through Mrs. Piper, I mean." "Oh," and he paused—relaxed—and his whole voice changed. "*That old fraud!*" and he sat down and began to laugh. "Why," I said, "I heard that you said there was no doubt about his being George himself, just as though he was at the other end of a rather poor telephone connection." "*That's a lie,*" he said; "nothing of the sort. I was finally persuaded to see Mrs. Piper, and found her a bright, shrewd, ill-educated, commonplace woman who answered glibly enough questions where guessing was easy, or where she might have obtained previous information. But whenever I asked anything that would be known only to George himself, she was either silent or entirely wrong. For instance, I asked as follows: 'Is this you, George?'—'Yes.'—'You know who I am?'—'Yes, my old friend, you, George?'—'Yes.'—'You know who I am?'—'Yes, my old friend John Fiske.'—'When did you see me last?'—'In Cambridge, at your house, a few months before I passed over.'—'What sort of house is mine?'—'A wooden house, two stories, hall in the middle, dining room on one side, library and study on the other.' And so it *was,* but *almost all the Cambridge houses are just that style.*

" 'Now," said Fiske, "that winter I had just published my book on philosophy, and George had amused himself by writing some very clever, very remarkable papers, in which he criticized my views quite severely. And, before publishing them, he was so afraid of hurting my feelings that the dear old boy wrote me to say he was coming to Cambridge to talk it over with me. He sent me his manuscript, which I read carefully, and then he came on by night from New York, and was at my house soon after breakfast. We talked philosophy until nearly twelve o'clock, when I started him home. Now I think if he remembered the date of the visit, and the house and arrangement of the rooms, he might have *had some slight remembrance of what we were talking about.*"

Of course you can use this letter in any way you wish.

Yours very sincerely,
Charles E. Pellew

As Charles's remarkable letter makes plain, Hodgson told outright lies about how Fiske had reacted to the séance he attended. John Fiske was a Harvard philosopher and historian, and a friend of William James. He was a devout theist and a believer in immortality, but he was also less gullible than James with respect to alleged psychic phenomena. Note how Mrs. Piper, who knew no Greek, took the word *Pater,* Greek for "Father" in the opening line of the Lord's Prayer, to refer to someone named Pat!

The tendency of believers to take vague statements uttered by a medium, and then fit circumstances to them, is brought out vividly by Rinn in giving some of Mrs. Piper's remarks that poor Hyslop considered evidential. Hyslop's dead father, speaking through Mrs. Piper, said that just before his death he had visited Hyslop. Hyslop called this evidential because his father had visited him several years before he died. The father's spirit spoke of a box of minerals he had owned as a boy. Hyslop scored this a hit because his father had owned a box of Indian arrowheads. In his book *Science and a Future Life* Hyslop said it took two years for Mrs. Piper to guess correctly what his uncle died from. Telepathy cannot account for Mrs. Piper's knowledge, Hyslop argued, because it took her twenty sittings to guess his uncle's name. "There was great difficulty in getting the name of my uncle James Carruthers," he wrote. "I had asked Mrs. Piper's spirit control to spell it out after failing in the first attempt. It was tried again the next day with no results." To a skeptic, this simply indicates that Mrs. Piper, at the time, didn't know the name.

Some notion of Hyslop's competence as an investigator can be gained from his practice of wearing a mask to conceal his identity when he entered a room for a séance, then removing it after Mrs. Piper went into a trance. Hyslop assumed that while in a trance Mrs. Piper could not see him even though her eyes were half-open. Before she awoke, he put the mask on again. Of course Hyslop had been introduced to Mrs. Piper by Hodgson, who could have provided the medium with all sorts of facts about him.

In *Modern Spiritualism,* Frank Podmore came to the following conclusion after going carefully over the verbatim reports of Mrs. Piper's séances with Hyslop:

> I cannot point to a single instance in which a precise and unambiguous piece of information has been furnished of a kind which could not have proceeded from the medium's own mind, working upon the materials provided and the hints let drop by the sitter.

Romaine Newbold, a philosopher at the University of Pennsylvania, after making many tests of Mrs. Piper, concluded: "In all the years of Mrs. Piper's mediumship, she made no revelation to science, her efforts in astronomy were utterly childish, her prophecy untrue. She never has revealed one scrap of useful knowledge. She never could reveal the contents of a test letter left by Dr. Hodgson."

Myers also left a sealed test letter for mediums to try to read. Myers himself, speaking through Mrs. Piper, was unable to read the letter as Hodgson's spirit could not read Hodgson's test letter. Myers's wife wrote to the London *Morning Post* (October 24, 1908) stating that she and her son found nothing in all the messages from Myers purporting to come through mediums that "we can consider of the smallest evidential value."

When Rinn asked Mrs. Piper's Dr. Phinuit if he had ever treated Esther Horton in Marseilles, George Pellew seized Mrs. Piper's hand and wrote "Esther Horton is very weak—cannot-cannot now—will try some other time." Rinn had invented the name, which of course meant nothing to Mrs. Piper. After Rinn explained the trap to Hodgson, he was never invited to another Piper séance.

The following *New York Times* editorial (July 9, 1909) gave an accurate summary of what everybody outside the small circle of believers thought of Mrs. Piper:

> We have no desire to deride the few men of learning in this age who hold to a spiritual conception of the universe, but when, like Sir Oliver Lodge and Professor James, they carry their theories so far as to accept, or at least dally with, supposed communications from the spirit world through trance mediums, their experiences will inevitably be compared with those of Robert Dale Owen and Luther Marsh. Owen received with an "open mind" the antics and sayings of the materialized Katy King, and lived to see the medium he had trusted thoroughly exposed as a common impostor. So did Marsh.
>
> Professor James is not willing to declare that the "Richard Hodgson" who maundered and chattered with the tongue of the medium Mrs. Piper is the veritable soul of his dead friend Dr. Richard Hodgson, but obviously he should like to believe it. To the practical mind, Mrs. Piper is either a

rank impostor, kindred to Browning's Sludge, and nearly all the other mediums who have forced themselves into public notice since the era of the Fox sisters, or a neurotic person subject to self-hypnosis.

Mrs. Piper's talk in trance, as quoted in the *Proceedings of the American Society for Psychical Research,* reads like the unutterable nonsense spoken by persons in hypnotic trance. Some of it must have sounded like the rambling of a phonograph out of order. But in the gift of evasion of direct questions to Richard Hodgson's spirit, it closely resembled the spirits called up in dark séances by all fraudulent mediums. The unseen ghosts of the Psychical Researchers are a poor, aimless lot, occasionally droll, but never convincing to anybody who has not made up his mind as to the honesty of the medium. Mrs. Piper is so ineffective as a medium, we are willing to believe that she is self-deluded. So are Professor James and Professor Hyslop.

On one occasion Hodgson asked Mrs. Piper to describe what a certain Mrs. Howard was doing at that moment. The control said she was pressing violets in a book, writing letters to two persons (who were named), then going upstairs to look in a drawer. These actions were corroborated by Mrs. Howard's daughter, except they all occurred on the day *before* the séance. (There was one error. Mrs. Howard put the violets in a drawer, not a book.) I was unable to learn if the daughter was present during the séance. If so, Mrs. Piper could have obtained the information by cold reading. Or did Hodgson inform Mrs. Piper in advance about the test, so that her servant woman could check with Mrs. Howard's servant? Surely either explanation is more plausible than Mrs. Piper's control clairvoyantly saw what Mrs. Howard did the day before.

Charles Peirce, James's skeptical philosopher friend, said that, when he attended one of Piper's séances, at no time did he think he was conversing with anybody except Mrs. Piper. Thomas W. M. Lund, chaplain of the School for the Blind, in Liverpool, made the following comment about a séance with Mrs. Piper in *The Proceedings of the Society for Psychical Research* (vol. 6, 1889/90, p. 534):

> With regard to my experience of Mrs. Piper, I do not feel that I saw enough to form data for any satisfactory conclusion. What impressed me most was the way in which she seemed to feel for information, rarely telling me anything of importance right off the reel, but carefully fishing, and then following up a lead. It seemed to me that when she got on a right tack, the nervous and uncontrollable movement of one's muscles gave her the signal that she was right and might steam ahead.

Lund goes on to say that among Mrs. Piper's usual mix of hits and misses she correctly told him his son was ill and that his wife planned to visit the son. However, he recalled that before the séance began he told Mrs. Lodge about his son's illness and his wife's plans "within earshot of Mrs. Piper." Here is how Mrs. Piper guessed the name of Lund's sister. "She then tried to find the name and went through a long list; at last she said it had 'ag' in the middle." After a favorable reaction, she said that the spirit taking over her vocal chords was named Maggie. When he asked Maggie why he wasn't there when she died, the control said "I'm getting weak now—*au revoir.*" Of course if Lund had not agreed that "ag" was in the name, the spirit would have continued along other lines. Incidentally, although Mrs. Piper knew Lund's name in advance of the séance, her control opened the sitting by asking, "Where's Mr. London?" Lund writes: "She made several attempts to arrive at my real name, Lund, but failed, saying that she couldn't pronounce it."

In later séances Lund's dead sister tried to explain why he was absent when she died, but the guesses were totally wrong. Here is how Lund summed up his final opinions:

> Altogether there was such a mixture of the true and false, the absurd and rational, the vulgar commonplace of the crafty fortune-teller with startling reality, that I have no theory to offer—merely the above facts. I should require much more evidence than I yet have, and with much more careful testing of it, to convince me (1) that Mrs. Piper was unconscious; (2) that there was any thought-reading beyond the clever guessing of a person trained in that sort of work; (3) that there was any ethereal communication with a spirit-world. I did not like the sudden weakness experience when I pressed my supposed sister for the reason of my absence at her death, and the delay wanted for giving a reply.

Even Myers, in the same issue of the *JSPR,* admitted there were striking differences between Mrs. Piper's honesty when awake, and the obvious dishonesty of her controls. He tells how her trances had a way of degenerating into sessions during which Dr. Phinuit's conversation consists "wholly of fishing questions and random assertions" which extract "information from the sitter under the guise of giving it."

One of the most bizarre of all cases involving Mrs. Piper concerned her attempt, like so many of today's psychics, to locate a missing person who had been reported dead. Dean Connor, the son of an assistant postmaster in Burling, Vermont, went to Mexico in 1894 and was believed to have died there. Dean's father had a vivid dream in which his son appeared and told him he was alive and held as a captive while someone else had been buried in his place. Hodgson heard about the dream and arranged for a friend of the Connor family to visit Mrs. Piper. In a trance, Mrs.

Piper said that the boy had been drugged, sent to a nearby mental hospital run by a Dr. Gintz, and a dead body had been put in the coffin. The control recommended that the coffin be opened and the body examined. So convinced was the sitter of Mrs. Piper's powers that he actually went to Mexico and had the body exhumed. He brought back from the decomposed corpse, which had not been embalmed, a sample of its hair. Doctors in Vermont thought it too dark to be the son's hair. Believers in Mrs. Piper were jubilant.

The *Boston Globe* was so taken by the story that it dispatched one of its reporters to Mexico to investigate. He there obtained conclusive evidence that Dean Connor had indeed died in a hospital, of typhoid fever, and had been buried. His body had not been embalmed because it was considered too expensive for the family. A nurse who had been in charge of Connor when he died said that the hair of typhoid victims often darkens after death. An injury to the son's left ring finger was visible on the skeleton. No trace could be found of a Dr. Gintz, or even of a nearby mental hospital. For more details about this weird series of events, check the summary in Rinn's book or look up fuller details in a book that the reporter, A. J. Philpot, wrote in 1897.

How did Hodgson respond to Philpot's investigation? He refused to believe the boy was dead. If he had the funds, he said, he would go to Mexico himself and find the lad alive. The *Boston Globe* then ran a headline on their first page offering to pay all of Hodgson's expenses for such a trip. Hodgson turned the offer down. You'll not find this story, or other stories about Mrs. Piper's abject failures, in any book by a believer in her powers. Nor are such failures cited by William James in his many articles about Mrs. Piper.

Although it is conceivable that cunning cold reading may account for all of Mrs. Piper's hits, I believe that, especially in her early years, she had other methods up her sleeves. We must not forget that she was constantly seeing friends and relatives of her clients. A vast amount of personal information can come through in the give and take of séance conversation, to be fed back to clients in later sessions. Because believers in Mrs. Piper were convinced she could recall nothing of what was said during a séance, it never occurred to them that Mrs. Piper might be lying, and that what she learned in one session could be used in a later one. We are told that much of the evidential data in her earlier séances was of such a personal nature it could not be published. Indeed, the large bulk of the records of her séances remains unpublished to this day, being stored in the archives of the SPR and the ASPR. Even the séances that James published were considerably chopped because James considered the omitted portions to be trivial and irrelevant. Maybe irrelevant to James—but not to skeptics who might find data from one séance turning up in another.

Mrs. Piper also could easily have obtained information from conversations among clients awaiting the start of a séance. Two or more visitors often chatter away, revealing all sorts of facts that could be overheard by the medium, or by her husband or one of her daughters on the other side of a wall. And it should not be forgotten that after years of practice Mrs. Piper may have developed a talent, like Sherlock Holmes, of basing shrewd deductions on a client's appearance, behavior, and way of speaking.

For a while investigators took the precaution of introducing clients to Mrs. Piper under names not their own. Since the clients came mostly from the area, many from the Harvard faculty, it would not be difficult for Mrs. Piper to recognize them from published photographs. Podmore relates an amusing incident. Professor J. E. Carpenter, from Oxford, was introduced to Mrs. Piper as Mr. Smith. But as soon as his wife entered the room, Mrs. William James greeted her as Mrs. Carpenter.

Did Mrs. Piper ever cheat by doing advance research on prospective clients? James and other investigators were of course aware of how easily mediums can obtain information about deceased persons, especially if they were prominent in their profession. Obituaries can be checked in newspapers and periodicals. Courthouses can yield valuable data on birth and marriage records, real estate sales, and so on. Reference books contain detailed biographical information that sitters will swear a medium could not possibly have known. The history of spiritualism swarms with instances of sitters insisting that no one but themselves knew this or that, only to have it turn out later that the fact was readily available in an obit or some other document. After his death, it was discovered that the American medium Arthur Ford—he converted Bishop James Pike to spiritualism—owned a vast collection of obituary clippings, which he called his "poems."

When Richard Hodgson began investigating Mrs. Piper he was so convinced she did secret research that, for several weeks, and much to Mrs. Piper's annoyance when she found out about it, he had detectives watch her and her husband. How effective was this effort? It seems unlikely that the Pipers were not early aware of such shadowing. How carefully was Mr. Piper watched? He is a dim figure about whom I have been unable to learn much. In her biography of her mother, Alta says little about her father beyond the facts that he loved outdoor sports (especially croquet) and music, played the piano and violin, and was strongly supportive of his wife's mediumship. Nowhere does Alta say how her father earned a living. He died in 1904 when Alta was twenty.

There are many instances in history of husbands secretly assisting mediums and psychics. The surgeon husband of Margery Crandon, another Boston medium, is a classic instance. Nina Kulagina's husband in Russia is always around in back rooms when Nina performs a miracle that requires a hidden confederate to pull invisible thread. What was to prevent Mr. Piper, before and after the shadowing, from going to libraries and doing other leg work? As far as I can tell, nothing.

And what about Mrs. Piper's two daughters? They were too young to help on their mother's first visit to England, but by the second visit they were in their twenties. Were the girls carefully monitored in the houses where they stayed or were they allowed to roam about? Amazing amounts of "evidential" data can be gathered from wastebaskets alone.

In her hagiography, Alta speaks of "servants" in their large home, as well as nurses and governesses. In 1885 they had an "old Irish servant" whose sister was a servant for a prominent Beacon Hill family, a family frequently visited by William James's mother-in-law. Yet when the mother-in-law first sat with Mrs. Piper, William was flabbergasted to learn that the medium had given her the names of members of his family! William and his wife later became good friends of the Pipers. On one occasion they shared a vacation in the White Mountains of New Hampshire, where Mrs. Piper went ever summer for a month or two of relaxation.

Did Hodgson and his detectives interview servants in the area? Did they visit Boston and Cambridge libraries with photographs of Mr. and Mrs. Piper to ask clerks if any of them were frequent patrons?

There are still other ways in which mediums can obtain evidential data. Mediums in a city get to know one another and cooperate. Among Arthur Ford's remains were copies of letters thanking other mediums, some in distant cities, for their help. People who like to attend séances usually visit many mediums. At the time there were scores of practicing mediums in Boston. They formed a network of professionals among whom valuable information could be passed back and forth. Of course no medium in such a network would ever admit knowing any of the others.

*   *   *

The strongest indictment that can be made against William James as a psychic researcher is that not once did he devise, or even consider devising, a sting operation. He was surely aware of how easily skeptics can set such traps. The psychologist G. Stanley Hall, for example, invented Bessie Beale, a fictitious person whose spirit Mrs. Piper had no difficulty reaching. Even James's invalid sister Alice—unlike her brother, a skeptic of things psychic—initiated a simple sting. James had asked for a lock of her hair to give to Mrs. Piper for use in some sort of séance, perhaps to determine the nature of Alice's illness. Alice sent her brother a lock of a deceased friend's hair. Here is how she exposed the hoax in a letter to William in 1886:

> I hope you wont be "offended," like Frankie, when I tell you that I played you a base trick about the hair. It was a lock, not of my hair, but that of a friend of Miss Ward's who died four years ago. I thought it a much better test of whether the medium were simply a mind-reader or not; if she is something more I should greatly dislike to have the secrets of my organisation laid bare to a wondering public. I hope you will forgive my frivolous treatment of so serious a science.

In the same letter Alice added: "I shall be curious to hear what the woman will say about the hair. Its owner was in a state of horrible disease for a year before she died—tumours, I believe."

If James reported the results to Alice, his letter apparently has not survived. At any rate, I know of no record that he left of any séance in which the hair played a psychometric role. James was probably too embarrassed to record it. So convinced was he of Mrs. Piper's honesty that he would have considered revealing such a sting to be an insult to a noble woman. Whether Alice's hoax succeeded or failed, Mrs. Piper and James's wife would never have forgiven him. If any reader knows of any report of Mrs. Piper's reaction to the hair, perhaps a document gathering dust in the ASPR archives, please tell me!

Alice had a low opinion of James's spiritualist friends. In one of her letters to William she calls Myers an "idiot." Here are her candid opinions as she jotted them down in her diary in February 1892, a week before she died of breast cancer:

> I do pray to Heaven that the dreadful Mrs. Piper won't be let loose upon my defenceless soul. I suppose the thing "medium" has done more to degrade spiritual conception than the grossest forms of materialism or idolatry: was there ever anything transmitted but the pettiest, meanest, coarsest facts and details: anything rising above the squalid intestines of human affairs? And o, the curious spongy minds that sop it all up and lose all sense of taste and humour!

James's aunt Kate was another relative deeply suspicious of Mrs. Piper and William's other spiritualist pals. She wrote to James's wife, also named Alice—the spongy-minded Alice—warning her against mediums. The letter was mentioned by Mrs. Piper in one of her trances. "Of course no one but my wife and I knew of the existence of this letter," James naively wrote. The "of course" typifies James's mind-set. It never occurred to him that his wife could have mentioned the letter to a friend or servant, and completely forgotten she did so. James himself could have mentioned the letter to someone and forgotten. Or their servant could have seen the letter. We know from an article by Mrs. Piper, which I shall come to in a moment, that her "maid of all work" was a friend of William James's servant!

In his best known essay, "The Will to Believe," James likens anomalies in science to the white crow that falsifies the assertion that all crows are black. "My own white crow," he wrote, "is Mrs. Piper." In the midst of all the undoubted humbug, he added, is "the presence . . . of really super-normal knowledge . . . in really strong mediums this knowledge seems to be in abundance, though it is usually spotty precisely because mediums, by normal means, can do no better than obtain spotty, disconnected, often inaccurate shreds of data."

James was a great man, but, like so many other intelligent men who take up psychic research, he had no comprehension of how easily bright persons, especially scientists, can be duped. A number of excellent books on how fake mediums operate were available in James's time. There is no evidence, however, he read any of them. Not once did he seek advice from a knowledgeable magician, such as England's John Maskelyne, whose *Modern Spiritualism* had appeared as early as 1876.

A year before he died James wrote "Confessions of a Psychical Researcher" for *American Magazine* (October 1909), an essay reprinted in his *Memories and Studies.* Said James:

> Mrs. Piper's control 'Rector' is a most impressive personage, who discerns in an extraordinary degree his sitter's inner needs, and is capable of giving elevated counsel to fastidious and critical minds. Yet in many respects he is an arrant humbug—such he seems to me at least—pretending to a knowledge and power to which he has no title, nonplussed by contradiction, yielding to suggestion, and covering his tracks with plausible excuses.

And yet James believed! "If spirits are involved," he wrote, they are "passive beings, stray bits of whose memory she [Mrs. Piper] is able to seize. . . ." James was aware of how Mrs. Piper's controls shamelessly fished for data, yet he could not avoid thinking that her messages were "accreted round some original genuine nucleus." Belief in psychic phenomena has lasted so long through the centuries, he argued foolishly, as so many believers still do, that there *must* be something to it. Something to astrology? To palmistry? Let me quote what I consider the most stupid remark in all of James's writings:

When a man's pursuit gradually makes his face shine and grow handsome, you may be sure it is a worthy one. Both Hodgson and Myers kept growing ever handsomer and stronger-looking.

*   *   *

When I began researching Mrs. Piper, I expected to find her a sincere woman whose skull contained split personalities that emerged in genuine trances. But the more I learned about her the more I became convinced that she was no more than a typical medium of the day, though cleverer than most in avoiding physical manifestations, which are so easily exposed, and in the art (for it is an art) of cold reading. There is no conceivable reason why the spirit of a dead person, chatting through a medium, would have to resort to flagrant fishing to obtain data that might prove he or she was a genuine discarnate. But cold reading is precisely what to expect from a clever mountebank who has no other way at the moment of obtaining evidential information. Even James once admitted that he sometimes wished Mrs. Piper could be caught in fraud because that would be the simplest way to explain her powers!

My low opinion of Mrs. Piper was clinched when I came across two references (there are probably many more) of Mrs. Piper performing a trick known to magicians as "eyeless vision." William James tells of an occasion when Mrs. Piper described the contents of a letter by holding it to her forehead, although it was not until two years later that she provided the writer's name. Oliver Lodge describes a séance during which Mrs. Piper was given a letter from a package, along with wrapping paper. She put the wrapping and the letter on top of her head, flicked away the wrappers, and partially read the letter.

We have learned how Mrs. Piper could not divine the contents of several sealed letters. When handed unsealed letters she did much better. Now, there is no sensible reason why a psychic should put a letter on the forehead or on top of the head before viewing it clairvoyantly, but there is an excellent reason for such action when a medium cheats. The usual technique goes like this. With eyes almost shut, the letter is held far to one side while the medium chatters away. Meanwhile, the eyes, hidden under their lids, shift to one side and steal quick glimpses of the letter. (If the letter is more than one page, of course it is hard to get a glimpse of the signature at the end.) Some mediums are blindfolded when they do eyeless vision, but Mrs. Piper never bothered with such precautions and would not even have known how to get around them. Spectators naturally assume that, while the medium divulges the letter's contents, she is viewing it paranormally for the first time, never dreaming that the letter was glimpsed some time before while their attention was diverted.

Lodge's account of how Mrs. Piper paranormally "read" the letter on top of her head strongly suggests that she had obtained only a quick glimpse of the letter's single page. She began by saying "Who's dear Lodge? Who's Poodle, Toodle, Poodle! Whatever does that mean?"

> Lodge: "I haven't the least idea."
> Mrs. Piper: "Is there J.N.W. here? Poole. Then there's Sefton. S-e-f-t-o-n. Poole, hair. Yours truly, J.N.W. That's it; I send hair. Poole. J.N.W. Do you understand that?"
> Lodge: "No, only partially."
> Mrs. Piper: "Who's Mildred, Milly? something connected with it, and Alice; and with him too, I get Fanny. There's his son's influence on it."

Lodge adds the following clarification.

> I found out afterwards that the letter began "Dear Dr. Lodge," contained the words "Sefton Drive" and "Cook" so written as to look like Poole. It also said "I send you some hair," and finished "yours sincerely, J.B.W."; the "B" being not unlike an "N." The name of the sender was not mentioned in the letter.

Apparently the references to a Mildred, Alice, and Fanny, and the son's influence, were no more than fishing remarks.

There are three possible explanations of Mrs. Piper's account of the letter: (1) while in trance she became a powerful clairvoyant; (2) Her spirit controls read the letter; (3) She cheated. Is not the third possibility the simplest and most plausible? But, you may argue, could she have deceived such astute observers as James and Lodge by such a simple technique? The answer is a thunderous yes. Both men were totally ignorant about how conjurers perform such feats. Even had they not been thoroughly convinced of Mrs. Piper's honesty, they would not have known what to look for when Mrs. Piper was handed the letter. Their scientific training was a liability, not an asset. To repeat: Electrons and laboratory animals don't cheat. Psychics do.

In 1901 Mrs. Piper wrote an extraordinary article for the *New York Herald* (Sunday, October 20). I have obtained a copy. It ran on two and one-half pages, with photographs of Mrs. Piper in her house and garden on Oakland Avenue in the Boston suburb of Arlington Heights. (The suburb had formerly been part of West Cambridge, near Harvard.) The headline over her article read: "I Am No Telephone To the Spirit World."

Mrs. Piper announced that she was resigning from the ASPR and retiring as a medium. Personal circumstances, which she did not specify, were making it impossible to continue her work. Besides, she wanted to be "liberated" from the ASPR, for which she had served as an "automaton" for fourteen years; she desired freedom for "other and more congenial pursuits." She wanted to tell the world that she had never heard of anything she said or wrote while in trance that could not have been either latent in her mind, or obtained by telepathy from the minds of a sitter or other persons living somewhere in the world. "I must truthfully say," she wrote, "that I do not believe that spirits of the dead have spoken through me. When I have been in a trance state . . . it may be that they have, but I do not affirm it." In her opinion telepathy was the most plausible explanation of her remarkable hits. Why could not information come from distant, living persons, she asked, like messages over a wireless telegraph, to be picked up by her subliminal self?

The article rambles, but it is well-expressed and gives evidence of a high intelligence and a woman of wide reading. She refers to St. Paul, and says that she hopes to enter heaven "directly" rather than through the "back door of spiritualism." At the end of the article she repeats a story about how savages were so impressed by a sundial that they built a roof over it. We are doing the same thing, she said, with our faith in God. "Break down the roof; let God in on your life!" Mrs. Piper was then under heavy fire from Christian preachers. Her references to God and the Bible may have been a calculated move to pacify them, or could have reflected a growing interest on her part in Christianity. Her parents had been Methodists, but when they moved to a town that had only a Congregational church, she attended that church with them. In 1910, in England, she was baptized and confirmed in the English Church.

Five days later the *Boston Daily Advertiser* published a brief statement by Mrs. Piper. She was upset over the headline above the *Herald* piece. She did not contradict anything in that article, but she did complain that her words had been misunderstood. She had not intended to deny unequivocally that the dead spoke through her, but only to say that, like William James, she was baffled by the sources of her utterances. She inclined to the view that it was her subliminal self speaking and that the evidential information brought forth was the result of her telepathic powers.

Mrs. Piper did not retire. For two more decades she continued to give séances, supervised by the ASPR, and continued to receive payments from England's SPR. Her communications by this time were almost entirely by automatic writing. New controls included George Eliot, Julius Caesar, and Madame Guyon, a seventeenth-century French mystic and automatic writer.

When Doyle visited her in 1922, he says in his history of spiritualism, she had lost all her powers. Skeptics suspect that the main reason for this was that better qualified researchers, such as psychologist G. Stanley Hall—he was a student of William James and a teacher of John Dewey—were subjecting her to rigorous experiments that earlier researchers were unwilling to make.

In her biography, Alta Piper attributes her mother's loss of power, from 1911 to 1914, directly to the "harsh" experiments conducted by Hall and his assistant Amy Tanner. So strict were the conditions that Impera-tor, Mrs. Piper's control, issued an "ultimatum that the power must be withdrawn for a time in order to repair 'the machine.' " Although her trances returned in 1915, from then until 1924 Mrs. Piper had only occasional sittings. The last parapsychologist to conduct experiments with her was Gardner Murphy, in 1924 and 1925. Unlike Hall, Murphy was a true be-liever in Mrs. Piper's powers.

Mrs. Piper died in 1950, age ninety-one, and almost totally deaf. She was then living in an old apartment house in a Boston suburb with her youngest daughter, Minerva. Her address was secret, and her phone number unlisted. The last article written about her was probably "America's Most Famous Medium," by Murray Teigh Bloom, in *The American Mercury* (May 1950). Bloom closed with these words:

> Few in the comfortable, old-fashioned apartment house know that the very old lady who occasionally goes out for a stroll with her nurse or gray-haired daughter is the simple Yankee housewife whose work once convinced leading scientists of two countries that there was indeed life after death.

Epilogue

I had finished this essay when psychologist Ray Hyman called my attention to a book I did not know existed. Books and articles about Mrs. Piper never mention it, nor is it cited by Alta Piper in her biography of her mother. The reason for such silence in obvious. The book was written by a skeptic, and is far and away the most valuable study ever made of Mrs. Piper. It is a book that deserves reprinting.

Studies in Spiritism, by Dr. Amy B. Tanner, was published by Appleton in 1910.[3] Tanner was an assistant to Dr. G. Stanley Hall, one of the most prominent and respected psychologists of his day, and at that time president of Clark University. Unlike William James and other investigators of Mrs. Piper, Hall was the first to perform experiments with Mrs. Piper that James would have considered unethical. As I noted earlier, these were the tests that Alta believed were responsible for her mother's temporary loss of powers.

Both Hall and Tanner approached Mrs. Piper with open minds. Tanner writes in her preface that before they began their investigation she believed in telepathy and did not rule out the possibility of spirit communication. Hall was more skeptical, though as a youth he accepted spiritualist claims and as an adult continued to believe in immortality. In 1909 he and Tanner had six sessions with Mrs. Piper, all recorded verbatim in her book. They ended their research persuaded that Mrs. Piper was probably not a charlatan, but a classic case of a person with multiple personalities who emerged from her unconscious mind during trances. Mrs. Piper was then at the height of her fame. Had the book accused her of fakery, Hall and Tanner could have been open to libel suits. If, however, you read carefully between the lines, there are subtle suggestions that Mrs. Piper may in some ways have practiced conscious deception.

One indication of this was the fact that, unlike other persons with subliminal personalities who take over in trances, Mrs. Piper's trances did not occur spontaneously. They never began when she was alone, or asleep, or daydreaming. She never walked or talked in her sleep. She was incapable of being hypnotized. Yet when a sitter who had paid for a séance was present, she had no difficulty going into a trance. I should add that persons who suffer from genuine trance seizures do not go in and out of trances in theatrical ways calculated to impress an audience.

An even stronger suggestion of fraud was the incredible role played by Mrs. Piper's right hand after direct-voice channeling had been entirely replaced by automatic writing. The fact that the hand functioned as a telephone to her controls was, as Hall remarks in his introduction, a miracle in itself. Sitters were asked to hold the hand, its palm close to their mouth, and to speak with a loud voice. Frequently the control would be unable to hear and would ask the sitter to talk louder, as if on a long distance telephone call. Occasionally the hand would explore a sitter's face or body.

My first thought was that the hand needed shouting because Mrs. Piper was getting a trifle deaf, but Hall and Tanner convinced me that the reverse was true. Although she sat with her head on pillows, face turned to one side and eyes seemingly closed, her hearing was extremely acute. As Hall writes, she reacted to everything audible—"noises on the streets, the rustle of clothing, the sitter's position, and every noise or motion, and our conversation, too. . . ."

By insisting that sitters address the hand in a loud voice, a strong impression was created that Mrs. Piper was "as much out of the game as if she were dead." If the hand could not hear unless a mouth was close to it and shouting, surely Mrs. Piper could not hear whispers or voices spoken in low tones. That Mrs. Piper was in a deep sleep was further strengthened by the long time, fifteen to twenty minutes, that it took her to come out of a trance. Convinced that the sleeping Mrs. Piper could hear nothing, sitters were free to move about the room and talk to one another. After a séance they would not even remember what they had said. Then when information from such whispered conversations came out in later séances, or even in the same séance, they would be amazed at how the control could possibly know such things!

It was often the case that nothing evidential emerged in a first sitting, to be followed by great successes in a later visit. Hints of revelations to come were commonplace during a first sitting, arousing a sitter's strong desire to come back and pay for other visits, often a series of many visits separated by weeks. This allowed plenty of time for sitters to forget their conversations; it also allowed Mrs. Piper time to find out more about a sitter's family.

Because I believe this conversation in the séance room to be Mrs. Piper's best kept secret, let me quote at length from Hall:

It is the ear, of course, that hears what is spoken into the hand. The establishment of this fact is of great significance. The clever trickster might have reasoned out a scheme of impressing the sitters with the idea that they must shout into the hand and that all else was lost, so that they would thus be thrown off their guard, while the intently listening ear would catch and utilise for the manual responses all that was said to each other. The keener the audition and the more deft the hand, the wider the range of oral impartation from whispering to shouting that would be profited by. With Mrs. Piper we believe this method was not a project of strategy or designed, but a slow, unconscious evolution. Thus, responses and statements are written that fairly smite with wonder the incautious and uncritical sitter, who naively allows himself to fall into the assumption which the method suggests that the control hears nothing but what is loudly spoken into the hand. The sitters have really thought aloud and communicated in low tones to others, feeling as secure against betrayal as if their thoughts were unspoken, and perhaps, indeed, not conscious that they had been put in articulate form. Thus, when natural answers come back, they seem veritable mind-reading or marvellous illustrations of the pellucidity of the sitters' souls to the celestial visitant.

Now, it is a very significant fact that stenographic records have rarely been kept, even of the *ipsissima verbs,* that are *consciously* said to the control by the sitters. Even our record, which was made as full as long hand could be, does not do this. This is because the feeling has been that the important things of the sitting came from the medium, when the exact reverse is true. Everything that is really significant comes from the sitters. Far less has there been any stenographic record of things said loud or low in the room, where there frequently are at least two if not more visitors present. Under the conditions of the sitting, the temptation is incessant to carry on considerable conversation, to express secret plans, and purposes and methods that betray answers; and all with the same feeling of security that we have, as I said, in speaking before the deaf. Such talk is, much of it, almost immediately forgotten, if, indeed, it was conscious even at the time. Yet in this is the source of supply from which the control garners most of its knowledge of us. There are, of course, inflections, too, movements, slight noises, etc., which are more or less significant. Often especially in our characterisations of both real and fictitious dead friends, we have only given the name and a few salient facts to the ear, adding various details in a low voice to Mr. Dorr and Dr. Tanner, while the hand was writing, which, however, insistently utilised these sources of information by incorporating reactions in the script, while we tried not to be remiss in the expressions of wonder which seemed to be the usual and proper thing under such circumstances.[4]

It is important to realize that such careless conversations in the séance room were never recorded. In early years, when Mrs. Piper channeled direct voices, only brief notes in longhand were taken, and in many cases were written down later from memory. Nor were any records made of such conversation in later years when only her right hand channeled. The absence of such records render all voluminous records of Mrs. Piper's séances almost valueless in trying to evaluate the kind of information she overheard. Today, of course, a serious investigator would tape-record the entire séance, which may be one reason why direct-voice mediums who bring evidential information from dead relatives are so hard to find. It is much safer to channel the voice of someone who lived thousands of years ago or who is on a distant planet!

I quote once more from Hall:

. . . Here then is a wide and copious margin in which suggestion can work. Never in our own or in other Piper sittings was any full record kept of what her interlocutors said. Still less have involuntary exclamations, inflections, stresses, etc., been noted, and even the full and exact form of questions is rarely, if ever, kept while the presence of a stenographer which we proposed was objected to. Thus unlimited suggestions are unconsciously ever being given off to be caught and given back or reacted to in surprising ways. If this method be a conscious invention on her part it shows great cleverness and originality, and if it be a method unconsciously drifted into, its great effectiveness could in fact be scientifically evaluated only by prolonged experiments in which a normal person should simulate her very peculiar kind of sleep. In fact, it often seemed that only her eyes were out of the game, and all her mental and emotional powers were very wide awake. A little practice convinced me that it is not hard to feign all this, and yet I am by no means convinced that she acted her sleep-dream, although that this could be done with a success quite equal to her own I have no shadow of doubt. If this is the case she is, of course, fraudulent, but if some of her faculties are really sleeping it is a unique and interesting case of somno-scripticism as her former practice of speaking instead of writing was of somno-verbalism, for both are species of the same genus of somnambulism. That Mrs. Piper-Hodgson's soul is awake and normal, our last sittings gave abundant evidence when she seemed to quite fall out of the Hodgson role and became angry.

Mrs. Piper's anger, as expressed by her Hodgson control (her right hand would pound the table), came after Hall revealed to Hodgson, in the sixth and final sitting, that he had been thoroughly flimflammed. Mrs. Piper had unconditionally agreed before the séances began that Hall could perform any kinds of experiments he desired. It seems likely she had no inkling of how far Hall would go in laying traps.

What Hall did—James should have done it earlier—was to present Hodgson with completely fictitious names. Although Hall had met Hodgson only once, Hall acted as if they were old friends. Hodgson reciprocated by calling Hall "old chap" and by recalling a wealth of events and discussions that had never happened. Hall invented a Bessie Beals. Hodgson had no difficulty locating her on the "other side." Indeed, he seemed as intimate with Hall as Mrs. Piper, in her waking state, mistakenly assumed he had been. Hodgson recalled everything Hall pretended had passed between them. When Mrs. Piper was given neckties to hold, neckties she was told belonged to Hodgson, Hall slyly substituted old neckties of his own. Hodgson, of course, never knew the difference.

In the final séance, Hall openly told Hodgson about his deceptions and did his best to persuade the control to admit he was not really Hodgson but only part of Mrs. Piper's brain. Both Hall and Tanner broke into laughter over Hodgson's confusions and evasions. This is the book's funniest chapter and probably the funniest séance ever recorded. At one point Hall said, "Now, . . . to oblige me, repeat the words 'I am not Hodgson.' " Hodgson refused. "No, I am Hodgson." Hall told him he was hurting the cause of spiritualism by pretending to be Hodgson and ordered him to "fade away." But Hodgson refused to fade, protesting that he would go only when he was ready. He finally faded, replaced by Rector who came on with "May the blessing of God rest on you."

"It may be that he [Hodgson] humoured me in my deceit to see how far I would go," Hall writes, "and let me fill full the measure of my turpitude of ruse and deception, but if so, why the flaming anger when I confessed my strategy?" Although Mrs. Piper insisted she never recalled anything that transpired during a séance, Hall had earlier noticed a coldness in her attitude toward him. After this final séance she betrayed no hint that she knew how damaging it had been to her. "She was evidently very curious to know," Tanner closes her account of this séance, "whether we were at all convinced and kept looking at both of us with a contemplative, questioning gaze, and when we said good-bye, and thanked her for her personal courtesy, the last thing that we saw was that same questioning gaze."

When Hall questioned Hodgson about events in his life on earth, events unknown to Mrs. Piper, he answered "only in platitudes or evaded. Would Hodgson, if living, have accepted such a tatterdemalion ghost of himself, and would he not have preferred death to such a pitiful prolongation of his personality?" Perhaps, suggests Hall with tongue in cheek, Hodgson's soul was in a "process of dissolution." He had already reached "an advanced stage of senile decrepitude. . . . He surely cut a sorry figure with us. He accepted each of the fictitious personages we invented. The figments of our fancy were quite as real to him as his own friends. . . . He could thus be fooled and imposed upon to the very top of our bent."

Mrs. Piper's hand did much more than just scribble almost unreadable messages. As Hall writes: "The hand points, nods for yes, shakes for no, quivers with impatience, listens, gestures for silence, beckons, with quite a vocabulary of signs." When a control first took over, the hand would suddenly clench. Controls called the hand, as well as Mrs. Piper's body, "the machine" through which they communicated. Mrs. Piper was known as "the light."

Hodgson constantly fished for information. He had a habit of suddenly injecting, from the blue, a meaningless name of a person, or initials, or a word. If these random interjections meant nothing to a sitter, they were simply ignored or forgotten. But if a sitter, often after much thinking, found some connection with his or her life, Hodgson would instantly follow up with more data. For example, a common name such as Robert or Kitty would be written. Almost everybody knew someone named Robert or Kitty. If the sitter could think of a relative or friend named Robert or Kitty, it would be the cue for Hodgson to go on. Otherwise, the name would be forgotten.

Mrs. Piper's most impressive séances took place when her husband was alive, and I strongly suspect that he did actual research for her. After his death, there was a marked falling off of "evidential" material in her séances when in my opinion she was forced to rely entirely on cold reading and information gained from conversations spoken in low tones during a séance.

*   *   *

If Mrs. Piper was in part a clever charlatan, as I am convinced she was, how does one explain such a curious personality? Although Mrs. Piper, after her husband's death, had no other means of supporting herself and her two daughters, I agree with Hall that money was not a primary motive. It is also possible she may sincerely have believed herself to be possessed of paranormal powers which she did her best to augment by trickery. It is, of course, impossible now, as it probably always was, to get inside Mrs. Piper's mind. Her daughter's hagiography is no help; it may even have been ghost-written. Writing about fraudulent mediums in general, Hall suggested that the primary motive is a

> morbid passion for deception . . . the real explanation of their success is to be chiefly found in the abnormal development of an inveterate inborn propensity to lie and mislead, which gives them a titilating sense of superiority on the one hand, and on the other the overpowering will to believe on the part of the faithful.

Those who were persuaded of Mrs. Piper's powers were invariably persons predisposed to believe. We know of her famous converts, but less familiar are the many prominent persons who were not impressed by her séances. Tanner gives a partial list. Geologist N. S. Shaler was unable to exclude fraud. George Darwin, a British astronomer, was convinced she had no paranormal powers. Professor A. Macalister (whom I have not been able to identify) considered her a "poor imposter." S. Weir Mitchell, an American physican and novelist, said that if he hadn't heard such praise from William James he would have considered Mrs. Piper a very stupid fraud. Harvard physicist John Trowbridge "was struck by a sort of insane cunning" in the way her controls groped for information. Harvard physiologist Henry Bowditch believed Mrs. Piper obtained advance information about him which during a séance her controls mistakenly applied to his uncle.

A Mrs. Howard Oakie wrote that nothing evidential came out in her first two sittings except "a great deal of hedging and guessing," but as she left the house she met two good friends on their way in. She was not impressed when, during her third session, Mrs. Piper produced a wealth of accurate information, but nothing that the two friends did not know.

"Spiritism," wrote Hall, "is the ruck and muck of modern culture, the common enemy of true science and of true religion, and to drain its dismal and miasmatic marshes is the great work of modern culture." More than eighty years have passed since he wrote those words, and hoped that Amy Tanner's book would help "turn the tide." Alas, it had no such effect. The muck is still with us, albeit in new forms, and the marshes are as far from drained as ever.

Notes

1. Palladino was a short, fat, Italian peasant who was caught cheating so many times that she herself finally admitted she resorted to trickery whenever the spirits failed to come. This admission had little effect on the faith of her followers. Hereward Carrington, who fancied himself a knowledgeable magician and even wrote a book on how mediums cheat, was her manager on a tour of the United States. He never doubted that she had genuine powers, one of which was her strange ability to produce a blast of cold air from a scar on her forehead. (She probably produced it simply by extending her lower lip and blowing upward.)

When James's colleague and friend, the Harvard philosopher Josiah Royce, learned that Eusapia had been caught using her feet to produce certain phenomena, he gleefully circulated the following jingle:

> Eeny, meeny, miney, mo.
> Catch Eusapia by the toe.
> If she hollers that will show
> That James's theories are not so.

2. "What real spirit," James wrote in one of his skeptical moods, "at last able to revisit his wife on this earth, but would find something better to say than that she had changed the place of his photograph?" Such a remark is typical of those made by sham fortune-tellers that have a high probability of being true, like saying "You have been thinking about buying a new car," or "You recently had a disturbing phone call."

3. James Hyslop was so infuriated by this book that he wrote a scathing 98-page review for the *Journal of the ASPR* (vol. 5, January 1911). Hyslop called the authors liars, idiots, troglodytes, and ignorant bunglers whose book swarms with omissions, distortions, and factual errors. Their crude methods, he states, "reduced Mrs. Piper to nervous prostration" so severe that for almost a year she was unable to enter a trance.

Neither Hall, Tanner, nor Tanner's book are mentioned in *William James on Psychical Research* (Viking, 1960), edited by Gardner Murphy and Robert Ballou, although it purports to be a definitive account of James's work with Mrs. Piper.

4. George B. Dorr was then the representative of England's SPR. As Hodgson had done for eighteen years, he served as Mrs. Piper's manager. All arrangements for séances had to be made through him, and he was usually present during the sittings.

References (Chronological)

William James. 1897. "What Psychical Research Has Accomplished," in *The Will to Believe*. Longmans, Green.

Amy E. Tanner. 1910. Studies in Spiritism. Introduction by G. Stanley Hall. Appleton.

William James. 1911. "Final Impressions of a Psychical Researcher," and "Frederic Myers' Services to Psychology," in *Memories and Studies,* Longmans, Green.

Conan Doyle. 1975. *History of Spiritualism.* George H. Doran, 1926, two volumes. Single volume edition, Arno.

Alta L. Piper. 1929. *The Life and Work of Mrs. Piper.* London: Kegan Paul. Introduction by Oliver Lodge.

Oliver Lodge. 1931. *Past Years.* Scribner's.

Murray Teight Bloom. 1950. "America's Most Famous Medium," in *The American Mercury,* May, p. 578–586.

Joseph Rinn. 1950. *Sixty Years of Psychical Research.* Truth Seeker.

Gardner Murphy and Robert Ballou, eds. 1960. *William James on Psychical Research.* Viking.

Frank Podmore. 1963. *Mediums of the Nineteenth Century,* vol. 2. University Books.

Leon Edel, ed. 1934. *Alice James.* Dodd, Mead. Retitled *The Diary of Alice James.* Penguin paperback, 1982.

Nandor Fodor. 1966. *An Encyclopedia of Psychic Science.* University Books. Citadel Paperback, 1974.

C. E. M. Hansel. 1966. *ESP: A Scientific Evaluation.* Scribner's. Revised and retitled *The Search for Psychic Power.* Buffalo: Prometheus.

Alan Gauld. 1970. "Mrs. Piper," in *Man, Myth, and Magic,* vol. 16. Marshall Cavendish.

Ruth Yeazell, ed. 1981. *The Death and Letters of Alice James.* University of California Press.

Ruth Brandon. 1983. *The Spiritualists.* Knopf.

Index